10

THOMAS MANN

〰〰〰〰〰〰〰

Joseph the Provider

———————

ALFRED A. KNOPF · NEW YORK · 1944

Originally published as JOSEPH, DER ERNÄHRER

Copyright 1943 by Bermann-Fischer, A.B., Stockholm

Copyright 1944 by Alfred A. Knopf, Inc., New York

Contents

VII. THE LOST IS FOUND

Joseph the Provider

PRELUDE IN THE UPPER CIRCLES

IN the upper circles of the hierarchy at this time there was felt, as always on such occasions, a mild yet poignant satisfaction, an agreeable sly sense of "I told you so," expressed in glances from under lowered lashes and round little mouths discreetly drawn down.

Once again had the cup run over; once more had patience been exhausted, justice fallen due; and quite against His own wish or will, under pressure from the Kingdom of the Stern (which, in any case, the world was unable to resist, since One had never succeeded in making it stand up on the unstable and yielding foundations of sheer mercy and compassion), He, the Almighty, in majestic affliction had seen Himself driven to step in and clean up; to overturn, to destroy, and only after that to even off again—as it had been at the time of the Flood and on the day of the rain of fire and brimstone, when the Salt Sea had swallowed up the wicked cities.

This time, of course, the concession to justice was not on such an appalling scale as in that earlier attack of remorse and the ensuing wholesale drownings. It did not compare with that other occasion when, thanks to the perverted sense of beauty of the people of Sodom, an unspeakable city tax had almost been exacted from two of us. No, this time it was not all mankind that had fallen into the pit; nor even some portion of it, the corruption of whose ways had cried to heaven. This was a matter of but one single specimen of the breed, albeit an uncommonly taking and self-complacent one, more than usually well equipped with the advantages of nepotism and long-standing design in his favour. And we had had our noses rubbed into him on account of a whim, a train of thought, only too familiar to the heavenly host, where it was the source of much bitterness, though also of the not unjustified hope that very soon the shoe would be on the other foot and the bitterness the portion of him who had set the train of thought in motion. "The Angels," so ran the train of thought, "are created after Our image, but yet not fruitful. The beasts, on the other hand, lo, they are fruitful, but not after Our likeness. Let Us create man—an image of the angels, yet fruitful withal!"

Fantastic. Worse than merely futile, it was far-fetched, extravagant, pregnant with remorse and bitterness. We were not "fruitful," not we! We were courtiers of the light, sober-minded chamberlains one and all; the story about our one-time going in unto the children of men was simply irresponsible gossip. But everything considered, and whatever interesting advantages the animal quality of fecundity might prove to have over and above its animality, at all events we "unfruitful ones" did not drink injustice like water, and One should see how far One would get with One's notions about fruitful angels: perhaps far enough to see that an Almighty with self-control and prudent forethought for His own peace of mind might better let matters rest once and for all at our decent and honourable form of existence.

Unlimited power, unlimited possibility of taking into one's head, producing out of it, and bringing into being by a mere "Let there be"— such gifts had, of course, their dangers. Even All-Wisdom might not be quite adequate to avoid all the blunders and waste motions in the practice of absolute qualities like these. Out of sheer restlessness and lack of exercise; out of the purest "much wants more"; out of a capricious craving to see, after the angel and the brute, what a combination of the two would be like; out of all these motives, and impelled by them, One entangled Oneself in folly and created a being notoriously unstable and embarrassing. And then, precisely because it was such an undeniable miscreation, One set One's heart upon it in magnificent self-will and made such a point of the thing that all heaven was offended.

Now, was it true that He had come on this idea all by Himself and of His own accord? Speculations to the contrary were rife in the hierarchy, albeit only in whispers and not susceptible of proof. Plausible, however, they were; and according to them the whole thing went back to a suggestion made by the great Shemmael, who at that time, before his luminous fall from on high, had stood very near the Throne. The idea sounded very like him—and why, forsooth? Because it was his business to realize and bring into the world evil, his very own thought, which nobody else either knew or cared about, and because the enrichment of the world's repertory through evil could be achieved in no other

4

way than just precisely by the creation of man. Among the fruitful animal creation evil, Shemmael's great invention, did not come into question, and certainly not among us unfruitful images of God. For it to come into the world, there was needed just the very creature which Shemmael, according to the hypothesis, had proposed: an image of God, which at the same time was fruitful—in other words, man. It did not necessarily follow that the Almighty had been hoodwinked. Shemmael, in his usual grandiose way, had probably not concealed the consequences of the proposed creation—in other words, the origin of evil—but had come out quite forthright and forcibly with it, though in our circles we guessed that he also said a lot about how much livelier it would make life for the Creator: for instance by the need to exercise mercy and pity, judgment and correction. Or by the appearance in the world of merit and demerit, reward and punishment—in other words, by the origin of the Good, a phenomenon bound up with that of Evil. The Good, indeed, had actually had to depend upon its opposite, waiting for existence in the limbo of the merely possible; thus it was clear that creation rested upon division, which had even begun simultaneously with the separation of light from darkness, and the All-power would only be consistent in going on from this exterior position to create the moral world.

The view was widespread in the hierarchy that this had been the argument by which the great Shemmael had flattered the Throne and won it over to his counsels—highly malicious counsels they were, of course; one could not help sniggering at their slyness, however much it had been disguised by the rude frankness the malice clothed itself in. With that malice, it must be said, the upper circles did not altogether lack sympathy. The core of Shemmael's malice lay here: if the beasts, though possessing the gift of fruitfulness, were not created in God's image, we of the hierarchy were not either, strictly speaking, since that property, God be praised, we were clean of. Now the properties of godlikeness and fruitfulness which we divided between our two groups were originally united in the Creator Himself and thus the new creation suggested by Shemmael would be the only one actually and literally after the Creator's own image. With this being, then—in other words, man —evil came into the world.

That was a joke to make anyone snigger. The very creature which if you like was nearer to the image of the Creator than any other brought evil with him into the world. Thus God on Shemmael's advice created

5

for Himself a mirror which was anything but flattering. Often and often in anger and chagrin He was moved to smash it to bits—though He never quite did, perhaps because He could not bring Himself to re-plunge into nothingness that which He had summoned forth and actually cared more about the failure of than He did about any success. Perhaps too He would not admit that anything could be a complete failure after He had created it so thoroughgoingly in His own image. Perhaps, finally, a mirror is a means of learning about oneself; and He was later to be confronted, in a son of man, a certain Abiram or Abraham, by the con-sciousness of that equivocal creature as a means to His own self-knowledge.

Man, then, was a result of God's curiosity about Himself. Shemmael had shrewdly divined the curiosity and had exploited it in his advice. Vexation and chagrin had been the inevitable and lasting effect—espe-cially in the by no means rare cases where evil was united with bold intelligence, logic, and pugnacity, as it was in Cain. The story of the first fratricide and his conversation with God after the deed was known in some detail to the upper circles and industriously circulated. God had not come off very well when He asked Eve's son: "What hast thou done? The voice of thy brother's blood crieth unto Me from the earth, which has opened her mouth to receive thy brother's blood from thy hand." For Cain had answered: "Yes, I have slain my brother and it is all very sad. But who created me as I am, jealous to that extent that under provocation my whole bearing is changed and I no longer know what I am doing? Art not Thou a jealous God, and hast Thou not created me after Thy image? Who put in me the evil impulse to the deed which I undeniably committed? Thou sayest that Thou alone bearest the whole world and wilt not bear our sins?" Not so bad. Quite as if Cain or Cajin had taken counsel beforehand with Shemmael, though probably the hot-headed rascal had needed no advice. Rejoinder would not have been easy. There could be only bitter laughter or a crushing blow. "Get out!" was what He had said. "Go thy ways! A fugitive and vagabond shalt thou be, but I will make thee a sign that thou belongest to Me and no one may slay thee." In short, Cain, thanks to his logic, came off better than unscathed; there could be no talk at all of punishment. Even that about the fugitive and vagabond was not serious: Cain settled in the land of Nod, eastward of Eden, and in peace and quiet begot his children, a work for which he was urgently needed.

At other times, as is well known, punishment descended, frightfulness was invoked, there was majestic affliction at the compromising conduct of the "most like" creature. Again there were rewards, extravagant rewards: we need only recall Hanok or Enoch and the incredible, between ourselves the quite irresponsible benefits that fell into the fellow's lap. In the circles and ranks the view was held—and cautiously passed about —that in the world below there was great lack of even-handed justice; that the moral world established by Shemmael's advice was not dealt with in a properly serious spirit. It did not need much, there were times when it needed nothing at all, to convince the hierarchy that Shemmael took the moral world much more seriously than He did.

It could not be disguised, even where it ought to have been, that the rewards, disproportionate as they were in some cases, were actually only a sort of rationalization of blessings which at bottom were nothing but an arbitrary playing of favourites, with almost no moral aspect at all. And the punishments? Well, for instance, just now in Egypt punishment and reduction to the ranks were taking place: there was compliance, apparently painful and reluctant, with the dictates of the moral world. A certain dashing and arrogant young darling, a dreamer of dreams, a scion of that stock which had hit on the idea of being a medium of self-knowledge to God, had come down to the pit, to the prison and the grave, and for the second time, because his folly had passed all bounds and he had let love—as before he had hate—get entirely out of hand. But we onlookers, perhaps we were deceiving ourselves in our satisfaction at this particular version of the fire and brimstone?

Just between ourselves we were not being deceived, at bottom not for a moment. We knew precisely or we accurately guessed that all this severity was for the benefit of the Kingdom of the Stern; that He was using the punishment, the instrument of the moral world, to break open a closed alley which had but one and that an underground exit to the light; that He—with all due respect—was perverting the punishment into a means of further elevation and favour. When we, in passing, made little O-shaped mouths with the corners drawn down, and shot little glances from under our eyelids, we did so because we saw through the whole thing. Disgrace as a vehicle to greater honour—the All-Highest's little game illuminated the past as well and shed light on the follies and flippancies which had given cause for punishment and "forced" Him to inflict it. And this light did not come from the moral world; for these

7

earlier failings, from wherever and whomever inspired, God knew, were also revealed as a medium and vehicle to new, extravagant exaltations.

In our circles we were convinced that we knew more or less about these devices, partaking as we did, to however limited an extent, in the Creator's all-knowledge: though even so, out of respect, we could make use of our knowledge only with the greatest caution, self-restraint, and dissimulation. In the merest whisper it might and should be added that the hierarchy thought it knew still more—of matters, steps, undertakings, intentions, manœuvres, secrets of the widest scope which it would have been wrong to brush aside as mere court gossip. There could be no mention, scarcely even so much as a whisper, and all that happened was the next thing to keeping silent: the slightest movement of lips just slightly curled, and that was all. What sort of matters were these, what were the rumours?

They had to do, of course, quite without comment, with this business of reward and punishment—with the whole complex question of favour, predilection, election, which had been raised with the birth of the moral world, the twin birth of Good and Evil. It had to do, further, with the not entirely authoritative but well-founded news, conveyed by all these barely moving lips, that Shemmael's counsel, his suggestion that God should create the "most like" creature—in other words, man; that this had not been the last piece of advice he had bestowed upon the Throne; that the relation between the latter and the fallen one had never been entirely severed or else at some later time had been resumed, no one knew how. Perhaps behind the backs of His court He had undertaken a journey to the Pit and there indulged in an exchange of ideas. Perhaps the exile, perhaps more than once, had found a way to leave his own place and speak again before the Throne. In any case he had clearly been in a position to continue his exposition, so cleverly seasoned by surprising candour, and to support it with fresh advice, which, however, as before, did not go deeper than to stimulate ideas already present and only requiring further persuasion.

In order to understand what was going on, we have to recall certain dates and facts which form the premise and prelude of our present story. I refer to that psychological soul-novel which was earlier the subject of discussion: that romance of the soul of man—primitive man—which, as formless matter, was from the very first one of the fixed premises, its "Fall" being the conditioned basis of everything that followed. We

8

might perhaps use the word "creation"; for surely the sin consisted in that the soul, out of a sort of melancholy sensuality surprising and shocking in a primitive principle proper to the higher world, let itself yield to a craving to penetrate in love matter which was formless and obstinately clung to its lack of form, for the purpose of calling up out of it forms through which it could compass fleshly desire. Surely it was the Highest who came to the rescue of the soul in that wrestling for love which was far beyond its power. He thereupon created the world, where things happen and can be told, the world of forms, the world of death. This He did out of sympathy for the straits of His erring partner and fellow fixed conditions. We may therefore even infer an affinity between them. If such an inference is to be drawn, we must not neglect to draw it, even if it sound impudent or blasphemous to speak in the same breath of error and weakness.

May we associate the idea of error with Him? A resounding No can be the only answer to such a question; it was in fact the answer of all the heavenly host, accompanied, of course, by that same discreet twist of all the little mouths. It would doubtless be going too far, it would be hasty, to consider that the Creator's tender and helpful pity for the erring was the same thing as error itself. That would be premature, because through the creation of the finite life-and-death world of form no least violence was done to the dignity, spirituality, majesty, or absoluteness of a God who existed before and beyond the world. And thus up to now one could not speak seriously of error in any full or actual sense of the word. It was different with the ideas, plans, and desires which were now supposed to be in the air, the subject of private conversations with Shemmael. The latter, of course, pretended to be presenting the Throne in all good faith with a perfectly new idea; whereas he was most likely quite aware that He was already more or less occupied with the very same one. Obviously Shemmael trusted to the widespread though mistaken belief that when two people hit on the same idea it must be a good one.

It is futile to go on beating round the bush. What the great Shemmael proposed, one hand on his chin, the other stretched in eloquent peroration toward the Throne, was the corporealization of the Most High, His embodiment in a chosen people not yet born but to be created. The idea was based on the model of other gods on this earth: folk and tribal gods, mighty in magic, full of fleshly vitality and energy. The word "vitality"

9

is well chosen; for the chief argument of the Pit, just as at the time of the creation, was that the spiritual, the above-and-beyond-the-world Creator would experience a great accession of vitality by following Shemmael's advice—only in a much more thoroughgoing and distinctly more fleshly sense. This, I say, was the chief argument: for the clever Pit had many more, and with more or less justice he assumed that all of them were already at work in the theatre of God's mind and only needed to be brought forward and stressed.

The field of the emotions to which they addressed themselves was ambition. It was ambition, certainly, towards degradation, ambition directed downwards; for in the case of the Highest, where there can be no striving upwards, there is only the other direction left. It was an ambition to mingle, a craving to be like the rest, a desire to stop being unusual. Nothing easier than for the Pit to harp on a certain sense of futility, a frustrating vagueness and universality which God must feel when He, a spiritual, supra-worldly world-god, compared Himself with the wonder-working and sensual appeal of primitive tribal gods. It was just this that would arouse an ambition to condescend mightily, to submit Himself to limitations which should result in a concentration of power; in short, to add the spice of sense to His existence. To exchange a lofty but somewhat anæmic spiritual all-sufficiency for the full-blooded fleshly existence of a corporeal folk-god; to be just like the other gods; it was this private hesitant seeking and striving which Shemmael met with his crafty counsel. To make all this clear, all this exposure and this yielding to infection, it is surely allowable to cite as a parallel that soul-novel, the soul's love-affair with matter and the melancholy sensuality which urged it on; in other words, its "Fall." Indeed, there is scarcely any need to cite, the parallel is so clear, even down to the creative help and sympathy which was then vouchsafed to the erring soul; surely it was this that gave the great Shemmael courage and maliciousness to make his proposal.

Malice, of course, and the burning desire to cause embarrassment were the innermost meaning of the suggestion. Man was already, simply as man and speaking generally, a source of constant embarrassment to the Creator; the situation must become intolerable through His fleshly union with a particular stock, through an increase of vitality which came to the same thing as becoming biological. All too well did the Pit know nothing good could come of an ambition heading downwards, of an attempt to be like the others; that is to say, to become a racial and folk-god—or at least not until after long wandering, embarrassments, disap-pointments, and embitterment. All too well did the Pit know, what surely God knew too, that after taking his fling at biological vitality as a tribal God and the doubtful if also full-blooded pleasures of a concen-trated earthly existence as a folk-incarnation, fed and worshipped and propped up by a technique of superstition; that upon all this there would inevitably follow the moment of remorse and reflection, the relin-quishing of all these stimulating limitations, the return of the One Beyond Time to beyond time, the resumption of all-power and spiritual all-competence. But what Shemmael—and he alone—cherished in his heart of hearts was the thought that this very about-face and return, comparable to the end of an era, must be accompanied by a certain chagrin, and the thought was a sweet savour on the tongue of the source of all malice.

By chance, or not by chance, it came about that the particular stock chosen and dedicated for a folk-embodiment was so constituted that the World-God, in that He became its corporeal deity, not only had to sur-render His superior rank above the other folk-gods of this earth and become like them but actually in power and honour fell considerably below them—at which the Pit rejoiced. In the second place, the whole declension to the state of folk-god, the whole experiment of biological sense-enjoyment, was from the very beginning against the better knowl-edge and deeper insight of the chosen stock itself. Indeed, it was not without the intensive spiritual co-operation of the chosen seed that God thought better of His plan, was converted and turned back to His superior other-worldly and beyond-the-worldly rank above all other gods. It was this that tickled Shemmael's malicious soul. To represent the godhead of this particular stock was on the one hand no great joy; it was not, as they say, "any great shakes," for among the various folk-gods it invariably took a back seat. But on the other hand and in con-sequence the quality common to the human race, of being an instrument of God's self-knowledge, here came out in peculiar strength. An urgent concern with the nature and status of God was native to it; from the very first it had the beginning of a lively insight into the Creator's other-worldness, universality, spirituality, His quality of being the theatre of the world but the world not His theatre (just as the story-teller is the theatre of the story, but the story not his theatre, which circumstance gives him the chance to deal with it). It was a seed capable of evolution, destined in time and with enormous effort to mature into full knowledge of God's true nature. May one assume that this was precisely the ground of its election? That the issue of the biological adventure was no better known to him who gave the counsel than to Him who received it? That He Himself consciously brought about the so-called chagrin and admonishment? Maybe we are driven to such a view. Anyhow, in Shemmael's eyes the point of the joke lay in the fact that the chosen seed was privately and subconsciously aware from the start that it knew better than the tribal God and exerted all this strength of its expanding reason to help Him out of His improper situation and back into the beyond-all, all-sufficing spiritual. Even so, the Pit's assertion remains unproved that the return from the Fall to the original position of honour could never have been possible without that human exertion and could never have happened save by its means.

The hierarchy was not far-sighted enough to go so far as this. It stopped at the gossip about secret conferences with Shemmael and the subject of these. But that was far enough to add fuel to the chronic angelic irritation with the "most like creature" and to the chosen seed now in process of evolution. It was far enough to make the hierarchy privately rejoice at the little flood and the rain of sulphur which He, greatly to His own distress, was obliged to visit upon a scion of the stock, despite His far-reaching designs in its favour, and with the ill-concealed purpose of making the punishment a vehicle to serve His plans.

All this was what they expressed, those little O-shaped mouths drawn down at the corners, and the scarcely perceptible jerk of the head by which the heavenly choirs drew attention to the figure standing, arms bound behind his back, in a sailboat propelled by oars over the river of Egypt and down to his prison. It was the scion of the Chosen Seed.

Chapter One

THE SECOND PIT

JOSEPH KNOWS HIS TEARS

JOSEPH too—by the law of correspondence between Above and Below —was thinking of the Flood. The two sets of thought met, or rather, if you like, moved parallel to each other far apart; for this young specimen of the human race, thinking them here on the waves of the Jeor, bowed down by the weight of events and the traditional procedure of punishment for guilt, was thinking with much more immediacy and associative energy than were the hosts above, who, having no experience of suffering, were just having a pleasant, refined little gossip.

But more of this later. The convict lay discomfortably in the plank compartment which served as cabin and storeroom to a smallish freight-boat built of acacia-wood, with a pitched deck. It was a so-called ox-boat, such as he himself had used taking goods up or down river when he was Mont-kaw's pupil. It was manned by four oarsmen, who had to take to their oars when the wind died down or was contrary and the swaying double mast was lowered. They stood on the platform of the forward deck; there was a steersman aft and two under-servants of Petepre acted as escorts, also served at the ropes and with the lead. Finally there was Khamat, the scribe of the buffet. To him had been entrusted the command of the ship and the transport of the prisoner to Zawi-Re, the island fortress. He carried on his person a sealed letter which the master had written about his erring steward to the warden of the prison, a captain of troops and "writer to command of the victorious army" named Mai-Sachme.

The journey was long and protracted—Joseph thought of that other, early one, seven and three years before, when for the first time he had voyaged on this river, with the old man who bought him, with Mibsam his son-in-law, Epher his nephew, and Kedar and Kedema his sons. In nine days they had come from Menfe, city of the Swaddled One, to No-

Amen, the royal city. But now they were going far beyond Menfe, yes, past On the Golden, and past Per-Bastet, the city of cats. Zawi-Re, the bitter goal, lay deep in the land of Seth and the red crown, that is to say in Lower Egypt, down in the desert, in a branch of the district of Mendes, which there is called Djedet. It was to the abominable goat-district they were carrying him; the thought gave his apprehensive and brooding melancholy an added pang. Yet it was not without a sense of destiny, a heightened emotion and lively play of thought. He was a son of Jacob and his real and only wife, and never all his life long would he be able to check this play—just as little now as a man of seven-and-twenty as when he was a simple inexperienced lad. And the kind of play dearest to his heart, most fascinating to his mind, was the play of allusion; so that when his life, so painstakingly introspected, seemed full of that quality, and its circumstances to show themselves suffused with correspondences to the motions of higher things, he was prone to feelings of satisfaction, since such correspondence could never really be wholly sad.

Sad enough in all conscience his circumstances were; and sadly musing he pondered them as he lay with his arms bound together at the elbows across his back, in his little compartment, on the roof of which the provender of the crew was heaped up, melons, ears of maize, and loaves of bread. He had returned to a hideously familiar state; again he lay helpless, in bonds, as once he had lain for three horrible days in the dark of the moon, in the hole of the well, with worms crawling and rustling about him, and fouled himself like a sheep with his own filth. True, his present state was a little less rigorous than before, because his fetters were not much more than a matter of form and for appearance's sake, being a piece of ship's rope they had forborne to tighten. But even so his fall was not less deep and breath-taking, the change in his life not less abrupt and incredible. That other time, the spoiled darling and pet of his father, always anointed with the oil of gladness, had been treated in a way he could never have dreamed of. This time it was Usarsiph, he who had mounted so high in the land of the dead, who was head overseer and dwelt in the special chamber of trust, who tasted all the charms and refinements of culture and arrayed himself in pleated royal linen—to this Usarsiph was his present treatment now meted out; he was sore smitten indeed.

Gone all the fine-folded linen, the modish apron and elegant sleeved coat, this being now become the evidence which spoke against him. They

14

had given him a single garment, the slave's hip-apron, such as the crew wore. Gone the curled wig, the enamelled collar, the arm-bands and necklace of red and gold. All this refinement and beauty was vanished away, not one poor ornament left, save on his neck the little packet with the amulet which he had worn in the land of his fathers and with which the seventeen-year-old lad had gone down to the pit. The rest was laid aside—Joseph used the significant words to himself, an allusive phrase, as the fact itself was an allusion and a matter of mournful order and correspondence. It would have been quite false, travelling whither he travelled, to wear breast and arm adornment. The hour of unveiling, of putting off of ornaments, was at hand, the hour of the descent into hell. A cycle had come round: a small cycle often completed; but also a greater, too, bringing round its like more seldom; for the revolutions of the two coincided with each other at the centre. A little year was returning on itself, a sun-year—insofar, that is, as the mud-depositing water had run off again and (not by the calendar but in practical reality) it was sowing-time, the time of ploughing and hoeing, the breaking up of the soil. When Joseph now and then got up from his mat and Khamat allowed him to walk on the caulked deck, with his hands on his back as though he held them there at will, he would stroll about or sit on a coil of rope, in the clear-carrying echoing air above the water and watch the peasants on the fertile shore performing their careful, life-and-death task of digging and sowing that was hedged about with so many taboos and penalties. A mournful task, for sowing-time is mourning-time, time when the Corn King is buried, when Usir is borne down to the dark and hope is seen but from afar. It is the time of weeping—Joseph wept a little himself at sight of the corn-burying little peasants, for he too was being buried again into the darkness and into hope only too far away—in token that a great year had come round as well and brought repetition, renewal of life, the journey into the abyss.

It was the abyss into which the True Son descends, Etura, the sub-terrestrial sheepfold, Aralla, kingdom of the dead. Through the pit he had come into the land below, the land of the rigour of death; now again the way went down into *bôr* and prison, towards Lower Egypt—lower it could not go. Days of the dark moon came again, great days which would become years, and during which the underworld had power over the Beautiful One. He declined and died; but after three days he would rise again. Down into the well of the abyss sank Attar-Tammuz as

15

evening star; but as morning star it was certain he would rise up out of it. This we call hope, and hope is a precious gift. Yet after all it has something forbidden about it, because it contracts the value of the hallowed present and anticipates the festal hours of the cycle, which are not yet at hand. Each hour has its honour, and he does not live aright who cannot despair. Joseph held this view. His hope, indeed, was the most certain knowledge; yet as a child of the moment he wept.

He knew his tears. Gilgamesh had wept them when he had scorned Ishtar's longing and she had "prepared tears" for him. He was thoroughly worn out from the sore trial he had endured, the pressure from the woman, the severe crisis of the climax and the utter downfall and transformation of his life. The first few days he did not ask Khamat's permission to walk on deck amid the colour and bustle of Egypt's great artery. He lay alone on the mat in his pen and wove a web of dreamlike thoughts. He dreamed tablet-verses.

Ishtar the raving bounded to Amo, King of the Gods, demanding revenge. "Thou shalt create the steer of the heavens, he shall stamp on the world, singe the earth with the fiery breath of his nostrils, wither and destroy the ground.

"The heavenly steer will I create, Lady Ashirta, for grievously art thou affronted. But chaff-years will come, seven in number, years of famine, thanks to this stamping and singeing. Hast thou provided food, heaped up provision, to meet the years of want?"

"Prepared have I for food, heaped up provisions."

"Then will I create and send the heavenly steer, for sore art thou affronted, Lady Ashirta."

What singular conduct! When Ashera burnt to destroy the earth because Gilgamesh shrank from her, and demanded from heaven the fire-breathing steer, there had not been much sense in accumulating food for the seven years' shortage the steer would cause. But anyhow that was what she had done, accepting the condition because she so burned for the avenging steer. What pleased and intrigued Joseph in the whole thing was just this precaution, which the goddess even at the height of her fury had to reckon with if she was to get her fire-breathing steer. Foresight, carefulness, these were familiar and ever important ideas to the dreamer, however often he might in his folly have done violence to them. And they were almost the first law of life in the land where he had grown up as by a spring, the land of Egypt. For it was a fearful land; its

16

folk engaged in endless effort, with every kind of magic and charm it could command, to close up all the crannies through which misfortune, great or small, might creep in. And he had now been for so long an Egyptian himself, his fleshly garment made of purely Egyptian stuff, that the national watchword of care and foresight had sunk deep into his soul, where it found its twin already at home. For it was deeply rooted in his native tradition, where the word "sin" had almost the same sense as want of foresight. It meant folly, it meant clumsy dealing with God, it was something to jeer at. Whereas wisdom meant foresight and care for the future. Had not Noah-Utnapishtim been called the exceeding wise one, simply because he had seen the Flood coming and provided for it by building the great ark? The ark, the great chest, the Arôn, wherein creations survived in the time of the Flood; to Joseph the ark was the first instance, the earliest pattern of all wisdom—in other words, of all knowledgeable foresight. And thus, by the route of Ishtar's fury, the trampling and fire-breathing beast, and the heaping up of provisions as a safeguard against want, Joseph's thoughts followed trains parallel to those in the upper sphere about the great Flood; of the little flood too he was reminded with tears, the one which had come upon him because while he had not, indeed, been so lost in folly as to betray God and cast himself out, yet he had certainly been guilty of woeful lack of foresight.

He acknowledged to himself his sin, just as he had done in the first pit, a great year before, and his heart was sore for his father Jacob, and bitterly ashamed before his face for having brought himself down again to the pit in the land whither he had been snatched. What a lifting up had come of that snatching and what a downfall and abasement had followed it, all due to the want of wisdom! The third—that is, the making-come-after—was so far away now that it was quite out of sight. Joseph's spirit was honestly crushed. Humbly he implored pardon of the spirit of his father, whose image had at the last moment saved him from the very worst. But to Khamat, the scribe of the buffet, and his guard, he was careful to betray no depression. Partly out of tedium, partly to enjoy the humiliation of a man who had risen so far above himself, Khamat often sat down by Joseph to talk; but Joseph treated him with hauteur and reserve. Yes, we shall see that after a few days, and simply by his way of knowing how to put things, he induced his guard to remove his bonds and let him move about freely, although Khamat thus ran the risk of sinning against his duty as guard and ought to have been afraid to do it.

"By Pharaoh's life!" said Khamat as he sat down in the pen beside Joseph's mat, "how you have come down in the world, ex-steward, and sunk beneath us all after you had so nimbly mounted above us! One can scarcely believe it. I can only shake my head to see you lying there like a Libyan prisoner or a man from the wretched Kush, with elbows pinioned behind his back. A man who got up so high and was head over all the house, and now you are, so to speak, delivered over to the devourer, the bitch of Amente. May Atum, Lord of On, have mercy on you! How you have bowed down your head to the dust—to use the jargon of your wretched Syria, which we have picked up from you, and by Khons we are not likely to pick up anything else, for not even a dog would take a piece of bread from your hand, so low are you fallen! And why, forsooth? Out of sheer frivolity and lack of discipline you were bent on playing the big man in a house like ours and could not bridle your reeking lust. And it had to be our sacred lady and mistress on whom you fixed your lewd desires, when, after all, she is almost the same as Hathor's self. That was shameless enough. Never shall I forget how you stood there before the master when he pronounced justice in his house, and hung your head because you found not the least word of excuse and knew not how to wash yourself clean of your guilt. How could you, when the torn garment spoke loud against you, which you had left in the mistress's hand when you vainly tried to overpower and assault her and it was plain you had even gone about the business very clumsily? It could not be worse! Do you remember how you came to me in the pantry to fetch the refreshments for the old pair in the upper storey? You were impudent enough even then; I warned you not to spill the drink over the old people's feet and I felt rather mortified when you behaved as though such a thing could not happen to you. Well now, you have spilled something on your own feet so they are all stuck together. Oh, no, I knew you wouldn't be able to hold the tray steady in the long run. But why couldn't you? Because, after all, you are a barbarian, a sand-rabbit, with no more self-control than the wretched Zahi, ignorant of our standards and knowledge of life here in the land of men; you could not truly lay to heart our precepts which teach that one may take his pleasures in the world but not with married women, because that is risky. But you in blind lust and unreason leaped at our mistress, and

18

you may thank your stars you were not put in corpse-colour at once—and that is the only thing you have to be thankful for."

"Do me the favour, Khamat, scholar of the book-house," said Joseph, "of not talking about matters you do not understand. It is frightful when a difficult and delicate matter gets to the ears of the masses though it is something much too ticklish for them to grasp. They all lick their lips and talk the greatest tripe about it—really it is intolerable how they go on, and worse for the subject-matter than even for the persons involved. It is naïve of you, and not very refined and does no credit to your renowned Egyptian culture to have you talk like this to me. Not because I was yesterday your overseer and you bowed down before me, for I am laying that aside. But, after all, you are to realize that I must know more and better about the affair between the mistress and me than you who can only see it from the outside and hear only gossip about it. So why should you question me about it? Furthermore, it is absurd for you to contrast the barbarous cravings of my flesh with the standard of Egypt, when, after all, these latter have no very good reputation themselves all over the world. And when you talk about assaulting and leaping and think no shame to apply such a word to me, you must be confusing me with that famous ram we are on our way to, to whom the daughters of Egypt yield themselves when he has his feast—and these are your fine cultural standards, forsooth! Let me tell you: it may come to pass that people will speak of me as one who preserved his chastity among a people whose lust was like the lust of the stallion and the ass—some day that may happen. Some day the virgins of the world may mourn for me before they wed, bringing me their maiden tresses and singing a melancholy ditty in which they lament my youth and recount the tale of one who withstood the hot solicitations of a female and so doing lost his life and his repute. As I lie here and ponder, I can well imagine such a tradition growing out of my story. Consider, then, how petty your comments must seem to me! And why, while rejoicing in my misfortunes, are you so surprised at them? I was Petepre's bought slave; now by his decree I am become Pharaoh's. So, after all, I am more than I was, I have added to my stature. Why are you so simple as to laugh at that? Very well, let us agree that for the moment my fortunes are on the decline. But is it a decline without honour and solemnity, does not this ox-boat seem to you like Usir's bark when it moves down to light the great sheepfold below and greet the dwellers in

19

the cave on his nightly ride? To me, let me tell you, it is strikingly like that. If you think I am parting from the land of the living, you may be right. But who shall say that my nose shall not smell the herb of life, and that I shall not rise the morrow morn over the rim of the world, even as a bridegroom goes forth out of his chamber and his radiance blindeth the eyes of the dull of sight?"

"Ah, ex-steward, I see you remain the same in all your misery. But the trouble is that nobody can tell what being the same really means. It is like the coloured balls which jugglers send flying out of their hands and catch again and you cannot see them as separate balls because they make a bright bow in the air. Where you get your cheek, no matter what happens to you, the gods only know, the ones you have dealings with; for god-fearing folk must get goose-flesh and pimples to hear you. You cannot get out of it by that rubbish about brides who dedicate their hair to your memory. That could happen only to a god. Or your comparing this boat, which is after all the vehicle of your shame, with Usir's evening-bark—would the Hidden One that you only compared the two! But you weave in the word 'strikingly'—you say this boat is strikingly like that bark, and you know how to convince a simple soul that it is really the very bark after all, and that you may really be Re when he is called Aton and changes into the bark of the night—and that gives one goose-flesh. But one gets it not only from laughing and shivering but also and even more from being angry, let me tell you, from disgust and bitterness like gall at your presumption; at the way you make bold to mirror yourself in the Highest and identify yourself with Him, so that you talk as if you were the same and go on making an arch of balls so that I blink my eyes in exasperation. Of course, it is open to anyone to say such things and to behave like that; but a decent person would not do it, he would be humble and pray. I sat down here to talk with you partly because I was sorry for you and partly because I was bored. But when you give me to understand that you are Atum-Re and Usir the great in his bark, at one and the same time, then I must leave you to yourself, for my gorge rises at your blasphemies."

"Take it as you must, Khamat of the book-house and the buffet. I did not ask you to sit down with me, for I like quite as well to be alone, maybe even a bit better, and I can amuse myself without you as you can see for yourself. If you knew how to entertain yourself as I do, you would not have come; but on the other hand you would not look askance

20

at the diversions I allow myself and you do not allow me. You make out that you do this out of pity; but actually it is nothing but ill will, and the pity is a sort of fig-leaf your ill will puts on—if you will pardon the far-fetched comparison! A human being entertains himself, he does not pass his life like the dumb brutes; that is the whole point, that and how far he goes in his diversions. You were not quite right to say that anybody might act the same as I; not everybody might. Not because decency forbids, but because he lacks any harmony with higher things, he has just been denied any affinity with them, it is not given him to pluck flowers of speech from the fields of heaven—if you will pardon me another figure. He sees in the Highest something quite different from what he sees in himself—in which, of course, he is perfectly right—and has no idea of serving Him, except with hymn-tunes, which are tiresome. If he hears anyone else praise Him in more intimate terms, he is green with envy and stands before the image of the Highest and weeps crocodile's tears and implores Him to forgive the blasphemy. That is a really silly pose, Khamat of the buffet, you should not be guilty of it. Give me my mid-day meal, for it is time and I am hungry."

"That I must, I suppose, if the time is here," answered the scribe. "I cannot let you starve. I have to deliver you alive to Zawi-Re."

Joseph could not feed himself with his elbows bound behind him, so Khamat had perforce to do it for him, there being no other way. Squatting beside Joseph, he had to put the bread in his mouth and then the beaker of beer to his lips; Joseph commented upon it at every meal.

"Yes, you squat here, long-legged Khamat, and feed me," said he. "It is kind of you too, even though you feel ashamed and show that you do not like it. I drink this to your health. At the same time I cannot help thinking how you have come down in the world, that you have to feed me and give me drink. Certainly you never had to when I was your overseer and you bowed before me! You have to serve me as never before, as though I were become more and you less. It is the old question: who is greater and more important, the watcher or the watched? But of course it is the latter. For is not even a king guarded by his servants, and is it not said of the just man: 'He shall give His angels charge over thee to keep thee in all thy ways'?"

And so after a few days Khamat said to Joseph: "Let me tell you, I am fed up with feeding you and having you open your beak like a young daw in the nest, and when you open it words come out that disgust me

21

even more. I am going to untie your bonds so that you are not so helpless and I need not be your slave and angel; that is not a scribe's job. When we come near your destination I will tie you up again and deliver you in bonds to the governor there, Mai-Sachme, a captain of troops. That is only proper. But you must swear to me not to tell that official that you were free in the meantime or that I have been lax in my duty; otherwise I shall be blamed."

"On the contrary, I will tell him you were a cruel warder and chastised me with scorpions every day."

"Nonsense, that is going much too far the other way. You never do anything but make fun of people. Of course, I don't know what is in the sealed letter I carry on my person and I am not sure what they mean to do with you. That is the worst of it, no one ever does know what to do with you. But you are to tell the governor of the prison that I treated you with tolerable severity and with firmness tempered with humanity."

"So will I do," said Joseph, and got his elbows free until they were far down into the land of Uto the Serpent and the seven-branched river in the district of Djedet and near to Zawi-Re, the island fortress. Then Khamat tied him up again.

THE GOVERNOR OF THE PRISON

Joseph's place of penance and second pit, which he reached after almost seventeen days' journey, and where by his own transcendental reckoning he was to spend three years before his head should be once more lifted up, was a group of gloomy buildings irregular in shape and covering almost the whole of the island that rose from the Mendesian arm of the Nile. It was a collection of cubical barracks, stables, storehouses, and casemates grouped around courts and passages surmounted at one end by a Migdol tower, the residence of the governor over the prison and the prisoners and commandant of the garrison, Mai-Sachme, a "scribe of the victorious army." In the middle of the whole rose the pylon of a Wepwawet-temple, whose standard was the sole relief to the eye in all that baldness. The whole was enclosed by a ring wall some twenty ells high, of unbaked bricks, with projecting bastions and platforms jutting out in the round. The landing bridge and the fortified and guarded gate lay somewhere at the side. Khamat stood on the bow of the ox-boat and waved his letter at the guards from afar. As they came under the gate he shouted that he was bringing a prisoner whom he must himself in person hand over to the troop captain and head of the prison.

Mercenaries, called Ne'arin, a military term adapted from the Semitic, lance-bearers with heart-shaped leather leaves on their aprons and shields on their backs, opened to the conveyance and let it through. To Joseph it seemed as though he were back in the times when he and the Ishmaelites were admitted through the gates of the fortress of Thel. Then he had been a boy, abashed before the marvels and abominations he saw in Egypt. Now he knew them all, the marvels and the abominations, he was Egypt hide and hair—apart from the reservations he confined to his private thoughts respecting the follies of the land whither he had been snatched—and he had got a good bit beyond his youth and was well into manhood. But now here he was, led on a rope, like Hapi, the living representation of Ptah in the court of his temple at Menfe: a captive in Egypt just like that sacred bull. Two of Petepre's people held the ends of his bonds and drove him in front of them. Behind them, Khamat addressed himself beneath the gate to an under-officer with a staff, who had probably given the order for admission, and was referred to a higher official coming across the court armed with a cudgel. This man took the letter, saying that he would take it to the captain, and told them to wait.

So they waited, under the curious gaze of the soldiery, in a little quadrangle, in the sparse shade of two or three spindling palm trees tufted with green at the top, their round reddish fruits lying about on their roots. The son of Jacob mused. He was recalling what Petepre had said about the governor of the prison into whose hand he was being given: that he was a man with whom one did not jest. Joseph's concern and suspense as he waited are easy to understand. At the same time he reflected that the titular captain probably did not know the man personally at all and had simply guessed that a man in charge over a prison was bound to be forbidding—a probable but not an inevitable conclusion. Joseph consoled himself with the thought that at least this was a human being with whom he would have to deal—and in Joseph's eyes that meant that he was somehow or other to be got on terms with; in God's name, however much he might be a born prison-keeper, yet by this means or that, from one angle if not from another, he *could* be jested with! Besides, Joseph knew his children of Egypt, the denizens of this land who against a background of deathlike rigidity and a religion of the tomb were blithe and inoffensive children at heart and easy to live with. Then the letter which the governor was now reading, where Potiphar told him about the man he was casting out, so that the governor could get an idea of his affair: Joseph was confident that the description would not turn out to be too dreadful; that it would not be calculated to evoke the man's grimmest qualities. His real confidence, however, was more of a generalization: it proceeded, as it is wont to do with children of the blessing, not from himself outwards but inwards upon himself and the happy mysteries of his own nature. Certainly he had got beyond the childish stage of blind confidence, where he had believed that everybody must love him more than they did themselves. What he continued to believe, was that it was given him to constrain the world and the men in it to turn him their best and brightest side—and this we can see was confidence rather in himself than in the world. In any case the two, his ego and the world, in his view belonged together, they were in a way one, so that the world was not simply the world, by and in itself, but quite definitely his world and by virtue of the fact susceptible of being moulded into a good and friendly one. Circumstances were powerful; but what Joseph believed in was their plasticity: he felt sure of the preponderant influence of the individual destiny upon the general force of circumstances. When like Gilgamesh he called himself a glad-sorry man, it was in the sense that he knew the happy side of his nature was capable of much suffering, but on the other hand did not believe in suffering— bad and black enough it was that it had proved too dense for his own light, or the light of God in him, to penetrate.

Such was the nature of Joseph's confidence. Generally speaking it was trust in God, and with it he armed himself to look Mai-Sachme, his taskmaster, in the face. In no long time he was set before him; for they were led through a low covered passage to the foot of the citadel, to a barred door manned by other guards in helmets with bosses on them. The grating presently opened and the troop-captain came out.

He was in the company of the high priest of Wepwawet, a lean baldpated man with whom he had been engaged in a game of draughts. The governor was a man of some forty years, a stocky figure in a cuirass which he had probably put on for the occasion, with little metal pictures of lions fastened on it like scales. He wore a brown wig, had round brown eyes under very heavy black brows, and a small mouth. His tanned and burnt face was darkened by a fresh growth of beard and his fore-arms were hairy. His whole expression was oddly unruffled, even sleepy; yet it was shrewd too, this expression, and the captain's speech was calm to the point of monotony as he came out from under the gate in conversation with the prophet of the warlike deity. They were obviously still discussing the moves in the game, upon which the newcomers had had to wait. In his hand the captain held the unsealed roll of the fan-bearer's letter.

He stood where he was, reopened and reread it; and when he lifted his face Joseph had a feeling that this was more than just a man's face, it was the very presentment of forbidding circumstance with the light of God striking through, the very face which life shows to the glad-sorry man. The black brows were threateningly drawn, yet a smile played about his small mouth. Now he banished smile and threat together out of his face.

"You had charge of the boat that brought you down from Wese?" he said in calm monotonous tones, turning round and raising his brows at the scribe Khamat. Upon the latter's assent he looked at Joseph.

"You are the former steward of the great courtier Petepre?" he asked.

"I am he," answered Joseph in all simplicity.

And yet this was rather a strong answer. He might have replied: "As you have said," or "My lord knows the truth," or more floridly: "Maat speaks out of your mouth." But in the first place just "I am he," spoken, of course, quite simply but with a sober smile, was a little incorrect; one did not speak in the first person to superiors but said "your servant," or with even greater self-disparagement "this servant here." And in the second place the "I" was too prominent: associated with the "he," it roused a vague suspicion that it referred to more than merely the stewardship which was all that was in question. There was an implication that question and answer did not quite match, that the answer over-lapped the question and might tempt the questioner to another question: "What are you?" or even "Who are you?" over and above that.

The truth is, Joseph's answer was a formula, old, familiar, and widely appealing from ages past. It was the time-honoured revelation of identity, a ritual statement beloved in song and story and play in which the gods had parts. In such a play it is used in order to string together a whole gamut of effects and plot sequences, from mere casting down of the eyes to being thundered at and flung to one's knees.

25

Mai-Sachme's placid features, the features of a man not prone to alarm, did show a faint confusion or embarrassment; it made the end of his small hooked nose turn whitish.

"Yes, yes, so you are," said he. Possibly at the moment he did not know himself just what he meant by that; and if so the fact that this man before him was the handsomest twenty-seven-year-older in the two lands may have contributed to his absence of mind. Beauty is impressive. Unfailingly it stirs a special kind of faint trepidation even in the most placid soul from whom fear in general is remote. A simple "I am he" uttered with a sober smile might be magnified by the beauty of the speaker into something a little unearthly.

"You seem to be a light-headed bird," went on the captain, "falling out of the nest out of sheer foolishness and lack of balance. Lived up there in Pharaoh's city where life is so full of interest that it could have been a perpetual feast-day for you, and for nothing and less than nothing you have got yourself sent down here to us where there is nothing too, nothing but nothingness. Here utter boredom reigns," said he, and gathered his brows in a momentary frown, accompanied however by a half-smile, as though smile and frown belonged together. "Were you ignorant," he went on, "that in the stranger's house one should not seek out the women with one's eyes? Have you not read the precepts in the Book of the Dead or the teachings and sayings of the holy Imhotep?"

"They are familiar to me," Joseph replied, "for I have read them countless times aloud and to myself."

But the captain, though he had asked for an answer, was not listening to it.

"That was a man," said he, turning to his companion, the chaplain, "a good companion for life, Imhotep the Wise! Physician, architect, priest, and scribe, all in one, Tut-anch-Djehuti, the living image of Thoth. I venerate the man, that I must say. If it were given me to be appalled, which it is not—perhaps I ought to say unfortunately, I am much too easy-going for that—but if I could I should certainly be appalled at such encyclopædic wisdom. He died long years ago, Imhotep the Divine; his like existed only in early times and in the morning of the two lands. His sovereign was an early king named Djoser, whose eternal dwelling he is known to have built, the stepped pyramid near Menfe, six storeys high, some hundred and twenty ells, but the limestone is poor. Ours up in the quarry where the convicts work is better stuff; the master

26

just had no better to his hand. But the art of building was only a small part of his knowledge and skill; he knew all the locks and keys to the temple of Thoth. Skilled in medicine he was too and adept in nature's matters, with knowledge of solids and liquids. He had a gentle hand with the sick and could relieve folk groaning and tossing with pain. He himself must have been very tranquil by nature and not prone to fear. Added to all this he was a reed in the hand of God, a writer of wisdom; but his talents worked together, not today a doctor and to-morrow a writer, but both in one and at the same time. I emphasize this because it is to my mind a surpassing virtue. Medicine and writing go well together, they shed light on each other and both do better by going hand in hand. A doctor possessed of the writer's art will be the better consoler to anyone rolling in agony; conversely, a writer who understands the life of the body, its powers and its pains, its fluids and functions, its blessings and banes, has a great advantage over him who knows nothing of such things. Imhotep was such a doctor and such a writer. A godlike man; they ought to burn incense to him. And I think when he has been dead awhile longer, they will. Anyhow, he also lived in Menfe, a very stimulating city."

"You need not blush before him, captain," replied the high priest. "For aside from your military service you practise the art of healing, you do good to those who wreathe and writhe, and besides that write very winningly in form and matter, while uniting all these branches in perfect serenity."

"Serenity by itself does not do it," answered Mai-Sachme, and the serenity of his own face with its shrewd round eyes altered a shade into the pensive. "Perhaps I just need to get good and scared once. But how could that happen?—And you?" he said suddenly. He lifted his brows and shook his head as he looked over at Petepre's two house-slaves who were holding the ends of Joseph's bonds. "What are you doing there? Are you going to plough with him or play horse like little boys? I suppose your ex-steward is to do time at hard labour with his limbs tied up like a calf for the slaughter? Untie him, stupids! Here we work hard for Pharaoh, in the quarry or on the new buildings, we don't lie about in bonds. What lack of understanding! These people," he explained aside to the man of God, "live in the belief that a prison is a place where one lies about in chains. They take everything literally, that is their way, and stick to the letter as children do. If they hear about somebody that

27

he lies in gaol, that being the phrase in common use, they firmly believe that the man has been plumped into some hole full of hungry rats and rattling chains, where he lies and steals days from Re. Such confusion of the word and the reality is to my way of thinking characteristic of low breeding and lack of education. I have often seen it in the rubber-eaters of the wretched Kush and even in the little peasantry of our own fields; not so much in the towns. To be sure, there is a certain poetry in the literal interpretation, the simple poetry of the fairy tale. There are, so far as I can see, two kinds of poetry: one springs from folk-simplicity, the other from the literary gift in essence. The second is undoubtedly the higher form. But in my view it cannot flourish cut off from the other, needing it as a plant needs soil, just as all the beauty of the higher life and the splendour of Pharaoh himself need the earth-mould of all our poverty-stricken existences in order to flower and flourish and be an amazement to the world."

"As scholar of the book-house," said Khamat, scribe of the buffet, who meanwhile had hastened to free Joseph's elbows with his own hands, "I have no part in any confusion between the phrase and the reality, and only for form's sake and for the moment, I thought I had to deliver the prisoner in bonds. He himself will tell you that during the greater part of the voyage I let him go free."

"That was no more than sensible," responded Mai-Sachme, "since there are differences between crimes. Murder, theft, trespass, refusal to pay taxes or conniving with the tax-collector, those are in a different class from offences where a woman is concerned, which require more discreet handling." He half unrolled the letter again and looked at it.

"Here," he said, "I see a woman comes into it; and as an officer and a pupil of the royal stables I cannot put it in the same boat with vulgar crimes. We have said that it is a sign of lack of elevation or maturity to take everything literally and not to distinguish between the phrase and the reality. But such a distinction is now and again unavoidable among the better sort of people. For instance it is said that in the house of strangers it is dangerous to cast eyes upon the women. Yet even so it is done, because wisdom is one thing and life another; and you might even say that the element of risk makes it to some extent honourable. Again, there are two parties to a love-affair, and that always obscures the issue a bit. From the outside it looks as though the case were clear; that is because one side—I mean the man, of course—always takes the

28

blame on himself, yet again it may be best to make a distinction in private between the phrase and the reality. When I hear of a woman being led astray by a man, I chuckle to myself, for it sounds like a joke and I think: By the great Triad! Because, after all, we know whose business seduction has been since the time of the gods and it was not the business of us stupid men. Do you know the story of the Two Brothers?" He turned to face Joseph, looking up at him with his round brown eyes, for he was considerably shorter as well as stoutish in build. He lifted his thick brows again as high as they would go, as though that would help to strike a balance.

"I know it well, my lord," answered Joseph. "For I had often to read it aloud to my master, Pharaoh's friend, and I also had to copy it out fair for him, with black and red ink."

"It will continue to be copied," said the commandant; "it is a capital invention not only in its style, which carries conviction even though the episodes are really almost incredible when one thinks them over calmly, for instance where the queen conceives through a splinter which flies into her mouth from the wood of the persea tree, which is too contradictory to medical experience to be taken literally. But despite that the story is lifelike, as when the wife of Anup leans against the youth Bata, finding him great in strength, and says to him: 'Come, let us have joy in each other for a little and I will make thee two feast-day garments,' and when Bata cries to his brother: 'Woe is me, she has turned all to ill!' and before his eyes cuts off his manhood with the blade of the sword-reed and gives it to the fishes to eat—that is thrilling. Later on, the narrative degenerates and becomes unbelievable; yet it is edifying too when Bata turns himself into the Hapibull and speaks: 'I shall be a wonder of a Hapi and the whole land will exult in me,' and makes himself known and says: 'I am Bata, lo, I live still and am the sacred bull of God.' Those are, of course, fantastic inventions; but yet how plastically life does sometimes pour itself into the most extraordinary forms of the creative fancy!"

He was silent awhile and stood placidly gazing off into space with his little mouth slightly open. Then he read a little more in the letter.

"You can imagine, Father," said he, lifting his head to the baldpate, "that an occurrence like this makes a more or less stimulating change for me in the monotony of this settled place where a man already settled by nature is in danger of falling asleep. What I usually get down here,

29

either already sentenced or for temporary custody before the scales of justice have finally settled and their case has not yet been tried, are all sorts of tomb-robbers, bush-rangers, purse-snatchers—and none of them help me to keep awake. A love crime is an exciting exception. For there can hardly be any doubt, so far as I know people of the most diverse way of thinking, agree that this is the most curious, exciting, and mysterious tract of all our human existence. Who has not had his surprising, thought-provoking experience in the realm of Hathor? Have I ever told you about my first love, which was at the same time my second?"

"Never, captain," said the chaplain. "The first and the second too? I wonder how that could have come about."

"Or the second, yet after all the first," responded the commandant. "As you like to put it. Again or for ever—who knows which is the right word? And it does not matter either."

Mai-Sachme stood there, his expression relaxed, not to say sleepy, his arms folded, the roll tucked under one of them; his head on one side, the heavy brows somewhat lifted under the brown bullet-eyes. His rounded lips moved with measured gravity and he began to narrate, there before Joseph and his guards, before the priest of Wepwawet and a number of soldiers who had gathered round:

"I was twelve years old, a pupil of the house of instruction in the riding-school of the royal stables. I was rather short and plump just as I am today, that is my stature and my state in my life before and after death. But my heart and mind were open. So one day I saw a maiden who was bringing her brother, a fellow-pupil of mine, his midday bread and beer, for his mother was ill. His name was Imesib, son of Amenmose, an official. But his sister, who brought him his rations, three pieces of bread and two jugs of beer, he called Beti, from which I gathered that her name was Nekhbet, which proved correct when I inquired of Imesib. For it interested me because she herself interested me and I could not keep my eyes off her so long as she was there. Not off her braids nor off her narrow eyes, nor her mouth like a bow, and especially not off her arms, which were bare and of that slender fullness that is so lovely— she made the greatest impression on me. But I did not know all day what the impression was—I found that out only at night, when I lay in the dormitory among my comrades, my clothes and sandals beside me, and under my head to serve as pillow according to the regulation my bag of writing tools and books. For we were not allowed to forget our books even in sleep; the contact with them was to keep them always in mind. But yet I did forget them, for my dreams had a way of shaping themselves quite independently of the books under my head. I dreamed explicitly and vividly that I was betrothed to Nekhbet, the daughter of Amenmose; our fathers and mothers had come to an agreement and she was soon to become my housewife and sister-bride, so that her arm would lie upon mine. I rejoiced beyond all measure, as I had never rejoiced in all my life before. My entrails rose up in joy on account of that contract, which was sealed by our parents bringing our noses close together, a most lovely feeling. But this dream was so lively, so natural, that it lagged not at all behind reality; and strangely enough even after I had wakened and washed myself it beguiled me into believing it. It has never happened to me before or since that a dream has been so vivid as to hold me in its power in my waking hours, so that I went on believing it. Well on into the morning I was still fondly and firmly convinced that I was betrothed to the maiden Beti, and only slowly, as I sat in the writing-room and the master thumped me on the back to liven me up, did my inward exultation subside. The bridge over into sobriety was formed by the reflection that the contract and the approaching of our noses had indeed been only a dream, but that nothing stood in the way of its immediate realization; that I only needed to have my parents come to an agreement with Beti's parents on our behalf. For quite a while it seemed to me that after such a dream my expectation of its fulfilment was only natural and nobody could be surprised at it. But gradually I arrived at the chilling and sobering thought that the realization of the dream which had seemed so real was only idle nonsense and as things stood frankly impossible. For of course I was nothing but a schoolboy, still beaten as they beat papyrus, only just at the beginning of my career as scribe and officer, and short and fat into the bargain, according to my constitution before and after death; and my betrothal to Nekhbet, who was probably three years older than I and might any day marry a man far above me in station and dignity, was revealed to me, with the fading of my dream happiness, as a thing of sheer absurdity.

"So," the official continued imperturbably, "I gave up an idea which would never have occurred to me save for that vivid and beautiful dream. And I went on with my studies in the house of instruction of the royal stables, frequently admonished by thumps on my back. Twenty years later, when I had long ago become a teacher-scribe to the victorious army, I was sent with three associates on a journey to Syria, in the wretched Cher, to muster and levy a tribute of horses, which were to be sent down in freight boats to Pharaoh's stables. So I travelled from the port of Khadati to the defeated Sekmen and to a town which, if I recall rightly, is called Per Shean, where we had a garrison, whose colonel gave a party to the people of the countryside and the remount scribes: an evening company with wine and flowers in a house of most beautiful doors. There were Egyptians there and city notables, men and women. I saw a maiden, a connection of this Egyptian house on the female side, for her mother was a sister of its mistress and she had come hither on a visit with male and female servants from far away in Upper Egypt where her parents lived, near the first cataract. Her father was a very rich trader from Suenet, who bought up the wares of the wretched Kasi, ivory, ebony, and leopard-skins for the Egyptian market. Now when I saw this girl, the daughter of the ivory-dealer, in all her youth, there happened to me for the second time in my life what had first happened so many years ago in the house of instruction: I could not keep my eyes off her, she made an exceptional impression on my mind and brought back in amazing likeness the joyous taste of that long-vanished betrothal dream, so that my entrails rose up for joy at sight of her just as before. But I was shy before her, although a soldier should not be shy, and for some time I shrank from finding out her name and who she was. But when I did so I learned that she was the daughter of Nekhbet, the daughter of Amenmose, who, quite shortly after I had seen her in my dream and been betrothed to her, had become the wife of the ivory-merchant of Suenet. But the maid Nofrure—so she was called—was not like her mother in her features or the colour of her braided hair or her complexion, being a good deal darker. At most her charming figure was like Nekhbet's—but how many girls have figures like that! Yet the sight of her roused in me at once the same deep feelings I had felt then and never again; so that one might say I had loved her already in her mother, as I loved the mother again in her. Indeed, I consider it possible, and in a way I expect, that if again after another twenty years I should meet by chance and unawares the daughter of Nofrure, my heart would melt to her irresistibly as once it did to her mother and her grandmother, and it will always and for ever be the same love."

"That is really a remarkable emotional experience," said the chaplain, charitably passing over the extraordinary fact that the captain had chosen to relate the tale at this moment, in however composed and level a tone. "But if the daughter of the ivory-merchant were to have a daughter, it would be a pity that she was not your child; then, even though your boyish dream on the pillow of books could never be realized, yet in Nekhbet's reincarnation or the return of your inclination to her, reality would have come into its own."

"Not so," replied Mai-Sachme, shaking his head. "Such a rich and beautiful maiden and a remount clerk, short and stout by nature and predestination, how could they go together? Most likely she has married a district baron or else somebody who stands under the soles of the Pharaoh, a steward of the treasure-house with the gold of favour round his neck. And you must realize that you stand in a fatherly relation, as it were, to a girl whose mother you once loved, so that the idea of marriage is not quite the thing. Besides, such thoughts as you suggest were shoved into the background with me by what you call the remarkable nature of the situation. That prevented me from taking a decision which would end in the grandchild of my first love becoming my own child. Was that anything actually desirable? It would have deprived me of the expectation in which I now live: that some day without knowing it I shall meet the daughter of Nofrure, the granddaughter of Nekhbet, and that she too will make on me the same wonderful impression. That is a possibility which leaves me something to hope for in my elder days; whereas if not, the course of my recurrent emotional experiences might have been cut off untimely."

"That may be," the priest agreed hesitantly. "But the least you could do would be to put on paper the story of mother and daughter, or rather your story about them, and use the reed to give it a charming form to the grateful enrichment of our literature. In my opinion you could just write out of your own fancy the third incarnation of that figure and of your love for it and make it seem as though it had already happened."

"I had made some beginnings," replied the captain coolly; "that is why I can tell the story so glibly, because I have already done some drafts of it. The thing is only that in order to include the meeting with Beti's granddaughter I have to set the story in the future and make myself out an elderly man, which is a strain and I shirk it, although by rights a soldier should not shirk. But the principal trouble is that I doubt whether by temperament I am not too steady-going to give to my tale the thrilling character it should have, as for instance in the model story of the Two Brothers. The subject is too dear to me that I should want to take the chance of botching it." He broke off with a guilty air and said: "But at the moment what I am doing is to induct the prisoner. How many beasts of burden," he asked, turning to condescend to Joseph, though with some difficulty on account of his shortness, "would it take, do you think, to carry food to five hundred stone-workers and porters, together with their officers and overseers?"

"Twelve oxen and fifty asses," answered Joseph, "might be about right."

"More or less. And how many men would you order to the rope to drag a block of stone four ells long by two wide and one thick, five miles to the river?"

"Counting the men needed to clear the road, the water-bearers to wet it under the sledges, and men to carry the rollers that need to be put underneath every now and then," said Joseph, "I should say at least a hundred."

"Why so many?"

"It is a good heavy block," answered Joseph, "and if you do not want to put oxen to it but men because men are cheaper, you should take enough of them so that midway one gang can spell the other at the rope. Then you do not have to reckon with deaths due to checked sweat or some of them straining their inwards or their wind giving out so that they roll about in agony."

"That is certainly to be avoided. But you forget that we have not only the choice between oxen and men, but there are all sorts of barbarians and folk of the desert of the red land, from Libya, Punt, and Syria—we have all that we can use."

"He who is here given into your hand," answered Joseph evenly, "is himself of such an origin, namely the child of a shepherd king of the Upper Retenu, where it is called Canaan, and has only been stolen down here into Egypt."

"Why do you tell me that? It is here in the letter. And why do you call yourself a child instead of a son? It sounds like self-indulgence and pampering, not becoming in a convict, even though his crime is not of a dishonourable kind but lies in the realm of the emotions. You seem to fear that I, because you are originally from the wretched Zahi, would harness you to the heaviest loads, until your sweat was checked and you died a dry death. That is an attempt, as indiscreet as it is clumsy, to

34

think my thoughts. I should be a poor prison governor if I did not know how to size up every man's parts and place him accordingly. Your answers show very plainly that you once oversaw the household of a great man and understand something about business. It seems you would like if possible to avoid having people exhaust themselves, even if they are not children—I mean sons of the black earth; this does not precisely run counter to my own wishes and shows some knowledge of economic thought. I will use you as overseer over a gang of convicts in the quarry, or perhaps in the inside service and the office; for of course you can reckon faster than the others how many measures of wheat can be put into a storeroom of this and this size, or how much spelt should be brewed to make so and so much beer or baked to make so much bread, and can turn one value into another, and things like that.

"It would be really a good thing," he added in explanation to the opener of Wepwawet's mouth, "for me to have some such assistance, so that I need not take everything on myself and could have more leisure for my efforts to put on paper in a good and even engrossing style my tale of the three love-affairs which were one and the same.—You people of Wese," he said to Joseph's attendants, "can now be off and set out on your homeward journey. You will be going upstream and you will have a north wind. Take your rope along with you, and make my compliments to Pharaoh's friend, your master.—Memi!" he gave order in conclusion to the man with the club who had ushered in the new arrival. "This slave of the King will do convict labour as assistant in the office; show him a place to sleep by himself and give him an upper garment and a staff of office. Very high he once stood, very low has he let himself be brought down here to us; now he must submit to the iron regimen of Zawi-Re. What superior parts he brings with him we will ruthlessly exploit, just as we do the physical strength of the lower sort. For they belong no longer to himself but to Pharaoh. Give him something to eat.— Till our next meeting, Father," he took leave of the chaplain and turned back to his tower.

Such was Joseph's first meeting with Mai-Sachme, the governor of the prison.

Now, like Joseph himself, you are reassured as to the particular kind of man this governor was into whose hands Petepre had given him. He was a man of peculiarly even and pleasing temper, and not for nothing has our all-illuminating narrative been in so little haste to take the spot-light from his undeniably stoutish figure, but has let it rest long enough upon him for the reader to get a clear picture of his hitherto unknown personality. And this for the reason that he has a not insignificant part, again very little known, to play in the tale which is here being retold with all possible correctness and verisimilitude. The fact is that after Mai-Sachme had been Joseph's superior and taskmaster for some years, he continued for a long time at his side and bore a part in the stage-management of great and glorious events, as we shall soon hear —and may the Muses strengthen me in the task of narration.

All this only in passing. But in speaking of the governor of the prison, the tradition uses the same formula earlier applied to Potiphar, that he "took nothing on himself," so that Joseph was soon responsible for all that happened in his second pit. We must pause upon this tradition, to interpret it aright; for it has not at all the meaning it had in the case of the sun-courtier and consecrated mountain of flesh who "took nothing on himself" simply because his whole being was nominal and titular; because he stood outside humanity and in a straitness of existence without prospect of change, remote from reality, and existence of the purest form. Whereas Mai-Sachme was a perfectly competent man, warmly if placidly interested in any number of things, particularly in people. He was a sedulous physician, who rose early every morning to inspect the discharge of the soldiers and convicts in his sick-bay. His workroom, in a well-guarded spot in the citadel tower of Zawi-Re, was a perfect laboratory, equipped with a herbarium, with mortars and pestles, phials and ointment-pots, tubes and stills. Here that same shrewd-sleepy face he had worn when on the first day he told the story of the three love-affairs bent over lotions, pills, and poultices or consulted the work "For the Benefit of Mankind" and other text-books of ripe wisdom for advice on the treatment of retention of urine, tumours of the neck, spinal rigidity, heartburn, and the like. As he read and pondered, his mind ranged over a whole area of general speculations: were the blood-vessels that ran in pairs from the heart to the separate limbs of the body and were so prone to hardening, choking, and inflammation that often they would not respond to treatment—were there only twenty-two of these blood-vessels or forty-six as he was more and more inclined to think? Were the worms in the body to whose destruction he applied his electuaries the cause of certain illnesses or more correctly their result—for instance by the stopping-up of one or more vessels a tumour was formed which had no outlet to discharge by and eventually became putrid and, of course, turned into worms?

It was a good thing the captain took these matters on himself although as a soldier they were less his province than that of his partner at draughts, the priest of Wepwawet. But the latter's knowledge of such physical matters was confined to the inspection and ritual slaughtering of the sacrificial animals, and his methods of healing were too dependent on charms and phylacteries—though of course these too were useful in their place, certainly in a case where the affection of an organ, say the spleen, or the spinal column, was clearly due to the fact that its special protecting deity had forsaken that member and left it to a hostile demon who was now creating his disturbing effect therein and must be forced by suitable invocations to void the field. For this purpose the chaplain had a cobra which he kept in a basket and by pressure on the neck could turn into a magic wand. His successes with the cobra sometimes inspired Mai-Sachme to borrow the creature. But on the whole the governor had the settled conviction that just magic by itself as a sufficing principle was seldom able to pull it off; it needed to be permeated and propped up by the grosser methods of profane knowledge, through which then it could produce its effect. For instance, Zawi-Re had suffered from a plague of fleas and the charms of the man of God had never reduced it, or so temporarily that the relief might have been only self-deception. It was only when Mai-Sachme, of course to the accompaniment of the spoken text, had sprinkled much natron-water and strewn much charcoal mixed with the powdered herb *bebet* that the pest subsided. It was the governor who ordered the lids of the food-stocks in the storehouses to be smeared with cat-fat, the mice being almost as much of a nuisance as the fleas. He had reckoned that the creatures would be frightened, thinking they were smelling the cat itself, and would leave the supplies alone, which proved to be the case.

The sick-bay of the fortress was always full of injured and ailing, for labour in the quarry, five miles inland, was hard labour indeed, as Joseph soon learned, since he often had to spend several weeks there to oversee a gang of soldiers and convicts in hewing, mining, cutting, and hauling operations. Soldiers and convicts were treated the same; the garrison of Zawi-Re, native and foreign, except for guard-duty did the same tasks as the convicts and felt the sting of the same lash. But at least where a soldier suffered from injury or exhaustion or his sweat struck inwards he was sent to the sick-bay somewhat sooner than a convict, who had to go on till he fell down, even to the third time of falling, for the first and second times were considered shamming.

Under Joseph's overseership, however, matters improved, beginning with his own gang. And at length the saying was fulfilled that the governor of the prison put all the prisoners into his hand. When he went out to the quarries it was as a sort of upper inspector and immediate representative of the commandant, and the improvement became general. For Joseph had in mind Jacob, his far-off father, to whom he was as dead, and how he had always disapproved of the Egyptian house of bondage. He decreed that a man even after falling down only twice should fall out and be fetched back to the island. For the first time he fell continued to be reckoned a sham, unless, of course, the man was dead.

So the lazaret was never empty of those who wreathed and writhed: a man might have broken a bone or "could no longer look down upon his belly" or his body might be covered with great swellings from infected fly- and gnat-bites; or his stomach, when one put one's finger on it, might go up and down like oil in a leather bottle; or stone-dust might cause inflammation and running from the eyes; all these cases the captain dealt with, shrinking from none; and for each, if the man was not already dead, he knew a remedy. The broken bones he splinted with little pieces of board, the inability of a man to look down upon his belly he sought to control with soothing poultices; the purulent discharge from bites he painted with goose-grease mixed with an emollient powdered herb; for the bloated abdomen he prescribed a chewing of berries of the castor-oil plant with beer, and for the frequent eye-inflammations he had a good salve from byblus. Probably there was always a trifle of "magic" to help out the medicines and defeat the insidious demon; but it consisted not so much in texts for application of the cobra wand as in the emanation from Mai-Sachme's imperturbable personality, which worked wonders of soothing on the patient, so that he was no longer frightened by his illness, that always having a bad effect. He ceased to writhe and unconsciously put on the captain's own facial expression—the rounded open lips, the brows drawn up with almost a quizzical air. So the patient lay and looked with equanimity towards healing or death. For this too Mai-Sachme taught them by his own attitude not to be afraid, and even when a man's face was already corpse-colour, his hands in their relaxed pose still expressed his doctor's teaching. Quietly, comprehendingly, with lifted brows and parted lips he lay, looking forward to the life after death.

So the lazaret was pervaded by serenity and absence of fear. Joseph sometimes entered it as the governor's right hand and even lent a hand, for he was soon transferred from the quarry to inside service. The words: "The governor of the prison committed to Joseph's hand all the prisoners that were in the prison, and whatsoever they did there he was the doer of it," are to be understood as meaning that Potiphar's former house steward, some six months after he entered Zawi-Re, had become, without any special title or promotion, the head manager and provisioner of the whole fortress. All the records and accounts went through his hands, and these, as everywhere else in the country, were endless: all purchases of oil, corn, barley, and cattle, all the giving out of supplies to the guards and convicts; all the operations in the brewery and the bakery of Zawi-Re; even the income and outgo of the Wepwawet temple; all matters connected with the dispatch of hewn stone from the quarries, and much, much else besides, came to be Joseph's business, greatly to the relief of those who had had charge of it before. He was accountable to the governor only, to that easy-going man with whom from the very beginning he had got on so well and continued to get on better and better.

For Mai-Sachme had learned that the words in which Joseph answered him at the first hearing had been uttered in very truth: the ancient, dramatic formula of self-revelation which had startled his phlegmatic soul and made him aware that the end of his nose had got cold. The impression had been uncommon, also very vague and general in kind. The captain was, in a way, grateful to Joseph for it, for on its basis he felt justified in his craving to be stirred out of his phlegm, and he looked forward to a satisfaction of the craving just as he did to the reappearance of the maiden Nekhbet in her grandchild and the ensuing third set of emotions; though he modestly and shrewdly sized himself

39

up as not worthy of such a shock. Vague and undefined too was Mai-Sachme's feeling that Joseph had uttered the truth in his self-revelation. He could not have said what was meant by the "he" in the always portentous formula "I am he"; he did not even know that he would not have known what it meant, because he had never found it desirable or necessary to consider the point. That is the difference between his obligations and ours. Mai-Sachme in his time, which was early from one point of view, though from another also very late, must be entirely absolved from any such responsibility. He may be allowed to go his placid way and limit himself, though with a modicum of trepidation, to feeling, faith, and divination. Our source has it that the Lord was with Joseph *and* gave him to find favour in the sight of the keeper of the prison. This "and" might be interpreted to mean that the favour which God showed to the son of Rachel consisted precisely in the kindliness his taskmaster conceived for him. But favour and kindliness are not precisely the same thing. It was not that God showed to Joseph the favour of making the captain's mind favourable to him. The sympathy and confidence—in a word, the trust —with Joseph's appearance and behaviour inspired in the prison-keeper flowed rather from the unerring instinct of a good man for the divine favour—that is, for the divine itself—which rested upon this convict's head. For it is, indeed, the mark of a good man that he is wise enough to perceive and reverence the divine. Here goodness and wisdom lie so close together that they actually seem to be the same.

What, then, did Mai-Sachme take Joseph for? For something right and proper, for the right and expected one, for the bringer of the new time. At first, only in the limited sense that this man convicted of an interesting crime and sent down to the humdrum hole where it had been the captain's lot to do service for years, and who knew how much longer, brought with him a definite break in the monotony. But when the commandant of Zawi-Re so sharply condemned and rejected any confusion between phrase and reality, his strictness may have sprung from his own involvement in that very confusion; indeed, if he did not take care, he might actually find himself guilty of mixing up the literal and the figurative. In other words, such faint stirrings, associations, intuitions as Joseph's traits called up were enough to make the governor round them out into full reality; which in Joseph's case meant the manifestation of the expected one, the bringer of salvation, who comes to end the reign of the old and monotonous and to usher in a new epoch amid the rejoicing of all humanity. But about this figure which Joseph suggested floated the nimbus of the divine; and in that again is inherent the temptation to mix up the metaphorical and the actual, the quality with that from which the quality is derived. But is that such a misguided temptation? Where the divine is, there is God. There is, as Mai-Sachme would have put it, if he ever did put anything, instead of divining and believing it, *a* god; in a disguise, of course, which outwardly and indeed mentally is to be respected, even though as a disguise it shows through, so to speak, and is not very convincing, because it is itself so very lovely and well-favoured. Mai-Sachme could not have been a child of the black earth without knowing that there are images of God, breathing images of the Deity, which must be distinguished from the inanimate ones and honoured as living images of God, like Hapi the bull of Menfe and like Pharaoh himself in the horizon of his palace. The governor's knowledge of this fact did contribute not a little to shape his speculations about Joseph's nature and appearance—and we know of course that, for his part, Joseph was not precisely keen on checking such speculations but on the contrary rather enjoyed making people sit up.

For the office and the book-keeping Joseph's presence was a perfect blessing. Tradition wrongs the captain when it says he took nothing on himself. But it was true that the office routine, so important in the eyes of his superiors in Thebes, had, as he well knew, been neglected for the pursuit of his tranquil passions of medicine and literature. Even his official reputation had already suffered on occasion, and letters full of polite, roundabout unpleasantness had come from the capital. And here Joseph proved to be the long-desired indeed, the bringer of change, the man of the "I am he." He put all the records in order, taught Mai-Sachme's scribes, much given to morra and skittles, that the higher preoccupations of their head were no reason why they should let dust accumulate on the necessary business of the place, but on the contrary were every ground for their own added diligence. Joseph saw to it that regular reports and accounts went off to the capital, where the authorities read them with pleasure. In his hand the staff of office became a cobra-snake stiffened to a magic wand. He needed only to tap a vat with it to say offhand: "That will hold fifty sacks of wheat"; and when they needed to know how many bricks it would take to build a ramp, he would put the staff to his forehead and then say: "It will take five thousand bricks." The first time that had been exactly right, the next time not

41

quite. But when he was quite right the first time, the success gilded the faultiness of the second guess and made that correct too.

In short, Joseph had not betrayed the captain in saying: "I am he." And when the book-keeping and the housekeeping came to no harm, Mai-Sachme often required his presence in the tower as well, where he compounded his drugs and made his literary essays. He liked to have Joseph about him, to discuss such matters as the correct number of blood-vessels and whether worms were the cause or the effect of disease. He set him to copy out the Tale of the Two Brothers, just as Joseph had done for his former master, in a de luxe edition on fine papyrus with red and black ink. Mai-Sachme found his assistant just the man for the job, not only because he could write a calligraphic script but also because the subject-matter was allied to Joseph's own fate. It was especially as a fool for love that Mai-Sachme found him so interesting. It was a field in which the governor's sympathies were warmly if sedately engaged—as indeed it is the chief theatre for the most fascinating exercise of the literary art. We can see how much time Jacob's son had to take from his administrative tasks—without neglecting them—to devote to Mai-Sachme's private avocations. They conferred for hours at a stretch how best to begin to commit to paper, in a pleasing, if possible even exciting, not to say thrilling style, the story of the governor's three-in-one-love-affair, which was still in part a tale of expectancy. The greatest and most discussed difficulty was this: if you included the third episode by anticipation, you would have to write the whole thing from the point of view of an old man of at least sixty; and that, they feared, would detract from the thrillingness, which, even as it was, was bound to suffer from the governor's natural temperament.

Then there was Joseph's own adventure which had brought him down to the prison. His affair with the sun-courtier's wife profoundly engaged Mai-Sachme's literary sympathies, and Joseph told him the whole story, taking care, of course, to spare the afflicted woman and not to minimize his own sins. These he described as being of the same nature as the ones he had earlier been guilty of against his own brothers and so against his father the shepherd king. So step by step he was brought back to the tale of his youth and origins; the captain's shrewd brown eyes got a strange and pregnant dissolving view into the backgrounds of this phenomenon, his aide, the convict Osarsiph. Mai-Sachme liked the fantastic name, obviously a made-up allusive combination. He spoke it feel-

42

ingly, like the good man he was, never taking it for the newcomer's own but rather for a disguise or an epithet, or a circumlocution of the "I am he."

He would have liked, with the enthusiasm of the born story-teller, to put to paper the tale of Potiphar's wife; and often he diverted himself with discussion about the best method. But when he tried, the result turned out to follow the pattern of the Two Brothers and he presently left off where he began.

The days went on, they multiplied, soon almost a year had gone round since Rachel's first-born came to Zawi-Re. Then there befell something in the prison, part of a series of important events in the great world. Not immediately, but after some lapse of time, this happening in the prison was to have extraordinary results and produce great changes for Joseph and for his friend and taskmaster, Mai-Sachme.

THE TWO FINE GENTLEMEN

One day, that is, Joseph betook himself, at his usual early hour, to the governor's tower, with some business papers for his chief's approval. The scene was always much like what happened between Petepre and the old steward Mont-kaw, and had the same ending: "Very good, very good, my friend." This time Mai-Sachme did not even look at the accounts, waving them away with his hand. His brows were even higher than usual, his lips more parted; it was plain that he was taken up with a particular occurrence, and, within the limits of his phlegm, wrought up.

"Another time, Osarsiph," he said, referring to the papers. "Now is not the moment. Let me tell you, in my prison things are not as they were yesterday and the day before. Something has happened, it happened before daybreak, very quietly, under special and secret orders. There has been a delivery of prisoners, a most embarrassing one. Two persons have arrived, under cover of darkness, for temporary arrest and safe-keeping—not ordinary persons, I mean they are very highly placed, or they were and may be again, but just now they have come down in the world. You have taken a fall yourself; but theirs is worse because they stood much higher. Listen while I tell you, but better not ask for details."

"But who are they?" asked Joseph all the same.

43

"Their names are Mesedsu-Re and Bin-em-Wese," answered the governor with reserve.

"Hark to that!" cried Joseph. "What sort of names are those? People don't have such names!"

He had good ground for surprise, for Mesedsu-Re meant "Hateful to the Sun-god" and Bin-em-Wese "Evil in Thebes." Those would have been strange parents who gave their sons such names!

The captain mulled about with some sort of decoction, without looking at Joseph.

"I thought," he said, "you knew that people are not necessarily named what they call themselves or are temporarily called. Circumstances can make names. Re himself changes his according to his circumstances. These gentlemen are called as I have called them, in their papers and the orders I received about them. Those are their names in the minutes of the action which will be brought against them, and they call themselves so according to their circumstances. You will not want to know more about it than that."

Joseph quickly considered. He thought of the revolving sphere, of the above that becomes below and again mounts upwards, by turns; of the laws of opposites, of how order is reversed and things turned upside down. "Hateful to the Sun-god"—that was Mersu-Re, "The Lord loves him"; "Evil in Thebes"—that was "Good in Thebes," Nefer-em-Wese. Through Potiphar he knew much about Pharaoh's court and the friends of the palace Merimat; and he recalled that Mersu-Re and Nefer-em-Wese were the names—quite overlaid with fulsome honorary titles—of Pharaoh's chief baker and supervisor of sweetmeats, with the title of Prince of Menfe, and of his overseer and scribe of the buffet, the head butler, Count of Abodu.

"The real names," said he, "of these given into your hands are probably 'What does my lord eat?' and 'What does my lord drink?' "

"Well, yes," responded the captain. "One only needs to give you an inch and you have an ell, as the saying goes. Or you think you have. Know what you know, and ask no further."

"What can have happened?" asked Joseph notwithstanding.

"Let be," replied Mai-Sachme. "They say," he went on, looking in the other direction, "that pieces of chalk were found in Pharaoh's bread, and flies in the good God's wine. How such responsible dignitaries come to be accused of such things and be sent up here awaiting investigation, under names corresponding to their circumstances, you can figure that out yourself."

"Chalk?" repeated Joseph. "Flies?"

"Before daylight," went on the captain, "they were put under strong guard on a boat bearing the sign of suspicion on prow and sail. They have been given me into strict though also suitable safe-keeping till their trial and till the verdict is pronounced. A most responsible and trying business. I have put them into the little vulture hut, you know, round the corner to the right by the back wall, that has a vulture with outspread wings on the ridgepole, it happened to be vacant—or rather, empty, for it is not furnished in the least as they are used to—and there they sit since early this morning, with some bitter beer, each of them on an ordinary camp-stool; and the vulture-house has no other amenities whatever. It is pretty hard on them; and what will be the end of their affair, whether they will soon be put in corpse-colour or whether the majesty of the good God will lift up their heads again, nobody can say. We have to behave in the light of this uncertainty, taking account within limits of their former station and to the extent of our powers. I will put you in charge of them, you will visit them twice or thrice a day, you know, and ask after their wants, if only for form's sake. Such gentlemen require good form; if we only ask what they would like, it does them some good, and it is less important after that whether they get it. You have the society graces, the *savoir faire*," said he (he used an Akkadian expression), "you can talk with them in a way that suits their own elegant conventions and their present circumstances too. My lieutenants here would be either too rough or too subservient. We have to keep the right balance. Respect with a shade of solemnity, that would be about my idea."

"I'm not so good at solemnity," said Joseph. "It is not my long suit. Perhaps I might make the respectfulness a little ironic, just slightly mocking."

"That might be good too," the captain responded. "When you inquire after their wishes, they see at once that you are not serious, and that of course they can't have things here the way they are used to them, or only sort of symbolically, as it were. Anyhow we cannot have them squatting there in an empty hut. We must put in two beds with head-rests, and at least one comfortable chair, if not two, with cushions for the feet; they can take turns sitting in it. And you must act as their vizier 'What

45

would my lord eat?' and their vizier 'What would my lord drink?' and go a little way towards satisfying their wishes. Say they want roast goose, you can give them stork. If they ask for cake you can give them shortbread, if they want wine let them have grape-juice. We will try every time to go half-way and at least show our willingness on all occasions. Go along now and pay them your respects—with any kind of colouring you think best. Beginning tomorrow, you should go morning and evening."

"I hear and obey," said Joseph, and betook himself down from the tower to the vulture hut.

The guards in front of it lifted their daggers with grins spreading over their peasant faces, for they liked him well. Then they drew back the heavy wooden bolt from the door and Joseph entered in to the courtiers. They squatted there in their little cubicle, bowed over their own stomachs, with their hands folded on top of their heads. He saluted them with the utmost refinement, though not in such an affected manner as he had seen in Hor-waz, the scribe of the Great Gate. However, it was a greeting à la mode, with raised arm and a smile and the formal wish that they might live the lifetime of Re.

They had sprung up as soon as they saw him, and overwhelmed him with questions and complaints.

"Who are you, young man?" they cried. "Are you well or ill disposed towards us? But at least you have come—at last somebody has come! Your manners are good, they suggest that you might feel with us and see how impossible, how intolerable, how indefensible our situation is! Do you know who we are? Have they told you? We are the Prince of Menfe, the Count of Abodu: Pharaoh's first inspector of bakestuffs and he who ranks even above the first scribe of the buffet, his sommelier-general, who hands him the cup on all the greatest occasions; the baker of bakers and the butler of butlers, master of the grape, in the garland of vine. Is this clear to you? Have you come here in this knowledge? Can you picture to yourself how we have lived, in pavilions faced with azurite and diorite, where we slept upon down and had special servants to scratch the soles of our feet? What will become of us in this hole? They have put us into this bare room, we have been sitting since before dawn behind bolts and bars, without the least attention paid to us. Curses on Zawi-Re! Curses, curses! There is nothing here, nothing! We have no mirror, we have no razors, no rouge-box, no bathroom, no place to

46

satisfy our necessities, so that we are forced to restrain ourselves, though they are more urgent than usual on account of the strain we have been under, and we have cramps—we, the arch-baker and the master of the vine! Is it given to your soul to feel that this situation of ours cries to heaven? Or do you only come to observe whether our misery has reached the uttermost?"

"High and noble sirs," answered Joseph, "calm yourselves! I am well disposed towards you, for I am the captain's mouthpiece and adjutant and trusted by him with the office of overseer. He has made me your servant, who am to ask after your commands, and as my master is good and even-tempered you may infer my own temperament from his choice of me. I cannot lift up your heads; that only Pharaoh can do, so soon as your innocence is made clear, which I assume with all due respect is present and can be made clear—"

Here he paused a little and waited. They both looked him in the face: one with eyes swimming in vinous emotion, yet hopefully; the other wearing a glassy stare wherein fear and deceit swiftly pursued each other.

One would have expected the baker to be like a bag of flour and the cup-bearer to resemble the slender vine. But on the contrary it was the cup-bearer who was full-bodied. He was short and plump, with a fiery red face between the wings of the kerchief drawn smoothly over his head, in front of which his thick ears adorned with stone buttons stood out. His chubby cheeks, alas, were now quite bristly with a stubble of beard; but they showed that when shaven and oiled they could shine right jollily. Even the present dejection and gloom on the chief butler's face could not quite extinguish its fundamental trait of joviality. The chief baker was by comparison tall and stoop-shouldered; his face was sallow, though perhaps again only by comparison; but also because it was framed by a sombre black coiffure, out of which his broad gold ear-rings peeped out. But there were unmistakably underworldly features in the baker's face: the longish nose was set somewhat awry, the mouth showed a one-sided thickening and lengthening, making it sag unpleasantly, and the lowering brows had a sinister, ill-omened expression.

We must not suppose that Joseph would have remarked the difference between the two faces with any easy partisanship for the good cheer of the one and just as easy dislike of the forbidding traits of the other. By tradition and training he would be prone to accord to both the jovial

47

and the jaundiced equal respect for their destinies. He would even go further and summon up more cordiality and courtesy towards the man whose features bore the stamp of the lower regions than to him who was already jolly by nature.

The beautifully pressed court costumes of the two with their ample adornment and gay-coloured ribbon bows were soiled and crumpled with travel; but each still wore in plain view the insignia of his high office: the butler a collar of gold vine-leaves and the baker an order of golden ears in the shape of a sickle.

"It is not I," repeated Joseph, "who can lift up your heads, nor is it the warden. All that we can do is to ease a little, as well as we can, the discomforts a heavy fate has inflicted on you. You will understand that a beginning has already been made, in that in your first hour here you wanted for everything. From now on, there will be something you do not lack; and that, after the complete deprivation, will seem sweeter to you than anything that you had when you still anointed yourself with the oil of gladness, but which, alas, this sorry place can never offer you. You see how well-meaning we were, my lords Count Abodu and Prince of Menfe, in making such a poor beginning. Within the hour you will have two bedsteads, simple ones but one apiece. An easy-chair, to use by turns, shall join the stools. A razor—unfortunately only a stone one, I apologize for it beforehand—will be at your service, and some very good eye-paint, black, shading into green, the captain himself knows how to prepare it and I am sure he will be delighted to give you some if I asked him. As for the mirror, again it was probably intentional to have it reflect your images not as you at present are but after you have washed up. Your servant, by which I mean myself, possesses a fairly clear copper mirror, and I will gladly loan it to you for the duration of your stay, which one way or the other can only be a brief span. It will please you that its frame and handle are shaped like the life-sign. As for bathing, you can get that done at the right of your hut by a couple of guards whom I will station there for the purpose; on the left side you can satisfy your necessities; that is probably just now the most pressing matter."

"Fine!" said the butler. "Just fine, for the present and in view of all the circumstances. Young man, you come like the rosy dawn after the night and like cooling shade after the heat of the sun. Health and strength to you and may you live long! The master of the vine salutes you! Lead us to the left side."

"But what did you mean," asked the baker, "by 'one way or the other' in connection with our stay and by 'a brief span'?"

"I meant by that," Joseph answered, "in any case, quite certainly, beyond a doubt—or something reassuring of that sort. That is what I meant."

And he took leave for the time of the two gentlemen, bowing somewhat more respectfully before the baker than before the butler.

Later in the day he came back, bringing a draught-board to amuse them, and inquired how they had dined. They answered more or less in the sense of "Oh, well . . ." and asked for roast goose. He promised they should have something of the kind, a roast waterfowl for instance and some sort of cake such as the poor place afforded. Further they might have an hour's target practice or a game at skittles under the eye of the guards on the court in front of the vulture-house: they had only to command. They thanked him very much and begged him to thank the captain as well for so thoughtfully arranging that they could now so greatly enjoy these indications of amelioration after the utter baldness of their beginning. They had conceived a great confidence in Joseph and kept him in talk as long as they possibly could, with thanks and complaints, both that day and the following one, each time he came to inquire after their welfare and their commands. But in all their volubility they did not depart from their silence on the ground of their presence here but showed the same reserve which Mai-Sachme had shown in his first talk about them with Joseph.

They suffered most on account of their new names, and repeatedly implored him not to believe that these were their real ones in any sense whatever.

"It is so very delicate of you, Osarsiph, dear youth," they said, "that you do not call us by the absurd names which they put on us when we were arrested. But it is not enough that you do not let them cross your lips; even to yourself you must not call us so; you must believe that we do not go by such indecent names, but quite the reverse. That would be a great help; for we are distressed lest these fantastic names which are written in indelible ink in our papers and the proceedings of our trials in the writing of truth should gradually take on reality and we be so called to all eternity."

"Do not distress yourself, my lords," answered Joseph; "that will all pass. After all, at bottom it is a kindness. They had given you a disguise to wear under your present circumstances, thus your real ones are not betrayed in the writing of truth. In a way it is not you at all who appear in the papers and indictments; it is not you who sit here, but 'Hated of God' and 'Scum of Thebes' who suffer under your deprivations."

They were inconsolable. "Ah, but it really is us, even though incognito," they lamented. "You are so tactful that you still give us the fine titles and decorations we wore at court: Distinguished in Menfe, Prince of the Bread, and His Eminence the Great Lord of the Winepress. But know, if you do not already, they took away all these names when they arrested us; we stand here practically as naked as when the soldiers pour water over us at the right of the hut—all we have left is 'Scum of the Earth' and 'Hated of God'—that is the horrible thing!"

And they wept.

"How ever is it possible," Joseph asked, looking away just as the captain had done, "how is it possible, how ever in all the world can it have happened that Pharaoh behaved to you like a leopard of Upper Egypt and like the raging ocean, and his heart brought forth a sandstorm like the mountains of the East, of such a sort that overnight you are shorn of your honours, arrested on suspicion, and snatched off down here to us?"

"Flies," sobbed the butler.

"Chalk," said the chief baker.

Both looked the other way but each in a different direction. However, there was not much resort in the hut for three pairs of eyes; their glances met by mistake, then quickly shifted, only to meet again whitherever they travelled. It was a depressing game and Joseph would have ended it by going away, as he saw that there was nothing to be got out of them save flies and chalk. They did not want to let him go, they kept trying to convince him how untenable was any suspicion of guilt, how preposterous the names Mesedsu-Re and Bin-em-Wese.

"I implore you, good youth from Canaan, dear Ibrim," said the butler, "listen and see, how could it ever be that I, Good-and-happy-in-Thebes, could have anything to do with such an affair? It is absurd, it is contrary to the order of things; it stands to reason that it only proceeds from misunderstanding and slander. I am the chief of the wine of life and carry the staff of the grape before Pharaoh when he goes in procession to the banquet and the blood of Osiris flows in streams. I am his herald, crying Hail and Health, swinging my staff above my head. I am the man

50

with the garland, of the vine-wreath on the head and the foaming beaker! Look at my cheeks, smoothed as they now are, albeit with a bad razor! Are they not like the bursting grape when the sun has brewed the sacred juice within it? I live and let live, crying all Hail and all Health! Do I look like one who measures the coffin for the God? Have I any resemblance to the ass of Set? One does not hitch that animal to the plough with the ox, one does not put wool and flax together in one garment; the vine does not bring forth figs. And what does not go together never can! I beg you to judge by your good common sense, as one who knows the laws of opposites and makes distinctions, who understands what is possible and what not; judge whether I can have any share in this guilt or partake at all in what is so impossible to me."

"I can see," said Prince Mersu-Re, the chief baker, looking the other way in his turn, "that the Count's words have not failed of their impression on you, man of Zahi and gifted youth. Indeed they were compelling; your judgment must inevitably speak in his favour. Therefore I also appeal to your sense of justice, convinced that you will not want for reason and worldly common sense in passing judgment in my own case. You have perceived that the suspicion we high officials labour under is inconsistent with the sacred office my friend here holds. So you will surely agree that one can even less reconcile it with the sacredness of mine, which is if possible still greater. It is in essence the oldest, the earliest, the most exemplary—a higher there may be, a deeper never. There is a consummateness about it as there is about everything from which a descriptive adjective derives; it is the holy, the very holiest of the holy! It speaks of the grotto and the cavern into which one drives swine to sacrifice, throwing torches down from above to feed the primeval fire, that it may burn to warm and expand the forces of production. Therefore I bear a torch before Pharaoh, not swinging it above my head but holding it seemly and priestlike before me and before him, when he goes to the table to eat the flesh of the buried god, which springs forth to the sickle from below and out of the depths that received the oath."

Here the baker gave a start, and the gaze of his staring eyes moved still further aside, until he was looking out of the left outside and the right inside corners. He kept beginning a sentence only to take it back and begin again, yet all the while he only talked himself deeper in. For his words were addressed downwards and he could not turn them round.

"Pardon me, I did not mean to say that," he began again, "at least I

51

did not intend to say it just like that; I do hope that you are not getting a wrong idea. You are a worldly-wise young man, and we would enlist your understanding in support of our innocence. I talk, but when I listen to my own words I am alarmed. I might be making you feel that I am invoking a sacredness so mighty, that is so great and so deep, that it is almost suspect itself, so to speak, and invoking it might even work the other way from what I want. I beg you, summon all your understanding, do not be confused into the idea that if the evidence is too strong that makes it weaker, or even makes it help to prove the opposite. That would be frightful, it would endanger the soundness of your judgment for you to come on such thoughts. Look at me! Even though I do not look at you, but at my arguments. I—guilty? I involved in such an affair? Am I not the very chief and lord of the bread, servant of the wandering mother who seeks her daughter with the torch, the fruit-bringer, the all-giver, giving warmness and greenness; who rejected the benumbing blood of the grape and gave the malt drink preference; who brought to mankind wheat and barley and first broke the clod with the curving plough; so that from milder nourishment milder customs sprang, whereas aforetime men ate roots and grasses and even one another? To her I belong, consecrate to her who in the wind on the threshing-floor winnows corn and chaff and separates honour from dishonour; the lawgiver who gives justice and regulates free will. Judge now in your wisdom if I could have engaged in such a sinister affair! Judge on the basis of unfitness, which does not so much rest on the fact that the affair is sinister; justice, like bread, being allied to the dark realm and to the womb of the earth below, where dwell the avenging goddesses; so that one might call it in its sacredness the watch-dog of the goddess, the more so since the dog is in fact sacred to her—and from that point of view you might also call me, who am sacred to her, a dog—"

Here he broke off with another frightful start and his eyeballs darted right over into the opposite corners. He asseverated that he had not meant to say what he had said, or at least not the way he had said it. But Joseph soothed them both, begging them not to take things so hard and not strain themselves on his account. He knew how to prize it, he said, and was honoured to have them tell him about their affair, or if not about the affair, at least the reasons why it could not have been their affair. But still less was it his affair to set himself as judge over them, for he was commanded only to be their servant, who inquired after their wishes, as they had been accustomed. Of course, they were also accustomed to having their wishes carried out, and that, much to his regret, he was largely unable to do. But at least they had the first half of what they were used to. And he asked if they would honour him with another command.

No, they said pensively, they knew of nothing; no other commands would be likely to occur to one, seeing that nothing came of them. Ah, but why must he leave them so soon? Would he not tell them how long he thought the investigation of the charges against them would take and how long they would have to lie in this hole?

He would tell them faithfully and at once, he replied, if he only knew. But naturally he did not. He could only make an entirely arbitrary and irresponsible guess; it would take thirty and ten days in all, at the most and the least, until their fate was decided.

"Ah, how long!" lamented the butler.

"Ah, how short!" cried the baker—but at once gave another frightful start and assured them that he also had meant to say how long. But the chief butler reflected and then remarked that Joseph's calculation had probably got some sense to it. For in thirty and seven and three days, counting from their arrival, it would be Pharaoh's beautiful birthday, well known as a day of justice and compassion; on that day, in all probability, their fate would be decided.

"I did not to my knowledge think of it," answered Joseph, "and did not make my calculations according. It was more of an inspiration, but seeing it turns out that Pharaoh's exalted birthday falls just on that day, you can see that my words are already beginning to be fulfilled."

OF THE STINGING WORM

With that he went, shaking his head over his two charges and their "affair," about which he now knew more than he could well admit. Nobody in the two lands might appear or assume to know more than was considered seemly for men to know, and this perilous knowledge was hushed up by the authorities in a cloud of circumlocution and secrecy, a screen of words about flies and pieces of chalk and unidentifiable made-up names like Hated of God and Scum of Weset. Nevertheless it was soon talked of through the length and breadth of the whole kingdom. Everybody, whether he used the prescribed circumlocutions or not, knew what was behind these minimizings and palliations. The story in all its shockingness did not lack popular appeal; one might even say that it had a ritual character, seeming as it did like the repetition in the present of events whose foundation lay far back in the past.

To put it bluntly, somebody had been conspiring against Pharaoh's life—this although the days of the majesty of that elderly god were well known to be numbered anyhow, and it is common knowledge that their inclination to unite again with the sun could not be arrested either by the advice of the magicians and physicians of the book-house or even by the mediation of Ishtar of the Way, which His Majesty's brother and father-in-law of the Euphrates, Tushratta, King over Khanigalbat or Mitanniland, had solicitously sent to him. But that the Great House, Si-Re, Son of the Sun and Lord of the Two Crowns, Neb-ma-Re-Amenhotep, was old and ailing and could scarcely breathe was no reason at all why he should not be conspired against; indeed, if you liked, it was a very good reason why he should, however dreadful, of course, such an enterprise remained.

It was a universally known fact that Re himself, the sun-god, had originally been King of the two lands, or rather ruler on earth over all men; and had ruled them with majestic brilliance and blessing so long as his years were still young, mature, or middle-aged, and even for some considerable period of time into his beginning and increasing age. But when he had got very old, and painful infirmities and frailties, though of course splendid in their form, approached the majesty of this god, he had found it good to withdraw from the earth and retire into the upper regions. For his bones gradually turned to silver, his flesh to gold, and his hair to genuine lapis lazuli, a very beautiful form of senescence, yet attended with all sorts of ailments and pains, for which the gods themselves had sought a thousand remedies but all in vain, since no herb that grows can avail against the diseases of gilding and silvering and lapidification, those troubles of advanced old age. Yet even under these circumstances the old Re had always clung to his earthly sovereignty although he must have seen that owing to his own weakness it had begun to relax, that he had ceased to be feared and even to be respected.

Now Isis, the Great One of the Island, Eset, a million-fold fertile in guile, felt that her moment was come. Her wisdom embraced heaven and earth, like that of the superannuated old Re himself. But there was

54

one thing she did not know or command, and the lack of it hampered her: she did not know the last, most secret name of Re, his very final one, knowledge of which would give power over him. Re had very many names, each one more secret than the one before, yet not utterly hopeless to find out, save one, the very last and mightiest. That he still withheld; whoso could make him name it, he could compel him and outdistance him and put him under his feet.

Therefore Eset conceived and devised a serpent, which should sting Re in his golden flesh. Then the intolerable pain of the sting, which only great Eset could cure who made the worm, would force Re to tell her his name. Now as she contrived it, so was it fulfilled. The old Re was stung, and in torments was forced to come out with one of his secret names after another, always hoping that the goddess would be satisfied before they got to the last one. But she kept on to the uttermost, until he had named her the very most secret of all, and the power of her knowledge over him was absolute. After that it cost her nothing to heal his wound; but he only got a little better, within the wretched limits in which so old a creature can; and soon thereafter he gave up and joined the great majority.

Thus tradition, known by heart to every child of Keme. It did suggest that Pharaoh had had something done to him; since he gradually got worse until his condition was so like that of the old god that one tended to mix them up. But there had been one particular individual who had taken the ancient tradition quite peculiarly to heart: a certain inmate of Pharaoh's house of women, the private and well-guarded pavilion of the greatest elegance adjoining the palace Merimat; whither Pharaoh still had himself carried now and then, of course only to chuck one or other of their graces under the chin, perhaps to defeat her on the board of thirty fields, and at the same time to enjoy the lute-playing, dancing, and singing of the rest of the sweet-scented troop. Often, indeed, he played a game with that very female who took so seriously the old legend of Isis and Re that she yielded to the temptation to re-enact it. Nobody, however well versed in the finer points of this story, can tell this woman's name. It has been obliterated from tradition, the night of everlasting forgetfulness shrouds it. And yet the woman had been in her time a favourite concubine of Pharaoh, and twelve or thirteen years before, when he still condescended to beget a child, she had borne him a son, Noferka-Ptah—this name is preserved—who as a scion of the godlike

55

seed received a special education, and on whose account she, a concubine, was privileged to wear the vulture head-dress. It was not quite so elaborate a one as that worn by Tiy, the great royal consort herself, but none the less a gold vulture cap. This cap, and her maternal weakness for Noferka-Ptah, went to the woman's head and were fatal to her. For the head-dress incited her to confuse herself with the wily Eset and to cherish ambitions hallowed by tradition and mixed up with her doting fondness for her little half-breed. The ancient records dazed her small and scheming brain, so that she made up her mind to have Pharaoh stung by a serpent, to instigate a palace revolt and set on the throne of the two lands not Horus-Amenhotep, the rightful heir, who was sickly anyhow, but the fruit of her own womb, Noferka-Ptah.

The first steps toward the goal of overturning the dynasty, bringing in a new time and elevating the nameless near-favourite to the rank of goddess-mother had been successfully taken. The plot was hatched in Pharaoh's house of women; but through certain officials of the harem and certain officers of the guard who had been eager for new things, connections had been established, on the one hand with the palace itself, where a number of friends, some of them highly placed—a head charioteer of the god, the chief of gens-d'armes, the steward of the fruit stores, the overseer of the King's herds of oxen, the head keeper of the King's ointments, and certain others—were won over for the enterprise; and on the other hand they got in touch with the outer world of the residential city, where through the officers' wives the male kindred of Pharaoh's graces were drawn in and engaged to stir up Wese's population with evil talk against the old Re, who by now was nothing at all but gold and silver and lapis lazuli.

In all there were two-and-seventy conspirators privy to the plot. It was a proper and a pregnant number, for there had been just seventy-two when red Set lured Usir into the chest. And these seventy-two in their turn had had good cosmic ground to be no more and no less than that number. For it is just that number of groups of five weeks which make up the three hundred and sixty days of the year, not counting the odd days; and there are just seventy-two days in the dry fifth of the year, when the gauge shows that the Nourisher has reached his lowest ebb, and the god sinks into his grave. So where there is conspiracy anywhere in the world it is requisite and customary for the number of conspirators to be seventy-two. And if the plot fail, the failure shows that

56

if this number had not been adhered to it would have failed even worse.

Now the present plot did fail, although it had had the benefit of the best models and all the preliminary steps had been taken with the greatest care. The head keeper of unguents had even succeeded in purloining a magic script out of Pharaoh's book-house and, following its instructions, had shaped certain little wax images; these were smuggled about here and there and were calculated to produce by magic a mental confusion and bewitchment such as must assure the success of the undertaking. It was decided to put poison in Pharaoh's bread or his wine or in both; and to use the ensuing confusion for a palace coup. Combined with a rising in the upper city, this was to have led to the proclamation of a new era and the elevation of the young bastard Noferka-Ptah to the throne of the two lands. And then all at once the lid blew off. Possibly at the last minute one of the seventy-two decided that by choosing the loyal part he would do better for his career and for the beauty and interest of the wall-paintings in his tomb. Or perhaps a police decoy had wormed himself into the councils from the start. Anyhow, a list had been put into Pharaoh's hands. It was painful enough reading, containing as it did the names of a number of really close friends of the god and visitors at his levee. The list was on the whole correct, though not quite free from errors and mistaken identities; and the prosecutions had been swift, quiet, and thorough. The Isis of the women's house was straightway strangled by eunuchs, her little son was sent into outermost Nubia and a secret commission met to investigate the whole scheme and each particular guilt. Meanwhile the persons thus exposed were labelled in one common epithet: "Abhorred of the two lands"; while cruel distortions were made of their personal ones, under which they disappeared into various custodies to await their fate in circumstances quite foreign to their usual habits.

And thus it was that Pharaoh's chief baker and chief butler had come down to the prison where Joseph lay.

JOSEPH HELPS OUT AS INTERPRETER

They had been sitting there now for thirty-and-seven days when Joseph one morning made his usual call to inquire how they had rested and to ask after their commands. He found the two gentlemen in a frame

57

of mind which might be called excited, depressed, and annoyed all at once. They had by now begun to get used to the simple life and had ceased to complain. After all, it is not necessary to life to live as they had lived, surrounded by malachite and diorite, with servants to scratch the soles of their feet. Indeed, with a bathing-place on their right and a retiring-place on their left, and some opportunity to shoot arrows and throw nines as a substitute for the lordly bird-shoot, life is not so bad after all. But today they looked definitely relapsed into their former spoilt-children state; as soon as Joseph appeared they exhausted themselves in the old bitter complaints: how after all they lacked for the most elementary conveniences and how their life here, however honest the effort they had made to come to terms with it, still continued to be a dog's life.

They had had dreams the night before, they said, in answer to Joseph's sympathetic questioning. Each of them had dreamed his own dream, and each dream had been of the most speaking vividness, highly impressive, unforgettable, and of quite peculiar flavour: dreams that unmistakably "meant something," wearing the sign "Understand me aright" on their brows. They fairly cried out for interpretation. And at home each of them had had his own interpreter of dreams, experts in all the monstrous brood of the dark hours, with eyes for every detail to which a claim of significance could be attached; equipped with the very best dream-books and expositions, Babylonian as well as Egyptian, and only needing to turn the leaves, if they themselves fell short of ideas. And when they were at a standstill and the books did not help them out, the two courtiers could call a convocation of temple prophets and learned scribes, by whose combined powers the matter could certainly be got to the bottom of. In short, in every such case they had been promptly, efficiently, and aristocratically served. But now, and here? They had dreamed: each of them his own special, striking, and poignant dream, each with a strange flavour of its own; their minds were full of them, and there was nobody in this accursed hole to interpret these dreams and serve them as they were used to be served. That was a deprivation far harder to bear than the loss of feather beds, roast goose, and bird-shooting; it made them feel their intolerable degradation even to tears.

Joseph listened and stuck out his lips a little.

"Well, gentlemen," said he, "to begin with, if it is any consolation to you to know that someone feels for you in your distress, then behold in me one who does so. But it might even be possible to do a little something about this lack that so upsets you. I have been appointed your servant and caretaker, and, so to speak, I am here as a general-purpose assistant. So why not after all for dreams as well? I am not quite unversed in the field, I may boast of a certain familiarity with dreams—do not take the word amiss, it is only apt, for in my family and tribe we have always been in the habit of having interesting dreams. My father, the shepherd king, while on his travels, had a first-class dream in a certain place, which clothed his whole being with dignity for the rest of his life; it was always an uncommon pleasure to hear him tell it. And in my previous life I myself had much to do with dreams. I even had a nickname for it among my brothers, who made a jest of this peculiarity of mine. You have had so much practice in putting up with things—how would it be if you put up with me and told me your dreams, in order that I might try to interpret them?"

"Yes, indeed," said they. "Very good. You are a most agreeable young man, and you have a way of looking dreamily into space with your charming, yes, even beautiful eyes, when you talk of dreams, that we could almost have confidence in your capacities. But even so, it is one thing to dream and quite another to interpret."

"Do not say so!" he responded. "Do not say it without qualification. For it may well be that dreaming is a single whole, wherein dream and interpretation belong together and dreamer and interpreter only seem to be two separate persons but are actually interchangeable and one and the same, since together they make up the whole. Whoever dreams interprets also; and whoever would interpret must have dreamed. Your Excellencies Lord Prince of the Bread and Hereditary Cup-bearer, you have lived under luxurious circumstances of unnecessary division of labour, so that when you dreamed, the interpretation was the business of your private soothsayers. But at bottom and by nature everybody is the interpreter of his own dream, and only out of sheer elegance does he have himself served with an interpretation. I will reveal to you the mystery of dreaming: the interpretation is earlier than the dream, and when we dream, the dream proceeds from the interpretation. How otherwise could it happen that a man knows perfectly when an interpretation is false, and cries: 'Away with you, ignoramus! I will have another soothsayer who interprets to me the truth'? Well, at least try it with me, and

59

if I blunder or do not interpret after your own knowledge, chase me away to hide my head in shame!"

"I will not tell mine," said the chief baker; "I am used to better service and I prefer to go without in this as in other things, sooner than take an unprofessional person as interpreter."

"I will tell mine," said the butler. "Truly I am so eager for an interpretation that I will gladly put up with what comes, especially since this young man shows some familiarity with the subject and narrows and veils his eyes in such a promising way. Young man, prepare to hear and to interpret; but pull yourself together, as I likewise must pull myself together to find the right words and not murder my dream in the telling. For it was so clear and lifelike and full of inimitable spice; for we know, alas, how a dream like that shrinks when you try to put it into words, and becomes the mummy and withered, swaddled image of that which it was when you dreamed it and it grew green and blossomed and bore fruit like the vine which was before me in this my dream—for it seems I have already begun to tell it. It seemed to me I was with Pharaoh in his vineyard and beneath the roof of the vaulted bower where Pharaoh was resting. And before me was a grapevine; I see it still, it was a marvellous vine and had three separate branches. You understand, it grew green and had leaves like human hands; but though the arbour was already hanging full of heavy bunches of grapes, this vine had not fruited yet, for that took place before my very eyes, in my dream. Lo, it grew before them and began to blossom, sending forth the most beautiful thick blooms among its foliage, and the three branches put out grapes that ripened visibly with the swiftness of the wind and their purple fruits were as bouncing as my own cheeks and bulged as nobody's cheeks in these parts. I rejoiced greatly and with my right hand I picked the grapes, for in my left I held Pharaoh's beaker, half full of cool water. And full of feeling I squeezed the juice of the grapes into the cup, remembering as I did so that you, young man, sometimes squeeze a little grape-juice into water and give it to us when we order wine. So I gave the cup to Pharaoh into his hand. . . . And that was all," he finished lamely, crestfallen and disappointed by his own words.

"It is not a little," answered Joseph, opening his eyes, which he had kept closed as he inclined his ear to the tale. "There was the cup, and clear water within it, and you yourself pressed the grape-juice into it from the vine with the three branches and gave it to the lord of the two crowns. That was a pure gift and there were no flies in it. Shall I interpret?"

"Yes, do!" cried the other. "I can scarcely wait!"

"This is the meaning," said Joseph. "The three branches are three days. In three days you will receive the water of life and Pharaoh will lift up your head and take away from you the name of shame so that you are once more called Justified in Thebes as before, and he will install you again in your office, so that you can give him the cup again into his hands as when you were his cup-bearer. And that is all."

"Splendid, capital!" cried the fat man. "That is a beautiful, an excellent, a masterly interpretation. I am served by it as never before in my life, and you, sweet youth, have done my mind an inestimable service. Three branches—three days—how you could have it so pat, you clever youth—and 'Honourable in Thebes' again as before, and everything as it used to be, and once more Pharaoh's friend! Thank you, thank you, thank you very, very much!"

And he sat there and wept for joy.

But Joseph said to him: "District Count of Abodu, Nefer-em-Wese! I have prophesied to you according to your dream—it was easily and gladly done and I rejoice that I could give you a happy interpretation. Soon you will be surrounded by hosts of friends, because you have been declared innocent; but here in these straits I shall be the first to congratulate you. I was your servant and steward for seven-and-thirty days and shall be so for three more, by the governor's orders; asking after your commands and giving you tokens of your accustomed amenities, so far as our limitations permit. I have come to you here in the vulture-house morning and evening, and been like an angel of God, if I may so express myself, into whose breast you could pour your troubles and be condoled with over the strangeness of your lot. But you have not asked me much about myself. And yet, like you, I was not born into this hole nor did I choose it for my habitation; I landed here, I know not how, put here as a slave of the King, condemned for a sin which is nothing but misrepresentation before God. Your minds were too full of your own misfortunes for you to have much feeling or interest left for mine. But forget me not, and my service to you, Count Chief Cup-bearer; think of me when you are back in all your former glory. Speak of me before Pharaoh and call to his attention that I am sitting here out of the sheerest misunderstanding, and beg in my behalf that he graciously remove me

61

out of this prison where I am so sorely against my will. For indeed I was stolen away, simply stolen as a boy from my home and brought down here to Egypt, stolen down into the pit—and am like the moon, when an opposing spirit stopped it in its course so that it could not move shining onwards before the gods its brothers. Will you do this for me, District Count Head Cup-bearer, and speak of me at Court?"

"Yes, of course, a thousand times yes!" cried the fat man. "I promise you that I will mention you at the first opportunity when I stand before Pharaoh, and will remind him each later time if his mind has not grasped it. It would be swinish of me indeed not to think and speak of you to your advantage; for whether you have stolen or are stolen is all the same to me; mentioned you shall be, and pardoned, sweet honey-youth!"

And he embraced Joseph and kissed him on the mouth and on both cheeks.

"But I also have dreamed," said the long man, "though the fact seems to have been forgotten here. I did not know, Ibrim, that you were such a skilled interpreter or I would not have rejected your aid. I now incline to tell you my dream in my turn, as well as it can be told in words, and you shall interpret it to me. Make ready to hearken."

"I hearken," answered Joseph.

"What I dreamed," said the baker, "was this, and was the following. I dreamed—but you can see how ludicrous was my dream, for how should I, the Prince of Menfe, who certainly never sticks his head into the oven, how should I, like a baker's apprentice, be delivering rolls and crescents? —but suffice it to say, there I was, in my dream, carrying on my head three baskets of fine rolls, one on top of the other, flat baskets fitting into each other, each full of all kinds of good things from the palace bakery; and in the top one lay uncovered the bakestuff for Pharaoh, the crescents and rolls. Then a flight of birds came swooping down on spread wing, their talons bared, their necks stretched out, their eyeballs goggling and glaring, and screeched as they came. And these birds in their boldness thrust down and ate of the food on my head. I would have lifted my free hand to wave it over the top of the basket and frighten the vermin away; but I could not, for my hand was as lamed. And they hacked at the food, and their flapping was all about me like a wind, and the bird-smell of them was piercing in its foulness." Here the baker started, as he always did, went pale, and tried to smile in the misshapen corner of his mouth. "That is," he said, "you must not imagine the birds and the

62

stench on the air nor their beaks nor their goggling eyes as too utterly disgusting. They were just birds, like any birds, and when I said they hacked—I don't remember whether I said that but I may have done— that was rather too strong a word, used to give you a feeling of my dream. I ought to have said they pecked. The little birds pecked from my basket; they probably thought I meant to feed them, the top basket being uncovered and no cloth over it—in short, the situation was very natural in my dream, except for me, the Prince of Menfe, carrying the bakestuff on my head, and of course that I could not wave my hand —though perhaps I did not want to because I liked the little birds to come. . . . And that was all."

"Shall I interpret?" Joseph asked.

"As you will," answered the baker.

"The three baskets," said Joseph, "are three days. In three days Pharaoh will take you out of this house and lift up your head from off you; that is, he will bind you to the post and shall hang you on a tree and the birds of the air will eat your flesh from off you. And that is all— unfortunately."

"What are you saying?" cried the baker, hiding his face in his hands. Tears sprang out from between his beringed fingers.

But Joseph comforted him, and said: "Do not grieve all too much, Excellence Chief Baker, neither do you dissolve, O master of the vine, in tears of joy. Rather accept with dignity what you both are and what comes to you both. For the world too, being round, has an upper and an under side; yet we should not make too much of this two-sidedness, for at bottom the ox is no better and no worse than the ass; they might easily change places, and together they make one whole. You can see by the tears you both are shedding that the difference between you two gentle- men is not so great. You, Your Eminence Master of the Feast, be not prideful, for you are only good in a manner of speaking and I suspect your innocence consists only in that nobody approached you from the side of evil, because you are a chatterbox and they did not trust you. So you remained ignorant of evil. And you will not be mindful of me when you come back into your kingdom, although you have promised to; I tell you this beforehand. Only very late will you do it, when you stub your toe on the memory of me. When you do, then remember how I told you so. But you, Master Baker, do not despair! For I think you joined the conspiracy because you thought it was respectably backed,

63

and you confused evil with good, as can easily happen. Lo, you are of the god when he is below, and your companion is of the god when he is above, and lifting up of the head is lifting up of the head, even though it be on the cross of Usir, on which, in fact, one sometimes sees an ass, in token that Set and Osiris are the same."

Thus Jacob's son to the two fine gentlemen. But three days after he had interpreted their dreams they were fetched out from the prison and the heads of both were lifted up: the chief butler in honour, the baker in shame, for he was put to death. But the butler completely forgot Joseph, because he hated even to think of the prison and so would not think of his former steward.

Chapter Two

THE SUMMONS

NEB-NEF-NEZEM

AFTER these events, Joseph remained for two more years in the prison and in his second pit. He had reached the mature age of thirty when he was hastily removed, yes, in the most breathless haste—for now it was Pharaoh's self who had dreamed. After the space of two years Pharaoh had a dream—in fact he had two dreams; but since they came to the same thing we may speak of them as one. The point is idle, by comparison with another: namely, that when we now speak of Pharaoh, the word has no longer, in a personal sense, the meaning it had when the chief baker and the chief butler dreamed their true dreams. For Pharaoh is always the word, and Pharaoh is always; but at the same time he comes and goes; just as the sun is always, yet likewise goes and comes. So now, that is to say very soon after the two gentlemen, Joseph's protégés, had in opposite ways had their heads lifted up, Pharaoh had gone and come. This had happened and much else besides, and Joseph had missed it, while he still lay in prison and in *bôr*, and only a faint echo of the resounding event reached him: namely, the change of reign, the lamentable passing of one day of the world and the exultant dawn of another, a new time, from which men expect a change for the better, no matter how good, humanly speaking, the former one may have been. On that day, they think and believe, right will drive out wrong, "the moon will come right" (as though it had never come right before!)— in short, from now on life would be one long season of laughter and amaze. All of which was reason enough for the whole population to hop on one leg and drink to excess for weeks—after, of course, a period of mourning in sackcloth and ashes, and that was by no means a hypocritical convention, but sincere grief over the going hence of the old time. For man is a creature prone to confusion.

As many years as his chief butler and the general intendant of his

65

bakeries had spent days at Zawi-Re, namely forty, had Amun's son, the son of Thutmose and the daughter of Mitanni's King, Neb-ma-Re-Amenhotep III-Nimmuria adorned his throne in splendour and built his palaces; then he died, he united himself with the sun, having had at the close of his life the disheartening experience with the two-and-seventy conspirators who had sought to lure him into the coffin. But now of course he had come to it anyhow, and a splendid coffin it was, studded with nails of pure beaten gold; he lay there, preserved in salt and bitumen, made to last to all eternity with juniper-wood, turpentine, cedar resin, styrax, and mastic, and wrapped in four hundred ells of linen bandages. Seventy days it took till the Osiris was ready. Then it was laid on a golden sledge drawn by oxen, that carried the bark holding the lion-footed bier roofed over by a canopy. Preceded by incense-bearers and water-sprinklers and accompanied by a host of mourners apparently overcome by grief, it was borne to its eternal dwelling in the hills, a many-chambered tomb equipped with every convenience. Before its door the ceremony was performed, the so-called "opening of the mouth," with the foot of the Horus-calf.

The Queen and the court were no longer walled in within the many-roomed abode, there to starve to death and moulder beside the dead. The days when that was considered necessary or proper were far in the past, the custom had lapsed and was forgotten—and why? What had they against it, and why was it remote from every mind? They indulged their fill in primitive observances, diligently made magic; stopped all the body openings of the exalted cadaver with charms against evil and faithfully performed the ceremony with the calf's-foot instrument, according to the time-honoured ritual. But to wall up the royal court—no, none of that, it was not done any more. It was not only that they did not wish to do it, that they no longer found it a good idea, as once they had. They did not even want to know that the custom had ever been practised or found good: neither the traditionally walled-in parties nor the wallers-in gave a single thought to the matter. Obviously it could no longer bear the light of day—call that light late or early as you will—and that is remarkable. Many people might feel that the remarkable thing was the fine old custom itself, the immurement of the living. But surely it is more remarkable that one day, by common, wordless, indeed uncon-scious consent, it simply ceased to come under consideration.

The court sat with its head on its knees, and all the people mourned.

66

Then they all lifted their heads, from the Negro borders to the delta and from desert to desert, and greeted enthusiastically the new epoch which should know no more wrong, in which "the moon would come right"; lifted their heads in exultant welcome to the son and successor, a charming though not beautiful lad, who if the reckoning was correct was only fifteen years old and still under the wardship of Tiy, the goddess-widow Horus-mother, who was still for some time to guide the reins of state. He was throned and crowned with the crowns of Upper and Lower Egypt; and there were great celebrations, in much weighty pomp, partly in the Palace of the West in Thebes, but the most solemn part at the place of the coronation, Per-Mont, whither young Pharaoh and his lady mother, lofty in feathers, with a splendid retinue, on the heavenly bark *Star of the Two Lands,* betook themselves upstream amid loud shoutings from the banks. When he returned thence, he bore the titles: "Strong Bull," "Favoured of the Two Goddesses," "Great in Kingship in Karnak," "Golden Falcon, who lifted the Crowns of Per-Mont," "King of Upper and Lower Egypt," "Nefer-Kheperu-Re-Wanre," which means "Lovely of form is he, who alone is and to whom he is the only"; "Son of the Sun, Amenhotep," "Divine Ruler of Thebes," "Great in Duration," "Living to all Eternity," "Beloved of Amon-Re, Lord of the Heavens," "High Priest of Him exulting in the Horizon by the Power of his name 'Heat-which-is-in-Aton.' "

Thus was young Pharaoh called after his crowning. The combination of titles, Joseph and Mai-Sachme agreed, was a compromise arrived at after long and tough bargaining between the court and the temple power. For the court inclined to Atum-Re's complaisant sun-sense; whereas Amun's jealous and oppressive temple power had reaped a few low bows before the traditionally Highest, but only in return for pretty transparent concessions to him at On in the point of the triangle. The royal boy, actually consecrated as "Greatest of Seers" of Re-Horakhte, had even woven the un- and anti-traditional doctrinal name Aton into the trailing garment of his title. His mother, the goddess-widow, called her strong fighting bull, who of course had no faintest resemblance to a bull, quite briefly, Meni. But the people, Joseph heard, had another name for him, a tender and delicate name: Neb-nef-nezem it called him, Lord of the Breath of Sweetness—it could not definitely be said why. Perhaps because it was known that he loved the flowers of his garden and liked to bury his small nose in their fragrance.

67

Joseph, then, in his pit, missed all these spectacles and the accompanying hubbub of rejoicing. The only sign of them down in the prison was the fact that Mai-Sachme's soldiers were allowed to get drunk three days running. Joseph was not present; he was not, so to speak, present on earth when the day changed, tomorrow became today, and the sun of tomorrow the sun of today. He only knew that it had happened; and from down below he cast his eyes up to the sun. He knew that Neb-nef-nezem's child- and sister-bride, another Princess of Mitanni, whom his father had wooed for him by letter from King Tushratta, had disappeared and taken her way westward almost as soon as she had arrived. Well, Meni, the strong fighting bull, was quite used to such disappearances. There had always been much dying all about him. All his brothers and sisters had died, some of them before his birth, some since, among them one brother; only a late-born little sister had survived, and she too had shown such a strong inclination westwards that she was almost never seen. Nor did he himself look as though he would live for ever and always, to judge from the sandstone images which the apprentices of Ptah made for him. But it was imperative that he should continue the line of the sun before he too went hence; so he had been married again in the lifetime of Nebmare-Amenhotep, this time to a daughter of the Egyptian nobility, Nefertiti by name, who had now become his exalted consort and mistress of the two lands, and to whom he had given the radiant title Nefernefruaton—"Beautiful beyond all beauty is Aton."

Joseph had missed the wedding feast too, and the sight of the rejoicing crowds on the banks. But he knew about it, and he took note of the young Highest. He heard for instance from Mai-Sachme, who got to know a good deal in the course of his duties, that Pharaoh, directly he had lifted the two crowns at Per-Mont, had given the order to complete with all speed the building of the house of Re-Horakhte-Aton at Karnak. His departed father had in fact already commissioned it. And special order was given to erect in the open court of the temple a mammoth freestone obelisk on a lofty base. The sun-meaning of this obelisk, referring to the doctrines of On at the point of the triangle, was quite obviously a challenge to Amun. Not as though Amun would have had anything against the neighbourhood of other gods, in and for itself. Round about his greatness there were indeed many houses and shrines at Karnak; for Ptah the swaddled one, Min the staring, Montu the falcon, and some others had shrines there, and Amun tolerated the worship of

68

them near him, and not only out of benevolence. For the multiplicity of the gods of Egypt was really an asset to his conservatism; always, of course, with the proviso that he, the weighty one, was king over them all, king of the gods, and that they waited upon him from time to time, in return for which he was ready, on proper occasion, to make them a return visit. But in this case there could be no waiting upon; there would be no image in the great new shrine and house of the sun, nothing but the obelisk, which threatened to be arrogantly tall. After all, it was no longer the time of the pyramid-builders, when Amun was small and Re very great in his light-places; when Amun had not yet taken Re into himself and become Amun-Re, god of the empire and king of the gods. Among these Re-Atum now, for his part and in his kind, might of course continue to exist, or rather, indeed, should continue to exist—but not in any presumptuous sense, not as a new god called Aton, setting himself up to philosophize about himself. That was fitting for Amun-Re alone, or, more correctly, not even for him; to think, indeed, was altogether unsuitable, and the settled position was that Amun and no other was king over the traditional multiplicity of the gods of Egypt.

But even under King Nebmare there had been a great deal of fashionable speculation at court; and now it looked as though it was going to take the upper hand. Young Pharaoh had given out an edict, and had it engraved on stone to commemorate the erection of the obelisk. It gave evidence of much subtilizing effort to define the nature of the sun-god in a new and anti-traditional way; to define it so sharply, indeed, that it suffered from tortuosity. "There lives," so the inscription ran, "Re-Hor of the horizon, who exults in the horizon in his name Shu, who is the Aton."

That was obscure, although it dealt with light itself and was meant to be very clear. It was complicated, although it aimed at simplification and unification. Re-Horakhte, a god among the gods of Egypt, had a threefold form: animal, human, and divine. His image was the image of a man with a falcon head, on which stood the disk of the sun. But also as a heavenly constellation he was threefold: in his birth out of the night, in the zenith of his manhood, and in his death in the west. He lived a life of birth, of dying, and of renewed generation, a life looking into death. But he who had ears to hear and eyes to read the writing on the stone understood that Pharaoh's doctrinal pronouncement did not wish the life of the god to be thus perceived as a coming and going, a becoming, passing, and becoming again, as a life done away with in death and thus phallic; all in all, not as life in so far as life is always done away with in death, but as pure being, the changeless source of light, subject to no ups and downs, out of whose image man and bird would at some far future time fall away, so that only the pure life-radiating sun-disk remained, called Aton.

This was understood, or not understood but at least energetically and excitedly discussed by such as had the necessary equipment to talk about it, also by such as entirely lacked the equipment and merely prattled. It was prattled about even as far down as into Joseph's pit; even Mai-Sachme's soldiers prattled about it, and the convicts in the quarry too, whenever they had breath enough; and this much at least everybody understood, that it was an offence to Amun-Re, as was likewise the great obelisk they had stuck in front of his nose, as well as certain more far-reaching orders of Pharaoh, having to do with the subtilizing definition in the inscription and really going very far indeed. Thus the great estate where the new house of the sun grew up was to bear the name Brightness of the Great Aton—yes, rumour even had it that Thebes itself, Wese, Amun's city, was henceforth to be called City of the Brightness of Aton; about this there was endless gossip. Even the dying in Mai-Sachme's hospital beds talked of it with their latest breath—quite aside from those who were only suffering from itch or pink-eye; so that the captain's rest-cure system was endangered.

The lord of the sweet breath, so it seemed, could not do enough to further his purposes and the purposes of the beloved god of his doctrine—in other words, the building of the temple; it was carried forwards with such haste and urgency that all the stone-masons from Jebu, the Elephant Isle, as far down as the delta, were set to work. And yet all this concentration failed to give the house of Aton the kind of structure suitable for an eternal dwelling. Pharaoh was in such haste, so ridden by impatience, that he gave up the use of the large blocks used for the tombs of the gods, because they were so hard to cut and haul. He gave order to erect the temple of changeless light out of small stones which could be tossed from hand to hand. Quantities of mortar and cement had thus to be used to smooth the walls for the painted bas-reliefs designed to shine there. Amun had made great fun of this, so one heard on all sides.

So it was that the course of events reached down into Zawi-Re and involved the son of Jacob, even though he was not present at them. For

Mai-Sachme's quarry had to furnish much stone for Pharaoh's hasty building, and Joseph had to be on hand with his overseer's staff to see that pick and crowbar were not idle, so that the governor of the prison should not get any flowery unpleasantness in his correspondence with the government. For the rest, he continued to endure his quite endurable punishment at Zawi-Re, by the side of his even-tempered chief. It was monotonous, like the captain's manner of speech, yet nourished by expectation. For there was much to expect, at hand and afar off—at first near at hand. Time passed for him as it does pass, in the usual way, which we may call neither quickly nor slowly, for it goes slowly, especially when one lives in expectation, yet if one looks back it appears to have gone very quickly. Joseph lived in Zawi-Re until he got to be thirty, without taking particular notice of it. Then came the breathless day and the winged messenger, a day which might have startled Mai-Sachme out of his calm and almost taught him to fear, if he had not already been expecting great things for Joseph.

THE EXPRESS MESSENGER

A bark arrived, with curving lotos prow and purple sail; it fairly flew up, so light it was, manned by five oarsmen on either side, and bearing the sign of royalty, an express boat from Pharaoh's own flotilla. It lay to neatly alongside the landing-stage of Zawi-Re, and a youth leaped ashore, slender and light as the boat that bore him, with lean face and long sinewy legs. His chest heaved beneath the linen garment, he was out of breath or at least he seemed to be, he behaved as though he were. There was no real reason for breathlessness; after all, he had come by boat, not run all the way. Anyhow, he ran, or flew, with extreme celerity through the gate and courtyard of Zawi-Re, opening a way for himself and preventing anyone from stopping him, by uttering a series of little shouts, not loud, but very disconcerting to the astonished and ineffectual guards in his path, and demanding to see the captain at once. He ran, then, or he flew, with such speed toward the citadel they pointed out to him that despite his slim build the pretended breathlessness might well have become real by the time he reached it. Certainly the little wings on the heels of his sandals and on his cap could not help him along, they were there merely in token of his office.

71

Joseph, occupied in the counting-house, saw this new arrival running, but paid him no heed, even when his attention was called to him. He went on turning over papers with the chief clerk until an underling came running, breathless too, with the order that Joseph was to drop everything, no matter how important, and present himself at once before the captain.

"I am coming," said he; yet finished first the paper he was going over with the clerk. Then, of course not loitering, but not running either, he betook himself to the captain in the tower.

The end of Mai-Sachme's nose was rather white when Joseph came into the dispensary. His heavy brows were drawn up higher than ever, his full lips parted.

"Here you are," he said with abated voice to Joseph. "You should have been here before. Hearken to this." He gestured toward the winged youth, who stood beside him, or rather did not stand, or not still, for his arms, head, shoulders, and legs kept moving in such a way that he seemed to run to and fro without stopping, in order to go on being breathless. Sometimes he stood on his toes, as though about to take flight.

"Your name is Osarsiph?" he asked in a low, hurried voice, keeping his quick, close-lying eyes upon Joseph's face. "You are the captain's aide who was in charge of certain occupants of the vulture-house here two years ago?"

"I am," answered Joseph.

"Then you must come with me just as you are," the other stated, with even more speaking play of limb. "I am Pharaoh's first runner, his swift messenger am I, and came with the express boat. You must straightway join me so that I can take you to court, for you are to stand before Pharaoh."

"I?" asked Joseph. "How could that be? I am too unimportant."

"Unimportant or no, it is Pharaoh's beautiful will and command. Breathless I bore it to your captain and breathless must you obey the summons."

"I have been put into this prison," responded Joseph, "certainly by way of a mistake, and in a manner of speaking I have been stolen down here. But here I am, a convict at hard labour, and though you cannot see my chains, yet I have them. How could I go out with you through these walls and gates on to your boat?"

72

"That has not the least thing in the world to do with it," hurried on the runner, "by comparison with the beautiful command, which makes all that vanish into thin air and in a trice bursts all your bonds. Before Pharaoh's wonderful will nothing can stand. But have no fear, it is more than unlikely that you will stand the test; much more than likely they will bring you back in short order to the place of your punishment. You will hardly be wiser than Pharaoh's greatest scholars and magicians of the book-house and shame the seers and soothsayers and interpreters of the house of Re-Horakhte, who invented the sun-year."

"That is in God's hands, whether He is with me or not," answered Joseph. "Has Pharaoh dreamed?"

"You are not here to ask but to answer," said the messenger, "and woe to you if you cannot. Then will you fall, I suppose, deeper than just back into this prison."

"Why am I to be thus tested," asked Joseph, "and how does Pharaoh know of me, that he sends forth his beautiful command down here to me?"

"You have been mentioned and named and called attention to in this crisis," the other replied. "On the way you may learn more; now you must follow me breathless, that you may straightway stand before Pharaoh."

"Wese is far," said Joseph, "and far is Merimat, the palace. However winged boat and messenger, Pharaoh must wait before his will is obeyed and I stand before him for my test. He might even have forgotten his beautiful command before I come, and himself find it no longer beautiful."

"Pharaoh is near," responded the runner. "It pleases the beautiful sun of the world to shine now in On, at the point of the delta; he has betaken himself thither in the boat *Star of the Two Lands*. In a few hours my bark will fly and flit to its goal. Up with you, then, not a word more."

"But I must have my hair cut first and put on proper clothes if I am to stand before Pharaoh," said Joseph. He had been wearing his own hair in the prison, and his clothing was only of the very common coarse linen. But the runner replied:

"That can be done on board as we flit and we fly. All has been provided. You imagine that one thing may delay another, instead of all being crowded into one time, in order to save it; but you know not what breathlessness is when Pharaoh commands."

73

So then Joseph turned to the captain to take his leave, and he called him "my friend."

"You see, my friend," said he, "how things stand and how they are to go with me after these three years. They hurry me out of the pit and draw me up out of the well—it is the old pattern. This courier thinks I shall come back down again to you, but I believe it not, and since I do not believe it, so will it not be. Fare thee well, and take all my thanks for the kindness and the peace which have made bearable this pause in my affairs, this penance and obscurity; for you have let me be your brother in the time of waiting. You were waiting for Nekhbet's third appearance and I was waiting upon my own business. Farewell, but not for long. Someone has thought of me after long forgetfulness, when he stubbed his toe against the memory of me. But I will think of you without forgetting; and if the God of my father is with me, whereof—not to offend Him—I do not doubt, then you too shall be drawn up out of this tedious hole. There are three beautiful things and three beautiful tokens which your servant cherishes in his heart: they are called 'snatching away,' 'lifting up,' and 'making to come after.' If God lift up my head, and I should fear to insult Him if I did not certainly expect it, then I promise you you shall come after and have a share in more stimulating circumstances than these, where your tranquillity will not be in danger of degenerating into sleepiness, and where the prospects for the third incarnation will be improved. Shall that be a promise betwixt thee and me?"

"Thanks in any case," said Mai-Sachme, and embraced him; a thing which up till now he could not have done and which, he vaguely felt, he would not be able to do later either, on opposite grounds. Only just now, at the moment of parting, was the right time. "For a minute," said he, "I thought I was quite upset when this man arrived hot-foot. But I am not, my heart beats evenly as ever—for how shall a thing one has been long expecting upset one? Calmness means nothing but that a man is prepared for every event and when it comes he is not surprised. But with feeling it is different; there is room for it even with self-control, and it touches me very much that you will think of me when you come into your kingdom. The wisdom of the Lord of Khnum be with you! Farewell!"

The courier, hopping from one foot to the other, had barely let the captain say his say to the end. Now he took Joseph by the hand, mani-

74

festly panting, and ran down with him from the tower, through the court and passages of Zawi-Re to the boat. They leaped aboard and off it went flying. And as it flitted and flew, Joseph, in the little pavilion on the after-deck, was shaved, rouged, and dressed while listening to the winged one's tale of what had happened at On, City of the Sun, and why he had been sent for. The thing was, Pharaoh had actually dreamed, and most portentously. But when the dream-interpreters were summoned, they had failed to give satisfaction and had fallen into disfavour. In the ensuing embarrassment the chief butler, Nefer-em-Wese, had spoken up and mentioned him—that is, Joseph—saying that if anybody could help out, perhaps he could, they might at least try it. What Pharaoh had actually dreamed, that the courier could not say, save in an obviously distorted and confused version, which had seeped through to the court from the council-chamber where the sages had suffered their discomfiture: the majesty of this god, it was said, had dreamed first that seven cows ate seven ears of corn and second that seven cows had been eaten by seven ears of corn—in short, a pack of nonsense such as occurs to nobody, even in a dream. Yet it was of some use to Joseph on his way, and his thoughts played about mental images of hunger and food, of need and supply.

OF LIGHT AND DARKNESS

What had really happened, leading up to the summoning of Joseph was this:

The year before—towards the end of the second year Joseph spent in the prison—Amenhotep, the fourth of his name, was sixteen years old and ceased to be a minor; the regency of Tiy, his mother, came to an end and the government of the two lands passed automatically to the successor of Nebmare the Magnificent. Thus ended a situation which the people and all those concerned had seen in the sign of the early morning sun, the young day born of the night, when the shining son is as yet more son than man, still belongs to the mother and is her fledgling, before he soars to the full height and strength of midday. Then Eset the Mother withdraws and yields up her sovereignty, although the maternal dignity still remains to her, the dignity of the source and fount of life and power, and always is the man her son. She gives over the power to him; but he exerts it for her, as she exerted it for him.

75

Tiy, the mother-goddess, who had been ruling and guarding the life of the lands since the years when her husband fell prey to the aging of Re, now removed from her chin the braided Usir beard which like Hatshepsut, Pharaoh with the breasts, she had been wearing, and surrendered it to the young son of the sun, whom it became almost as oddly when on occasions of high ceremony he assumed it. On such he was also obliged to appear with a tail; that is, to fasten a jackal's tail to his apron at the back. This animal attribute belonged to the strict and primitive ceremonial costume of His Majesty, and still formed an item in the sacred and jealously preserved ritual, though nobody any longer knew why it was there. However, they did know at court that young Pharaoh hated it. Wearing it even had a bad effect on his digestion; inclined His Majesty to feel quite sick and made him look pale or even green in the face; though, frankly speaking, even without the tail that was a feature of the attacks to which his health was subject.

Unless all observers erred, the shifting of the royal power from the mother to the son had been accompanied by much misgiving: would not one do better to put it off or void it altogether, leaving the young sun under the shelter of the mother's wing for good and all? The mother of the god herself entertained these doubts; her chief councillors had them, and a mighty man of our acquaintance, Beknechons, sought to feed and further them: Beknechons of the strict observance, great prophet and first priest of Amun. He had not, strictly speaking, been a servant of the crown or, as many of his predecessors had done, united the office of high priest with that of the head of the administration of the two lands. King Nebmare, Amenhotep III, had seen himself called upon to separate the spiritual from the secular arm and set up laymen as viziers of the North and the South. But as the mouth of the imperial god, Beknechons had a right to the ear of the regent, and she lent it to him graciously, though aware that it was to the voice of political rivalry that she lent it. She had had a decided share in her husband's decision to separate the two functions and in that way to achieve the necessary result of damming back the weight of the College of Karnak and preventing a preponderance of power which—and not only since yesterday—had been a threat to the royal house. It had inherited the problem from early days. Tutmose, Meni's great-grandfather, had dreamed his promise dream at the feet of the Sphinx and freed her from the sand, naming as his father the lord of the prehistoric giant statue, Harmakhis-Khepere-Atum-Re,

76

to whom he owed his crown. But this, as everybody understood and as Joseph too had learned to understand, was nothing but the hieroglyphic circumscription of the very same position: the religious formulation of political self-assertion. And it escaped nobody that this fresh definition of Aton as a new constellation in the firmament, a process begun back at the court of the son of Tutmose and dwelt on so lovingly in his little grandson's thoughts, had as its aim to prize Amun-Re loose from his arbitrary and despotic union with the sun, to which he owed his universal character, and reduce him to the rank of a local power, as the city god of Wese, which he had been before his political *coup*.

We fail to recognize the indivisibility of the world when we think of religion and politics as fundamentally separate fields, which neither have nor should have anything to do with each other; to the extent even that the one would be devalued and exposed as false if any trace of the other were to be found in it. For the truth is that they change but the garment, as Ishtar and Tammuz wear the veil by turns, and it is the whole that speaks when one speaks the language of the other. And it speaks besides in other tongues: for instance through the works of Ptah, the creations of taste, skill, and love of ornament; for to consider these as things apart, quite outside world-indivisibility and having nothing to do with either religion or politics, would be equally foolish. Joseph knew that young Pharaoh, on his own initiative, without any maternal prompting, devoted the most zealous, even jealous attention to the fostering of beauty and ornament in his world, in intimate connection with the effort he made to think into existence the god Aton in all his purity and truth. He cherished surprising ideas of change, of relaxation of the conservative tradition, feeling sure that his dearly loved god would have it so. The cause lay close to his heart, he fostered it for its own sake, in accordance with his convictions about what was true and pleasing in the world of form. But had it on that account nothing to do with religion and politics? Since the memory of man, or, as the children of Keme loved to say, since millions of years, the world of art had been regulated by pretty stiff religious conventions, now imposed and continued in force by Amun-Re in his chapel or by his powerful priesthood for him. To relax or indeed wholly to remove these fetters for the sake of a new truth and beauty which the Aton-god had revealed to Pharaoh was a blow in the face to Amun-Re, the head and front of a religion and politics indissolubly bound up with certain pictorial conceptions consecrated by time. In young Pharaoh's disintegrating theories on the subject of the pictorial arts, the world-whole spoke the language of good taste, one language among many, in which it expresses itself. For with the world-whole and its unity the human being has always and ever to do, whether he knows it or not.

He might know it, Amenhotep, the boy king; but the world-whole was manifestly too much for him. His strength seemed to be too slender, he suffered too much. Often he was pale or green, even when he did not have to wear the jackal's tail; he was so tortured by headaches that he could not keep his eyes open; often and often he had to give up his food. He was obliged to lie in the dark for days—he whose whole love was the light, the golden bond between heaven and earth, those rays ending in the caressing, life-giving hands of his father Aton. Of course, it was matter for grave concern when a reigning king was constantly prevented by such attacks from fulfilling his representational duties: such as offering sacrifice, dedicating this and that, receiving his wise men and councillors. But unfortunately there was even worse: one could never tell what attack might suddenly seize His Majesty in the middle of these duties, in the presence of dignitaries or even of masses of people. Pharaoh, holding his thumbs clamped round by the other four fingers and rolling his eyeballs back under half-closed lids, might fall into a not quite normal unconscious state, not lasting very long but still a disturbing interruption to the business in hand. He himself explained these incidents as abrupt visitations from his father the god; and he feared much less than he desired to receive them. For he returned from them with his daily life enriched by first-hand instruction and revelation on the true and beautiful nature of Aton.

Thus it need cause us neither surprise nor doubt to learn that when the new son reached his majority the point was discussed whether it might not be better to leave him under the maternal wing and let things go on as they were. But the idea came to nothing, despite Amun's representations in its favour. However much there was for it, there was too much against it. For to admit that Pharaoh was so ill, or so sickly, that he could not take over the government was contrary to the interests of the hereditary sun-rulers and might give rise to dangerous notions in the kingdom and the tributary states. Moreover, Pharaoh's attacks were of a nature which forbade their use as a reason for continuing his minority: they were holy, they contributed to his popularity rather than other-

78

wise; it would be unwise to make them the ground for a prolongation of his minority; it was much better to exploit them against Amun, whose private intention to unite the double crown with his own feather head-dress and himself found a new dynasty lurked in the background of every situation.

And so the maternal bird turned over to her son the full authority of the zenith of his manhood. But looking very closely, we can see that he himself, Amenhotep, had conflicting feelings on the whole subject. He felt pride and joy in his new powers, but he felt embarrassment as well; all in all he might have preferred to remain under his mother's wing. There was one reason why he looked forward with positive horror to his majority, and it was this: every Pharaoh at the beginning of his reign, by fixed tradition, personally undertook, as commander-in-chief, a mili-tary campaign of war and plunder, into either the Asiatic or the Negro lands. And upon its glorious conclusion he was solemnly received at the border and escorted back to his capital, where he offered as tribute to Amun-Re, who had thus set the princes of Zahi and Kush under his feet, a goodly share of the swag. Pharaoh had also with his own hand to slay a half-dozen prisoners of war, as high as possible in rank—in case of need they were elevated for the purpose.

Of all such ceremonies the lord of the sweet breath knew himself to be utterly incapable. He was attacked by facial twitchings, pallor, and greenness whenever they were mentioned or even whenever he thought of them. He loathed war; it might be Amun's business but was far from being that of "my father Aton," who in one of those holy and question-able attacks of Meni's had expressly revealed himself to his son as the "Prince of Peace." Meni could neither take the field with steed and chariot, nor plunder, nor make presents of booty to Amun, nor slay in his honour princely or theoretically princely captives. He neither could nor would do any of that, even ostensibly and for form's sake; and he refused to be pictured on temple walls and arches shooting arrows from a lofty war chariot at terrified foes or holding a bunch of them with one hand by the hair of their heads and with the other brandishing the bludgeon. All that was to him—that is to say, to his god and so to him—intolerable and impossible. It must be clearly understood by court and state that the inaugural campaign of plunder would not take place; that after all it could be somehow got round, by good will and good words. One could say that all the lands of the globe already lay at Pharaoh's

79

feet, and tribute poured in so promptly and copiously that any warlike demonstration was superfluous; that indeed it was Pharaoh's wish to signalize his accession by the absence of such events.

But even after this easement Meni's feelings continued to be mixed. He did not conceal from himself that as a reigning monarch he came into immediate contact with the whole world and all its languages and ways of expressing itself, whereas up till then he could regard it from the one point of view which he preferred, the religious one. Not taken up with earthly affairs, among the flowers and trees of his gardens he could dream of his loving god, think him forth, muse upon him, and consider how his essence could best be comprehended in one name and represented by a single image. That had been strain and responsibility enough; but he loved it, and gladly bore with the headaches it gave him. Now he had that to do and to think about which gave him headaches he did not love at all. Every morning, with sleep still in all his members, he received the Vizier of the South, a tall man with a little chin beard and two gold neck-rings, named Ramose. The man greeted him with a fixed form of address, like a litany, very florid and long-winded, and then for endless hours badgered him with rolls of marvellously executed writings about current administrative problems: judicial business, sentences, tax registers, plans for new canals, foundation-stone laying, building supplies, opening of quarries and mines in the desert, and so on and on, instructing Pharaoh in Pharaoh's beautiful will in all these matters. After that with upraised hands he would marvel at the beauty of Pharaoh's will. It was Pharaoh's beautiful will to take such and such journeys into the desert, to designate the right spots for wells and post-stations, after they had been picked out beforehand by people more competent in such matters. It was his admirably beautiful will to summon the city Count of El-Kab to come before his face for a hearing upon why he so unpunctually and insufficiently paid his official assessments of gold, silver, cattle and linen into the treasury at Thebes. The next day it was his exalted will to set out for miserable Nubia, to lay a cornerstone or preside at an opening of a temple—usually one dedicated to Amun-Re and thus in Meni's mind by no means compensating for the exhaustion and headache brought on by the journey.

At best, the obligatory temple service, the cumbersome ritual of the imperial god, took up a great part of his time and strength. Outwardly it was his beautiful will to perform it; but inwardly it was the reverse;

for it prevented him from thinking of Aton, and also it inflicted on him the society of Beknechons, Amun's autocratic servant, whom he could not abide. In vain had he tried to have his capital city called "City of the Brightness of Aton." The name was not taken up by the people, the priests prevented them, and Wese was and remained Nowet-Amun, the city of the Great Ram, who by the strong right arms of his royal sons had reduced foreign lands to subjection and made Egypt rich. Even thus early, Pharaoh was secretly playing with the idea of removing his residence from Thebes, where the image of Amun-Re shone from every column and arch, column and obelisk and was a vexation to his eyes. Certainly he did not yet think of founding a new city all his own, wholly dedicated to Aton; he only contemplated transferring the court to On at the top of the delta, where he felt more at home himself. There, in the vicinity of the sun-temple, he had a pleasant palace, not so brilliant as Merimat in the west of Thebes, but provided with all the comforts his delicate health required. The court chroniclers had often to record the journeys of the good god by boat or wagon down to On. True, it was the seat of the Vizier of the North, who had under him the administration and judiciary functions of all the districts between Asyut and the delta, and who in his turn lost no time in giving him headaches. But at least at On Meni was spared burning incense to Amun under the supervision of Beknechons; and he very much enjoyed talking with the learned shiny-pates from the house of Atum-Re-Horakhte about the nature of the glorious god his father and his inner life, which despite his vast age was so fresh and lively that it proved capable of the most beautiful variations, clarifications, and developments; if one may so express it, there emerged out of the old god, with the aid of human brain-power, slowly, yet ever more completely, a new, unspeakably lovely one, namely the wonderful, universally illuminating Aton.

Oh, that one might give oneself wholly to him and be his son, midwife, herald, and confessor, instead of being King of Egypt as well, and successor of those who had enlarged the boundaries of Keme and made it an empire! He was tied fast to them and to the deeds they had done; he was vowed to them and to all their acts; probably the reason why he could not endure Beknechons, Amun's man, was that he was right when he constantly emphasized the fact. In other words, young Pharaoh himself, in his most private self-examination, suspected it: he suspected first that it was one thing to found an empire and another to help a

81

world-god into being; and second that the latter occupation might easily be in some kind of contradiction to the regal task and responsibility of preserving and sustaining the achievements of the past. And the headaches which made him shut his eyes when the Viziers of the North and the South set upon him with imperial business were connected with suspicions to the effect (or not quite to the effect, but moving in that direction) that they, namely the headaches, were not caused so much by fatigue and boredom as by a vague but disquieting insight into the conflict between devotion to the beloved Aton theology and the duties of a King of Egypt. In other words, they were conscience and conflict headaches. Knowing them for what they were only made them worse instead of better, and increased his nostalgia for his former state of protection under the wing of maternal night.

Doubtless not only he but the country too would have been better off. For an earthly land and its prosperity are always better taken care of by the mother, however much the spiritual side may be so in the hands of the son. This was Amenhotep's private conviction, and it was probably the feeling of Egypt itself, the Isis belief in the black earth which she instilled into it. Meni made a mental distinction between the material, earthly, "natural" welfare of the earth and its mental and spiritual weal; he vaguely feared that the two concerns might not only not coincide but even conflict rather fundamentally. To be charged with both of them at once, to be both priest and king, was the source of many headaches. The material and natural well-being and prosperity were the business of the king, or, even better, it was the business of a queen, of the mother, the great Cow—in order that the priest's son in freedom and without responsibility for material well-being might dwell on the spiritual side and spin his sun-thoughts. His royal responsibility for the material side oppressed young Pharaoh. His kingship was for him bound up with the black Egyptian loam between desert and desert—black and fertile from the impregnating water. Whereas his passion was the pure light, the golden sun-youth of the heights—and he had no good conscience about it. The Vizier of the South, who got all the reports, even about the early rising of the dog-star which heralds the swelling of the waters—this Ramose, then, constantly called his attention to the latest news on the state of the river, the prospects of a good rise, the fertilization, the harvest. To Meni, however attentively, yes, conscientiously he listened, it seemed as though the man would much rather give his reports as he used

82

to, to the mother, the Isis-Queen. She knew more about these things, they were better off in her hands. And yet for him too, as for his lands, everything depended on a blessing-issue in the dark fields of fertility. Failure or deficiency, if it came, reflected on him. Not for nothing did Egypt's people have a king who was God's son and so in God's name represented an assurance against stoppages in holy and necessary processes upon which nobody else had any influence. Mistakes or damages in this department of the black earth meant that his people were disappointed in him, whose mere existence should have prevented them. His credit was shaken and, after all, he needed all he could get, that he might make to triumph the beautiful teaching of Aton and his nature of heavenly light.

That was the difficulty and the dilemma. He had no bond with the blackness below, loving alone the upper light. But if things did not go smoothly and well with the blackness that fed them all, he lost his authority as teacher of the light. And so young Pharaoh's feelings suffered from a split when the motherly night took away her wing from above him and handed him over the kingdom.

PHARAOH'S DREAM

Well then, Pharaoh had betaken himself once more to instructive On out of unconquerable yearning to escape from the empire of Amun and commune with the shiny-pates of the sun-house about Harmakhis-Khepere-Atum-Re, Aton. The court chroniclers, puckering their lips and obsequiously crouching, mincingly entered in the record His Majesty's beautiful resolve; and how thereupon he mounted a great car made of electrum, together with Nefertiti, called Nefernefruaton, the Queen of the lands, whose body was fruitful and whose arm was about her consort; and how he had radiantly taken his beautiful way, followed in other cars by Tiy, the mother of God, Nezemmut, the Queen's sister, Baketaton, his own sister, and many chamberlains and ladies-in-waiting with ostrich-feather fans on their backs. The heavenly bark *Star of the Two Lands* had also been used by stretches; the chroniclers had set down how Pharaoh, sitting under his canopy, had eaten a roast pigeon, also held the bone out to the Queen and she ate from it, and how he put into her mouth sweetmeats dipped in wine.

83

At On, Amenhotep entered his palace in the temple district and slept there dreamlessly the first night, exhausted from the journey. The following day he began by sacrificing to Re-Horakhte with bread and beer, wine, birds, and incense. After that he listened to the Vizier of the North, who spoke before him at length, and then, regardless of the headache that had brought on, devoted the rest of the day to the much-desired talks with the priests of the God. These conferences, which at the moment greatly occupied Amenhotep's mind, had been taken up with the subject of the bird Bennu, also called Off-spring of Fire, because it was said that he was motherless, and moreover actually his own father, since dying and beginning were the same for him. For he burned himself up in his nest made of myrrh and came forth from the ashes again as young Bennu. This happened, some authorities said, every five hundred years; happened in fact in the temple of the sun at On, whither the bird, a heron-like eagle, purple and gold, came for the purpose from Arabia or even India. Other authorities asserted that it brought with it an egg made of myrrh, as big as it could carry, wherein it had put its deceased father, that is to say actually itself, and laid it down on the sun-altar. These two assertions might subsist side by side—after all, there subsists so much side by side, differing things may both be true and only different expressions of the same truth. But what Pharaoh first wanted to know, what he wanted to discuss, was how much time had passed out of the five hundred years which lay between the bird and the egg; how far they were on the one hand from the last appearance and on the other from the next one; in short, at what point of the phœnix-year they stood. The majority opinion of the priests was that it must be somewhere about the middle of the period. They reasoned that if it was still near its beginning, then some memory of the last appearance of Bennu must still exist and that was not the case. But suppose they were near the end of one period and the beginning of the next; then they must reckon on the impending or immediate return of the time-bird. But none of them counted on having the experience in his lifetime so the only remaining possibility was that they were about the middle of the period. Some of the shiny-pates went so far as to suspect that they would always remain in the middle, the mystery of the Bennu bird being precisely this: that the distance between the last appearance of the Phœnix and his next one was always the same, always a middle point. But the mystery was not in itself the important thing to Pharaoh. The burning question to be discussed, which was the object of his visit, and which then he did discuss for a whole half-day with the shiny-pates, was the doctrine that the fire-bird's myrrh egg in which he had shut up the body of his father did not thereby become heavier. For he had made it anyhow as large and heavy as he could possibly carry, and if he was still able to carry it after he had put his father's body in it, then it must follow that the egg had not thereby increased in weight.

That was an exciting and enchanting fact of world-wide importance. In young Pharaoh's eyes it was worthy of the most circumstantial exposition. If one added to a body another body and it did not become heavier thereby, that must mean there were immaterial bodies—or differently and better put, incorporeal realities, immaterial as sun-light; or, again differently and still better put, there was the spiritual; and this spiritual was ethereally embodied in the Bennu-father, whom the myrrh egg received while altering its character thereby in the most exciting and significant way. For the egg was altogether a definitely female kind of thing; only the female among birds laid eggs, and nothing could be more mother-female than the great egg out of which once the world came forth. But Bennu the sun-bird, motherless and his own father, made his own egg himself, an egg against the natural order, a masculine egg, a father-egg, and laid it as a manifestation of fatherhood, spirit, and light upon the alabaster table of the sun-divinity.

Pharaoh could not talk enough with the sun-calendar men of the temple of Re about this event and its significance for the developing nature of Aton. He discussed deep into the night, he discussed to excess, he wallowed in golden immateriality and father spirit, and when the priests were worn out and their shiny pates nodded, he was still not tired and could not summon resolution to dismiss them—almost as though he were afraid to stay alone. But at last he did dismiss them, nodding and stumbling to their rest, and himself sought his bedchamber. His dressing and undressing slave was an elderly man, assigned to him as a boy, who called him Meni although not otherwise informal or lacking in respect. He had been awaiting his master for hours by the light of the hanging lamp and now quickly and gently made him ready for the night. Then he flung himself on his face and withdrew to sleep on the threshold. Pharaoh for his part nestled into the cushions of his exquisitely ornate bed, which stood on a dais in the middle of the room, its headboard decorated with the finest ivory-work displaying figures of

85

jackals, goats, and Bes. He fell almost at once into an exhausted sleep. But only for a short time. After a few hours of profound oblivion he began to dream: such complicated, impressive, absurd, and vivid dreaming as he had not done since he was a child with tonsillitis.

In his dream he stood on the bank of Hapi the Nourisher, in a lonely, marshy, uncultivated spot. He had on the red crown of Lower Egypt, the beard was on his chin and the jackal's tail fastened to his upper garment behind. Quite alone he stood, heavy-hearted, and held his crooked staff in his hand. Then there was a rippling noise not far from the shore and seven shapes mounted from the stream: seven cows came on shore; they had probably been lying in the water like buffalo cows. They moved in a straight line one behind another, seven without the bull, for no bull was there, only the seven cows. Magnificent cows they were, white ones, black ones with lighter backs, grey with lighter belly, and two dappled—fine smooth fat kine with bursting udders, long-lashed Hathor-eyes, and high curving lyre-shaped horns. They began to graze contentedly among the reeds. The King had never seen such fine cattle, not in the whole country. Their sleek well-fed bodies were something to see and Meni's heart would have rejoiced at the sight if it had not felt so heavy and full of care—feelings which presently gave way, indeed, to actual horror and fear. For these seven were not all: still more cows came out of the water, joining those to these, seven more cows climbed upon the bank, again without the bull, for what bull could have cared to join with such as these? Pharaoh shuddered at the kine; they were the ugliest, leanest, most starveling cows he had ever seen in his life— their bones stood out on their wrinkled hides, their udders were like empty bags with stringlike teats. They were an alarming and upsetting sight, the wretched creatures seemed scarcely able to keep their legs. And yet their behaviour was so bold, so aggressive and sudden—one could never have expected the like from such decrepit beasts, yet truly it was all too natural, since it was the recklessness of starvation. Pharaoh watches: the haggard herd advances on the bonny one, the calamitous cows leap on the well-favoured ones as cows do when they play the bull; the poverty-stricken devour and swallow the well-fed and simply wipe them off the earth. Afterwards they stand there on the spot as lean as ever before, without one single sign of being any fuller.

Here this dream ended and Pharaoh started from his sleep in a perspiration of fear; sat up with throbbing heart and looked about in the

86

mildly lighted chamber. It had been only a dream; yet so immediate, so speaking, that its urgency was like that of the starving kine and lay cold in the limbs of the dreamer. He had no wish for his bed again; stood up, drew on his white woollen robe, and moved about in the room, musing on the dream and the pressing nature of that obviously absurd yet so vivid nonsense. Gladly would he have waked the slave to tell it to him, or rather to try if what he had seen could be reproduced in words. But he was too kindly to disturb the old man, who had had to wait up so long the night before. He sat down in the cow-footed armchair beside the bed, drew closer about him the moonbeam softness of his white wool robe, and dozed off again, his feet on the footstool, squeezed into the corner of the chair.

But scarce was he asleep when he dreamed again; again—or still—he stood on the bank in beard and crown and tail, and now there was on it a ploughed strip of black earth. And he beholds the loam disturbed, the crust rises, curls over, a stalk pricks forth, and one, two, even up to seven ears spring swiftly from it, one after another, all on one stalk: full, fat ears, bursting with golden fullness. How blithe the heart could feel at such a sight! Yet cannot, for, lo, the stalk keeps on shooting forth ears; seven ears more, poor, pathetic, dead, and dry, scorched by the east wind, blackened with mildew and blight; and as they push out raggedly below the full ones, the fine large ears vanish as though into the poor lean ones. Truly it was like that: the wretched ears swallowed up the fat, just as before the ill-favoured cows had devoured the sleek ones. And grew neither fuller nor better favoured than before. This Pharaoh saw with his bodily eyes, started up in his chair, and once more found it all a dream.

A confused, ridiculous enough dream, wordless and senseless. Still it came so close, it so urgently assailed his mind with its burden of warning, that Pharaoh could not sleep again. Nor did he even wish to, till happily the dawn soon broke, but went on shifting between bed and chair, musing on the dream—or the twin dreams grown on one stalk—and its clear and pressing demand for clarification. Already he was firmly resolved not to let such a dream pass over silently and keep it to himself. He would make an occasion of it, he would sound an alarm. In it he had worn the crown, the crozier, and the tail, beyond a doubt these were king-dreams of imperial import, vastly suggestive and significant.

87

They must be made public and everything possible done to get to the bottom of them and study them on the basis of their obviously alarming meaning. Meni was greatly wrought up over his dreams, he hated them more with every minute that passed. A king could not put up with such dreams—although on the other hand they could not come to anyone but a king. While he, Nefer-Kheperu-Re-Wanre-Amenhotep, sat on the throne such things must not happen: no such abominable cows must eat up such fine fat ones; or such wretched blighted ears consume such swelling golden ones. Nothing must happen in the realm of events corresponding to this frightful picture-language. For it would reflect upon him, his prestige would suffer; ears and hearts would be closed to the annunciation of Aton, and Amun would gain thereby. Danger threatened the light from the black earth, danger from the material side threatened the spiritual-ethereal, there was no doubt about that. His excitement was great; it took the form of anger, and the anger swelled up into a great resolve that the danger must be revealed and recognized for what it was in order to meet it.

The first person to whom he told the dream—as much as it lent itself to telling—was the old man who now came to dress him, arrange his hair, and wind the head-dress round it. He only shook his head in amaze and then gave it as his view that the dream came from the good god going to bed so late after he had heated his brain with all that wool-gathering, as he popularly and simple-mindedly put it. Very likely he unconsciously thought of the dreams as a sort of punishment for having kept his old servant up so late. "Silly old goat," Pharaoh had said, half laughing, half angry. He gave him a light slap on the cheek and went to the Queen. But she was feeling sick, being pregnant, and paid little heed. Then he sought out Tiy, the mother goddess, and found her at her dressing-table in the hands of her maids-in-waiting. To her too he told the dream, finding it not at all easier to tell as time went on, but harder instead. Nor did he get from his mother much consolation or encouragement. Tiy was always rather mocking when he came to her with his kingly cares; and he was so convinced that this was a heavy care that he began by saying so. And at once the bantering smile appeared on the maternal face. King Nebmare's widow had, after mature reflection, of her own free will laid down the regency and given over to her son the ruling power of his majority; but she could never quite conceal her jealousy, and the painful thing for Meni was that he saw it all, this bitter reaction which he himself evoked did not escape him, while he sought to soften it by childlike pleas for counsel and help.

"Why does Your Majesty come to me, the rejected?" she would say. "You are Pharaoh, so be Pharaoh and stand on your own feet instead of on mine. Confide in your servants the Viziers of the South and the North when you do not know what to do, and let them tell you what is your will if you do not know it; but not in me, for I am old and have retired."

She behaved like that about the dream too. "I am too much out of the habit of power and responsibility, my friend," she had told him with a smile, "to be able to judge whether you are right in giving so much weight to this matter. 'Hidden is the darkness,' so it is written, 'when ample is the light.' Let your mother hide herself. Let me even hide my opinion whether these dreams are worth while or befitting your state. They ate them up? They devoured them? Some cows ate up some other cows? Some withered ears some full ones? That is no dream vision, you cannot see it or form a picture of it, either awake or I should say asleep either. Probably Your Majesty dreamed something quite different and you have put in its place this monstrous picture of impossible greediness."

In vain Meni assured her that he had positively seen it precisely like that with the eyes of his dream and that its clarity had been full of meaning which cried out for interpretation. In vain he spoke of his inner threat, of the harm which might come to the "teaching"—in other words, to Aton—if the dream were to interpret itself unhindered; that is to say, be fulfilled and take the actual shape of which it had been the prophetic garment. He had again the impression that at bottom his mother had no heart for his God; that it was only with her reason, namely on political and dynastic grounds, that she sided with him. She had always supported her son in his tender love, his spiritual passion for Aton. But again today, as for a long time, he saw—and thanks to his sensitiveness he always saw—that she did it only out of calculation, exploiting his heart as a woman would who saw the whole world exclusively from the point of view of statesmanship, and not, as he did, from the religious first and foremost. That troubled Meni and wounded him. He left his mother, having heard from her that if he really thought his cow-and-corn vision important to the state, he could apply to Ptah-em-heb, the Vizier of the South, at the morning audience. Besides, there was no dearth of dream-interpreters on the spot.

He had already sent for the interpreters and now impatiently awaited them. But before receiving them he had to see the great official who came to report on the affairs of the "Red House," in other words the business of the treasury of Lower Egypt. Immediately after the greeting hymns Meni interrupted him and made him listen to the story of the dreams, related in nervous, tormented tones; hesitating, seeking for the right words, he demanded that the man express himself on two points: first, whether he, like his master, considered the narrative to have political significance, and second, if so, in what way and what connection. The official did not know what to answer; or rather he had answered in a lengthy speech of very well-turned phrases that he did not know how to answer and did not know what to say about the dreams—after which he had tried to return to treasury business. But Amenhotep kept him to the subject of the dreams, obviously unwilling and unable to talk about anything else or listen to it, only to want to make him understand how speakingly impressive or impressively speaking they were—and he did not leave off until the wise men and seers were announced.

The King, full of his night's experience—indeed, possessed by it as he now was—turned his levee into a first-class ceremony—and yet after all it turned out to be a lamentable failure. He not only ordered Ptah-em-heb to remain present, but also arranged that all the court dignitaries who had accompanied him to On should attend the audience of interpretation. There were some dozen high-ranking gentlemen: the great steward of the palace, the keeper of the King's wardrobe, the overseer of the fullers, the so-called sandal-bearer of the King, a considerable office; the head wig-keeper of the god, who was likewise "guardian of the enchanted empires," in other words of the two crowns, and privy councillor of the royal jewels; the groom of all Pharaoh's horses; the new head baker and Prince of Menfe, named Amenemopet, the first steward of the buffet, Nefer-em-Wese, once temporarily called Bin-em-Wese, and several fan-bearers on the right hand of the god. All these had to be present in the audience and council hall; they stood round in two groups on either hand of Pharaoh's splendid seat, which was on a raised dais under a baldachin borne by slender beribboned poles. The prophets and dream-interpreters were brought before him, six in number, all of whom were in more or less close relation with the temple of the horizon-dweller and of whom a few had taken part in the phœnix-council of the day before. People of their sort no longer prostrated themselves on their bellies to kiss the ground, as had once been the custom, before the throne-chair. It was still the same chair as in the time of the pyramid-builders and even much earlier: a box-like arm-chair with a low back and a cushion on the floor in front; only there was rather more ornamentation than in primitive times. But even although the chair had become more splendid and Pharaoh more mighty, one no longer kissed the ground before them. Here as in the case of the living burial of the court in the dead king's tomb, it was no longer good *ton*. The soothsayers merely lifted their arms in reverential wise and murmured in rather unrhythmical confusion a long formula of respect and greeting, wherein they assured the king that he had a form like his father Re and illumined the two lands with his beauty. For the radiance of His Majesty penetrated into the dungeons and there was no place which escaped the piercing glance of his eye, nor one whither the fine hearing of his million ears did not reach, he heard and saw all, and whatsoever issued from his mouth was like the words of Horus in the horizon as his tongue was the scale of the world and his lips more precise than the little tongue on the just scale of Thoth. He was Re in all his members, they said, in uneven and confused chorus, and Khepere in true form the living image of his father Atum of On in Lower Egypt —"O Nefer-Kheperu-Re-Wanre, Lord of Beauty, through whom we breathe!"

Some of them finished before the others. Then they were all silent, and listened. Amenhotep thanked them, told them first in general on what occasion he had called them together, and then began, before this assemblage of some twenty either elegant or learned persons to relate his egregious dream—for the fourth time. It was painful to him, he flushed and floundered as he spoke. His insistent sense of the portentous significance of his tale had decided him to make it public. Now he regretted the decision, for he did not conceal from himself that what had been—and to him still was—so serious sounded laughable when he repeated it aloud. Really, why should such fine fat cattle let such miserable weak ones calmly eat them up? Why and how should one set of ears of corn devour another set? But it had been so to him in his dream, so and not otherwise. The dreams had been fresh, lifelike, and impressive at night; by day and put into words they were like badly prepared mummies, with distorted features; nobody could want to reveal them. He was embarrassed and came laboriously to an end. Then he looked shyly and expectantly at the dream-seers.

They had nodded their heads meaningfully; but gradually one after another they stopped nodding and began a side-to-side motion, a series of wondering head-shakes. These were very singular and almost unique dreams, they explained through their elders; the interpretation was not easy. Not that they despaired of it—the dream was still to be dreamed that they could not expound. But they must ask for time to consider and the favour of withdrawing for counsel. And compendiums must be fetched for consultation. There was nobody so learned as to have the whole technique at his fingers' ends. To be learned, they permitted themselves to remark, did not mean to have all knowledge in their heads; there would not be room for it; no, it meant to be in possession of the books in which the knowledge was written, and that they were.

Amenhotep granted them leave to take counsel. The court was told to hold itself in readiness. The King spent two whole hours—the wait lasted that long—very restlessly. Then the sitting was resumed.

"May Pharaoh live a hundred years, beloved of Maat, lady of truth, in response to his love of her who was without guile." She stood in person at the side of the experts as they pronounced their results and brought their interpretation before Pharaoh, Protector of the Truth. In the first place: the seven fat kine meant seven princesses, which Nefernefruaton-Nofertiti, the Queen of the Lands, would in time bear. But that the fat kine had been devoured by the lean ones meant that these seven daughters would all die in Pharaoh's lifetime. That did not mean, they hastened to add, that the King's daughters would die young. To Pharaoh would be vouchsafed such a length of days that he would outlive all his children, however long they lived.

Amenhotep looked at them open-mouthed. What were they talking about, he asked them, in a diminished voice. They answered, it had been granted them to deliver the meaning of the first dream. But this interpretation, he had responded, in a still smaller voice, had no sort of reference to his dream, it simply had nothing to do with it. He had not asked them whether the Queen would bear him a son and successor or a daughter and more daughters. He had asked them for the interpretation of the sleek and the ill-favoured kine.—The daughters, they replied, were the interpretation. He should not expect to find cows in the interpretation of a dream about cows. In the interpretation the cows were turned into princesses.

Pharaoh no longer had his mouth open, he had it very tightly closed, and opened it only a very little when he ordered them to go on to the second dream.

Very well, the second, they said. The seven full ears were seven flourishing cities which Pharaoh would build, but the seven shrunk and scrubby ones were—the ruins of them. It was well known, they hastily explained, that all cities inevitably fell into ruins in time. Pharaoh himself would survive so long that he would see with his own eyes the ruins of the cities he had built.

But here Meni's patience came to an end. He had not had enough sleep; the repeated telling of the dreams, lessening in impressiveness each time he told them, had been painful; the two hours' wait unnerving. Now he was so filled with the idea that these interpretations were sheer boggling and miles away from the true meaning of his visions that he could no longer control his anger. He put one more question: did the books say the same as the wise men had said? But when they replied that their contributions were a suitable synthesis of what was in the books, together with the promptings of their own powers of combination, he sprang from his chair. During an audience that was unheard of, the courtiers shrugged and put their hands over their mouths. Meni, tears in his voice, called the fearfully startled prophets bunglers and ignoramuses.

"Away with you!" he cried, almost sobbing. "And take with you, instead of the plenteous gold which my Majesty would have conferred on you if truth had come out of your mouths, the disfavour of Pharaoh. Your interpretations are cheating and lies, Pharaoh knows it, for it was Pharaoh who dreamed, and even though he does not know the meaning, he does know how to distinguish between real interpretation and such worthless stuff as this. Out of my sight!"

The pallid scholars were led out by two palace officials. But Pharaoh, without sitting down, had declared to his court that their failure would not lead him to let the matter rest. The gentlemen had unfortunately been witnesses to a mortifying failure, but by his faith and his sceptre, on the very next day he would call up other experts, this time from the house of Djehuti, the scribe of Thoth the ninefold great, lord of Khnumu. From the adepts of the white peacock was to be expected true and worthy interpretation of that which, the inner voice had told him, must be explained at all costs.

The second hearing took place next day under the same circumstances. It went off even worse than the first. Again young Pharaoh, with much inward constraint, halting in his speech, made public exhibition of his dream-mummies and again among the luminaries there had been great nodding and then great head-shaking. Not two but three hours had King and court to wait on the issue of the private consultation; and then the experts were not even agreed among themselves, but divided as to the meaning of the dreams. Two interpretations, the eldest among them announced, existed for each dream, and these, certainly, were the only ones possible, or even thinkable. According to one theory the seven fat kine were seven kings of Pharaoh's seed, the seven lean ones seven princes of misery who would make head against them. All this lay in the distant future. Alternatively the fat kine might be so many queens whom either Pharaoh himself or one of his late successors would take into his women's house, and who, as indicated by the lean kine, would unhappily all die, one after the other.

And the ears of corn?

The seven golden ears meant in one version seven heroes of Egypt, who in a later war would fall by the hand of seven hostile and—as shown by the thin ears—much less powerful warriors. The others stuck to it that the seven full and seven barren ears were children, in all fourteen of them, which Pharaoh would get from those foreign queens. But quarrels would break out among them, and, thanks to superior guile, the seven weak children would destroy the seven stronger ones.

This time Amenhotep did not get up from his seat of audience. He sat there bent over, burying his face in his hands; the courtiers to right and left of the canopy inclined their ears to hear what he was muttering. "Oh, muddlers, muddlers!" he whispered over and over; then beckoned to the Vizier of the North, who stood nearest him, and gave him a whispered order. Ptah-em-heb discharged this task by announcing to the experts in a loud voice that Pharaoh wanted to know if they were not ashamed of themselves.

They had done their best, they replied.

Then the Vizier had to bend over again to the King, and this time it appeared he had received the order to tell the wonder-workers they were to leave the audience. In great confusion, looking one at another as

94

though to ask whether the like had ever been known before, they departed. The court, remaining, stood about perplexed, for Pharaoh still sat there, bent over, shielding his eyes with his hand. When at length he took it away and sat up, affliction was painted upon his face, and his chin quivered. He told his courtiers he would gladly have spared them, and only reluctantly plunged them into pain and grief, but he could not hide the truth; their lord and King was profoundly unhappy. His dreams had borne the unmistakable stamp of political significance, and their meaning was a matter of life and death. The expositions he had been given were ineffectual twaddle; they did not in the least fit the dreams, nor could the dreams recognize themselves in the interpretations, as dream and interpretation must recognize each other. After the failure of these two full-dress attempts he was forced to doubt whether he was to be able to get any interpretation corresponding to the truth, which he would at once recognize. But that meant to be forced to leave the dreams to interpret themselves without any preventive measures and proceed to their evil consummation, quite possibly involving religion and the state in irreparable injury. Danger threatened the lands; but Pharaoh, to whom it was apparent, would be left alone, without counsel or aid.

The oppressive silence lasted for only a moment after Pharaoh finished speaking. For then it happened that Nefer-em-Wese, the chief cupbearer, after a long struggle with himself, came forward from the group of the King's friends and besought the favour of speaking before Pharaoh. "I do remember my faults today": thus tradition makes him begin his speech, we know the words, they still echo today in our ears. But the chief butler meant not faults which he had not committed, for he had once come unjustly into prison and had not shared in the plot to have the aged Re bitten by Eset's serpent. He meant a different fault: namely, that he had explicitly promised somebody to mention him but had not kept his word for that he had forgotten the somebody. Now he thought of him, and he spoke of him before the baldachin. He reminded Pharaoh —who scarcely remembered it himself—of the "ennui" (for so he put it, with a deprecating foreign word) he had had at one time two years before, under King Nebmare, when there had been a mistake in identity and he, together with another man, whom it were better not to name, an accursed of God, whose soul had been destroyed with his body, had been sent to Zawi-Re, the island fortress. There a youth had been assigned to him as steward, a Khabirite from Asia, the captain's aide, with the fantastic name of Osarsiph, son of a shepherd king and friend of God in the East, born of a beautiful woman, as one could tell just by looking at him. This youth, then, had the greatest gift in the field of dream-exegesis, which he, Excellent-in-Thebes, had ever seen in all the days of his life. For they had both dreamed, his guilty fellow-prisoner and himself the innocent one: very weighty, portentous dreams, each his own dream, and been extremely embarrassed for their true meaning. Then this Osarsiph, without making much of his talent beforehand, had interpreted their dreams quite easily and offhand, and announced to the baker that he would come to the gibbet, but to himself that on account of his utter innocence he would be taken back again into favour and put back into his office. And exactly so it had come to pass, and today he, Nefer, was mindful of his fault, namely that he had not long before called attention to and pointed out this talent that existed under a cloud. He did not hesitate to express the conviction that if anyone were able to interpret Pharaoh's important dreams, it was this youth, presumably still vegetating in Zawi-Re.

There was a stir among the friends of the King; something stirred also in Meni's face and form. A few more questions and answers, quickly exchanged between him and the fat man—and then the high command went forth, the first and swiftest messenger was straightway to hasten by flight of boat to Zawi-Re and with the minimum of delay to fetch back the soothsaying youth to On, before Pharaoh's countenance.

Chapter Three

THE CRETAN LOGGIA

THE PRESENTATION

WHEN Joseph arrived in the City of the Blinking, thousands-of-years-old On, it was once more seed-time, time of the burial of the god, as it had been when he came for the second time to the pit and lay in it three great days under tolerable conditions thanks to Mai-Sachme, the even-tempered captain. Everything fitted in: precisely three years had passed, they were at the same point in the circle, the week of the twenty-second to the last day of Choiak, and the children of Egypt had just celebrated once more the feast of the harrowing and the setting-up of the sacred backbone.

Joseph was glad to see golden On again. As a lad three-and-ten years before he had passed through it with the Ishmaelites on the way whither they led him and they had all got themselves instructed by the servants of the sun in the beautiful figure of the triangle and the mild nature of Re-Horakhte, lord of the wide horizon. Once more his way led through the wedge-shaped city of instruction with its many glittering sun-monuments. At the messenger's side he went toward the top of it and the great obelisk at its apex where the two sides cut each other; its golden, all-outglittering peak and cap had already greeted them from afar.

Jacob's son, who for so long had seen nothing but the walls of his prison, had no leisure to use his eyes and enjoy the sights of the busy city and its folk. Not only that none was given him by his guide, the winged messenger, who lost not a second and ever urged him on to more breathless haste. His own temperament and feelings left him no time for gazing. Once it had been Petepre before whom it was vouchsafed him to speak in the garden, the highest in that immediate circle, and everything had depended on it. Now it was Pharaoh himself, the All-Highest here below, before whom he should speak, and now even more depended on it. But what depended on it was being helpful to the Lord in His

97

plans, not clumsily to thwart them. That would be a great folly and a disgraceful denial of the world-order out of want of trust. Only a wavering faith that God meant to lift him up could be a cause for unskilfulness or poor grasp of the opportunity presented. Thus Joseph, while of course bent on the coming event, so that he had no eyes for the busy bustling streets, yet awaited it with a self-confidence devoid of fear, being strong in that faith which he knew was the basis of all devout and adroit dealing: namely, that God meant well and lovingly and momentously by him.

We, as we go along with him, sharing his suspense even though we well know how everything fell out, we shall not reproach him for self-confidence, but take him as he was and as we have long known him to be. There are some chosen ones full of doubt, humility, and self-reproach, unable to believe in their own election. They wave it away in anger and poorness of spirit, trusting not their own senses, even feeling some injury done to their unbelief when after all they find themselves lifted up. And there are others to whom nothing in the world is more natural than their own election: consciously favoured of the gods, not at all surprised at whatever elevation and consummation come their way. Whichever group of chosen ones you prefer, the self-distrustful or the presumptuous, Joseph definitely belonged to the second. Yet let us at least be glad that he did not belong to the third, which likewise exists: hypocrites before God and man, who behave unworthily even to themselves and in whose mouth "the grace of God" conceals more arrogance than all the blessing-confidence of the unabashed.

Pharaoh's temporary quarters in On lay east of the sun-temple, connected with it by an avenue of sphinxes and sycamores on which the god proceeded when he went to burn incense before his father. The dwelling-house had been conjured up by a blithe, gay fancy; not built of stone, which was suitable only for eternal dwellings, but made of brick and wood like other dwellings, though of course as charmingly and gracefully conceived as only the highest culture of Keme could dream of, surrounded in its gardens by the protection of the blindingly white wall, in front of whose elevated entrance, on gilded flagpoles, gay pennants floated in a light breeze.

It was past midday, the meal-time already over. The messenger had not rested even by night, yet it took the forenoon too before they reached On. There was a bustle on the square before the walled gate. Many of

the citizenry of On had got up and gone thither only to stand about and
wait to see the sights. Groups of police guards and charioteers barred
the way, standing to chat while their steeds snorted, pawed, or even
sometimes gave out a high clear whinny. Then there were all sorts of
hawkers and pedlars selling coloured sweetmeats and cakes, little
scarabs, and inch-high statuettes of the King and Queen. Not without
difficulty did the messenger and his charge make a way for themselves.
"A guest, a guest, way by the King's command!" he cried again and
again, trying to frighten the people by his professional breathlessness,
which he had resumed on landing. He cried out again to the servants running towards him in the inner court; they raised their eyebrows and
made signs of assent and led Joseph to the foot of a staircase. A palace
official stood on the top of it guarding the entrance to a pavilion and
looked down at them dull-eyed. He was something like an under-steward.
To this man the messenger cried up the stairs in winged words that he
was bringing the soothsayer from Zawi-Re who had been sent for hither
in the utmost haste. Whereupon the man, still dull, measured Joseph
from head to foot, as though even after this explanation he had something to say about whether he would let him in or no. Then he beckoned
them up, still with the air of himself deciding not to refuse. Hastily the
messenger once more charged Joseph that he must pant and gasp for
breath when he came before Pharaoh, to impress the King with the fact
that he had run the whole way to his countenance without pause. Joseph
did not take him seriously. He thanked the long-legged one for fetching
and accompanying him and mounted the stairs to the official, who did
not nod but shook his head by way of greeting, but then invited Joseph
to follow him.

They paced the gaily coloured vestibule, which had landscapes on the
walls and four ornamental columns wound with ribbons; and arrived
at a fountain hall likewise shining with pillars, this time of rare polished
woods. Here there was a guard of armed men. It opened in front and
at the sides into wide pillared passages. The man led Joseph straight
ahead through an antechamber with three deep doors in a row and they
entered through the middle door, into a very large hall, with perhaps
twelve columns supporting a sky-blue ceiling painted full of flights of
birds. A little open house in red and gold, like a garden belvedere, stood
in the centre, in it a table surrounded by armchairs with coloured
cushions. Aproned servants were sprinkling and brushing the floor, clear-

ing away fruit-plates, looking after the incense vases and lamps, on tripods alternating with wide-handled alabaster vases. They rearranged the chased gold beakers on the buffet and plumped up the cushions. It was clear that Pharaoh had eaten here and then withdrawn to some place to rest, either in the garden or somewhere in the house beyond. To Joseph this was all much less new and astonishing than his guide probably supposed, for he looked at him sideways from time to time.

"Do you know how to behave?" he asked as they left the hall on their right and entered a court with flower-beds and four basins let into the pavement.

"More or less, if I have to," answered Joseph with a smile.

"Well, you have to now," retorted the man. "You know at least how to salute the god?"

"I wish I did not," replied Joseph, "for it would be pleasant to learn it of you."

The official kept a straight face for a moment, then abruptly and unexpectedly he laughed. Then he pulled his long face that had gone so suddenly broad, and was sober again.

"You seem to be a sort of joker," he said, "a rascal and horse-thief who can make a man laugh at his tricks. I suppose your gift of interpreting is a trick too, like something you see a quack do at a fair?"

"Oh," answered Joseph, "I can't tell you much about interpreting; I haven't had much to do with it, it is not my line, it just happens by accident, and up to now I have not made much of it. But since Pharaoh called me in such haste on account of it, I have begun to think better of it myself."

"That is meant for me, I take it?" asked the man. "Pharaoh is young and gentle and full of kindness. That the sun shines on a man is no proof that he is not a rascal."

"It not only shines on us, it makes us shine," answered Joseph as they went on. "Some in one way, some in another. May you shine in yours!"

The man looked at him sideways. Then he looked straight ahead; but after that, suddenly, as though he had forgotten something and had to give another look at what he had seen before, he turned his head back to Joseph; at length the latter was compelled to return the side glance. He did so smiling and with a nod, as one who would say: "Yes, yes, don't be surprised, you are seeing straight." Quickly and as it were startled, the man turned away again and stared before him.

From the court with the flower-beds they reached a passage lighted from above, where the wall on one side was painted with scenes of harvesting and sacrifice, while the other through columned doorways gave glimpses of various rooms. Here was the entrance to the hall of council and audience; the guide pointed it out to Joseph as they passed. He had become more talkative; he even told his companion where Pharaoh was to be found.

"They went into the Cretan loggia after luncheon," he said. "They call it that because some such foreign artist from across the sea did the paintings. He has the chief royal sculptors with him now, Bek and Auta, and is instructing them. And the Great Mother is there. I will hand you over to the chamberlain in the anteroom and have him announce you."

"Yes, let us do so," said Joseph; there was no more than that to what he said. Yet as they went on, the man at his side first shook his head and then again suddenly fell into a soundless, prolonged chuckle, almost spasmodic, which visibly shook his diaphragm in sudden jolts. He seemed not to have quite got it under control when they reached the antechamber at the end of the passage. A little stooped courtier in a wonderful frilled apron, with a fan on his arm, detached himself from the crack of a portière embroidered with golden bees, where he had stood listening. The guide's voice still shook with suppressed chuckles; it went up and down quaintly as he announced his companion to the chamberlain tripping mincingly toward them.

"Ah, the much-heralded know-it-all!" said the little creature, in a high pipe, with a lisp. "He who is wiser than all the scholars of the book-house! Good, good, exquisite!" said he, still stooping, either because he was born like that and could not stand up straight, or because the exaggerated punctilio of court life had fixed him in this posture. "I will announce you, announce you at once, why shouldn't I? The whole court is waiting for you. I will interrupt Pharaoh, whatever he is saying, in the middle of his instruction to his artists, to tell him you have arrived. Maybe that surprises you a bit, eh? Let us hope it does not bewilder you and make you utter follies—though you may easily utter them anyhow without that. I call your attention beforehand to the fact that Pharaoh is extraordinarily sensitive to any stupidities told him about his dreams. I congratulate you. Your name was—?"

"My name was Osarsiph," answered the other.

"You mean your name is Osarsiph, of course. Extraordinary, to be called that all the time. I will go to announce you by your name. Merci, my friend," said he, with a shoulder-shrug, addressing Joseph's guide. The man went away, and the chamberlain slipped through the curtains.

From inside subdued voices could be heard: a youthful one, gentle and shy at once. It paused. Probably the hunchback had minced and lisped himself close to Pharaoh's ear. Now he came back, his eyebrows high, and whispered:

"Pharaoh summons you."

Joseph went in.

A loggia received him, not large enough really to be called, as they did call it, a garden-house, but of most unusual beauty. Its roof was supported by two columns inlaid with coloured glass and sparkling stones and wound with painted garlands so well executed that they seemed real. The floor was laid in tiled squares of alternating design, cuttlefish and children riding on dolphins. The whole place looked out through three large openings upon gardens all of whose loveliness it thus embraced. There were glorious beds of tulips, strange exotic flowering shrubs, and paths strewn with gold-dust that led to lily-ponds. The eye ranged far out into a perspective of islands, bridges, and kiosks and met the glitter of the faïence decorations on a distant summer-house. The loggia itself glowed with colour. The side walls were covered with paintings unlike anything elsewhere in the country; strange peoples and customs were depicted; obviously these were landscapes from the islands of the sea. Women in gay stiff clothing sat or moved about, their bosoms bare in their tight bodices, their hair curling above the ribbon on their foreheads and falling on their shoulders in long plaits. Pages attended them, in strange elaborate costume, and handed drink from tapering jugs. A little prince with a wasp waist, particoloured trousers, and lambskin boots, a coronet with a gay gush of feathers on his curly head, strutted complacently between rankly blossoming grasses and shot with his bow and arrow at fleeing game which leaped away with all four hooves clear of the ground. Acrobats turned somersaults over the backs of raging bulls for the diversion of ladies and gentlemen looking down from balconies.

In the same exotic taste were the objects of art and fine handicraft: bright enamelled earthenware vases, ivory reliefs inlaid with gold, embossed drinking-vessels, a steer's head in black basalt with gold horns and rock-crystal eyes. As Joseph entered and raised his hands his serious and modest gaze went the round of the scene and the persons of whose presence there he had been told.

Amenhotep-Nebmare's widow sat directly facing him with her back to the light, throned on a lofty chair with a high footstool, in front of the middle window embrasure. Her bronze-tinted skin, dark against the white garment, looked even darker in the shadow. Yet Joseph recognized her unusual features, having seen them various times on the occasion of royal progresses: the fine little aquiline nose, the curling lips framed in furrows of bitter worldly knowledge; the arching brows, lengthened with the pencil above the small, darkly gleaming, coolly measuring eyes. The mother did not wear the gold vulture-cap in which Joseph had seen her in public. Her hair was surely already grey, for she must have been at the end of her fifties. But it was covered by a silvery mob-cap which left free the gold band of a strap over brow and temples, and from the crown of her head two royal serpents—two of them, as though she had taken over that of her husband now with God—wreathed down and reared themselves in front of her brow. Round plaques adorned her ears, of the same coloured precious stones that composed her necklace. The small, energetic figure sat very straight, very upright and well-knit, so to speak in the old hieratic style, the forearms on the arms of her chair, the little feet set close together on the footstool. Her shrewd eyes met Joseph's as he entered, but turned away again towards her son after gliding swiftly down the newcomer's figure, in natural and even correct indifference, while the deep-graven bitter lines round her prominent lips shaped a mocking smile at the boyish curiosity in his face as he looked towards the eagerly awaited and recommended arrival.

The young King of Egypt sat in front of the left-hand painted wall, in an armchair with lions' feet, richly and softly cushioned and with a slanting back from which he bent briskly forward, his feet under the seat and holding its arms with his thin, scarab-decked hands. It must be added that this posture of tense expectancy, as though to spring from his chair, this turn to the right while the veiled grey eyes went as wide open as they possibly could to look at the new interpreter of his dreams: this expressive series of changes did not happen all at once, but was carried out by stages and lasted a full minute; at the end it really looked as though Pharaoh had lifted himself from his seat and was resting all his weight on the hands clutching the chair-arms—their knuckles stood out white. And thus an object which had been in his lap—some sort of stringed instrument—fell with soft ringing and twanging to the floor, quickly retrieved and handed back by a man who stood before him, one of the sculptors he was instructing. The man had to hold it out awhile until the King took it, closing his eyes and sinking back into the cushions in the same attitude which had obviously been his when talking with his artists. It was extraordinarily relaxed and easy, even too easy, for the chair-seat was hollowed out to hold the cushions, and the cushions were too soft, so that he could not help sinking down. Thus he sat, not only leaning back but also very low, with one hand hanging loosely over the back of the chair, and with the thumb of the other hand lightly touching the strings of the strange little harp in his lap. His linen-covered knees were drawn up and crossed, so that one foot went to and fro rather high in the air. The gold strap of the sandal ran between his great and his second toe.

THE CHILD OF THE CAVE

Nefer-Kheperu-Re-Amenhotep was at that time just the age that Joseph—now standing before him a man of thirty—had been when he was "feeding the flocks with his brethren" and beguiled his father of the many-coloured coat. In other words, Pharaoh was seventeen years old. But he seemed older; not only because in his climate men ripen faster; not only because of his delicate health; but also because of his early obligations to the universe, the many impressions that, coming from all quarters of the heavens, had assailed his mind and heart, and finally because of his zealous and fanatical concern anent the divine. In describing his face, under the round blue wig he wore today over the linen cap, the thousands of years' gap must not prevent the apt comparison: he looked like an aristocratic young Englishman of somewhat decadent stock; spare, haughty, weary, with a well-developed chin which yet somehow looked weak, a nose with a narrow, rather depressed bridge which made even more striking the broad, sensitive nostrils; and deeply, dreamily overshadowed eyes with lids he could never open quite wide —their weary expression was in disconcerting contrast to the unrouged, morbid brilliancy of the full lips. There was a complicated and painful mixture of intellectuality and sensuality in this face, still in its boyish stage, with a suggestion of arrogance and recklessness. Pretty and well-favoured it was not at all, but of a disturbing attractiveness; it was not surprising that Egypt's people had a great tenderness for their Pharaoh and gave him flowery names.

Not beautiful either, indeed quite odd, and unconformable to tradition was Pharaoh's figure. It scarcely reached middle height; that was plain as it lay there in the cushions, clearly defined in its light, choice, costly raiment. The relaxed posture did not indicate a lack of manliness but was a sustained attitude of opposition. There were the long neck and thin arms, the narrow, tender chest half covered by a collar of priceless stones, the arms encircled by chased gold bands; the abdomen, rather prominent from childhood, with the apron beginning well below the navel and reaching high up in the back, the rich frill in front trimmed with the uraeus and ribbon fringes. Add to all this that the legs were not only too short but otherwise out of proportion, the thighs being distinctly too big while the legs looked almost as thin as a chicken's. Amenhotep charged his sculptors not to disguise this peculiarity but even, for the sake of truth, to exaggerate it. His hands and feet, on the contrary, were most delicate and aristocratic in shape, especially the hands, with their long fingers and sensitive expression. They had traces of unguent at the base of the nails. It was something to ponder on, that the ruling passion of this spoilt lad, who obviously took for granted all the privilege and luxury of his state, was knowledge of the Highest; Abraham's descendant, standing at one side and looking at Pharaoh, marvelled to see in what divers sorts of humanity, strange and remote one from another, concern for God could manifest itself on earth.

"So, good Auta"—Joseph noted the gentle reserved tones he had heard from outside, rather high-pitched, rather slow, but at times falling into a more impetuous measure—"make it as Pharaoh has directed, pleasing, living, fine, as my Father above would have it. There are still errors in your work—not mistakes of technique, for you are very capable, but mistakes of spirit. My Majesty has shown them to you and you will correct them. You have done my sister, sweet Princess Baketaton, too much in the dead old style, contrary to the Father whose will I know. Make her sweet and easy, make her according to the truth, which is the light, and in which Pharaoh lives, for he has set it in his inmost heart! Let one hand be putting to her mouth a piece of fruit, a pomegranate, and her other hand be hanging down easily—not with the palm turned stiffly to the body but the rounded palm turned backwards, thus will the god have it that is in my heart and whom I know as no other knows him because I have come of him."

"Your servant," answered Auta, wrapping the clay figure with one hand while he raised the other arm towards Pharaoh, "will make it exactly as Pharaoh commands and has instructed me to my great joy who is the only one of Re, the beauteous child of Aton."

"Thank you, Auta, my warm and loving thanks to you. It is important, you understand? For as the Father is in me and I in him, so shall all become one in us, that is the goal. But your work, conceived in the right spirit, can perhaps contribute a little to all becoming one in him and me.—And you, good Bek—"

"Remember, Auta," the deep, almost masculine voice of the goddess-widow made itself heard at this juncture from her high seat, "always remember that it is hard for Pharaoh to make us understand him, and that he probably says more than he means in order that our understanding may follow him. What he means is not that you are to show the sweet Princess Baketaton as eating, as biting into the fruit; rather you should only put the pomegranate into her hand and make her slightly lift her arm so that one may assume she will probably put the fruit to her mouth. That will be enough of the new and is what Pharaoh means you to understand when he says you are to make her eat it. You must also subtract a little from what His Majesty said about the hanging hand, that you are to turn the palm entirely to the back. Turn it just slightly away from the body, half turn it, that is what is meant—and that will make you praise and blame enough. This simply to make things clear."

Her son was silent a space.

"Have you understood?" he asked then.

"I have," answered Auta.

"Then you will have understood," said Amenhotep, looking down at the lyre-shaped instrument in his lap, "that the great mother of course said somewhat less than she meant, in seeking to lessen the effect of my words. You can carry the hand with the fruit rather far towards the mouth. As for the other hand, it is, of course, only a half turn if you turn her palm away from her body towards the back, for nobody carries the palm turned entirely outwards. And you would be offending against truth if you made it like that. Thus you can see how wisely the mother has qualified my words."

He looked up from the instrument with a mischievous smile showing

106

the teeth, too small, too white, too translucent between his full lips. He looked over at Joseph, who smiled back at him. The queen and the craftsman smiled too.

"And you, good Bek," he went on, "go, as I have commissioned you, to Jebu, into the elephant land, and fetch some of the red granite that is produced there; a goodly amount of the very finest quality, the kind with a glittering of quartz and shot through with black, you know, which my heart loves. Lo, Pharaoh will adorn the house of his father at Karnak that it may excel Amun's house, if not in size, then in the preciousness of the stones, and the name 'Brilliance of the great Aton' be more and more usual for his district, until perhaps Weset itself, the whole city, may take on one day the name 'City of the Brilliance of Aton' in the popular mouth. You know my thoughts, and I confide in your love of them. Go, then, my good man, travel at once. Pharaoh will sit here in his cushions and you will travel far away upstream and bear the burdens it costs to get the red stone out and down and ship it to Thebes. So is it, and thus so be it. When will you set out?"

"Early tomorrow," answered Bek, "when I have taken care of home and wife; and love to our sweet Lord the beauteous child of Aton will make as light my travel and travail as though I sat in the softest cushions."

"Good, good; and go now, my men. Pack up and go each to his task. Pharaoh has weighty business; only outwardly does he rest in his cushions, inwardly he is in a high state of tension, zealous and full of cares. Your cares are indeed great, but small in comparison with his. Farewell!"

He waited until the craftsmen had done their reverence and withdrawn but meanwhile he looked at Joseph.

"Come nearer, my friend," he said, as the bee-studded curtain closed behind them, "pray come close to me, dear Khabiru from the Retenu, fear not, nor startle in your step, come quite close to me! This is the mother of god, Tiy, who lives a million years. And I am Pharaoh. But think no more of that, lest it make you fearful. Pharaoh is God and man, but sets as much store by the second as the first, yes, he rejoices, sometimes his rejoicing amounts to defiance and scorn, that he is a man like all men, seen from one side; he rejoices to snap his fingers at those sour-faces who would have him bear himself uniformly as God."

And he actually did snap his slender fingers in the air.

"But I see you are not afraid," he went on, "and startled not in your steps, but pace them with calm courage towards me. That is good to see, for in many the heart turns over when they stand before Pharaoh, their spirit forsakes them, their knees give way and they cannot distinguish life from death. You are not giddy?"

Joseph, smiling, shook his head.

"There can be three reasons for that," said the boy king. "Either because your descent is noble, or because you see the human being in Pharaoh, as it pleases him when it comes about within the frame of his divinity. Or it may be you feel that a reflection of the divine rests upon you, for you are wonderfully lovely and charming, pretty as a picture. My Majesty noted it directly you entered, although it did not surprise me, as I have been told you are the son of a lovely woman. For after all it indicates that He loves you who creates beauty of form through Himself alone, who lends the eyes love and power of vision through and for His beauty. One may call beautiful people the darlings of the light."

He looked at Joseph with satisfaction, his head on one side.

"Is he not wonderfully pretty and well-favoured, like a god of light, little Mama?" he asked Tiy, who sat leaning her cheek against three fingers of her little dark hand that blazed with gems.

"You have summoned him because of the wisdom and power of interpretation he is supposed to have," she answered, looking into space.

"They belong together," broke in Amenhotep quickly and eagerly. "Pharaoh has considered much and perceived much on this point; he has discussed it with visiting ambassadors often from afar and foreign lands, magi, priests, and initiates who brought him from east and west news of the thoughts of men. For where all must he not hearken and what all not observe: to test, to choose, and make useful the usable that he may perfect the teaching and establish the image of truth according to the will of his Father above! Beauty, little Mama, and you, dear Amu, has to do with wisdom through the medium of light. For light is the medium and the means, whence relationship streams out on three sides: to beauty, to love, and to knowledge of truth. These are one in him, and light is their three-in-oneness. Strangers bore to me the teaching of the beginning god, born of flames, a beautiful god of light and love, and his name was 'first-born brilliance.' That is a glorious, a useful contribution, for therein is displayed the unity of love and light. But light is beauty as well as truth and knowledge, and if you would learn the medium of truth, then know that it is love.—Well, now, they say of you that when you hear a dream you can interpret it?" he asked Joseph. His face was suffused with the colour of embarrassment at his own extravagant and fanatical words.

"It is not I who does this, O my lord," answered Joseph. "It is not I who can do it, it is God alone, and He does it sometimes through me. Everything has its time: dreams, and the interpretation of them. When I was a lad I dreamed and my brothers were angry and chid me. Now when I am a man has come the time of interpretation. My dreams interpret themselves to me, and certainly it is God who gives it to me to interpret the dreams of others."

"So you are a prophetic youth, a so-called inspired lamb?" inquired Amenhotep. "You seem to belong in that category. Will you fall down dead with your last words after you have announced the future to the King, and die in a spasm, that he may give you solemn burial and have your prophecies inscribed to be handed down to posterity?"

"Not easily," said Joseph, "is the question of the Great House to be answered; not with yes and not with no, at best with both. It amazes your servant and goes to his heart that you are pleased to see in him a lamb, an inspired lamb. For I am used to this name since a child: my father the friend of God used to call me 'the lamb,' because my lovely mother, the star-maid for whom he served at Sinear, across the river flowing the wrong way, and who bore me in the sign of the virgin, was named Rachel, which means mother sheep. But this does not justify me, great lord, in accepting your idea unconditionally or in saying 'I am.' For I am and am not just because I am I. I mean that the general and the typical vary when they fulfil themselves in the particular, so that the known becomes unknown and you cannot recognize it. Do not expect me to fall down dead with my last word just because that is the established pattern. This your servant, whom you summoned from the grave, does not expect it, for it belongs only to the typical and not to me, the variation from the typical. Nor shall I foam at the mouth, like the typical prophetic youth, if God shall give it to me to prophesy to Pharaoh. When I was a lad, I probably did twitch, and gave my father great concern by rolling my eyes like those who run naked, babbling oracles. My father's son has put that away from him since he came to years; he holds now with divine reason, even when he interprets. Interpretation is spasm enough, one need not slaver as well. Plain and clear shall be the interpretation, and no aulasaukaulala."

He had not looked toward the mother as he spoke, but out of one corner of his eye he saw that she nodded assent on her high seat. Her brisk, low, almost masculine voice, issuing from that fragile form, was heard to say:

"The stranger speaks what is worth hearing and heartening to Pharaoh."

On that Joseph could only continue, for the King was silent for the moment and hung his head with the sulky look of a chidden child. Joseph, thus encouraged by Tiy, went on:

"In my unworthy opinion, a composed manner in interpreting is due to the fact that it is an I and a single individual through whom the typical and the traditional are being fulfilled, and thereby, in my feeling, the seal of divine reason is vouchsafed to them. For the pattern and the traditional come from the depths which lie beneath and are what binds us, whereas the I is from God and is of the spirit, which is free. But what constitutes civilized life is that the binding and traditional depth shall fulfil itself in the freedom of God which belongs to the I; there is no human civilization without the one and without the other."

Amenhotep nodded to his mother with lifted brows; he began to applaud, holding one hand straight up and striking the palm with two fingers of the other.

"Do you hear, my little Mama?" said he. "This is a youth of great insight whom My Majesty has sent for to come hither. Remember, pray, that by my own resolve I called him to come. Pharaoh too is very gifted and advanced for his years, but it is doubtful whether he could have made up and expressed these things about the binding pattern of the depths and the dignity which comes from above.—So you are not bound to the binding pattern of the foaming lamb," he asked, "and you will not bruise the heart of Pharaoh with the traditional announcements of horrible misery to come, the invasion by foreign peoples, and how that which is undermost shall be turned uppermost?" He shuddered. "We all know about that," he said, his lips going a little white. "But My Majesty must spare himself a little, he cannot well bear the wild and savage, he is in need of tenderness and love. The land has gone down to destruction, it lives in uproar. Bedouins rove over it. Poor and rich change places, all law is annulled, the son slays the father and by his brother is slain, wild beasts of the desert drink at the springs, one laughs the laugh of death, Re has turned away his face, no one knows when midday is, for one knows not the shadow on the dial; beggars consume the sacrifices, the King is taken and snatched away; one only consolation abides, that by the might of him who shall deliver all shall be better once more. Pharaoh, then, need not hear this song again? May he hope that the modification of the traditional by the particular will exclude such horrors?"

Joseph smiled. It was now that he made the famous reply, both courteous and shrewd:

"God shall give Pharaoh an answer of peace."

"You speak of God," probed Amenhotep. "You have done so several times. Which god do you mean? You are from Zahi and from Amu, so I assume that you mean the ox whom in the East they call Baal the Lord?"

Joseph's smile became detached. He even shook his head.

"My fathers, the God-dreamers," said he, "made their covenant with another Lord."

"Then it can only be Adonai, the bridegroom," said the King quickly, "for whom the flute wails in the gorges and who rises again. You see, Pharaoh knows his way about among the gods of all mankind. He must know and try all and be like a gold-washer who dredges the kernel of truth out of much absurdity, that it may help to perfect the teaching of his adored father. Pharaoh finds it hard, but good, very good, a royal task. My good parts have made me work that out. Who has hardship must also have ease, but only he. For it is disgusting to have only ease; yet to have only hardship is not right either. At the great feast of tribute in the beautiful balcony of audience My Majesty sits next to my lovely consort and the ambassadors of the people. Moors, Libyans, and Asiatics bring a ceaseless train of gifts from all the world, bar gold and gold in rings, ivory, silver vases, ostrich feathers, oxen, byssus, leopards and elephants in procession; and just so the Lord of the Crowns sits in the beauty of his palace and receives in fitting ease the tribute of all the thought of the inhabited earth. For as My Majesty was already pleased to say, the singers and seers of strange gods succeed one another, coming to my court from all the regions of the earth together: from Persia, where the gardens are renowned and where they believe that some day the earth will be flat and even and all men have one species, speech, and law;

from India, the land where the incense grows, from star-wise Babel and the islands of the sea. They all visit me, they pass over before my seat, and My Majesty has intercourse with them as he now has with you who are a special kind of lamb. They offer me the early and the late, the old and the new. Sometimes they leave strange souvenirs and divine signs. Do you see this toy here?" And he lifted the round stringed object from his lap and held it out to Joseph.

"A lyre," the other assented. "It is fitting that Pharaoh holds in his hand the symbol of goodness and charm."

This he said because the hieroglyph for the Egyptian "Nofert," which means both goodness and charm, is a lyre.

"I see," responded the King, "that you have understanding of the arts of Thoth and are a scribe. I suppose that belongs to the dignity of the I, wherein the binding pattern of the depths fulfills itself. But this object is a sign of something else besides goodness and charm, namely of the artfulness of a strange god, who may be a brother of the Ibis-headed or his other self, and who invented the toy as a child when he met a certain creature. Do you know the shell?"

"It is a tortoise-shell," said Joseph.

"You are right," assented Amenhotep. "This sly-boots of a child-god met this wise creature born in the hollow of the rocks and it fell a sacrifice to his quick wit. For he impudently robbed it of its hollow shell and put strings across and fastened on two horns as you can see, and it became a lyre. I will not say this is the very same toy the mischievous rascal made. The man who brought it and gave it to me, a seafarer from Crete, does not say that. It may only have been made in memory of the first, in jest or piety, for this was only one of various tales the Cretan told of the swaddling-babe of the cave. It seems this infant was always getting up out of his hole and swaddlings to play pranks. He stole—it is almost unbelievable—the cattle of the sun-god, his elder brother, away from the hill where they pastured, when the sun-god had gone down. Fifty of them he took and drove them about, across and across, to confuse their hoof-marks. His own steps he disguised, binding on them enormous sandals woven of branches, so that there were giant footprints that he left behind, and thus none at all. And that was quite fitting. For he was indeed an infant and yet a god; and so those vast vague footprints were quite as they should be. The cattle he drove away and hid them in a cave, a different one from the one where he was born—there are many in those parts. But first he slaughtered two cows by the river and roasted them at a huge fire. These he ate, the suckling babe; it was the meal of a giant child and went with the footprints."

Amenhotep went on, lying back relaxed in his chair: "This done, the thievish child slipped back to his parent cave and into his swaddlings. But when the sun-god came up again and missed his cattle, he divined, for he was a soothsaying god, and knew that only his newborn brother could have done the deed. Hot with anger he came to him in his cave. But the little thief, who had heard him coming, cuddled himself into his swaddlings that smelled sweet of his godhead, made himself very small, and counterfeited the slumber of innocence. In his arms he held his invention, the lyre. And of course the hypocrite knew how to lie like the truth when the sun-god, undeceived by his wiles, taxed him with the theft. "Quite other concerns have I," he lisped, "than this you think: sweet sleep and mother's milk, the swaddlings round my shoulders and warm baths." And then he swore, the seafarer said, a great round oath that he knew nothing of the cattle.—Do I bore you, Mama?" he interrupted himself, and turned to the goddess on her throne.

"Since I am freed from the cares of the governing of this land," she replied, "I have much time to spare. I can as well while it away listening to stories of strange gods. Yet truly the world seems upside down to me: it is usually the king who lets himself be narrated to, and now Your Majesty narrates himself."

"Why should he not?" responded Amenhotep. "Pharaoh must instruct. And what he has learned he is always urged to teach at once to others. What my mother really objects to," he went on, and stretching two fingers towards her he seemed as it were to explain to her her own words, "is, no doubt, that Pharaoh delays to relate his dreams to this understanding and inspired lamb, that he may at last hear the truth about them. For that I shall get true interpretation from him I am almost certain even now, owing to his person and some things he has already said. My Majesty is not afraid, for he has promised that he will not prophesy in the manner of the mouth-foaming youth or horrify me with such tales as that beggars will consume the offerings. But do you not know and have you not seen the wonderful way the mind has: that a man, when the fulfilment approaches of his most coveted wish, will of his own free will hold off a little from the consummation? 'Now it is at hand anyhow,' he says, 'and only waits on me; I may just as well put it off a little, for

113

the desire and the wish themselves have grown dear to me, in a way, and it is too bad about them.' That is a way human beings have, and Pharaoh too, who sets great store by being a human being himself."

Tiy smiled.

"As your beloved Majesty does it, we shall call it beautiful. Since this soothsayer may not well ask, I will: did the naughty suckling's perjury avail, or what happened next?"

"This," answered Amenhotep, "according to my source: the sun-brother brought the thief in bonds before their father, the great god, that he should confess and the god punish him. But here too the rascal lied with the utmost guile and spoke piously out of his mouth. 'Highly I honour the sun,' he lisped, 'and the other gods and you I love, but fear him here. Protect, then, the younger and help poor little me!' So he misrepresented himself displaying his baby side, winking the while at his father out of one eye, so that he could only laugh aloud at the arch rogue. He ordered him to show his brother the cattle and deliver back the stolen property, to which the infant agreed. But when the elder brother heard of the two slaughtered cows he was wroth anew. Now while he threatened and fumed, the little one played on his lyre—this thing here—and his singing went so sweet to the sound of the lyre that the elder brother's scolding died away and the sun-god thought only of getting the instrument for his own. And his it became, for they made a bargain: the cattle remained to the thief, the lyre the brother carried away—and keeps it for ever."

He stopped speaking and looked down at the toy in his lap.

"In right instructive way after all," said the mother, "Pharaoh has put off the fulfilment of his most ardent wish."

"Instructive it is," gave back the King, "for it shows that child gods are only disguised children—disguised out of sheer mischief. He came out of his cave whenever he chose, as a gay and gifted youth, skilled in devices, never at a loss for flexible stratagems, a helper to gods and men. What new things did he not invent, in the belief of the people: writing and reckoning, culture of the olive and of shrewd persuasive speech; not shrinking from deceit, yet deceiving with great charm. My seafaring man, whose patron he was, esteemed him highly. For he was the god of favourable chance, so the man said, and of smiling inventiveness; shedding blessing and well-being—whether honestly or even a bit dishonestly won, the way life is; a leader and guide through the wind-

114

ings of this world, turning back with lifted staff to smile. Even the dead he guides, the man said, in their kingdom of the moon—and even dreams, for he is lord of sleep, who closes the eyes of man with his staff, a gentle magician with all his slyness."

Pharaoh's gaze fell on Joseph, as he stood before him, the pretty and charming head bowed or even bent on one shoulder, looking sideways up at the paintings on the wall, with an unforced and absent smile which seemed to say he need not absolutely listen to all this.

"Are the tales of the mischievous god known to you, soothsayer?" asked Amenhotep.

Joseph quickly changed his pose. He had behaved with pointed lack of courtly manners and now showed that he was aware of it. He even did so in somewhat exaggerated fashion; so that Pharaoh, who always noticed everything, got the impression not only that this startled return to the present moment was assumed, but that it had been put on to create that very impression. He waited, keeping his veiled grey eyes, as wide open as he could make them, directed on Joseph.

"Known, highest Lord?" the young man asked. "Yes and no—if you will permit your servant the double answer."

"You seek often for such permission," said the King, "or rather you simply take it. All your speaking turns on the Yes and at the same time on the No. Is that likely to please me? You are the mouth-foaming youth and you are not, because you are you. The mischievous god is known to you and he is not, because—why? Was he known to you or not?"

"To you too, Lord of the Crowns, he has always been known—in a way; for did you not call him a distant brother of the Ibis-headed, Djehuti, the moon-friendly scribe, or indeed his other self? Was he known to you or not? He was familiar—that is more than known, for in it the Yes and No cancel each other out and are one and the same. No, I did not know the child of the cave and master of pranks. My father's oldest servant, the wise Eliezer, was my teacher: he who could say that the earth sprang to meet him on the bridal journey for the saved sacrifice, my father's father—pardon, pardon! All this leads too far afield, your servant cannot narrate the world to you at this hour. And yet the words of the great mother still ring in his ear: it is the custom in the world for the king not to narrate but to be narrated to. Of such pranks as these I might know several, to show you, you and the great mistress, that the spirit of the rogue-god has always been at home among my people and is familiar to me."

Amenhotep looked across at his mother with a light nod which meant: "Well, what shall we make of him?" Then he answered Joseph:

"The goddess permits you to tell us one or two of them, if you think you can amuse us, before the interpreting."

"Our breath cometh from you," said Joseph, with an obeisance. "I use it to divert you."

And with folded arms, but often lifting his hand in a descriptive gesture, he spoke before Pharaoh and said:

"Rough was Esau, my uncle, the mountain goat, twin of my father, who forced the passage before him when they were born. Red and shaggy of hair was he, a bungler; my father was smooth and fine, tent-bred and son of his mother, clever in God, a shepherd, while Esau a hunter was. Always was Jacob blest, since before the hour when my forebear, father of both, resolved to bestow the handed-down blessing, for he declined unto death. Blind the old man, his ancient eyes would no longer obey him, only with hands he saw, feeling not seeing. Before him he summoned the red one, his eldest, longing to love him. 'Go, shoot me game with thy bow,' he said, 'my forthright, hairy first-born, cook me a savoury meat that I may eat and then bless thee, strengthened thereto by the meal.' Red one went off to the hunt. Meanwhile the mother wrapped the younger in goatskins round his smooth limbs and gave him a mess, spiced and seasoned, from goat's flesh. With it he went to the master into the tent and spake: 'Here am I back, my father, Esau, thy hairy one, having hunted and cooked for thee. Eat then, and bless thy first-born!' 'Come now to me, come near to thy father, my son,' spoke the blind old man, 'that I may feel with my seeing hands if you are truly Esau, my hairy one, for it is easy to say.' And felt with his hands and felt the fell of the goat where the skin was bare, and there it was rough, like Esau; red it was not, but that the hands could not see and the old eyes would not. 'Yes, there can be no doubt, it is you,' said the old man then, 'from your fleece it is plain to me. Rough or smooth, so it is, and how good that one needs not the eyes to perceive, for the hand sufficeth! Esau art thou, then feed me that I may bless thee!' So did he smell and eat, and he gave to the wrong one, who yet was the right one, the fullness of blessing one might not recall. Then came Esau from hunting, puffed up and boastful at this his great hour. He cooks and seasons his game where all eyes can see him and bears it within to his father inside the tent. But there in the tent was he cheated and mocked as a humbug, truly he was the wrong right one, since the right wrong one had come before him through mother's guile. Only a barren curse he received since naught else was left after the blessing was spent. What jesting and laughing were there, when he sat down wailing aloud with his tongue hanging out, and the fat tears plumped down into the dust, the cozened clodpate whom the clever one tricked, skilled and familiar in all!"

Mother and son both laughed, the one in a sonorous alto, the other clear and rather piping. Both shook their heads.

"What a grotesque tale!" cried Amenhotep. "A barbaric farce, capital in its way, if rather depressing too; one hardly knows how to take it, it makes you feel like laughing and crying, both at once. The wrong right one, you say, and the wrong one that was the right one? That is not bad; it is so crazy that it is witty. But may the higher goodness preserve us all from being both right and wrong, so that we need not sit blubbering in the end, with our tears plopping into the dust! What do you think of the mother, little Mama? Wrapping goatskins round the smoothness, and helping the old one and his seeing hands to bless the right one, in other words the wrong one. Tell me if you do not find this an original lamb whom I have summoned before my presence. My Majesty permits you to relate another jest, Khabire, that I may see whether the first was not good just by chance, and whether this spirit of clever roguery is really better than known to you, because familiar. Let me hear!"

"What Pharaoh commands," Joseph said, "is already done. The blessing one had to flee before the wrath of the cheated; travel he must, and travelled to Naharin in the land of Sinear, where relatives dwelt: Laban the clod, a sinister man of affairs, and his daughters, the one red-eyed, the other more lovely than stars in the sky. So she became his all, and more to him than all save only God. But the hard taskmaster made him serve seven years for the starry maid. They passed like days, but then the uncle gave to him first in the dark the other unloved, and only much later the true bride, Rachel the mother sheep, who bore me with more than natural pains, and they called me Dumuzi, the true son. This only in passing. Now, when the star-maid was healed after bearing, my father would be away with me and the ten whom the maids and the wrong one had borne him; or he made as though he would go to his uncle, who was unwilling, for Jacob's blessing-hand was a profit to Laban. 'Give me, then, all the pied sheep and goats of the flocks,' said he to his uncle. 'They shall be mine, but yours all those of one colour. Such is my modest condition.' So then they sealed their bargain. But what then did Jacob do? Took wands from the trees and bushes and peeled white stripes in the bark, so they were pied. These he laid in the troughs where the flocks came to drink and mated after the drinking. Always he made them see the pied wands at this business, which worked on them through their eyes so that they dropped pied young, which he took. So he grew rich out of all count and Laban was laid by the heels through the wit of the roguish god."

Again the mother and son were much diverted. They laughed and shook their heads; a vein stood out on the King's sickly forehead and tears were in his half-shut eyes.

"Mama, Mama," said he, "My Majesty is very, very much amused. Striped staves he took and gave them the pattern through their eyes— ring-straked and speckled, we say, and ring-straked and speckled Pharaoh could laugh himself at a jest like that! Does he still live, your father? That was a rogue! And so you are the son of a rogue and a lovely one?"

"The lovely one was a thief and rascal too," Joseph supplemented his tale. "Her loveliness was no stranger to stratagems. For love of her husband she stole her gloomy father's images, thrust them into the camel's bedding, and sat on it and said in her beguiling voice: 'I am unwell with my periods and cannot stand up.' But Laban searched in vain, to his own chagrin."

"One on top of the other!" cried Amenhotep, his voice breaking. "Listen to me, Mama. You owe me an answer whether I have not summoned before me a highly original subtle and sportive lamb. Now is the moment," he suddenly decreed; "now is Pharaoh ready to hear from this wise youth the interpretation of his difficult dreams. Before these tears of merriment are quite dry in my eyes, I will hear it. For as long as my eyes are still wet from this rare laughter, I fear not the dreams nor their meaning, whatever it is. This son of jesters will tell Pharaoh neither such stupidities as did the pedants of the book-house, nor yet any frightful things. And even though the truth he tells be bad, yet these lips so given to smiling can scarcely shape it so as to turn straightway these tears of laughter to tears of mourning. Soothsayer, is there need of any vessel or apparatus for your task? A cauldron, perhaps, to receive the dreams, out of which their meaning shall rise?"

"Nothing at all," answered Joseph. "I need nothing between heaven and earth for my affair. I just go ahead and interpret as the spirit moves me. Pharaoh needs only to speak."

The King cleared his throat and looked over in some embarrassment at his mother, excusing himself by a little bow for her having to hear the tale all over again. Then, blinking with his laughter-wet eyes, for the sixth time he conscientiously related his now stale dreams.

PHARAOH PROPHESIES

Joseph listened unaffectedly, in a respectful posture; while the King spoke he kept his eyes closed, but in no other way did he betray the profound abstraction and concentration of his being upon what he heard. He did something else too; he kept them shut for a little while after Amenhotep had finished and was waiting, holding his breath. He even went so far as to let the King wait a little, while he stood there, not looking but aware of the attention focused upon him. It was very still in the Cretan loggia; only the goddess mother gave a ringing cough and played with her ornaments.

"Are you sleeping, lamb?" Amenhotep asked at last in a tremulous voice.

"No, here am I," answered Joseph, as without undue haste he opened his eyes before Pharaoh. Even then he seemed to look through him instead of at him, or rather his gaze, resting on the King's figure, broke there and turned inwards in contemplation—and all that became the black Rachel-eyes very well.

"And what say you to my dreams?"

"To your dreams?" Joseph answered. "To your dream, you mean. To dream twice is not to dream two dreams. You dreamed but one dream. That you dreamed it twice, first in one form and then in the other, has only the meaning of emphasis: it means that your dream will certainly be fulfilled and that speedily. Furthermore its second form is only the explanation and more precise definition of the meaning of the first."

"That is just what My Majesty thought in the beginning!" cried Amenhotep. "Mother, what the lamb says was my own first thought,

that the two dreams are at bottom only one. I dreamed of the goodly
cattle and then the ghastly ones, and then it was as if somebody said to
me: 'Did you understand me? This is the meaning.' And then I dreamed
of the ears, the full and the blasted ones. As a man will seek to express
himself and then try again, 'In other words,' he says, 'so and so.' Mama,
here is a good beginning which this prophetic boy has made, without
foaming at the mouth. Those botchers from the book-house bungled at
the very start and nothing good could come after that. Continue, prophet.
What is the single meaning of my double royal dream?"

"Single is the meaning, like the two lands, and double the dream
like your crown," Joseph replied. "Is not that what you meant just now
though you did not quite say it, yet said it not quite by chance? You
betrayed what you meant in the words 'my royal dream.' Crown and
train you wore in your dream, as I darkly perceived. You were not
Amenhotep, but Nefer-Kheperu-Re, the King. God spoke to the King
in his dream. He revealed his future purposes to Pharaoh that Pharaoh
may know and plan accordingly."

"Absolutely," cried Amenhotep. "Nothing was clearer to me. Mother,
nothing was more certain from the beginning than what this peculiar
kind of lamb has said: that it was not I who dreamed, but the King, in
so far as the two can be separated, and in so far as not even I was necessary in order that the King should dream. Did not Pharaoh know it and
swore to you at once next morning that the double dream was important
for the realm and therefore absolutely must be interpreted? But it was
sent to the King not as the father of the lands but because he is also
the mother of them; for the sex of the King is double. My dream had
to do with matters of life and death and with the black underworld. I
knew it and I know it. But yet I know no more," he suddenly bethought
himself. "Why is it My Majesty utterly forgot that he knows nothing
more and that the interpretation is still to seek? You have a way,"
he turned to Joseph, "of making it seem as though everything is all
beautifully clear whereas so far you have only told me what I knew
already. What means my dream, what would it show to me?"

"Pharaoh errs," Joseph responded, "if he thinks he does not know.
His servant can do no more than to prophesy to him what he already
knows. Did you not see the cows as they came up out of the water in a
row, one after the other, and followed in one another's steps, first the

fat and then the lean, so that there was no break in the row? What are they that come up out of the casket of eternity, one after the other, not together but in succession, and no break is between the going and the coming and no interruption in their line?"

"The years!" cried Amenhotep, snapping his fingers as he held them up.

"Of course," said Joseph. "It needs not to rise out of any cauldron nor any rolling of eyes nor foaming at the mouth to tell us that the cows are years, seven and seven. And the ears of corn which sprouted one after the other, and to the same number: shall they be something quite different and vastly hard to guess?"

"No!" cried Pharaoh and snapped his fingers again, "they are years too!"

"As divine reason would have it," answered Joseph, "to which all praise and honour shall be given. But why the cows should have become ears, seven fruitful and seven barren—now indeed the cauldron must be fetched. Large round as the moon, that the answer may rise out of it and tell us what the connection is between cows and ears and the reason why the first seven cows were so fat and second seven so lean. Pharaoh will be so kind as to send for a cauldron and tripod!"

"Get along with your cauldron!" cried the King. "Is this a time to talk of cauldrons, as though we needed anything of the sort! The connection is as plain as a pikestaff and clear as a gem of the first water. There is a connection between the goodness and the badness of the cows and the ears: one means good crops and the other bad ones." He paused, staring out into space before him. "Seven fat years will come," he said in a sort of transport, "and then seven lean ones."

"Without fail or faltering," said Joseph, "for it was told you twice."

Pharaoh directed his gaze upon his lamb.

"You have not fallen dead after the prophecy," he said with a certain admiration.

"Were it not evil and punishable to say so," Joseph responded, "one might put it that it is wonderful Pharaoh does not fall dead, for Pharaoh has prophesied."

"No, you are just saying that," contradicted Amenhotep. "You made it seem as though I myself interpreted because you are a child of stratagems and descended from rogues. But why could I have not done it before you came? I only knew what was false but not what was true. For true is this interpretation, that I know in my very soul; my own dream knows itself again in the interpretation. Yes, you are indeed an inspired lamb, but you certainly have your own little ways. You are no slave of the binding pattern of the depths, you did not prophesy first the curse-time and then the blessing-time but the other way round, first the blessing and then the curse—and that is very original of you!"

"It was you yourself, Lord of the Two Lands," answered Joseph, "and on you it depended. You dreamed, first of the fat kine and ears and then of the lean ones; and you yourself are the only original."

Amenhotep worked himself up out of the hollow of his chair and sprang to his feet. He strode to his mother's seat, moving swiftly on those odd limbs of his—the heavy thighs and thin lower parts showed plainly through the batiste garment.

"Mama," he said, "now we have it! My king-dreams are now interpreted to me and I know the truth. When I think of the erudite rubbish that was passed off to My Majesty—the daughters, the cities, the kings, and the fourteen children—I feel as much like laughing as I felt like weeping before when I was desperate at its poverty. Now, thanks to this prophetic youth, I know the truth and I can simply laugh at it. But the truth itself is serious enough. My Majesty has been shown that seven fat years will come in all Egypt and after that seven years of dearth, such that one will quite forget the previous plenty, and famine will consume the land, just as the lean kine consumed the fat, and the blasted ears the golden ones; for such was the message: that one would know no more of the fullness that was before the famine-time, for its harshness will consume our memory of the fullness. This is what was revealed to Pharaoh in his dreams, which were one dream and which came to him because he is the mother of the lands. That it remained dark to me until this hour is what I can scarcely understand. Now it is brought to life by the aid of this genuine but peculiar lamb. It was necessary, in order that the King might dream, that I should be; in the same way it was necessary that he should be, in order that the lamb might prophesy; our being is only the meeting-place between not-being and ever-being; our temporal only the medium of the eternal. And yet not only that. For we must ask—it is the problem which I should like to put before the thinkers of my Father's house—whether the temporal, the individual, and the particular get more worth and value from the eternal, or the eternal more from the particular and temporal. That is one of those beautiful questions which permit of no solution, so that there is no end to the contemplation of them from dewy eve to early dawn."

Seeing Tiy shake her head, he broke off.

"Meni," said she, "Your Majesty is incorrigible. You kept on at us about your dreams, which you thought were so important to the realm that they must be interpreted without fail, so that they could not fulfil themselves unhindered. But now that you have the meaning, or think you have, you act as though everything were all settled, you forget the meaning even as you utter it, to get lost in the most remote and impossible speculations. Is that like a mother? I could not even call it fatherly; and I can scarcely wait until this man here has gone back where he came from and we are alone, to admonish you indignantly from my maternal throne. It is possible that this soothsayer knows his craft and that what he says may happen. It has happened in the past, that good and poor seasons have alternated, that then the Nourisher has run low and time after time he has denied his blessing to the fields, so that want and famine consumed the lands. It has happened, it has actually happened seven times running, as the chronicles show. It can happen again, and therefore you have dreamed it. But perhaps you have dreamed it because it is going to happen again. If that is what you think, then, my child, your mother is astonished that you can rejoice over the interpretation and even flatter yourself that in a way you made it yourself. And now, instead of summoning all your counsellors and wise men together to consider how to meet the threatening evil, you go off into such extravagant abstractions as this about the meeting-place of the not-being and the ever-being!"

"But, dear little Mama, we have time!" cried Amenhotep, with a lively gesture. "Where there is no time, then of course one cannot take any; but we can, for before us lies a fullness of it. Seven years! That is the great thing; the fact to make us dance and rub our hands together: that this highly individual lamb was not bound to the hateful pattern and did not prophesy the accursed time before the blessing-time, but the blessing-time first, and for as long as seven years. Your rebuke would be just if the bad time, the time of the withered kine, were due to begin tomorrow. Then there would certainly be no time to lose in thinking about expedients and preventive measures—although My Majesty is free to confess he knows no adequate measures against failure of crops. But seven years of fatness are granted us in the kingdom of the black earth, during which the love of the people for their Pharaoh-mother will flourish like a tree, under which he can sit and teach his father's teaching. So I do not see why on the very first day—your eyes are speaking, soothsayer," he broke off, "and you have such a very piercing look; have you anything to add to our common interpretation?"

"Nothing," answered Joseph, "save a plea that you permit your servant to go now to his own place, back to the prison where he was serving and into the pit out of which you took him for the sake of your dream. For his task is done and his presence is no longer fitting in the places of the great. In his hole will he live and feed upon the golden hour when he stood before Pharaoh, the beautiful sun of the lands, and before the great mother, whom I name in the second place only because language will have it so, which belongs to time and must deal with one thing after the other, unlike the world of images, where two can stand side by side. But speech and naming belong to time; thus the first mention belongs to the King; yet truly the second is not the second, for was not the mother before the son? So much in the succession of things. But whither my smallness now returns, there will I continue in my thoughts this intercourse with the great, to mingle in which were culpable of me. Pharaoh was right, I shall say to myself in the silence, to rejoice in the reversed order and the beautiful respite before the time of cursing and the years of drought. But how right was not the mother too, who was before him with the view and the warning that from the very first day of the blessing-time and from the very day of the interpretation there must be much taking of thought against the coming of evil! Not to avoid it, for we avoid not the purposes of God; but to anticipate and provide against it by proper foresight. For the term of blessing which is promised us means in the first place a stage wherein to take breath to bear the affliction. But in the second place it means time and space to take steps, at least to clip the wings of the raven of calamity; to take note of the coming evil to work against it, and so far as possible not only to keep it in bounds but perhaps to derive from it a blessing to boot. This or something like it shall I be saying to myself in my dungeon, since it would be worse than improper for me to inject my thoughts into the converse of the great. What a great and splendid thing, shall I whisper to myself, is the wisdom which can convert even misfortune into blessing! And how gracious is God, that He granted to the King, through the medium of his dreams, such a wide survey over time—

not only over seven, but over fourteen years! Therein lies the provision, and the command to provide. For the fourteen years are but one time, made up of twice seven though it is; and it does not begin in the middle but at the beginning, in other words with today, for today is the day of surveying the whole. And to survey it all is to provide for it all."

"All this is very odd," remarked Amenhotep. "Have you been speaking, or have you not? You have been speaking while you did not speak but only let us hear your thoughts, those, that is, which you only think to think. But it seems to me it is the same as though you had spoken. In other words, you contrived a little device, to say something that had not yet been said."

"Everything must have its first time," Joseph replied. "But foresight is not new. And there has been for very long the shrewd employment of what time is granted. If God had put the bad time before the blessing-time and it began tomorrow, there could be no counsel nor could any avail. What the chaff-time wrought among men could not be made good by the fullness to follow. But now it is the other way on, and there is time—not to waste, but to make good the coming want and to balance the fullness and the lack, by saving the fullness to feed the lack. The order of the dream was meant to instruct us: the fat kine come up first, then the lean; which means that he who makes the survey is called and commanded to feed the lack."

"You mean we must heap up provision and gather it into bins?" asked Amenhotep.

"On the very largest scale," said Joseph with decision. "In quite other measure than has ever been in the time of the two lands! And the master of the survey shall be the taskmaster of the fullness. He shall control it with strictness; the people's love for him will teach them the economy of plenty. Then, when the dearth comes, and they find that he can give, how will their love and trust increase! Under that spreading tree he may sit and teach. And the master of the survey shall be the vicar and shadow-spender of the King."

As he spoke, Joseph's eyes chanced to meet those of the great mother, the little dark figure sitting upright and hieratic upon her raised seat with her feet together. Those shrewd, sharp eyes, gleaming black out of the shadow, were fixed upon him, and the lines about her full lips shaped a mocking smile. He dropped his lids gravely before this smile, yet not without a respectful twinkle.

125

"If I have heard aright," said Amenhotep, "you think, like the great mother, that without any loss of time I should summon my advisers to a council, that they may decide how to deal with the abundance to make it serve the lack?"

"Pharaoh," answered Joseph, "has had no great luck with the councils he summoned to interpret the double dream dreamed by his double crown. He interpreted himself, he found the truth. To him alone was the prophecy sent and the whole situation made clear; on him alone is it incumbent to administer the supplies and husband the plenty which will come before the drought. The measures which must be taken are unprecedented in method and scope; whereas a council is prone to decide on a middle and traditional course. Therefore he alone who has dreamed and interpreted must be the man to decide and execute."

"Pharaoh does not execute his decisions," Tiy the mother coolly made herself heard. She gazed through and past both of them as she spoke. "That is an ignorant conception. Even granted that he make his own decision about what to decide according to his dream—in other words, granted that the decision is to be made in accordance with the dream—he will then put the performance of it into the hands of his administrators who are there for the purpose: the two Viziers of the South and North, the steward of the storehouses and stalls, and the head of the treasury."

"Precisely so," said Joseph, with an appearance of astonishment, "did I think in my hole to tell myself, in the imaginary conversation I was carrying on. Indeed, those very words, even 'ignorant conception' did I put into the mouth of the great mother and turned them against myself. I am swollen with pride to hear her utter just what I would have made her say, down there and only to myself. I will take back her words with me into my prison; there, living and feeding upon the memories of this exalted hour, I will answer in spirit and say: 'Ignorant are all my conceptions, save perhaps one only: the thought that Pharaoh himself, the beautiful sun of the two lands, should himself carry out what he decides and not leave the performance of it to tried and tested servants, saying: "I am Pharaoh! Be as myself, receive from me full powers for the task wherein I have tried and tested you; for you shall be the middleman between me and men, as the moon is middleman between sun and earth. So shall you turn to blessing this threat to me and to the two lands." ' No, my ignorance is perhaps not so all-embracing; for in this matter and in my own mind I clearly hear Pharaoh speak and say these words, yet not to many, but to one. And again, no man hearing my words, I will say: 'Many counsellors make many counsels; therefore let there be but one, as the moon is one among the stars and is the middleman between above and below, who knows the dreams of the sun. The first of the extraordinary measures must be the choice of him who shall put them into action. Otherwise they will be not extraordinary but middling, usual, and inadequate. And why? Because they will not be put into action with faith and knowledgeable foresight. Tell the many your dreams, they will both believe and disbelieve; part of each will have faith and part foresight, but all these parts together will not make up the complete faith or foresight which is necessary and can be only in one. Therefore let Pharaoh look for a wise and understanding man in whom dwells the spirit of his dreams, the spirit of seeing and the spirit of providing, and set him over the land of Egypt. Say to him: "Be as I am," that he may be as it says in the song: "Unto the borders of the land 'Twas he who saw it all." And let him administer the abundance of the years of plenty with a strictness never seen before, that the King may have shade to sit in during the time of dearth.' Such are my words which I shall be saying to myself in my pit; for truly to utter them here before the gods would be the grossest indiscretion. Will Pharaoh now dismiss his servant from his sight, that he may go out of the sun into his shadow?"

Joseph made a turn towards the bee-studded hangings and a gesture thitherwards, as though asking if he might pass through. The eyes of the goddess-mother looked sharply at him, and the worldly-wise lines round her mouth deepened to a mocking smile. He saw, but purposely did not look back at her.

"I DON'T BELIEVE IN IT"

"Stay," said Amenhotep. "Wait a little, my friend. You have played very prettily upon this instrument of yours, this pretext that one may speak without speaking, not speak and yet speak withal, while getting a hearing for your thoughts. You have not only put My Majesty in the way of interpreting his own dream, but also you have pleasured me with this novel device of yours. Pharaoh cannot let you go unrewarded, surely you cannot think that. The only question is, how can he reward you?

About that My Majesty is not yet clear. For instance, to give you this tortoise-shell lyre, the invention of the lord of mischief, that, I think, would be too little, and surely you think so too. Yet take it at least, for the moment, my friend, take it in your arms, it becomes you there. The god of contrivance gave it to his soothsaying brother; you are a soothsayer too, and full of contrivance into the bargain. But I am think-ing of keeping you at my court, if you will stop, and of making some fine title for you, such as First Dream-interpreter of the King, something very imposing, to cover up your real name and make it quite forgot. But what is your real name? Ben-ezne, perhaps, or Nekatiya, I suppose?"

"What I am called," Joseph answered, "I was not called, and neither my mother, the starry virgin, nor my father, the friend of God, called me so. But since my hostile brothers flung me in the pit and I died to my father, being stolen away down here, what I am has taken on another name: it is now Osarsiph."

"Most interesting," pronounced Amenhotep. He had settled back into the cushions of his too-easy-chair, while Joseph, the seafaring man's gift in his arms, stood there before him. "So you think one should not always be called the same, but suit his name to his circumstances, ac-cording to what happens to him and how he feels? Mama, what say you to that? I think My Majesty likes it well, for I am always pleased by new views; whereas those who know only outworn ones open their mouths in astonishment, as wide as I do when I yawn at theirs. Pharaoh himself has too long been called by his present name, and for long it has been out of tune with what he is and how he feels. In fact for some time he has cherished the idea of putting aside the old and mistaken name and taking a new and more accurate one. I have never spoken of this to you, Mama, because it would have been awkward for me to tell you just by ourselves. But in the presence of this soothsayer Osarsiph, who him-self once had another name, it is a good opportunity to speak. Certainly I will do nothing rash, it will not happen from one day to the next. But happen it must, and soon; for what I am now called becomes daily more a lie and an offence to my Father above. It is a disgrace, in the long run it is not to be borne, that my name contains the name of Amun the throne-robber, who gives out that he consumed Re-Horakhte the Lord of On and the ancestor of the kings of Egypt, and who now reigns as Amun-Re, the god of the Empire. You must understand, Mama, that in the long run it is a sore offence to My Majesty to be named after him, instead of by a name pleasing to Aton; for out of him have I issued, in whom is united what was and what shall be. Lo, Amun's is the present, but the past and future are my Father's, and we two are old and young both, we are of times past and times to come. Pharaoh is a stranger in the world, for he is at home in the early time, when kings raised their arms to Re their father, the time of Hor-em-akhet, the time of the Sphinx. And at home he is in the time that shall come, of which he is the fore-runner; when all men shall look up to the sun, the unique god, their gracious father according to the teaching of the son, who knows his precepts, since he came out of him and his blood flows in his veins. Come hither, you!" said he to Joseph. "Come and look!" And he drew the batiste from his thin arm and showed the other the blue veins on the inside of the forearm. "That is the blood of the sun!"

The arm shook visibly, although Amenhotep supported it with the other hand; for the other hand shook too. Joseph looked respectfully at the exhibit and then drew back a little from the royal seat. The goddess-mother said:

"You excite yourself, Meni, and it is not good for Your Majesty's health. You should rest, after the interpretation and all this exchange of views, and take a little time from the time that is given you, to let your decisions ripen, not only concerning measures against what may come, but also about the very serious proposal to change your name, which you seem to be considering; while at the same time you are thinking about a proper reward for this soothsayer. Do go and rest!"

But the King was unwilling. "Mama," he cried, "I do beg you most ardently not to ask that of me, just in the middle of such a promising train! I assure you, My Majesty is perfectly well and feels no trace of fatigue. I am so excited that I feel well, and so well that I feel excited. You talk just like the nurses in my childhood; when I felt my liveliest, then they said: 'You are overtired, Lord of the Two Lands, you must go to bed.' It could only make me savage, I could have kicked with rage. Now I am grown, and I thank you most respectfully for your care of me. But I have the distinct feeling that this present audience can lead to further good and that my decisions can better ripen here than in my bed, and in talk with this skilled soothsayer, to whom I am grateful, if for no other reason, for giving me the opportunity to speak of my intention to take a real name, which contains the name of the unique one, namely Ikhnaton, that my name may be pleasing to my Father.

Everything should be called after him and not after Amun; and if the Lady of the Two Lands, who fills the palace with sweetness, the sweet Titi, is soon brought to bed, then the royal infant, whether prince or princess, shall be called Merytaton, that it may be loved by him who is loved. No matter if I draw down on my head the anger of the mighty one of Karnak, who will come and make representations and harangue me with threats of the anger of the Ram! Him I can endure—all I can endure for the sake of my love to my Father above."

"Pharaoh," said the mother, "you forget that we are not alone. Matters which need to be dealt with in wisdom and moderation are probably best not discussed in the hearing of a soothsayer from the people."

"Let that be, Mama," replied Amenhotep. "He is in the way of noble lineage, that he has himself given us to understand—the son of a rogue and a lovely one, which is definitely attractive to me; while that he says he was even as a child called the lamb, that also indicates a certain refinement. Children of the lower classes are not given such nicknames. And besides, I get the impression that he is able to understand much, and give answer to much. Above and beyond all this, he loves me and is ready to help me, as he has done already in interpreting the dreams and also by reason of his original view that one should call oneself according to one's own circumstances and feelings. It would all be very fine, if I liked a little better the name by which he chooses to be known. . . . I would not wish to be unfriendly or distress you," he turned to Joseph, "but the kind of name you have taken pains me: Osarsiph, that is a name of the dead, as when we call the dead bull Osar-Hapi; it bears the name of the dead lord, Usir, the frightful, on the judge's throne and with the scale, who is only just but without mercy, and before whose tribunal the terrified soul trembles and shakes. This old creed has nothing in it but fear, it is dead itself, it is an Osar-creed, and my Father's son believes not in it."

"Pharaoh," the mother's voice came again, "I must once more appeal to you and warn you to be cautious and I need not hesitate to do so in the presence of this foreign interpreter, since you grant him such extended audience and take as a sign of his higher origins his mere assertion that as a child he was called the lamb. So he may hear that I warn you to be wise and moderate. It is enough that you go about to decrease the power of Amun and set yourself against his universal rule, in that wherever possible you take from him step by step the unity with Re the horizon-dweller, who is the Aton. Even to do this takes all the shrewdness and policy in the world, and a cool head besides, for heated rashness comes of evil. But let Your Majesty beware of laying hands on the people's belief in Usir, King of the lower regions, to which it clings more obstinately than to any other deity, because all are equal before him, and each one hopes to go in unto him with his name. Bear in mind the prejudice of the many, for what you give to Aton by diminishing Amun, you take away again by offending Usir."

"Ah, I assure you, Mama, the people only imagine that they cling so to Usir," cried Amenhotep. "How could it really cling to a belief that the soul which goes up to the judge's seat must pass through seven times seven regions of terror, inhabited by demons who cross-examine it as it passes in some three hundred and sixty several magic formulas, each harder to remember than the last, yet the poor soul must have them all by heart and be able to repeat each one in the right place, otherwise it does not pass and will be devoured before ever it reaches the judgment seat. And if it does get there, it has every prospect of being devoured if its heart weighs too light in the scale; for then it is delivered over to the monstrous dog of Amente. I ask you, where is there anything in all that to cling to?—it is against all the love and goodness of my Father above. Before Usir of the lower regions all are equal—yes, equal in terror. Whereas before my Father all shall be equal in joy. With Amun and Aton it is the same. Amun too, with the help of Re, will be universal and will unite the world in worship of him. There they are of one mind. But Amun would make the world one in the rigid service of fear, a false and sinister unity, which my Father would not, for he would unite his children in joy and tenderness."

"Meni," said the mother again, in her low voice, "it would be better for you to spare yourself and not speak so much of joy and tenderness. You know from experience that the words are dangerous to you and put you beside yourself."

"I am speaking, Mama, of belief and unbelief," answered Amenhotep; once more he worked himself out of the cushions and stood on his feet. "Of these I speak, and my own good mind tells me that disbelief is almost more important than belief. In belief there must be a sizable element of disbelief; for how can a man believe what is true so long as he also believes what is false? If I want to teach the people what is true, I must first take from them certain beliefs to which they cling.

Perhaps that is cruel, but it is the cruelty of love, and my Father in the sky will forgive me. Yes, which is more glorious, belief or disbelief, and which should come before the other? Believing is a great rapture for the soul. But not believing is almost more joyous than belief —I have found it so, My Majesty has experienced it, and I do not believe in the realms of fear and the demons and Usiri with his frightfully named ones and the devourer down there below. I don't believe in it! Don't believe, don't believe," Pharaoh sang and trilled, skipping on his misshapen legs, whirling round with arms outstretched and snapping the fingers of both hands.

After that he was out of breath.

"Why did you give yourself such a name of death?" he asked, gasping, as he came to a stop beside Joseph. "Even if your father thinks you are dead, after all you are not."

"I must be silent to him," answered Joseph, "and I vowed myself to silence with my name. Whoever is thus dedicate and set apart, he is among the dead. You cannot separate the depths from the holy and consecrated, they belong together; and just therefore lies upon him the gleam of light from above. We make offerings to the depths; yet therein lies the mystery, that in so doing we only rightly make them to the heights. For God is the whole."

"He is the light and the sweet disk of the sun," said Amenhotep with emotion, "whose rays embrace the land and bind them in love—he makes the hands grow faint with love, and only the wicked, whose fate is directed below, have strong hands. Ah, how much more would things in the world go by love and goodness if not for this belief in the lower and in the devourer with the crushing jaws! No one shall persuade Pharaoh that men would not do much or consider much pleasing to do if their fate were not directed downwards. You know, the grandfather of my earthly father, King Akheperure, had very strong hands and could span a bow which no one else in all the lands could span. So he went out to slay the kings of Asia and took seven of them alive. He fastened them to the prow of his ship by the heels—their hair hung down and they glared straight ahead with their upside-down bloodshot eyes. And that was only the beginning of all that he did with them, which I will not go into, but he did it. It was the first story my nurses told me as a child, to instil in me a kingly spirit—but I started shrieking out of my sleep with what they instilled and the doctors from the book-house came and instilled an antidote. But do you suppose Akheperure would have done all that to his foes if he had not believed in the realms of horror and the spectres and the frightfully named ones of Usiri and the dog of Amente? Let me tell you: men are a hopeless lot. They know how to do nothing that comes from within themselves, not even the very least thing occurs to them on their own account. They only imitate the gods, and whatever picture they make of them, that they copy. Purify the godhead and you purify men."

Joseph did not reply to all this until he had looked across to the mother and read in the eyes she rested on him that a reply from him would please her.

"Harder than hard," he said then, "it is to reply to Pharaoh, for he is gifted beyond measure, and what he says is true, so that one can only nod and murmur: 'Quite right,' or else keep still and let the echo die of the truth he uttered. Yet we know Pharaoh would not have speech die away and cease at the truth. Rather he desires that it free itself and go on, past the truth and perhaps to further truth. For what is true is not the truth. Truth is endlessly far and all talk is endless too. It is a pilgrimage into the eternal and looses itself without rest, or at most after a brief pause and an impatient 'Right, right,' it moves away from every station of the truth, just as the moon moves away from each of her stations in her eternal wanderings. All of this brings me—whether I will or no, and whether it is fit or unfit in this place—to the grandfather of my earthly father, whom at home we always called by a not quite so earthly name and named him the moon-wanderer, though we knew quite well that actually his name was Abiram, which means high father. He came from Ur in the Chaldees, the land of the great tower. He did not like it there and could not endure it—he could never endure it anywhere and hence the name we gave him."

"You see, Mother," the King broke in, "that my soothsayer has good origins in his way? Not only that he himself was called the lamb, but also he had a great-grandfather to whom they gave a name not of this earth. Mixed races and people from the lower classes do not usually know their great-grandfathers. So he was a seeker after truth, your great-grandfather?"

"So untiring," responded Joseph, "that in the end he discovered God and made a pact with Him that they should be holy the one in the other. But strong he was in other ways too, a strong-handed man; when robber kings came on from the East, burning and plundering, and took away his brother Lot a prisoner, then with swift resolve he went out against them with three hundred and eighteen men and Eliezer, his oldest servant, making three hundred and nineteen, and thrust at them with such force that he drove them beyond Damascus and freed his brother Lot out of their hands."

The mother nodded and Pharaoh cast down his eyes.

"Did he take the field," he asked, "before he had discovered God or afterwards?"

"It was in between," answered Joseph, "while he was working on his task and without loss of power from the combat. What can be done with robber kings that burn and plunder? You cannot give them the peace of God, they are too stupid and bad. You can only bring it to them by first smiting them hip and thigh until they know that the peace of God has strong hands. But you owe it to God that things shall go on earth at least half-way according to His will and not entirely according to the will of burners and plunderers."

"I see," said Amenhotep in boyish annoyance, "if you had been one of my guardians, you too would have told me stories about hair floating upside down in the wind and rolling eyes full of blood."

"Could it come to pass," Joseph inquired as though of himself, "that Pharaoh should err and despite extraordinary gifts and maturity be wrong in his thought? I can scarcely believe it; yet it seems to happen and is a sign that he has his human as well as his godlike side. Those who burdened his young heart with tales of warlike prowess," he went on, always speaking as though to himself, "they, of course, stood for war and lust of the sword for their own sakes. Now your soothsayer here, descended from the moon-wanderer, he would seek to bring to war word of the peace of God; while to peace he would put in a word for courage as a dealer between the spheres and go-between 'twixt above and below. The sword is stupid; yet I would not call meekness wise. Wise is the mediator who counsels courage in order that meekness may not be revealed as stupid in the sight of God and man. Would I might say to Pharaoh this that I think!"

"I have heard," said Amenhotep, "what you have been saying to yourself. It is the same as before: the little trick you have invented, that you may speak aloud to yourself and that no one else has any ears. You are holding the seafaring man's gift in your arms—perhaps the little invention comes to you from it, and the spirit of the mischievous god speaks through your words."

"It may be," responded Joseph. "Pharaoh speaks the word of the hour. It may be, it is possible, we should not quite reject the idea that the quick-witted god is present with us and would make Pharaoh mindful of him and aware that it was he who brought up the dream to him from below to where he sits in his palace. For he is a guide to the world below and, with all his gay spirits, the friend of the moon and the dead. He puts in a friendly word with the upper world for the lower and with the lower world for the upper, he is a gentlemanly go-between 'twixt heaven and earth. Violence and abruptness are hateful to him and better than any-one else he knows that one can be right and yet wrong."

"You are coming back to your uncle," asked Amenhotep, "the wrong right one whose big tears rolled down in the dust while all the world laughed at him? Let that story be. It is amusing but it makes me uneasy. Perhaps it is true that what is funny is always at the same time a little sad, and that we only breathe freely and happily at the pure gold of serious things."

"Pharaoh says it," answered Joseph, "and may he be the right one to say it! Serious and stern is the light and the power which streams up from below into its clarity—power it must surely be and of masculine kind, not mere tenderness; otherwise it is false and premature and tears will follow."

He did not look over at the mother after he spoke—at least not full in the face. But enough so that he could see whether she nodded approval. She did not nod, but he thought she looked steadily at him, which was perhaps even better.

Amenhotep had not been listening. He leaned back in his chair, in one of those exaggerated attitudes of his, deliberately aimed at the old style and the rigidity of Amun. One elbow leaned against the chair-back, his other hand was on his hip, thrust out by the weight he put on that leg, the other one resting lightly on its toes. He went back to his own last words.

"I think," he said, "My Majesty said something very good, which merits attention. I mean about jest and earnest, one oppressing and the other blessing. The moon mediates between heaven and earth. True, but the mediation is of the jesting kind, uncanny, ghostly. Whereas all the beams of my father Aton are golden earnest without guile, bound up in truth, ending in tender hands, which caress the creation of the father. God alone is the whole roundness of the sun, from which the truth pours itself out upon the world, and unfaltering love."

"The whole world hearkens to Pharaoh's words," answered Joseph, "and no one fails to hear a single one of them when he teaches. But that may easily happen to others, even when their words should by chance be just as much worth taking to heart as his. But never will it happen to the Lord of the Crown. His golden words put me in mind of one of our stories, namely how Adam and Eve, the first human beings, were frightened by the approach of the first night. They feared that the earth would again become void and formless. For it is the light which divides things and puts each in its place—it creates space and time, while night brings back disorder again, the chaos and the void. So the two were terribly frightened when the day died at the red even and darkness crept up on all sides. They beat their brows. But God gave them two stones: one of the deepest black, the other like the shadow of death. He rubbed the two together for them and lo, fire sprang out, fire from the bosom of the earth, the inmost primeval fire, young as the lightning and older than Re. It fed on dry leaves and burned on, making night plain for the two."

"Very good, very good indeed!" said the King. "I see that not all your tales are jests. Pity you do not also speak of that great joy of the first morning, when God lighted up their whole world anew and drove away the frightful shapes of darkness; for their delight must have been very great. Light, light!" he cried. Springing from his relaxed position, he stood up and began to move to and fro in the room, now fast, now slowly, now lifting both bebanded arms over his head, now pressing his two hands to his heart.

"Blessed light, that created for itself the eyes which see it, created sight and thing seen; the becoming-conscious of the world which knows of itself only through the light, which distinguishes in love. Ah, Mama, and you, dear soothsayer, how glorious above all glory and how unique in the all is Aton my Father, and how my heart beats with fullness of pride because I came forth from him and before all others he gave me to understand his beauty and love! For as he is unique in greatness and goodness, so am I his son unique in love to him, whom he has entrusted with his teaching. When he rises in the eastern horizon of heaven and mounts out of the land of God in the east, glitteringly crowned as king of the gods, then all creatures exult. The apès adore with lifted hands and all wild creatures praise him, running and leaping. For every day is his blessing-time and a feast of joy after the cursing-time of the night, when his face was turned away and the world sunk in self-forgetfulness. It is frightful when the world forgets itself, though it may be well for its refreshment. Men sleep in their chambers, their heads are wrapped up, their nostrils stopped, and none seeth the other; stolen are all the things that are under their heads while they know it not. Every lion cometh forth from his den, all serpents they sting. But thou hast raised them up, their limbs bathed, they take their clothing, their arms uplifted in adoration to thy dawning. Then in all the world they do their work. The barks sail upstream and downstream alike. Every highway is opened because thou hast dawned. The fish in the river leap up before him, and his rays are in the midst of the great sea. Though he is afar, yet his rays are upon the earth as in the sea and fix all creatures with his love. For unless he were so high and far, how should he be over all and everywhere in his world which he has linked and spread out in manifold beauty: the countries of Syria and Nubia and Punt and the land of Egypt; thou hast set a Nile in the heavens that he may fall for them, making floods upon the mountains like the great sea and watering their fields among their towns as he springs for us out of the earth and makes fertile the desert that we may eat. Yes, how manifold, O Lord, are thy works! Thou makest the seasons in order to create all thy works with million shapes, that they live in you and fulfil their life-span, which you give, in cities, towns, and settlements, on highway or on river. Thou settest every man in his place, thou suppliest their necessities. Everyone has his possessions and his days are numbered. Their tongues are divers in speech, their ways are varying, but you embrace them all. Some are brown, others red, others black, and still others like milk and blood. And in all these hues they reveal themselves in you and are your manifestations. They have hooked noses or flat or such as come straight out of the face, they dress in gay colours or white, in wool or linen, according as they know or think; but all that is no reason for them to laugh or to be spiteful, rather only interesting and solely a ground for love and worship. Thou fundamentally good God, how joyful and sound is all that thou createst and nourishest and what heart filling delight hast thou instilled into Pharaoh, thy beloved son who proclaims thee! Thou hast made the seed in man and giveth life to the son in the body of the woman, thou soothest him that he may not weep, thou good nurse and nourisher! Thou makest of what the flies live on and of the like the fleas, the worm, and the offspring of the worm. It would be enough for the heart and even well-nigh too much that the creature is satisfied in his pasture, that trees and plants are in sap and blossoms spring in praise and thanks, while count-less birds flutter above the marshes. But when I think of the little mouse in its hole where thou preparest what it needs, there it sits with its beady eyes and cleans its nose with its paws—then my eyes run over. And I may not think at all of the little chick that cries in the eggshell, out of which it bursts when he has made it ready—then it comes out of the egg to chirp with all its might and runneth about before Him upon its two feet with the greatest nimbleness—especially may I not be mindful of this, else I must dry my face with finest batiste, for it is flooded with tears of love.—I should like to kiss the Queen," he suddenly cried, and stood still with his face turned up to the ceiling. "Let Nefertiti be sum-moned at once, she who fills the palace with beauty, the mistress of the lands, my sweet consort!"

ALL TOO BLISSFUL

Jacob's son was almost as weary with standing before Pharaoh as when he had played dumb waiter for the old pair in the garden-house. And young Pharaoh, for all his delicacy of feeling for the gnats, the chicks, the little mouse, and the offspring of the worm, seemed to have no thought for Joseph's discomfort. His delicacy was of a regal kind, it had lapses. To neither him nor the mother-goddess on her high seat did the idea occur—and probably it could not—to tell him to sit down awhile. His limbs had great longing and there were many charming little stools in the Cretan loggia to invite him thereto. It was hard; but when one knows what is involved, one just takes the hardship for granted and stands firm—and here we have a good instance of a literally correct usage.

The goddess-widow took it on herself to clap her hands when her son announced his desire. The chamberlain from the anteroom sidled sweetly through the bee-curtain. He rolled up his eyes when Tiy flung at him: "Pharaoh summons the great consort!" and disappeared again. Amenho-tep stood at one of the great bay-windows with his back to the room and looked out over the gardens, his chest and his whole body heaving with the violence of the homage he paid to the sun and its works. His mother was looking towards him with concern. But only a few minutes passed before she appeared whom he had summoned—she could not have been far away. A little door, invisible among the paintings, opened in the right-hand wall, and two maidservants fell on their faces on the threshold. Between them the Queen of the lands appeared, with swaying tread, faintly smiling, her eyes cast down, the long, lovely neck thrust anxiously out: the bearer of the seed of the sun. She did not speak. Her hair was covered with a blue cap, which hung in a bag behind, elongating the shape of the head; her large, thin, finely turned ears were uncovered. Navel and thighs showed through the ethereal pleatings of her flowing garb, the bosom was covered with a shoulder drapery and a flower-collar glittering with enamel and gems. She moved with hesitant steps towards her young husband, who approached her still panting with access of feeling.

"Here art thou, golden dove, my sweet bed-sister," he said with trembling voice; embraced and kissed her on eyes and mouth, so that the two cobras on their foreheads kissed too. "I had to see thee, if only for a moment to show thee my love—it came over me while talking. Was my summons a burden to thee? Art thou at the moment not suffering from thy present sacred condition? My Majesty does wrong, perhaps, even to ask; for I might thereby rouse and recall thy nausea with my words. You see how the King has understanding of all. I would have been so grateful to the Father if you had today been able to keep our excellent breakfast by you. But no more of that. Here thrones the eternal mother, and this man with the lyre is a foreign magician and soothsayer who has interpreted for me my politically important dream and can tell such amusing tales that I may keep him by me, in a high office at court. He lay in prison, owing to some mistake, such as can sometimes happen. Nefer-em-Wese too, my cup-bearer, was once in prison by mistake, while his companion there, the late chief baker, was guilty. Of two that lie in prison, one always seems to be innocent, and of three, two. This I say as a man. But as god and king, I say that prisons are necessary, notwithstanding. And as man I kiss you, my sacred love, on your eyes, your cheeks and mouth; be not surprised that I do it in the presence not only of the mother but also of the soothsaying stranger, since you know that Pharaoh loves to show himself as he is before men. I think to go even further in this direction. You do not know about that yet, nor does Mama, therefore I take this opportunity to tell you. I am considering a pleasure voyage on the royal barge *Star of the Two Lands*. The populace, urged by curiosity and also partly by my royal command, will follow along the banks in crowds, and there in their sight, my sacred treasure, without having got permission from Amun's first priest beforehand, I will sit with you under the canopy and hold you on my knee and kiss you right soundly and often before all the people. That will annoy him of Karnak, but the people will exult, and it will not only show them our great happiness but also instruct them in the essence, spirit, and goodness of my Father above. I am glad that I have now mentioned this plan of mine. But do not think I sent for you on this account, for I only happened to come on the thought as I was speaking. I called you simply and solely out of sudden unconquerable longing to show you my tenderness, and now I have done so. Go, then, my crowning joy! Pharaoh is overwhelmed with affairs and must take counsel on matters of high import with his dear and eternal little Mama and with this young man, who, you must understand, comes of the stock of the inspired lamb. Go, and take great care of yourself, guarding against all jars to your person. Divert yourself with dancing and song. The babe, whatever it is, shall be called Merytaton, when you are happily brought to bed—that is, if you find it good, and I see you do. You always find everything good that Pharaoh thinks. If only the whole world would think well of what he thinks and teaches, it would be better for it. Adieu, swan's throat, little dawn-cloud, golden-seamed! Adieu and au revoir!"

The Queen swayed away again. Behind her the picture-door closed and became invisible. Amenhotep, embarrassed by his own emotions, turned back to his throne chair.

"Happy lands," said he, "to which such a mistress is vouchsafed, and a Pharaoh whom she makes so happy! Am I right to say that, Mama—do you agree with me, soothsayer? If you stop on at my court as interpreter of the King's dreams, I will marry you off, that is my firm intention. I will myself choose the bride, befitting your office, from the higher circles. You do not know how delightful it is to be married. For My Majesty, as my idea about the pleasure-voyage in public will have shown you, it is the very image and expression of my human side, on which I lean more than I can say. For look, Pharaoh is not proud—and if he is not, then who in all the world should be? But in you, my friend, I feel a sort of pride, with all your charm of manner—I say a sort, for I do

140

not know its cause and can only suspect it has to do with what you told us, that you are in some way set apart and consecrate to silence and the deeps, as though the sacrificial garland lay on your brow, made of an herb called touch-me-not. It was just this that gave me the idea to bestow you in marriage."

"I am in the hand of the highest," answered Joseph. "What he does will be beneficent. Pharaoh knows not how necessary to me was my pride to protect me from evil-doing. I am set apart for God alone, who is the bridegroom of my race and we are the bride. But as it says of the star: 'In the evening a woman, in the morning a man,' so I suppose it is here too, and out of the bride steps forth the wooer."

"Such a double nature may be fitting for the son of the sly one and the lovely one," said the King, with a worldly-wise air. "But now," he added, "let us speak seriously of serious matters. Your God, who and what is He? You have neglected or avoided giving me a clear understanding. The forefather of your father, you say, discovered Him? That sounds as though he had found the true and only God. Is it possible that so remote from me in space and time a man divined that the true and only God is the sun's disk, the creator of sight and seen, my eternal Father above?"

"No, Pharaoh," Joseph answered, smiling. "He did not stop at the sun disk. He was a wanderer, and even the sun was but a way-station on his painful wandering. Restless was he and unsatisfied—call it pride if you will; for thereby you seal your censure with the sign of honour and necessity. For it was the pride of the man, that the human being should serve only the Highest. Therefore his thoughts went out beyond the sun."

Amenhotep had flushed. He sat bent forward, his head in the blue wig stretched out on its neck; with the tips of his fingers he squeezed and kneaded his chin.

"Mama, pay attention! By all you hold dear, pay strict attention," he breathed, without turning the fixed gaze of his grey eyes away from Joseph. His suspense was so great that it seemed he would tear away the veil which dimmed them.

"Go on, you!" said he. "Wait! Stop, no, go on! He did not stop? He went out beyond the sun? Speak! Or I will speak myself, though I know not what I should say."

"He made things hard for himself, in his unavoidable pride," Joseph

141

said. "For this he was anointed. He overcame many temptations to worship and adore, for he longed to do so, but to worship the Highest one alone, for only this seemed right to him. Earth, the mother, tempted him; she who preserves life and brings forth fruit. But he saw her neediness, which only heaven can supply, and so he turned his face upwards. Him tempted the turmoil of the clouds, the uproar of the storm, the pelting rain, the blue lightning-flash driving down, the thunder's rattling roar. But he shook his head at their claims, for his soul instructed him they were all of the second rank. They were no better, so his soul spake to him, than he himself—perhaps lesser indeed, although so mighty; and though they were above him it was simply in space, but not in spirit. To pray to them, so he felt, was to pray too near and too low; and better not at all, he said to himself, than too near or low, for that was an abomination."

"Good," said Amenhotep, almost soundlessly, and kneaded his chin. "Good! Wait! No, go on! Mama, pay attention!"

"Yes, how many great manifestations did not tempt my forefather!" Joseph went on. "The whole host of the stars was among them, the shepherd and his sheep. They were indeed far and high, and very great in their courses. But he saw them scattered before the beams of the morning star—and she indeed was surpassing lovely, of two-fold nature and rich in tales, yet weak, too weak for that which she heralded; she paled before it and vanished away—poor morning star!"

"Spare your regrets!" ordered the King. "Here is matter for triumph. For tell me what it was she paled before, and who appeared, whom she had heralded?" he asked, making his voice sound as proud and threatening as it could.

"Of course, the sun," Joseph replied. "What a temptation for him who so longed to worship! Before its cruelty and its benignity all peoples of the earth bowed down. But my ancestor's caution was unlimited, his reservations endless. Peace and satisfaction, he said, are not the point. The all-important thing is to avoid the great peril to the honour of humanity, that man should bow down before a lower than the highest. 'Mighty art thou,' he said to Shamash-Marduk-Bel, 'and mighty is thy power of blessing and cursing. But something there is above thee, in me a worm, and it warns me not to take the witness for that which it witnesses. The greater the witness, the greater the fault in me if I let myself be misled to worship it instead of that to which it bears witness. Godlike is the witness, but yet not God. I too am a witness and a testimony: I and my doing and dreaming, which mount up above the sun towards that to which it more mightily bears witness than even itself, and whose heat is greater than the heat of the sun.' "

"Mother," Amenhotep whispered, without turning his eyes from Joseph, "what did I say? No, no, I did not say it, I only knew it, it was said to me. When of late I had my seizure, and revelation was vouch-safed me for the improvement of the teaching—for it is not complete, never have I asserted that it was complete—then I heard my Father's voice and it spoke to me saying: 'I am the heat of the Aton, which is in Him. But millions of suns could I feed from my fires. Callest thou me Aton, then know that the name itself stands in need of improvement. When you call me so, you are not calling me by my last and final name. For my last name is: the Lord of the Aton.' Thus Pharaoh heard it, the Father's beloved child, and brought it back with him out of his attack. But he kept silent, and even the silence made him forget. Pharaoh has set truth in his heart, for the Father is the truth. But he is responsible for the triumph of the teaching, that all men may receive it; and he is concerned lest the improvement and purification, until at last it consist only of the pure truth, might mean to make it unteachable. This is a sore concern which no one can understand save one on whom as much responsibility rests as on Pharaoh. For others it is easy to say: 'You have not set truth in your heart, but rather the teaching.' Yet the teaching is the sole means of bringing men nearer the truth. It should be improved; but if one improve it to the extent that it becomes unavailable as a medium of truth—I ask the Father and you: will not only then the reproach be justified that I have shut up the teaching in my heart to the disadvantage of the truth? Pharaoh shows mankind the image of the revered Father, made by his artists: the golden disk from which rays go down upon his creatures, ending in tender hands, which caress all creation. 'Adore!' he commands. 'This is the Aton, my Father, whose blood runs in me, who revealed himself to me, but will be Father to you all, that you may become good and lovely in him.' And he adds: 'Pardon, dear human beings, that I am so strict with your thoughts. Gladly would I spare your simplicity. But it must be. Therefore I say to you: Not the image shall you worship when you worship, not to it sing your hymns when you sing; but rather to him whose image it is, you understand, the true disk of the sun, my Father in the sky, who is the Aton, for the image is not yet he.' That is hard enough; it is a challenge to men; out of a hundred, twelve understand it. But if now the teacher says: 'Still another and further effort must I urge upon you for the sake of truth, however much it pains me for your simplicity. For the image is but the image of the image and witness to a witness. Not the actual round sun up there in the sky are you to think of when you burn incense to his image and sing his praise —not this, but the Lord of Aton, who is the heat in it and who guides its course.' That goes too far, it is too much teaching, and not twelve, not even one understands. Only Pharaoh himself understands, who is outside of all count, and yet he is supposed to teach the many. Your forefather, soothsayer, had an easy task, although he made it hard for himself. He might make it as hard as he liked, striving after truth for his own sake and the sake of his pride, for he was only a wanderer. But I am King, and teacher; I may not think what I cannot teach. Whereas such a one very soon learns not even to think the unteachable."

Here Tiy, his mother, cleared her throat, rattled her ornaments, and said, looking ahead of her into space:

"Pharaoh is to be praised when he practises statesmanship in matters of religious belief and spares the simplicity of the many. That is why I warned him not to wound the popular attachment to Usir, king of the lower regions. There is no contradiction between knowing and sparing, in this connection; and the office of teacher need not darken knowledge. Never have priests taught the multitude all they themselves know. They have told them what was wholesome, and wisely left in the realm of the mysteries what was not beneficial. Thus knowledge and wisdom are together in the world, truth and forbearance. The mother recommends that it so remain."

"Thank you, Mama," said Amenhotep, with a deprecating bow. "Thank you for the contribution. It is very valuable and will for eternal ages be held in honour. But we are speaking of two different things. My Majesty speaks of the fetters which the teaching puts upon the thoughts of God; yours refers to priestly statecraft, which divides teaching and knowledge. But Pharaoh would not be arrogant, and there is no greater arrogance than such a division. No, there is no arrogance in the world greater than that of dividing the children of our Father into initiate and uninitiate and teaching double words: all-knowingly for the masses, knowingly in the inner circle. No, we must speak what we know, and witness what we have seen. Pharaoh wants to do nothing but improve the teaching, even though it be made hard for him by the teaching. And still it has been said to me: 'Call me not Aton, for that is in need of improvement. Call me the Lord of the Aton!' But I, through keeping silent, forgot. See now what the Father does for his beloved son! He sends him a messenger and dream-interpreter, who shows him his dreams, dreams from below and dreams from above, dreams important for the realm and for heaven; that he should awake in him what he already knows, and interpret what was already said to him. Yes, how loveth the Father his child the King who came forth out of him, that he sends down a soothsayer to him, to whom from long ages has been handed down the teaching that it profits man to press on towards the last and highest!"

"To my knowledge," Tiy coldly remarked, "your soothsayer came up from below, out of a dungeon, and not from above."

"Ah, in my opinion that is sheer mischief, that he came from below," cried Amenhotep. "And besides, above and below mean not much to the Father, who when he goes down makes the lower the upper, for where he shines, there is the upper world. From which it comes that his messengers interpret dreams from above and below with equal skill. Go on, soothsayer! Did I say stop? If I did, I meant go on! That wanderer out of the East, from whom you spring, did not stop at the sun, but pressed on above it?"

"Yes, in spirit," answered Joseph, smiling. "For in the flesh he was but a worm on this earth, weaker than most of those above and below him. And still he refused to bow and to worship, even before one of these phenomena, for they were but witness and work, as he himself was. All being, he said, is a work of the highest, and before the being is the spirit of whom it bears witness. How could I commit so great a folly and burn incense to a witness, be it never so weighty—I, who am consciously a witness, whereas the others simply are and know it not? Is there not something in me of Him, for which all being is but evidence of the being of the Being which is greater than His works and is outside them? It is outside the world, and though it is the compass of the world, yet is the world not its compass. Far is the sun, surely three hundred and sixty thousand miles away, and yet his rays are here. But He who shows the sun the way hither is further than far, yet near in the same measure, nearer than near. Near or far is all the same to Him, for He has no

145

space nor any time; and though the world is in Him, He is not in the world at all, but in heaven."

"Did you hear that, Mama?" asked Amenhotep in a small voice, tears in his eyes. "Did you hear the message which my heavenly Father sends me through this young man, in whom I straightway saw something, as he came in, and who interprets to me my dreams? I will only say that I have not said all that was said to me in my seizure, and, keeping silent, forgot it. But when I heard: 'Call me not Aton, but rather the Lord of the Aton,' then I heard also this: 'Call on me not as "my Father above," for that is of the sun in the sky; it must needs be changed, to say: "My Father *who art in heaven*"!' So heard I and shut it up within me, because I was anxious over the truth for the sake of the teaching. But he whom I took out of the prison, he opens the prison of truth that she may come forth in beauty and light; and teaching and truth shall embrace each other, even as I embrace him."

And with wet eyelashes he worked himself up out of his sunken seat, embraced Joseph, and kissed him.

"Yes, yes!" he cried. He began to hurry once more up and down the Cretan loggia, to the bee-portières, to the windows and back, his hands pressed to his heart. "Yes, yes, who art in heaven, further than far and nearer than near, the Being of being, that looks not into death, that does not become and die but is, the abiding light, that neither rises nor sets, the unchanging source, out of which stream all life, light, beauty, and truth—that is the Father, so reveals He Himself to Pharaoh His son, who lies in His bosom and to whom He shows all that He has made. For He has made all, and His love is in the world, and the world knows Him not. But Pharaoh is His witness and bears witness to His light and His love, that through Him all men may become blessed and may believe, even though now they still love the darkness more than the light that shines in it. For they understand it not, therefore are their deeds evil. But the son, who came from the Father, will teach it to them. Golden spirit is the light, father-spirit; out of the mother-depths below power strives upward to it, to be purified in its flame and become spirit in the Father. Immaterial is God, like His sunshine, spirit is He, and Pharaoh teaches you to worship Him in spirit and in truth. For the son knoweth the Father as the Father knoweth him, and will royally reward all those who love Him and keep His commandments—he will make them great and gilded at court because they love the Father in the son who

146

came out of Him. For my words are not mine, but the words of my Father who sent me, that all might become one in light and love, even as I and the Father are one. . . ."

He smiled, an all too blissful smile; at the same time grew pale as death; putting his hands on his back, he leaned against the painted wall, closed his eyes, and so remained, upright indeed, but obviously no longer present.

THE WISE AND UNDERSTANDING MAN

Tiy, the mother, came down from her chair into the hall and approached the rapt one with short, decided steps. She looked at him a moment, gave him a quick little tap with the back of one finger across his cheek, of which he was obviously unconscious, and turned to Joseph.

"He will exalt you," said she, with her bitter smile. Her pouting mouth and the lines round it were probably incapable, by their shape, of any smile but a bitter one.

Joseph, in some alarm, was looking over at Amenhotep.

"Do not be distressed," she said. "He does not hear us. He is unwell, he has his affliction, but it is not serious. I knew it would end like this when he would keep on talking about joy and tenderness; it always ends the same way, although sometimes it is more severe. When he began on the mice and chickens I was sure how it would turn out, but I was certain when he kissed you. You must take it in the light of his special susceptibility."

"Pharaoh loves to kiss," Joseph remarked.

"Yes, too much," she answered. "I think you are shrewd enough to see that there is danger for a kingdom which supports within it a too powerful god and without it many envious tributaries, who plot revolts. That was why I was willing you should speak to him of the stout-heartedness of your ancestors, who were not debilitated by all their thoughts on God."

"I am no man of war," said Joseph, "nor was my ancestor save under great pressure. My father was a pious dweller in tents and prone to contemplation, and I am his son by his first and true wife. True, among my brethren who sold me are several who are capable of considerable barbarity; the twins were war-heroes—we called them twins, though there

147

is a whole year between them—and Gaddiel, son of one of the concubines, wore more or less harness, at least in my time."

Tiy shook her head.

"You have a way," she said, "of talking about your people—as a mother I should call it spoilt. All in all, you think pretty well of yourself, it seems; you feel you could stand a good deal of promotion?"

"Let me put it like this, great lady," said he, "that none surprises me."

"So much the better for you," she answered. "I told you that he would exalt you, probably quite extravagantly. He does not know it yet, but when he comes to himself he will."

Joseph said: "Pharaoh has exalted me in that he honoured me with his talk about God."

"Rubbish," said she, impatiently. "You put him on to it, you led up to it from the start. You need not play the innocent before me; or pretend to be the lamb they called you who spoiled you when they brought you up. I have a political mind, it is no use to make pious faces to me. 'Sweet sleep' forsooth, and 'mother's milk, warm baths, and swaddling bands'! Stuff and nonsense! I have nothing against politics, on the contrary; and I do not reproach you for making the best of your hour. Your talk of God was a talk of gods as well; and your story not bad at all, the one about the god of mischief and worldly-wise advantage."

"Pardon, great mother," said Joseph, "it was Pharaoh who told that tale."

"Pharaoh is receptive and suggestible," she responded. "What he said, your presence evoked. He felt you, and spoke of the god."

"I was without falseness against him, great Queen," said Joseph. "And I will remain so, whatever he may decide about me. By Pharaoh's life, I will never betray his kiss. It is long since I received the last kiss. That was at Dothan in the vale, my brother Jehudah kissed me before the eyes of the children of Ishmael, my purchasers, to show them how highly he valued the goods. That kiss your dear son has wiped off with his own. But my heart is full of the wish to serve and help him as well as I can and as far as he empowers me to do it."

"Yes, serve and help him," said she, coming quite close with her firm little person and putting her hand on his shoulder. "Do you promise it to his mother? You see the great and high responsibility I have with the child—but you understand. You are painfully subtle; you even spoke of the wrong right one, and—he is so sensitive—he got the point when you suggested that one can be right and yet wrong."

"It was not known or recognized before," answered Joseph. "It is a destiny and a basis for destiny that a man can be right on the way and yet not the right one for the way. Until today there was no such thing; but from now on there will be. Honour is due every new foundation: honour and love, if one is as worthy love as your lovely son!"

From Pharaoh's direction came a sigh; the mother turned toward him. He stirred, blinked his eyes, and stood up straight. Colour came back to his lips and cheeks.

"Decisions," they heard him say, "decisions must be made. My Majesty made it clear that I had no more time and must return at once to my immediate kingly concerns. Pardon my absence," he said with a smile as he let his mother lead him back to his seat and sank into the cushions. "Pardon me, Mama, and you too, dear soothsayer. Pharaoh," he added, with a meditative smile, "had no need to excuse himself, for he is untrammelled, and besides, he did not go but was fetched. But he excuses himself all the same, out of ordinary politeness. But now to business. We have time, but we have none to lose. Take your seat, eternal mother, if I may respectfully beg you. It is not proper for you to stand when your son is sitting. Only this young man with the lower-regions name might stand before Pharaoh for a little while longer, during the discussion of matters growing out of my dreams. They came from below too, but out of concern for that which is above; but he seems to me to be blest from below up and from above down. So you are of the opinion, Osarsiph," he asked, "that we must husband the fullness against the ensuing scarcity and collect enormous stores in the barns to be given out in the barren years, in order that the upper should not suffer with the lower?"

"Just so, dear master," answered Joseph. The term was quite foreign to etiquette, and at once brought the bright tears to Pharaoh's eyes. "That is the silent message of the dreams. There cannot be enough barns and granaries; there are many in the land, but yet all too few. New ones must be built everywhere so that their number is like the stars in the skies. And everywhere must officials be appointed to deal with the harvest and collect the taxes—there should be no arbitrary estimate which can always be got round with bribes, but instead there must be a fixed ruling —and heap up grain in Pharaoh's granaries until it is like the sands

149

of the sea; and provision the cities so that food is laid up for distribution in the bad years and the land does not perish of hunger and Amun reap the benefits, who would misinterpret Pharaoh to the people, saying: 'It is the King who is guilty and this the punishment for the new teaching and worship.' I said distribution; but I do not mean it so that the corn should be handed out once and for all, but we should distribute to the poor and the little people and sell to the great and rich. Poor harvests mean a hard time, and when the Nile is low prices are high; the rich shall buy dear and all those shall stoop who still think themselves great as Pharaoh in the land. For only Pharaoh shall be rich in the land of Egypt, and he shall become silver and gold."

"Who shall sell?" cried Amenhotep in alarm. "God's son, the King?"

But Joseph answered: "God forbid! It shall be the wise and understanding man whom Pharaoh must search out among his servants: one filled with the spirit of planning and foresight, master of the survey, who sees all even unto the borders of the land and beyond, because the borders of the land are not his borders. Him let Pharaoh appoint and set him over the land of Egypt with the words: 'Be as myself'; so that he husband the abundance as long as it goes on and feed the dearth when it comes. Let him be as the moon between Pharaoh our lovely sun and the earth below. He shall build the barns, direct the host of officials, and establish the laws governing the collection. He shall investigate and find out where it is to be distributed gratis and where sold, shall arrange that the little people shall eat and listen to Pharaoh's teaching, and shall harass the great in favour of the crown, that Pharaoh become over and over gold and silver."

The goddess-mother laughed a little from her chair.

"You laugh, little Mama," said Amenhotep. "But My Majesty finds really interesting what our foreseer here foresees. Pharaoh looks down from above on these things below, but it interests him mightily to see what the moon brings about on earth in her jesting, spectral way. Tell me more, soothsayer, since we are in council, about this middleman, this blithe ingenious young man, and how he should go to work once I have appointed him."

"I am not Keme's child and not the son of Jeor," answered Joseph; "indeed, I came from abroad. But the garment of my body has long been of Egyptian stuff, for at seventeen I came down here with my guide which God appointed for me, the Midianites, and came to No-Amun, your city. Although I am from afar, I know this and that about the affairs of the land and its history: how everything came about and how the kingdom grew out of the nomes, and out of the old the new, and how remnants of the old still defiantly persist, out of tune with the times. For Pharaoh's fathers, the princes of Weset, who smote the foreign kings and drove them out and made the black earth a royal possession, these had to reward the princes of the nomes and the petty kings who helped them in their campaigns, with gifts of land and lofty titles, so that some of them still call themselves kings next after Pharaoh, sit defiantly on their estates, which are not Pharaoh's, and resist the passage of time. All this being well known to me, I have no trouble in showing how Pharaoh's middleman, the master of the survey and of the prices, shall act and how use the occasion. He will fix the prices for the whole seven years to the proud district princes and surviving so-called kings when they have neither bread nor seed but he has abundance of them. They shall be such a kind of prices that their eyes will run over with tears and they shall be plucked to the last pin-feather; so that their land shall finally fall to the crown as it ought and these stiff-necked kings be turned into tenants."

"Good!" said the Queen-mother energetically in her deep voice.

Pharaoh was much amused.

"What a rascal, your young middleman and moon-magician!" he laughed. "My Majesty would not have thought of it, but he finds it capital. But what shall this man, my regent, do about the temples, which are rich to excess and oppress the land; shall he harass them too and fleece them properly as a rogue should? Above all, I would wish that Amun might be plundered and that my man of business would straightway lay the common taxes on him who has never had to pay!"

"If the man is as extremely sensible as I expect," replied Joseph, "he will spare the temples and leave the gods of Egypt alone during the years of plenty, since it has always been the custom for the gods' property to be left untaxed. Above all, Amun must not be exasperated against the work of provision and not agitate among the people to oppose the storage of supplies, telling them it is directed against the god. When the hard times come, then the temple will have to pay the prices of the master of the prices; that is enough. It will not profit from the success of the crown's enterprise; Pharaoh shall become heavier and more golden than all of them if the middleman even half-way understands his affair."

"Very sensible," nodded the mother-goddess.

"But if I do not deceive myself in the man," went on Joseph, "and why should I since Pharaoh will choose him?—then the man will cast his eye even beyond the borders of the land and see to it that disloyalty is suppressed and the vacillating firmly attached to Pharaoh's throne. When my forefather Abram came down into Egypt with his wife Sarai (which means queen and heroine), when they came down, there was famine at home where they lived and high prices in the lands of the Retenu, Amor and Zahi. But in Egypt there was plenty. And shall it be different now? When the time of the lean kine comes for us here, who says there will not be scarcity up there too? Pharaoh's dreams were so heavy with warning that their meaning might apply to the whole world and would be a thing something like the Flood. Then the peoples would come on pilgrimage down to the land of Egypt to get bread and seed-corn, for Pharaoh has it heaped up in abundance. People will come hither, people from everywhere and from who knows where, whom one had never expected to see here; they will come driven by need and come before the lord of the survey, your business man, and say to him: 'Sell to us, otherwise we are sold and betrayed, for we and our children are dying of hunger and know not how to live longer unless you sell to us out of your substance.' Then will the seller answer them and go about with them according to what sort of people they are. But how he will go about with this and that city king of Syria and Phœnicia, that I can trust myself to prophesy. For I know that neither of them loves Pharaoh his lord as he should, and is unsteady in his loyalty, carrying water on both shoulders and even pretending submission to Pharaoh, but at the same time making eyes at the Hittites and bargaining for his own advantage. Such as these will the overseer make humble when the time comes, I can see that. For not alone silver and wood will he make them pay for bread and seed-corn; they will be obliged to deliver up their sons and daughters as payment or as a guarantee to Egypt if they want to live; thus they will be bound to Pharaoh's seat, so that one can depend on their loyalty and duty."

Amenhotep bounced for joy on his chair, like a child.

"Little Mama," he cried, "think of Milkili, the King of Ashdod, who is more than wobbling and so evil-intentioned that he loves not Pharaoh from his whole heart but even plots treachery and defection—I have had letters to that effect. Everybody wants me to send troops against Milkili and dye my sword; Horemheb, my first officer, demands it twice daily.

But I will not do it, for the Lord of the Aton will have no bloodshed. But now you hear how my friend here, the son of the roguish one, suggests how we can force the loyalty of such bad kings and bind them firmly to Pharaoh's seat without shedding of blood and just in the way of business. Capital, capital!" he cried, and struck his hand repeatedly on the arm of his chair. Suddenly he grew serious and got up solemnly from his seat; but then, as though seized by misgiving, sat down again.

"It is difficult," he said pettishly. "Mama, I do not know how to arrange about the office and rank which I shall confer on my friend and middleman, the person who shall concern himself with the collection and distribution of provisions. The government is unfortunately fully staffed, all the best offices are taken. We have the two viziers, the overseers of the granaries and the King's herds, the chief scribe of the treasury, and so on. Where is the office for my friend, to which I can appoint him, with a suitable title?"

"That is the least of your difficulties," returned his mother calmly. She even turned her head aside as though the matter were indifferent to her. "It happened often in earlier times, and even in more recent ones; there is an established tradition, which could be resumed any day, if it pleased Your Majesty, to set between Pharaoh and the great officials of the state a go-between and mouthpiece, the head of all the heads and overseer of all the overseers, through whom the King's word went forth, the representative of the god. The chief mouthpiece is something quite customary. We need not see difficulties where there are none," she said, and turned her head even further away.

"And that is the truth!" Amenhotep cried. "I knew it, I had just forgotten it, because there had been no occupant of the office for so long, no moon between the heaven and the earth, and the Viziers of the North and the South were the highest. Thank you, little Mama, thank you most warmly and cordially."

And he got up again, very grave and solemn of countenance.

"Come nearer to the King," he said, "Osarsiph, messenger and friend! Come here beside me, and let me tell you. The good Pharaoh fears to startle you. I beg you to steel yourself for what Pharaoh has to say. Steel yourself beforehand, even before you have heard my words, so that you will not fall in a faint and feel as though a winged bull were bearing you up to the skies. Have you prepared yourself? Then hear! You are this man! You yourself and no other are he whom I choose and raise to a place here by my side, to be chief overseer over all, into whose hands the highest power is given, that you may husband the plenty and feed the lands in the years of famine. Can you wonder at this, can my decision take you utterly by surprise? You have interpreted me my dreams from below, without cauldron or book, just as I felt one must interpret them, and you did not fall dead afterwards as inspired lambs are wont to do. To me that was a sign that you are set apart to take all the measures which, as you clearly recognize, follow from the interpretation. You have interpreted to me my dreams from above, precisely according to the truth of which my heart was aware, and have explained to me why my Father said that he did not wish to be called Aton, but the Lord of the Aton, and you have enlightened my soul on the doctrinal difference between 'my Father above' and 'my Father *who is in* heaven.' You are not only a prophet but a rogue as well; you have shown me how by means of the lean years we can fleece the district kings who no longer fit into the picture, and bind the wavering city kings of Syria to Pharaoh's seat. God has told you all this; and because of it no one can be so understanding as you, and there can be no sense in my seeking far and near for another. You shall be over my house, and all my people shall be obedient to your word. Are you very much surprised?"

"I lived long," answered Joseph, "at the side of a man who did not know how to be surprised, for he was steadiness itself. He was my taskmaster in the prison. He taught me that steadiness is nothing but being prepared for everything. So I am not overwhelmingly surprised. I am in Pharaoh's hand."

"And in your hands shall be the lands, and you shall be as myself before all the people," said Amenhotep with feeling. "Take this in the first place," said he. With nervous fingers he jerked and pulled a ring over his knuckle and thrust it upon Joseph's hand. It was an oval lapis lazuli of exceptional beauty, in a high setting. It glowed like the sunlit heavens, and the name Aton within the royal cartouche was engraved on the stone. "That shall be the sign," Meni went on with passion, once more growing quite pale, "of your plenary power and representative status, and whoever sees it shall tremble and know that each word you utter to one of my servants, be he the highest or the lowest, shall be as my own word. Whoever has a request to Pharaoh, he shall come first before you, and your word shall be kept and obeyed because wisdom and reason stand at your side. I am Pharaoh! I set you over all the land of Egypt, and without your will shall no one stir hand or foot in the two lands. Only by the height of the royal seat shall I be higher than you, and lend you of the loftiness and splendour of my throne. You shall drive in my second chariot, just behind mine, and they shall run alongside and shout: 'Take care, take your heart to you, here is the Father of the Lands!' You shall stand before my throne and have the power of the keys, unlimited. . . . I see you shake your head, little Mama, you turn it away and I hear you murmur something about extravagance. But there can be something splendid about extravagance, and just now Pharaoh is bent on extravagance. You shall have a title and style confirmed to you, lamb of God, such as was never before heard of in Egypt; and in it your death-name shall disappear. We have of course the two viziers; but I will create for you the as yet unknown title of Grand Vizier. But that will not be nearly enough; for you shall be called in addition Friend of the Harvest of God, and Sustainer of Egypt, and Shadow-spender of the King, Father of Pharaoh—and whatever else happens to occur to me, though just now I am so happy and excited that nothing else does. Do not shake your head, Mama, let me this one time have my fun; for I am extravagant on purpose and consciously. It is grand that it will happen as in the foreign song that goes:

Father Inlil has named his name Lord of the Lands.
He shall administer all realms over which I hold sway,
All my obligations shall he take to himself.

His land shall flourish, he himself shall be in health.
His word shall stand firm, what he commands shall not be changed,
Not any god shall alter the word of his mouth.

As it goes in the song and as the foreign hymn says, so shall it be, and it gives me infinite pleasure. Prince of the Interior and Vice-God: so shall you be called at the investiture. We cannot undertake your gilding here, there is no adequate treasure-house out of which I can reward you with gold, with collars and chains. We must go back at once to Weset, it can only be there, at Merimat in the palace, in the great court under the balcony. And a wife must be found for you from the best circles—that is, of course, a whole lot of wives, but first of all the first and true one. For it is settled that I am going to see you married. You will find

155

out what a pleasure that is!" And Amenhotep clapped his hands with the eager unrestraint of a child.

"Eiy!" he called breathlessly to the chamberlain who came crouching forward. "We are leaving. Pharaoh and the whole court are going back to Nowet-Amun today. Make haste, it is a gracious command. Make ready my boat *Star of the Two Lands,* I will travel on it with the eternal mother, the sweet consort, and this elect one, the Adon of my house, who from now on shall be as myself in Egypt. Tell it to the rest. There will be a tremendous gilding!"

The hunchback had of course been close to the portières the whole time, he had listened with all his might, but he had not trusted his ears. Now he was forced to believe; and we can imagine how he fawned like a kitten and bridled and kissed his fingertips.

Chapter Four

THE TIME OF ENFRANCHISEMENT

SEVEN OR FIVE

IT is well that this conversation between Pharaoh and Joseph—which led to the lifting up of the departed one, so that he was made great in the West—this famous and yet almost unknown conversation which the great mother who was present, not unaptly called a conversation of gods about God, has now been re-established from beginning to end in all its turnings, windings, and conversational episodes. Well that it has been set down with exactitude once and for all, so that everyone can follow the course which in its time it pursued in reality; so that if some point or other should slip the memory, one need only turn back and read. The summary nature of the tradition up till now almost makes it, however venerable, unconvincing. For instance upon Joseph's interpretation and his advice to the King to look about for a wise and knowledgeable and forethoughted man, Pharaoh straightway answers: "Nobody is so knowledgeable and wise as you. I will set you over all Egypt." And overwhelms him on the spot with the most extravagant honours and dignities. There is too much abridgement and condensation about this, it is too dry, it is a drawn and salted and embalmed remnant of the truth, not truth's living lineaments. Pharaoh's inordinate enthusiasm and favour seem to lack foundation and motivation. Long ago when, overcoming the shrinking of our flesh, we pulled ourselves together for the trip down through millennial abysses, down to the regions below, to the field and the fountain where Joseph was standing; even so long ago what we were actually after was to listen to that very conversation and to bring it back with us in all its members as it really came to pass and took place at On in Lower Egypt.

Of course, there is really nothing against condensation in itself. It is useful and even necessary. In the long run it is quite impossible to narrate life just as it flows. What would it lead to? Into the infinite. It would be beyond human powers. Whoever got such an idea fixed in his head would not only never finish, he would be suffocated at the outset—entangled in a web of delusory exactitude, a madness of detail. No, excision must play its part at the beautiful feast of narration and recreation; it has an important and indispensable role. Here, then, the art will be judiciously practised, to the end of getting finally quit of a preoccupation which, though after all it has a distant kinship with the attempt to drink the sea dry, must not be driven to the extreme and utter folly of actually and literally doing so.

What would have become of us, for instance, when Jacob was serving with the devil Laban, seven and thirteen and five—in short, twenty-five years, of which every tiniest time element was full of a life-in-itself, quite worth telling? And what would become of us now without that reasonable principle, when our little bark, driven by the measuredly moving stream of narration, hovers again on the brink of a time-cataract of seven and seven prophesied years? Well, to begin with, and just among ourselves: in these fourteen years things were neither quite so definitely good nor so definitely bad as the prophecy would have them. It was fulfilled, no doubt about that. But fulfilled as life fulfils, imprecisely. For life and reality always assert a certain independence, sometimes on such a scale as to blur the prophecy out of all recognition. Of course, life is bound to the prophecy; but within those limits it moves so freely that one almost has one's choice as to whether the prophecy has been fulfilled or not. In our present case we are dealing with a time and a people animated by the best will in the world to believe in the fulfilment, however inexact. For the sake of the prophecy they are willing to agree that two and two make five—if the phrase may be used in a context where not five but an even higher odd number, namely seven, is in question. Probably this would constitute no great difficulty, five being almost as respectable a number as seven; and surely no reasonable man would insist that five instead of seven could constitute an inexactitude.

In fact and in reality the prophesied seven looked rather more like five. Life, being living, put no clear or absolute emphasis on either number. The fat and the lean years did not come up out of the womb of time to balance each other so unequivocally as in the dream. The fat and lean years that came were like life in not being entirely fat or entirely lean. Among the fat ones were one or two which might have been described as certainly not lean, but to a critical eye as certainly no more than very moderately fat. The lean ones were all lean enough, at least five of them, if not seven; but among them there may have been a couple which did not reach the last extreme of exiguity and even half-way approached the middling. Indeed, if the prophecy had not existed they might not have been recognized as years of famine at all. As it was, they were blithely reckoned in along with the others.

Does all this detract from the fulfilment of the prophecy? Of course not. Its fulfilment is incontestible, for we have the fact—the facts of our tale, of which our tale consists, without which it would not be in the world and without which, after the snatching away and the lifting up, the making to come after could not have happened. Certainly things were fat and lean enough in the land of Egypt and adjacent regions, years-long fat and years-long more or less lean, and Joseph had plenty of chance to husband the plenty and distribute the crying lack, and like Utnapishtim-Atrachasis, like Noah the exceeding wise one, to prove himself a man of prudence and foresight, whose ark rocks safe on the flood. In loyal service to the highest he did this as his minister, and by his dealings he gilded Pharaoh over and over again.

THE GILDING

But for the present it was himself who was gilded; for to "become a man of gold" was the phrase the children of Egypt used for what now happened to him when by Pharaoh's gracious command—together with this god, the Queen-mother, the sweet consort, and the princesses Nezem-mut and Baketaton—he had made the journey upstream on the royal bark *Star of the Two Lands* back to Weset, amid the plaudits of the crowded shores. There with the sun-family he made his entry into the palace of the west, Merimat, set in its gardens and with the lake of its gardens, at the foot of the high-coloured desert hills. There he received spacious quarters, servants, raiment, and everything for his comfort and pleasure and as early as the second day the state function of the investiture and gilding was held, beginning with the ceremonial progress by the court when the purchased slave did actually drive in Pharaoh's second car directly behind the monarch and surrounded by his Syrian and Nubian bodyguard and fan-bearers, separated from the car of the god only by a troop of runners who cried: "Abrekh!" and "Take care!"

and "Grand Vizier!" and "Behold the father of the land!" By this
means it was made known to the populace what was going on and who
that was in the second car. At least they saw and understood that Pharaoh
had made someone very great, for which he must have had his own
reasons, even if only it was his gracious will and whim, that being quite
reason enough. Moreover, since the idea of a dawning of a new age and
great improvement in all things was somehow always bound up with
such an investiture and lifting up, Weset's people exulted greatly on
the house-tops and hopped on one leg along the avenues. They shouted:
"Pharaoh! Pharaoh!" and "Neb-nef-nezem!" and "Great is Aton!" And
you might even distinguish this name pronounced with a softer sound:
"Adon! Adon!" doubtless referring to Joseph. For it had probably
leaked out that he was an Asiatic, and it seemed proper—particularly
to the women—to hail him by the name of the Syrian "Lord" and
bridegroom, not least because he whom they thus distinguished was so
very young and handsome. It should be added here that among all his
titles it was this name which stuck. And in all the land of Egypt he was
called Adon all his life, in speaking both to and of him.

After this fine procession they were all ferried across the river to the
west bank and back to the palace, where there was now to take place
the ceremony of the gilding, always wonderful and this time simply
irresistible to the eye and the heart. Its course was as follows: Pharaoh,
and She-who-filled-the-palace-with-love, Nefernefruaton the Queen,
showed themselves at the so-called audience-window, actually not a
window but a sort of balcony giving on an inner court of the palace,
a pillared terrace in front of the great reception hall. It was magnificently
constructed of malachite and azure and adorned with bronze uræi. But
in front of this was still another little structure supported on enchant-
ingly garlanded lotus columns. Its broad balustrade was covered with gay
cushions, and on these Their Majesties leaned to fling down the gold
presents of every shape and sort, handed them by officers of the treasure-
house, upon the lucky man standing below on the terrace. The present
recipient, of course, was no other than Joseph the son of Jacob. The
scene and all that went with it were never forgotten by those who once
saw it. Everything swam in a sea of colour and pomp, of extravagant
favour and fervid ecstasy. The splendid fretwork of the architecture,
the banners flapping in the breeze, under a sunny sky, from the gay
gilded and painted wooden columns; the blue and red whisks and fans

of the ranking retainers who filled the court, dressed in flowing gala aprons, bowing and scraping, cheering and paying homage; women striking tambourines; boys with the youth-lock told off to jump for joy without stopping; the hosts of scribes in their customary obsequious posture, writing down with their reeds everything that happened; the view through three wide-open gates into the outer court, full of vehicles whose prancing horses carried tall coloured plumes on their heads and behind them the drivers, facing the scene with them, bowing low and lifting their arms; looking in on all this from outside the red and yellow mountains of Thebes, dark blue and violet in their shadowy depths; and on the splendid ceremonial estrade the godlike pair, fragile and smiling in their languid elegance, wearing their high caplike crowns with the drapery protecting the back of their necks: uninterruptedly, with obvious enjoyment tossing out of an inexhaustible store the shower and dower of valuables on the favoured one below, strings of gold beads, gold in the shape of lions, gold arm-bands, gold daggers, gold fillets, collars, sceptres, vases, hatchets, all out of fine gold—the recipient of course could not catch them all, so he had two slaves to heap up in front of him on the ground a veritable golden hoard, glittering in the sunshine amid the onlookers' admiring cries—yes, this was certainly, take it all in all, the prettiest scene imaginable; and were it not for the inexorable laws of abridgement and condensation it would be described here in much greater detail.

Jacob in his time had amassed treasure during his life with Laban the devil in the land of no return. On this day his darling did so too, in the merry land of the dead into which he had died and been sold. For certainly all that gold exists only in the lower world. Here in this very spot and space of time he became a well-to-do man simply by dint of the gold of favour. We know that foreign kings, trading with Pharaoh for gold, were wont to say that in Egypt that metal was no more precious than the dust in the streets. But it is an economic error to think that gold decreases in value the more there is of it.

Yes, that was a red-letter day for the snatched-away and set-apart one, a day full of worldly blessing. One could wish that Jacob the father might have beheld it, feeling as he gazed a mixture of pride and dismay in which the first would have outweighed the second. Joseph did wish it; and later he said: "Tell the father of all my glory in Egypt!" He had had a letter from Pharaoh that day, not written by the King himself, of course, but by the "actual scribe," his secretary, by Pharaoh's order. It was somewhat stiff, but as a calligraphic production quite delightful, and in its content most gracious. It said:

"Command of the King to Osarsiph, the overseer of that which the heavens give, the earth produces, and the Nile brings forth, superintendent of all things in the whole land and actual administrator of works. My Majesty has heard with pleasure the words which a few days before this, in the conversation which the King was pleased to hold with you at On in Lower Egypt, you spoke about heavenly and earthly things. On that happy day you greatly rejoiced the heart of Nefer-Kheperu-Re with that which he really loves. My Majesty heard these words from you with extraordinary pleasure, in that you linked the heavenly with the earthly and through your concern for the one at the same time showed great concern for the other, and also contributed to the teaching of my Father who is in heaven. Truly you know how to say what pleases My Majesty extraordinarily, and what you say makes my heart to laugh. My Majesty also knows that you rejoice to say what My Majesty likes to hear. O Osarsiph, I say to you times without end: Beloved of his lord! Rewarded of his lord! Favourite and ordained of his lord! Truly the Lord of Aton loves me, since he has given you to me! As true as Nefer-Kheperu-Re lives eternal, whenever you utter a wish, be it orally or in writing to My Majesty, My Majesty will straightway see it granted."

And in anticipation of such a wish, in Egyptian thought the most pressing concern of all, the latter ended by saying that Pharaoh had given orders for the immediate excavation, construction, and decoration of an eternal dwelling, in other words a tomb for Joseph in the western hills.

After the exalted one had read this paper, there took place before the assembled court, in the great columned hall behind the balcony of audience, the great ceremony of the investiture; at which Pharaoh, besides the signet ring already given and all the gold showered upon him, hung a particularly heavy gold necklace of favour round Joseph's neck over his immaculate court garment—which of course was not made of silk as we in our ignorance might think, but of the finest royal linen. The Vizier of the South read the letters patent which Pharaoh had conferred, and the style and titles under which henceforth Joseph's death-name should be hidden. Most of these we already know from Pharaoh's own lips and from the formal letter with its official superscription: "Admin-

162

istrator of what the heavens give," and so forth. The most impressive were probably "the King's shadow-dispenser," "friend of the harvest of God," "nourisher of Egypt" ("Ka-ne-Keme" in the language of the country). "Grand Vizier," although unprecedented, and "universal friend of the King," as distinguished from "unique friend," sounded pale beside them. But it did not stop there, for Pharaoh was bent on extravagance. Joseph was called "Adon of the royal house," and "Adon over all Egypt." He was called "chief mouthpiece" and "prince of medi-ation," "increaser of the teaching," "good shepherd of the people," "double of the King," "vice-Horus." There had not been such a thing before, the future has never repeated it, and probably it could only happen under the dominion of a young king prone to impulsiveness and bursts of extravagant resolve. There was another title still, but that was more like a personal name and intended not so much to cover as to replace Joseph's own. Posterity has speculated much about it, and even the most respectable tradition gives an inadequate or misleading interpretation. It is said that Pharaoh called Joseph his "Privy Coun-sellor." That is an uninformed version. In our script the name would have appeared as Dje-p-nut-ef-onch, which the glib-lipped children of Egypt pronounced Dgepnuteefonech, with the palatal *ch* on the end. The most prominent part of the combination is *onch* or *onech,* the sign for which in picture-writing is (⚚), which means life and which the gods held under the noses of men, especially their sons the kings, that they might have breath. The name, then, which was added to Joseph's many titles, was a name of life. It meant: "The god" (Aton, one did not need to specify) "says: Life be with thee!" But even that was not its whole meaning. It meant, for every ear that heard it, not only "Live thou thyself," but also "Be a life-bringer, spread life, give living-food to the many!" In a word, it was a name that meant satisfaction, suffi-ciency; and in that character above all had Joseph been exalted. All his titles and styles, in so far as they did not refer to his personal relation to Pharaoh, contained in some form or other this idea of the preservation of life, the feeding of the country; and all of them, including this excel-lent and much disputed one, could be comprehended in a single epithet: the Provider.

When Jacob's son had had these strings of titles hung around his neck he was overwhelmed with congratulations. I leave to your imagination the honeyed homage and adulation that followed. Human beings mostly have an itch to accept the arbitrary caprice, the incomprehensible election, the tremendous "I favour whom I favour," going beyond all possible calculation, even disarming envy itself and imparting a kind of sincerity to the words of the veriest toady. Nobody could really understand why Pharaoh was thus exalting this still youthful stranger, but everybody blissfully gave up trying. True, the art of soothsaying was held in honour; it was a partial explanation that Joseph had chanced to distinguish himself in this field and had come off better than the very best domestic product. Moreover Pharaoh's weakness for those that "heard his words" was well known; those, that is, who entered into his theological ideas and realized that interest in them, whether real or assumed, was rewarded by the tenderest gratitude. Here, too, this extraordinary chap both seemed favoured by fortune and also apparently had some inherited talent for the sort of thing Pharaoh loved. In any case, it was clear that in dealing with their lord he had kept his wits about him; with the result that he had been whisked upstairs and now ranked high above them all. They bowed before his successful cunning no less than before the royal will. They bowed and scraped with a vengeance, they kotowed and kissed hands for all they were worth. One man among the unique friends of the King, who fancied himself as a writer, had even composed a panegyric in Joseph's honour and he sang it accompanied by soft chords on the harp. It went like this:

> Thou livest, thou art hale, thou art sound.
> Thou art not poor, thou art not wretched.
> Thou abidest like the hours.
> Thy plans abide, thy life is long.
> Thy speech is choice.
> Thine eye sees what is good.
> Thou hearest what is pleasing.
> Thou seest good, thou hearest pleasantness.
> Thou shalt be placed among the counsellors.

Thou standest firm, thy foe falls down.
Who speaks against thee is no more.

Pretty mediocre. But for something written by one of themselves the court found it capital.

Joseph took all this as one whom no preferment surprises: gravely, courteously—though at times, owing to the distraction of his thoughts, the situation verged on the painful. For he was distraught, his mind was not here in Pharaoh's hall. It was in a house of hair on a far hill; or in the grove of the Lord near by, with his own little brother from the true mother. To that little lad with the helmet-like hair he was telling his dreams. Or he sat beneath the awning on the harvest field with companions to whom likewise he related his dream; or at Dothan in the vale by a certain well, whither he had come by no gentle means. And thus preoccupied he almost failed to acknowledge the salutation of a certain courtier to whom such neglect would have been most painful.

In other words, among the troop of gratulants was Nefer-em-Wese, who had once been called just the opposite, the Master of the Vine. We can feel the fat man's bewilderment and dismay at the tricks life plays, as he waited to congratulate, under such undreamed-of, such incredibly altered circumstances, his young steward of earlier and evil days. He might hope that the new favourite was friendly disposed and would not "speak against him," since to him, Nefer, he owed his summons and his great opportunity. But on the other hand the fat man guiltily realized that he had done nothing until the very eve of the prophesying to call attention to Joseph and then only because the occasion had so to speak hit him in the eye. He thought that perhaps Joseph cared as little as himself to be reminded of the prison; so he confined himself to the cautious familiarity of winking one eye, which might mean anything; and had the gratification of seeing Adon wink back.

Here and now may be the right time to speak of another possible—and how pregnant—meeting of old friends, and to justify a silence which has not always been preserved by those who have concerned themselves with Joseph's history. I refer to Potiphar or Potiphera, more correctly Petepre, the great eunuch, Joseph's former owner, master and judge, who with such good will threw him into prison. Was he too present at the gilding and the reception and did he too pay Joseph homage at court—thus expressing, perhaps, the respect of a man incapable of a certain thing but knowing how to value it, for another man who was capable of it yet also capable of renouncing it? To describe such a meeting is alluring indeed—but alas, nothing of the sort took place. The painfully beautiful motif of reunion plays a triumphant role in our present tale; we shall hear much that is undreamed of, much that is moving on this very theme. But in this place there is only silence and the silence of our accepted version at this point in the story of the sun chamberlain and particularly of his honorary wife, the pathetic Mutem-inet—this silence is not simply omission unless negation can be regarded in that light: the express statement that something did *not* happen; in other words, that Joseph, after his departure out of the courtier's house, never again met either its master or its mistress.

The people, and to please them the poets, an all too easy-going breed, have spun out in a variety of ways this tale of Joseph and Potiphar's wife, which was only an episode, if an important one, in the life of Jacob's son. Any possibility of more to follow was, of course, completely excluded by the final catastrophe. But they have written sentimental continuations and given it a predominant place within the Joseph story. In their hands it becomes a sugary romance with a proper happy ending. According to these poetasters, the temptress—who goes by the name of Zuleika, a fact at which we can only shrug our shoulders—after she had got Joseph into prison, withdrew full of remorse into a "hut" and there lived only for the expiation of her sins. Meanwhile through the death of her husband she became a widow. But when Yussuf (meaning Joseph) was about to be freed out of the prison, he had refused to have his "chains" removed until the female aristocracy of the country had come before Pharaoh's throne and borne witness to his innocence. Accordingly the entire nobility of the sex had come before the King and with one voice the whole lovely bevy had announced that Joseph was the prince and pattern of purity, the very freshest ornament in her crown. After which Zuleika took the floor and made public confession that she alone had been the offender, and he an angel. The shameful crime was hers, she frankly avowed it; but now she was purified and gladly bore the shame and disgrace. Even after Joseph's elevation she continued to do penance, growing old and grey in the process. Only on the festal day when Father Jacob made his alleged triumphal entry into Egypt—and thus at a time when Joseph was actually the father of two sons—did the pair meet again. Joseph had forgiven the old woman, and as a reward

166

heaven had restored all her former seductive beauty; whereupon Joseph had most romantically married her, and thus, after all these tribulations, her old wish came true, and they "put their heads and feet together."

All that is just Persian musk and attar of roses. It has nothing whatever to do with the facts. In the first place, Potiphar did not die so early. Why should the man have died before his time, whose peculiar constitution saved him from using up his powers, who lived entirely for his own inner satisfactions and often went bird-shooting to freshen himself up? The silence of history upon his fate after the great day of the house judgment certainly indicates his disappearance from the scene—but why draw the conclusion that he died? We must remember that while Joseph was in prison, there had been a change of rulers, and on such occasions it is the rule that the court or some part of it changes too. We know that Petepre had had his troubles as nominal head of troops without any real authority; now, after the burial of Nebmare the magnificent he withdrew into private life, with the title and rank of unique friend. He went no more to court, needed to do so no longer in any case; and on the day of Joseph's gilding he must have refrained, obviously out of the sense of delicacy that was so strong in him. Afterwards they never did meet; the reason being, in part at least, that as master and overseer of the department of supplies Joseph, as we shall see, had his residence not at Thebes but at Memphis. Potiphar's tact was probably responsible for the rest. If, in the course of years, a chance encounter did take place, on one or other ceremonial occasion, we may be sure it went off without the flicker of an eyelash, with perfect discretion and the most deliberate ignoring of the past on both sides. It is just this situation that is reflected in the silence of the authorized tradition.

The same thing applies to Mut-em-enet, and on equally good grounds. Joseph did not see her again. That is quite clear; but just as clear is it that she did not withdraw into any penitential hut. Nor did she ever publicly accuse herself of shamelessness—if she had it would have been a lie. This great lady, the instrument of Joseph's trial, which he passed by no means brilliantly, but still passed; after the shipwreck of that desperate attempt to escape into the human from her honorary existence, she was forced back finally and for ever into the form of life which before her affliction had been the normal and familiar one to her. Indeed, she now practised it with more pride and concentration than ever. By reason of the surpassing wisdom Potiphar had shown at the time of the catastrophe, their relations had gained in warmth rather than the reverse. He had given judgment like a god, elevated above and beyond the frailties of the human heart; she was grateful to him, and from that day onwards was a blameless and devoted wife. She did not curse the beloved for the agony that he had brought upon her or she had brought upon herself. No, the agonies of love are set apart; no one has ever repented having suffered them. "Thou hast made rich my life—it burgeons"— so had Eni spoken in the midst of her travail; it is clear that love has its own quality of torment, not always incompatible with heartfelt gratitude. At least, she had lived and loved. Unhappily, of course; but is there really such a thing as unhappy love? And shall we not put aside as stupid and officious any pity we may feel for Eni? She asked for none; and she was much too proud to pity herself. Her life had had its flowering, the renunciation was stern and final. The lines of her body, for a time those of a witch for love, quickly recovered their normal state. That was no longer the swanlike beauty they had owned in youth; it was rather an expression of the nunlike in her nature. Yes, Mut-em-enet from now on was a cool moon-nun, chaste-bosomed, irreproachably elegant, and —it must be added—extremely bigoted. We all remember how in the season of her painful blooming she had burned incense with the beloved before the world-wide, omni-friendly Atum-Re of On, Lord of the Wide Horizon, and prayed that he would smile upon her passion. That was all over. Her own horizon had closed round her again, and narrow, rigid, and devout it was. Her whole devotion now went to him rich in bulls of Ipet-Isowet, and to his conservative sun-sense; more than ever she lent her ear to the spiritual counsel of his head baldpate the great Beknechons, who hated all change and frowned on all speculation. Thus she was the more estranged from the court of Amenhotep IV, where a tender, all-embracing, ecstatic cult had begun to be the mode. In Mut-em-enet's eyes it had nothing whatever to do with religion. She was all for the sacred static, the eternal equilibrium of the scales, the stony stare into for-ever-and-ever; and she celebrated it when in her tight-skirted Hathor dress she rattled her clappers before Amun in measured dance-step, and from her shrunken bosom gave out her still admired voice to swell the choir of her noble sisterhood. And yet at the bottom of her soul there abode a treasure of which she was secretly prouder than of all her religious or worldly honours and, whether confessedly or not, would never have surrendered. A treasure buried very deep; yet ever

168

it sent a warm glow upwards into the grey daylight of her resigned state. Of course the chill knowledge of defeat was there present too, in slight measure; but weak compared to the warmth from below, which imparted to her worldly and religious pride an indispensable element of the human—the pride of life. It was a memory—not so much of him who, as she had heard, was now become lord over all Egypt. He was an instrument—as she, Mut-em-enet, had been an instrument. Almost independent of him was her sense of having justified her own existence, her secret knowledge that she had once blossomed and burned, once suffered and loved.

LORD OVER EGYPT

Lord over Egypt: I use the phrase in the spirit of a convention, which could never go far enough in deification to satisfy itself; and in the sense of that beautiful extravagance which Pharaoh defended in favour of the interpreter of his dreams. However, it is not recklessly or fancifully used in this place, but rather with a full sense of loyalty to truth. For here in this account I am not drawing a long bow but merely telling what happened; and these are two very different things, whichever one you may happen to prefer. Exaggeration does, of course, get a more striking temporary effect; but surely a critical and considered narrative is of more real profit to the listener.

Joseph became a very great lord at court and in the country, no question of that; and the confidential relations between him and the monarch after the talk in the Cretan garden room, his position as a favourite, left the limitations to his authority somewhat vague. But he was never actually lord over Egypt, or as saga and song sometimes express it, Regent of the Lands. His elevation, which was fabulous enough, and his inordinate row of titles could not alter the fact that the administration of the country whither he had been snatched remained in the hands of the crown officials, some of whom had held office under King Neb-ma-re. It would be excessive to suppose that the administration of justice, for instance, came under the authority of Jacob's son, which from time immemorial had been the business of the high judge and vizier and now of the two viziers. The same is true of the field of foreign policy, which might indeed have had better results if Joseph had taken it over than those which history records. We must not forget that at bottom he was not interested in the glory of the kingdom, however much he had become Egyptian in his outward walks and ways. And that whatever energetic benevolence he displayed to the inhabitants, however wisely he served the public good, his inward eye ever remained directed upon the personally spiritual, the private which was yet of such world-shaking significance; on the furtherance, in short, of plans and purposes which had little to do with Mizraim's weal or woe. We may be certain that he had at once brought Pharaoh's dreams and what they foretold into relation with his own plans and purposes. Certainly he made them fit into his ideas about expecting and preparing the way; in fact, we cannot deny that his attitude before Pharaoh's throne was a thought too eager, almost enough so to cool the sympathy which we would wish to preserve for Rachel's child, if we did not keep it in mind that Joseph regarded it as his duty to further such plans and to be as helpful as he possibly could to God in carrying them out.

Well, whatever the interpretation in fact of all his string of titles, he was duly installed as minister of agriculture and supplies; and in this capacity he carried through important reforms, among them the ground-rent law which has particularly impressed itself on history. But he never overstepped the limit of his field, however likely it is that the affairs of the treasury and the administration of the granaries were too closely connected with his own operations for his authority not to have reached out into them; for all that, designations like Lord over the Land of Egypt and Regent of the Lands remained fanciful ornamentations upon the actual situation. And something else must be taken into account too. Under the conditions that obtained during the first and decisive ten to fourteen years of his tenure of office—conditions in anticipation of which he had been installed—the importance of his particular responsibilities increased so extraordinarily as to put all the others in the shade. The famine which five to seven—more likely five—years after his elevation broke over Egypt and the neighbouring provinces made the man who had foreseen it, and knew how to help people through it, easily the most important figure in the kingdom, and his activities of more living importance than any other's. It may well be a fact that judgment, if it is fundamental enough, leads back to a recognition of the soundness of the popular verdict; this being the case, we will say no more than that Joseph's position, at least for a period of years, was equal in fact to that of a lord over the land of Egypt, without whose voice no one could stir hand or foot in the two lands.

For the present, immediately after his investiture he undertook by boat and car a journey of inspection through the country, accompanied by a staff of secretaries chosen by himself, mostly young men not yet fossilized by the jog-trot of office. He did this to acquire first-hand knowledge of the black earth and, before he took any concrete measures, to make himself in actual fact master of the survey. The conditions of property were peculiarly vague and undefined. Theoretically, the soil like everything else belonged to Pharaoh. The lands, including the conquered or tributary provinces as far as the "wretched land of Nubia" and the borders of Mitanniland were Pharaoh's private property. But the actual state domains, the "estates of Pharaoh" as special crown lands, were distinct from the estates which earlier kings had presented to their great men, as well as from the property of small nobles and peasants which passed as personal property of their proprietors, although, to be exact, the situation was more in the nature of leasehold and rental, while preserving the right of inheritance. The only exceptions were the temple lands, especially the acres of Amun, which were all freehold and tax-free; and those remnants of an older structure made up of special immunities, proprietary rights of single district princes who were still powerful and behaved as though they were independent; inherited estates which stood out here and there all through the kingdom like islands of an obsolete feudalism, and like the acres of the church expected to be considered the unqualified property of their owners. But whereas those latter were on principle left in peace by Joseph's administration, he went after the obdurate barons tooth and nail, from the very beginning; he included their estates without more ado in his system of taxation and reservation and in time arrived at simple expropriation in favour of the crown. It is not correct to say that the peculiar agrarian constitution of the so-called new kingdom, a phenomenon so striking to other peoples—namely, that in the lands of the Nile all the soil except the properties of the priesthoods belonged to the King—was created by the measures taken by Jacob's son. For what he did only completed a process well on the way, by defining, regularizing, and legalizing, so that they became clear to the people, conditions which had existed before his time.

His travels did not extend to the Negro lands or to the districts of

171

Syria and Canaan, as he sent commissioners into these regions instead; even so, his tour of inspection took between two and three times seventeen days, there was so much to inspect and have recorded. Then he went back to the capital, where he established himself with a staff in a government building on the Street of the Son and from there, well before the harvest, issued in Pharaoh's name the famous land law which was immediately proclaimed throughout the country. Universally and without respect to person or crop failure it fixed the produce tax at one fifth, to be delivered into the royal storehouses punctually and without notice —or if with notice certainly in peremptory terms. At the same time the children of Egypt could see that all over the country, in the cities large and small and the regions roundabout, these storehouses were enlarged and increased in number by the labours of a large force of workmen. Certainly it looked as though there were more than were needed, because at first, of course, many of them stood empty. Yet more and more were built, for the undue number, so it was said, was reckoned on the abundance which had been foretold by the new Adon of distribution and friend of the harvest of God. Wherever you went you saw the skittle-shaped corn-bins standing in close rows or grouped into squares around courts. They opened on top to receive the corn and had stout doors below to empty it out by and they were built with unusual solidity on terraced platforms of pounded clay to protect them from damp and mice. There were also numerous underground pits for the storage of grain, well lined, with almost invisible entrances, guarded by police.

It is pleasant to report that both measures—the tax law and the construction of the big magazines—enjoyed decided popularity. Taxes there had always been, of course, in many forms. Not for nothing had old Jacob, who had never been in Egypt but had built up an emotional picture of it, been used to talk about the Egyptian house of bondage; even though his mistrust took too little account of the conditions peculiar to the country. The labour of the children of Keme belonged to the King, that was taken for granted; and it was used to erect enormous tombs and incredibly ostentatious public buildings, yes, certainly it was used for that. But it was even more in demand for works of necessity: for all the digging and hoisting operations indispensable to the prosperity of this peculiar and extraordinary land of oases; for keeping the waterways in good condition, digging ditches and canals, manning the sluices, strengthening the dams—all these things were a matter of the general welfare and could not be left to the imperfect intelligence and improbable personal industry of subordinates. Therefore the government kept its children's noses to the grindstone, they had to work for the state. And when they had worked, then they had to pay taxes on what they had done. They had to pay taxes for the canals, lakes, and ditches they used, for the irrigation machinery and sluices which served them, and even for the sycamore trees which grew on their fertilized soil. They paid for house and farmyard and everything that house and farmyard produced. They paid with skins and copper, with wood, rope, paper, linen; and always since time immemorial with corn. But the taxes were levied at the very uneven discretion of the regional administrators and village overseers, according to whether the Nourisher, that is to say Hapi, the river, had been great or small—and that, of course, was sensible enough. But between connivance on the one hand and extortion on the other there was much room for bribery and favouritism and good reason to complain. We may say that from the first day Joseph's administration tightened the reins on the one hand and loosened them on the other. That is, he put all the emphasis on the corn rent and looked very leniently at other debts. The people might keep their linen of the first, second, and third quality, their oil, copper, and paper, if only the corn delivery, the fifth of the bread-grain harvest, was conscientiously handed over. This explicit and universal tax provision could not be regarded as oppressive in a country where the fertility is on the average thirtyfold. Moreover, it had a certain legendary charm and metaphysical appeal, since it had been shrewdly and intentionally taken from the sacred intercalary figure of the five extra days after the three hundred and sixty making up the year. And lastly it pleased the people that Joseph unhesitatingly levied the tax on the still recalcitrant district barons as well and forced them to make up-to-date improvements on their properties for the good of the state. For the reactionary spirit of these men operated to keep their estates in a condition far behind the times: the irrigation system was clumsy and inadequate; they retained it partly out of laziness but mostly out of defiance; and thus the soil yielded less than it should have done. To this gentry Joseph emphatically prescribed the repair of their water systems, recalling as he did so a certain Saleph, an uncle of Eber, about whom Eliezer had told him, that he was the first man to "turn the brooks on to his property," and thus was the inventor of irrigation.

Now as for the new erections, the extraordinary measures taken to heap up the surpluses: the Egyptian national idea of thrift and foresight is probably the best explanation of the fact that Keme's children liked them well. Joseph's own personal tradition of the Flood and the brilliant idea of the ark which saved the human race as well as all animal creation from complete extinction, was in harmony here with the instinct for security and defence deep-rooted in this very vulnerable civilization which had waxed old despite the precarious circumstances under which it lived. Egypt's children even tended to see something magic about Joseph's storehouses. They themselves were practised in fending off evil and malicious demons by setting up some kind of impediment, impenetrable as possible, in the way of magic symbols and signs. Thus in their minds the ideas of foresight and magic were easily interchangeable; they found it not hard to see even such prosaic arrangements as Joseph's corn-bins in the light of enchantments and spells.

In a word, the impression prevailed that Pharaoh, young himself, had made a lucky hit when he installed in office this young father of the harvest and shadow-dispenser. His authority was destined to wax exceedingly in the course of the years; but even now it was favoured by the circumstance that this year the Nile had been very great, and a far greater crop than usual was harvested under the new management, particularly of wheat, green rye, and barley; and abundance of durra-corn could be gleaned from the stalks. We may have our doubts about including in the seven years one of which the prosperity was already certain when Joseph took office. It may not be allowable to count it as one of the years of the fat kine. But it was later so counted—probably in an attempt to bring the number of the blessing years up to seven, though even so they did not quite reach that figure. In any case, it was pleasant for Joseph that he took over the business under conditions of prosperity and plenty. Popular psychology always has been and always will be, quite self-respectingly, without rhyme or reason. If a minister of agriculture takes office in a period of prosperity, public opinion is quite capable of thinking he is a good minister.

Thus, when Jacob's son drove through the streets of Weset, the populace greeted him with lifted hands and shouted: "Adon! Adon! Ka-ne-Keme! Live for ever, friend of the harvest of God!" Many even cried: "Hapi! Hapi!" and carried their right hands, thumb and forefinger pressed together, to their mouths—which was going rather far, and

174

must be ascribed in large part to their childish enthusiasm for his handsome person.

But he very seldom drove out, being exceedingly busy.

URIM AND THUMMIM

Whatever we do in life is determined by fundamental tastes and sympathies, by deep-lying private destinies which colour our whole existence and dye all our doing. These are responsible for our acts—these and not any of the reasonable grounds we are likely to adduce to others and to ourselves. The King's chief mouthpiece and overseer of all his stores, a short time after he entered office—very much against Pharaoh's wish, who would gladly have kept his new friend near him for discourse about his Father who was in heaven and with his help to labour on the improvement of the teaching—moved his residence and all his offices from Nowet-Amun, the capital, to Menfe in the north, home of the Swaddled One. The external but probably quite justifiable ground for the change lay in the fact that thick-walled Menfe was "the balance of the lands," the centre and symbol of the equilibrium of Egypt and well suited for the residence of the master of the survey. Of course, that about the balance of the lands was not strictly accurate; Menfe lay really quite far north, near On, the city of the blinking and the cities of the seven mouths. If one reckoned that Egypt reached only to the Elephant Isle and the island Pi-lak and did not count Negritia, then the city of King Mira, where his beauty lay buried, was by no means the balance of the lands, but lay as much too far north as Thebes lay too far south. Nevertheless, age-old Menfe continued to be thought of as the balance; and it was axiomatic that it held a commanding position and was a point of vantage for both upstream and down. At any rate, such was the argument upon which the Egyptian Joseph based his decision, and Pharaoh himself could not deny that the trade with the Syrian port cities, when they sent down into the granary, as they called the land of the black earth, to buy grain, was easier from Menfe than from Per-Amun.

All this was perfectly true. And yet these were only the external, the rational grounds for Joseph's decision to get Pharaoh's permission to live in Menfe. The real and decisive reasons were in his heart, where they lay

175

so deep and reached so far that they involved his whole attitude to life and death.

It is long, long since, but we can all remember how once as a lad, alone and dispirited, at odds with his brothers, he had looked down from the hill by Kirjath Arba upon the moon-white town in the valley and upon Machpelach, the twofold hollow, the rock-tomb which Abram had bought and where the bones of his ancestors rested. We recall the strange medley of feelings in his soul aroused by sight of the tomb and of the populous town lying there asleep: feelings of piety, which is reverence for death and the past, mingled with a half-mocking, half-fascinated drawing to the "city" and the busy human life which all day long filled the crooked streets of Hebron with clamour and reek, and at that hour lay snoring in its chambers with its knees drawn up. It may seem bold and arbitrary to connect such feelings, which after all were so early and so momentary, with the considered conduct of his present age. And probably still more rash to make the latter depend on the former. Yet there is some evidence in favour of the association: I mean the remark which Joseph later made to the old man, his purchaser, when they were together in Menfe, the metropolis. He had idly said that he liked the place, whose dead had not to ferry over the water because they were already west of the river; and remarked that among the cities of Egypt this one pleased him most. That was entirely characteristic of Rachel's eldest, far more than he realized himself. He had taken great pleasure in the way the little people of Menfe, in a mocking spirit preserved in the midst of their monotony, had blithely shortened the ancient grave-name of the city Men-nefru-Mire to Menfe. And this pleasure was almost Joseph himself, it revealed the deepest depth of his nature. We call that feeling of his by the name of sympathy, a rather tame word for so profound an emotion as it actually is. For sympathy is a meeting of life and death; true sympathy exists only where the feeling for the one balances the feeling for the other. Feeling for death by itself makes for rigidity and gloom; feeling for life by itself, for flat mediocrity and dull-wittedness. Wit and sympathy can arise only where veneration for death is moderated, has, so to speak, the chill taken off by friendliness to life; while life, on the other hand, acquires depth and poignancy. This happened in Joseph's case; and his shrewd and friendly temper was the result. This was the blessing, the double blessing with which he was blessed from the heights above and the depths which lay beneath; the blessing which Jacob, his father, launched into on his death-bed, behaving as though he then gave and conferred it, whereas after all he was only reasserting an already accomplished fact. Any attempt to examine the moral foundations of our exceedingly complicated world requires a certain amount of learning. Of Jacob it had always been said that he was "*tam*," meaning that he was upright, and that he dwelt in tents. But *tam* is an equivocal word, not properly rendered by "upright." It is both positive and negative, it is yes and no, light and darkness, life and death. It turns up again in the curious formula "Urim and Thummim," where in contrast to the light, affirmative Urim it obviously stands for the dark, death-shadowed aspect of the world. Tam, or Thummim, is the light-and-dark, the upper and the under world at once and by turns; and Urim only the light, as distinguished in pure usage. So "Urim and Thummim" does not actually express a contradiction; it only exhibits the mysterious truth that when one separates a part from the whole of the moral world, the whole always stands opposed to the part. It is not so easy to make head or tail of the moral world, first of all because what is sunshiny in it refers to the underworldly. Esau, for instance, the Red One, was distinctly a sun-man of the lower world. And Jacob, his younger twin, set off against Esau as a mild moon-shepherd, did, we must remember, spend the better part of his life in the underworld with Laban, and the means he used there to become gold and silver are very inaccurately described by the word "upright." Urim he was certainly not; but *tam* precisely describes him: a glad-sorry man, like Gilgamesh. And Joseph was that too, whose rapid adaptation to the sunny underworld of Egypt as little indicates a Urim-nature pure and simple. "Urim and Thummim" might be rendered as yes—yes-no; that is, yes-no with the coefficient of a second yes. Mathematically speaking, after the yes and the no have cancelled each other out, only the second yes is left; but the purely mathematical has no coloration at all, or at least it ignores the dark tone of the resultant yes, which is obviously an after-effect of the eliminated no. All that is, as I said, involved. We do better merely to repeat that in Joseph life and death met, and the result was that sympathy which was the profounder reason why he asked Pharaoh's permission to live in Menfe, that sprightly metropolis of tombs.

The King had first of all taken thought for the eternal dwelling of his "universal friend," and it was already under way. He now gave Joseph a residence in the dearest quarter of Menfe: a sunny dwelling-house, with garden, reception-hall, fountain court, and all the amenities of that late-early time, not to mention a host of Nubian and Egyptian servants, for kitchen, vestibule, stable, and hall, who swept and garnished and sprinkled the villa and adorned it with flowers, under the supervision of —guess whom? But of course even the slowest in the uptake must have known long ago. For Joseph kept his word more punctually and punctiliously than Nefer-em-Wese, the cup-bearer, had kept his: he straightway honoured the promise he had made to somebody when they parted: that he would send after him and take him to himself whenever he should be lifted up. While he was still in Thebes, immediately after he got back from his tour of inspection, with Pharaoh's approval he wrote to Mai-Sachme, the warden at Zawi-Re, and invited him to be his house steward and head of his house and of all those matters which such a man as Joseph now was could not take on himself. Yes, he who had once been overseer in Petepre's house and to whom a so much greater charge had now fallen, he himself had an overseer over everything that was his: wagons and horses, storerooms, house servants, scribes, and slaves. And that was Mai-Sachme, the imperturbable, who was not startled when the letter of his former convict reached him, if only because it was not given him to be startled. Nevertheless, he did not even wait for his successor to arrive at the prison, but betook himself by leaps and bounds to Menfe—a somewhat out-of-date city, of course, quite over-crowded by Thebes in Upper Egypt, but in comparison with Zawi-Re immensely stimulating. Imhotep, the wise, the many-sided, had lived and worked there; and now Imhotep's great admirer had been beckoned hither to a splendid post. Mai-Sachme put himself at once at the head of Joseph's house, assembled the staff, bought, furnished, and bestowed; so that when Joseph came down from Wese and Mai-Sachme met him at his own beautiful gateway, he found his house equipped in every detail as the residence of a great man. He even found an infirmary ready for such as would wreathe and wind, and a pharmacy where his overseer might mix and triturate to his heart's content.

The meeting was most cordial, though of course the two could not embrace in view of the surrounding staff. The embrace had taken place once for all when they parted, in the only moment proper to it, when Joseph was no longer Mai-Sachme's servant but not yet Mai-Sachme's lord. The steward said:

"Welcome, Adon; lo, here is your house. Pharaoh gave it, and he whom you command commanded it, down to the smallest detail. You need only go to the bath, be anointed, sit down, and eat. But I thank you very much for thinking of me and pulling me out of my tedium directly you sat in glory, and now everything has come out as your servant always imagined it would, and you have called me to share your varied and diverting life, which I shall strive to deserve."

Joseph replied:

"And in my turn I thank you, you good soul, for answering my call and being willing to be my housekeeper in this new life. It came as it has come, because I never offended my father's God by the smallest doubt that He would be with me. But do not call yourself my servant, for we shall be friends as we were before, when I was beneath your feet; and together shall we meet the good and bad hours of life, the exciting and the unexciting. There will certainly be both, and I need you most for the exciting ones. For your careful oversight I thank you in advance. But it must not consume you to the extent that you have no leisure to guide the reed in your study as you love to do, to find the right and fitting form for the story of the three love-affairs. Great is the writer's art! But truly I find it greater yet to live in a story; this that we are in is certainly a capital one, of that I am more and more convinced the longer I live. And now you are in it with me because I brought you; and when in the future people hear or read of the steward who was with me and at my side in exciting moments, they will know that this steward was you, Mai-Sachme, the man of poise."

THE MAIDEN

Once in the beginning God made a deep sleep to fall upon the man he had set in the garden in the East, and while the man slept God took out one of his ribs and closed the place up with flesh. But out of the rib He made a woman, in the opinion that it was not good for man to be alone, and presented her to the man that she should be about him for company and help. And it was very well meant.

Our teachers have painted this presentation in very fine colours: thus and so, they say, it happened; they behave as though they knew all about it—and it may be they really do know. God washed the woman, they assure us, He washed her clear, for naturally she was a bit sticky, anointed her, rouged her face, curled her hair, and at her urgent plea adorned her head, neck, and arms with beads and precious stones, among them sardonyx, topaz, diamond, jasper, turquoise, amethyst, emerald, and onyx. He brought her, thus embellished, before Adam, with a choir of thousands of angels singing and playing on their lutes, to present her to the man. Then there was a feast and a feasting, that is to say a festal meal, of which it seems God Himself most affably partook, and the stars danced together, to the music they themselves made.

That was the first great wedding feast; but we do not hear that it was also straightway a marriage. God made the woman for a helper to Adam, simply in order that she might be about him, and had obviously thought no more about it. That she should bear children in suffering He only inflicted upon her after she and Adam had eaten of the tree and their eyes had been opened. Between the feast of the presentation and the time when Adam knew his wife and she bore him the farmer and the shepherd, in whose footsteps Jacob and Esau walked, between these comes the story of the tree and the fruit and the serpent and the knowledge of good and evil. For Joseph too it came in this order. He too knew the woman only after he had learned what good and evil are, of a serpent who would have given her life to teach him what is very, very good but yet evil. But he resisted her, and had the art to wait until it was good and no longer evil.

How can we help thinking sadly of the poor serpent now, at the moment when the sun-dial points to the hour of Joseph's marriage, which he made with another woman and put heads and feet together with her instead of with the serpent? I have sought to forestall that natural sadness by speaking first of her, how that by now she had become once more a cool moon-nut, to whom the whole affair no longer mattered. It is easier to think of her thus; our faint remaining bitterness is quenched in the picture of her as the bigoted priestess she had now become. Besides, her tranquillity was in no danger of being disturbed by the wedding, for that took place not in Thebes but far away at Joseph's house in Menfe. Pharaoh, who had been zealous in the affair from the beginning, came down in person to the festivities and most affably sat by while the stars danced in their courses. He quite literally took on the role of God, being profoundly convinced that it is not good for man to be alone. He had told Joseph almost at once how pleasant it was to be married, and, unlike God, he spoke from experience, for he had Nefertiti, his little dawn-cloud, gold-edged, whereas God was always alone and His concern was only for all mankind. But Pharaoh, like God in this, had concern for Joseph too. So as soon as he had exalted him, he began to look about for a state alliance, which was to be just that; that is to say, very aristocratically and politically conceived, yet pleasant and enjoyable too—not such a simple combination. But as God for Adam, so Pharaoh produced his creature the bride, led her to Joseph to the sound of harps and cymbals, and himself took part in the wedding feast.

Now who was this bride, Joseph's graceful consort, and what was her name? Everybody knows; but that does not lessen the pleasure of telling or hearing it. It may be possible that somebody had forgotten it or no longer knows that he knows it, and would not know what to say if asked. Her name, then, was Asenath, the maid, daughter of the sun-priest at On. Yes, Pharaoh had gone high, higher he could not have gone. To marry the daughter of the head priest among those who served Re-Horakhte—it was a thing unheard of, it bordered on sacrilege, although of course the girl was destined in any case for marriage and motherhood, and nobody in the least wanted her to live a cloistered life and die unwed. On the other hand, however desirable and proper it was that she be wed, yet whoever should capture her was thought of as a dark, equivocal phenomenon; he was an abductor, and she was not given but snatched—that was the attitude in her circle, though actually everything went off with the utmost propriety and according to all the conventions. But never parents in the world made more to-do about handing a child over to a husband. The mother in particular was or affected to be quite beside herself. She could not talk enough about her inability to grasp what was happening; she wrung her hands and behaved as though she herself had been or was going to be raped. She even made vows of vengeance, though less because she really meant them than because they were the proper thing under the circumstances. Now, the reason for all this was that the virginity of the daughter of the sun, though in the last analysis destined for the common lot, was invested with the shield and buckler of a peculiar sacredness and inviolability. She was uniquely girdled with the virgin girdle, she was the virgin of virgins, the idea, so to speak, of a virgin: quite especially and exclusively maid, the essence of maidenhood. In her case the common noun became proper: "Maiden" she was called all her life; and the husband who should make theft of her maidenhead would be to the average mind committing a godlike crime, though actually less criminal for being so godlike. The relation of the son-in-law to the parents of the girl, particularly to the hand-wringing mother, might be in private perfectly friendly; but in public it was a case of strained relations, in order to bear out the theory that in a sense they never consented to let their daughter belong to her husband. Indeed, in the marriage contract the condition was expressly stated that the child should not live all the year round with her sinister brigand, but should return and live as a maid with her parents for a certain by no means small part of each year. But here again the condition was symbolic rather than literal; its fulfilment only meant that the bride, in quite normal and regular way, paid visits to her parents' house after she was married.

If the high-priest and his wife had had several daughters, still these arrangements would refer primarily to the eldest, and to the others in much lesser degree. But sixteen-year-old Asenath was their only child. Think, then, of what godlike violence and unnatural crime was this man guilty who wedded her! Her father, Horakhte's chief prophet, was of course not the same gentle old greybeard who at the time of Joseph's first visit to On, with the Ishmaelites, had occupied the golden chair at the foot of the great obelisk in front of the winged disk of the sun. He was that man's elected successor, likewise gentle, benevolent, and blithe of countenance; for thus had every servant of Atum-Re to be by virtue of his office; and if he was not by nature thus, then by some necessary disguise he had to become so by second nature. Chance willed it that this priest, as we are aware, had the same name as Joseph's former owner, the courtier of light, namely Potipherah or Petepre—and what name could be better for him in his office than "The sun gave him"? The name indicates that he was born and destined for the office. Presumably he was the son of that old man in the little gold cap, and Asenath, accordingly, his granddaughter. As for her name, written Ns-nt, it was connected with the goddess Neith from Sais in the Delta; it meant "She who belongs to Neith," and the maiden was under the special protection of that armed goddess, whose emblem was a shield with two arrows fastened crosswise on it, and who even in human guise usually wore a cluster of arrows on her head.

Asenath did. Her hair, or rather the conventional wig she wore over it, the construction of which left it a little uncertain whether it was a

182

coiffure or a head-dress, was always adorned with arrows either thrust through or fastened on top; while the shield, in token of her peculiar virginity, appeared as an ornament, at throat or waist or on her arm-bands, accenting, together with the crossed arrows, the inviolable character of her maidenhood.

Despite all this armour and outward emphasis upon her inward resistance, Asenath was a charming child, highly sweet-natured, gentle and biddable, obedient to the wishes of her aristocratic parents, to Pharaoh's will, and to her husband's—even to the point of having none of her own. It was precisely this combination of sacred and inviolate purity with a definite tendency to let people do what they would with her, a tolerant acceptance of her feminine lot, which was the essence of Asenath's character. Her face was typically Egyptian in shape, small-boned, with somewhat prominent lower jaw; but it did not lack individuality. The cheeks still had their child-like roundness, the lips were full too, with a soft hollow between mouth and chin; the forehead chaste, the little nose perhaps a thought too thick; the large, beautifully painted eyes had that peculiarly fixed and expectant gaze which is typical of the deaf; but Asenath was not deaf, her gaze only reflected her inner expectancy. It was as though, with conscious readiness and acceptance, she was waiting for the hour of her destiny to strike. This faint unearthliness in her face was more than made good by the dimple coming and going in one cheek as she talked—the whole effect was rarely charming.

Charming and a little unusual her figure was too, as seen through the spun air of her garment: the waist exceptionally small and wasplike, the hips and abdominal cavity by contrast ample and spreading, a good womb for child-bearing; the breasts stood out like little twin bucklers, the arms were slender and shapely, with large hands which she habitually held with the fingers spread out. Portrait of a maiden in amber—such was the whole impression Asenath gave.

Until her marriage she had led among flowers a life like theirs. Her favourite spot was the lake shore in her father's temple grounds, a rolling meadowy stretch carpeted with narcissus and anemones where she loved to wander by the mirrorlike waters with her playmates, the little daughters of the priests and the aristocracy of On. There she plucked her flowers, sat in the grass, and wound her garlands, her listening look fixed upon space, the brows lifted, the dimple coming and going in her chin, wholly expectant of what should come. And then it came: for one day Pharaoh's messengers appeared on the scene. From Potipherah, father and priest, heavily nodding assent, and from the mother, who was quite beside herself and wrung her hands, they demanded the virgin Asenath for wife to Dgepnuteefonech, Vice-Horus and shadow-dispenser of the King. She herself, possessed by the one idea of her existence, flung up her arms to heaven imploring aid. But they snatched her round her tiny waist and tore her away.

All that was just a farce, a symbolic performance dictated by convention. For not only were Pharaoh's wishes law, but a marriage with his favourite and first mouthpiece was highly honourable and desirable and the parents could not have looked higher for their child than Pharaoh had looked for Joseph; so there was no reason at all for desperation or even for grief going beyond the natural pain of parents at parting from their only child. But there had to be much ado made over Asenath's virginity and the theft of it; it was necessary to portray the bridegroom as a sinister character, however pleased the parents had reason to be and in fact probably were. Pharaoh had expressly given out that virginity here espoused virginity: that the bridegroom too was in his way a virgin, long wooed and set apart, a bride whence now the wooer issued. To this end he had had to arrange matters with the God of his fathers, the bridegroom of his race, whose jealousy he had long spared but now no longer spared, or spared only in so far as he was making a very special kind of marriage, a proper virgin marriage—if that helped matters any. We, of course, need feel no concern, despite all the implications of the step; for Joseph was making an Egyptian marriage, a marriage with Sheol, an Ishmael marriage, and thus a marriage not without a precedent, though a doubtful one, in need of all the consideration which, it appears, it was sure to receive. Our teachers and expounders have many of them taken exception to this marriage of Joseph's and even sought to deny the fact. In the interest of purity they have put it about that Asenath was not the child of Potipherah and his wife but a foundling and no other than the offspring of Jacob's own unhappy daughter Dinah, exposed and found floating in a basket. According to this theory, Joseph took his own niece to wife; which even if it were true would not greatly improve matters, because half of Dinah's child was flesh and blood of the fidgety Sichem, a Baal-worshipping Canaanite. Anyhow our reverence for our teachers must not prevent us from pronouncing the story of the child in the basket to be what it is, an interpolation and pious fraud. Asenath

184

the maiden was the real child of Potipherah and his wife, of pure Egyptian blood, and the sons she was to present to Joseph, his sons and heirs Ephraim and Manasseh, were, whether we like it or not, simply half-Egyptian by blood. And even that was not all. For by his marriage with the daughter of the sun Israel's son came into close relations with the temple of Atum-Re—priestly relations in fact, as had been part of Pharaoh's plan when he arranged the marriage. It was almost unthinkable that a man as high in government preferment as Joseph was should not at the same time have performed a higher priestly function and drawn a temple revenue, and—again whether we like it or not—Joseph, as Asenath's husband, did both. In other words and to put it rather baldly, he had an income from the idolaters. To his official wardrobe henceforth belonged the priestly leopard-skin and under certain circumstances he was liable to burn incense officially before an image—that of the falcon Horakhte with the sun-disk on its head.

These things have been well understood by but very few people; to have them thus clearly stated may come as a shock. But it is quite clear that for Joseph the day of enfranchisement was now come; and we may be sure that he had known how to reach an understanding with Him who had parted him from his own, transplanted him to Egypt, and made him great there. Perhaps we have here an application of the philosophy of the triangle, according to which a sacrifice at the alabaster table of the complaisant Horakhte meant no derogation from any other godhead. And after all this was not just any temple; it was the temple of the god of the far horizon; Joseph might put to himself that it would have been a mistake, a piece of foolishness, in other words a sin, to ascribe to the God of his fathers a narrower horizon than to Atum-Re. And finally we must not forget that the Aton had of late emerged out of this god; in the conversation between Pharaoh and Joseph it had transpired that one properly invoked him not by the name Aton but as the Lord of Aton; not as "our Father above" but as "our Father who art *in* heaven." All this may have passed comfortably through Joseph's mind when on certain rare occasions he put on his leopard-skin and went to burn incense.

All in all Rachel's eldest, Jacob's parted darling, was definitely a very special case. The indulgence vouchsafed him took account of the things of this world; and that in turn prevented things from ever coming to a tribe of Joseph as it did to a tribe even of Issachar, Dan, and Gad. His role, his place in the plan, was that of a man set in the great world to be, as we shall see, guardian, provider, and saviour of his own. There is every reason to think that he was aware of this function, at least emotionally, and thought of his own exiled and cosmopolitan existence not as that of an outcast but as that of a man set apart for a purpose. Undoubtedly this is the explanation of his supreme confidence that the Master of the Plan would treat him with due consideration and forbearance.

JOSEPH TAKES A BRIDE

Well then, Asenath the maiden, accompanied by twenty-four selected slaves, was sent up to Menfe to her virgin marriage in Joseph's house. The high-priestly pair, bowed down with grief at this incredible abduction, travelled up from On; and Pharaoh himself travelled down from Nowet-Amun, to partake in the mysteries of the wedding feast, personally to present this exceptional bride to his favourite and as an experienced married man to assure him of the amenities procured by the married state. It should be said that twelve of the twenty-four young and beautiful maidservants who came with Asenath and with her passed into the possession of the sinister bridegroom (involuntarily one thinks of the retinue which in former times used to attend a king living into his tomb), twelve of them were there to make music, dance, and jubilate, the other twelve to lament and beat their breasts. For the wedding ceremonies as they were celebrated in the torch-lit fountain court and adjacent rooms of Joseph's palatial house had a strongly funereal flavour; that we do not go into them with the last degree of exactitude is due to a kind of consideration for old Jacob back there at home, deluding himself in the belief that his darling was treasured up in death and permanently seventeen. Jacob would assuredly have flung up his hands at the sight of much that happened at the wedding. It would have confirmed him in his honest prejudices against Mizraim, the land of mud, prejudices which we would wish to respect and so do not describe the occasion with such particularity as to imply that we approve of what went on.

Behind his back we may agree that there does exist a certain relation between death and marriage, a bridal chamber and a tomb, a murder and the abduction of a virgin. It is no great strain to think of a bridegroom as a god of death. And there is a likeness between the fate of

the maiden, who, a veiled sacrifice, steps across the serious divide between maidhood and wifehood, and the fate of the seed-corn buried
in the darkness there to rot and then out of corruption to come back to
the light as just such another seed-corn, virgin and new. The resemblance
is an accepted one; just as we admit the ear mown down by the sickle
to be a painful parable of the daughter snatched out of her mother's arms,
who herself was once virgin and sacrifice, once also mown down by the
sickle and now in her daughter's fate reliving her own.

The sickle in fact played a prominent part in the decorations provided
by Mai-Sachme for the great occasion. The symbolism of the corn, the
grain, and the sown field was ingeniously used in the fountain court and
the peristyle round it; as likewise in the entertainment offered the guests
before and after the ceremony: men strewed corn on the pavement and
poured water on it out of jars, with ritual shoutings; women bore vessels
on their hips, one side filled with corn, the other with a little burning
torch. Since the festivities were in the evening there were many torches
everywhere throughout the rooms, which were hung with coloured draperies and garlands of myrtle. The torches were of course; yet there
was such lavish use of them that here too the decoration verged on the
symbolic. A torch in fact is used to give light where there is no daylight.
The bride's mother, Potiphar's wife (if one may speak of her thus without confusion), entirely shrouded in a deep-violet mantle, a perfect
tragic muse, carried part of the time a torch in each hand or even two
in one hand. And everyone, male and female, bore torches in the great
procession which was the climax of the evening. Torch in hand, they
moved in a long line through all the rooms in the house and then into
the fountain court, where Pharaoh, the most exalted guest, sat in an easy
attitude between Joseph and Asenath (also shrouded in a violet veil).
In the fountain court the procession broke up into an ingenious and
remarkable dance—or rather broke out, for the flaming smoking line
of dancers remained still one behind another and moved in a ninefold
spiral to their own left around the fountain. In all the labyrinthine in-
volutions the line was kept by a red ribbon running through the hands
of the dancers; which did not prevent them from executing their crowning marvel of pyrotechnic skill, for the blazing torches themselves
danced, tossed and caught from outside to inside of the ninefold coil,
without a single one missing its goal or falling to the ground.

One must have seen that, in order to share the writer's temptation to describe it in more detail than suits with the thought of the old man at home. He would surely have taken some pleasure in the skilful dance at least, purely as a spectacle, certainly much more than in some other manifestations. He saw things through a father's eye; and he would have disapproved—to put it mildly—of the prominent part played by the maternal element at his son's wedding; by the mother of Asenath, storming and threatening and figuring in her own person both the bereft and the beraped. Again, most of the men and youths taking part in the grand procession and the spiral dance were dressed as women in garb like the bride-mother—and that, of course, in the eyes of the good Jacob would have been a Baal-abomination. Apparently they were considered to represent her and to enter into her feelings; for the same violet veil flowed about them and they gave vent in the same way to anger, taking the torch in the left hand in order to shake the right fist in the air; the gesture was the more alarming because these figures wore masks, which bore no resemblance to the matronly countenance of Potiphar's wife, but had an expression of affliction and wrath to curdle one's blood. Some of them had stuffed out their mourning garments to look as though they were advanced in pregnancy; that is, they represented the mother, still—or once again—bearing the maiden sacrifice beneath her heart, or else the maiden there bearing a new sacrifice-maiden—probably they were not clear just what they did mean. Men and youths who thus distended their bodies—no, that would certainly have been nothing for Yakob ben Yitzschak. Nor must any further description of the wedding feast be construed as approval of the goings-on. But for Joseph, set apart and severed into the great world, the time of licence had come; his marriage itself was one great licence and we report on its details in the indulgent and forbearing spirit the occasion demands.

There was in short a certain abandon and on the other hand a savour of the grave—bespoken for instance by the myrtle wreaths with which all the guests and all the rooms in the house were adorned. Some of the guests even carried whole bunches of myrtles in their hands. For the myrtle is sacred both to love and to the dead. But the great procession had an equal number of performers with cymbals and tambourines, displaying joyous exultation in the same measure as the others did the postures and gestures of grief, as though they were walking in a funeral train. It must be added that each kind of performance showed various stages. For instance, certain groups of mourners merely wandered to

188

and fro with satchels and staves; they went aimlessly up to and past the royal seat, the wedding pair, and the high-priestly parents, without actual lamentation or shedding of tears. In the same way there were various degrees of rejoicing, some of them quite dignified and pleasing; as, for instance, a group would advance to the seats of honour bearing jugs of graceful shape, and turn them ceremonially upside down to east and west, chanting antiphonally: "Overflow!" "Receive the blessing!" So far so good. But often, and more and more as the evening wore on, the laughter and rejoicing rather coarsely betrayed the real idea at the bottom of a wedding feast, the thought of what was naturally to follow. One might put it that the idea of abduction and murder and the idea of fertility came together and flowed into licence; so that the air was full of offensive innuendo, of winking, obscene allusions, and roars of laughter. Animals had been led about in the procession, among them a swan and a stallion, at sight of which the bride's mother shrouded herself more closely in her purple veil. But what shall we say to the appearance of a pregnant sow, actually with a rider in the shape of a fat, half-naked old woman with an equivocal cast of countenance who gave out a stream of bad jokes! This offensive old female played a familiar, popular, and important role in the whole performance. She had accompanied Asenath's mother from On and had been whispering lewd jokes the whole time into the lady's ear in order to cheer her up on the journey. This was her function and her role. She was called the comforter; in the prevailing high spirits the name was constantly shouted at her and she answered with coarse gestures. During the whole evening she scarcely stirred from the side of the theoretically inconsolable one, striving none the less to console her—that is, to make her laugh by whispering an inexhaustible flow of indecency into her ear—and she succeeded too, because that was the pattern: the offended, furious, and ostensibly outraged mother did really from time to time titter into the folds of her veil at what she heard. Then all the assemblage laughed too and applauded the "comforter." But as the mother's anger and grief were only put on, being largely a matter of convention, we may assume that the tittering too was merely a concession to old practice and that she would herself have felt only disgust at the antics of the comforter. At most her amusement might be as much and as little unfeigned as is the natural and not conventionally exaggerated grief of a mother at losing her only daughter to a husband.

Enough has been said to justify the good sense of not going into the details of Joseph's wedding feast. Even if we sin against our own intentions, that does not mean we approve. The young pair themselves, clasping hands across Pharaoh's knees, were almost indifferent to the whole scene, looking at each other instead of at the indispensable scenes enacted before their eyes. Joseph and Asenath were attracted to each other from the first, and felt delight each in the other's company. Of course, this was a prearranged state marriage, and into such an arrangement, at least at first, love does not come. It has to find itself, and with well-constituted people it does so in time. The mere knowledge that they belong together helps; but in this case other circumstances favoured the growth of feeling. Over and above her natural passive readiness, Asenath the maid had gone some way toward accepting her lot in the person of this abductor and murderer of her maidenhead, who had clutched her round a waist that seemed to be made tiny on purpose, and made off with her into his realm. Already she felt drawn to Pharaoh's dark, handsome, wise, and kindly minister, and did not doubt that liking could grow into a stronger bond; while the thought that he would be the father of her children was like a mussel-shell in which the pearl of love should grow. Not otherwise was it with Joseph. The set-apart one, in this situation of special licence, admired God's large, worldly-wise freedom from prejudice—as though the eternal wisdom had not always taken account of his own worldliness—and left it to Him to cope with the delicate question what relation the children of Sheol who would be born of this marriage were to bear to the Chosen Seed. But we cannot blame this virgin wooer that his thoughts were less on the expected children than they were on the till now forbidden mysteries to which they would owe their existence. What had once been evil and forbidden was now good. But look upon this being through whom evil becomes good; look well upon her, and especially because she has such listening eyes and so speaking an amber-tinted shape as had Asenath the maiden, and you will be sure that you will love her; nay, that you already do.

Pharaoh walked between them when at last the feast ended and the procession re-formed. It now included all those present, who with jubilation and lamentation, with myrtle-strewing and the fist-shaking of the masked mothers, took their way to the bridal chamber, where the newly-wed pair were put to bed among flowers and fine linen. The sow-rider stood just behind the daughter of the sun-priest as the parents, murmuring the prescribed sayings, took leave on the threshold of Asenath the maid. Over the bride's shoulder the old hag murmured such things as made the anguished mother laugh amid her tears. And shall we too not both laugh and weep, is there not food for both laughter and tears, in the thought of what nature has contrived for mankind, and after what fashion she wills that they seal their love—or, in case of a state marriage, of course, learn to love? The sublime and the ridiculous flickered in the lamplight of this wedding night where virginity met virginity and wreath and veil were torn—a difficult work of tearing it was. For this was a shield-maid whom the dark arms embraced, expressly so designated, an obstinate virgin; and in blood and pain Joseph's first-born was conceived, Manasseh, a name which means: "God has made me forget all my connections and my father's house."

CLOUDS IN THE SKY

It was the year one of the fat kine and the full ears. Of course the customary reckoning was from the year of the god's accession; but among the children of Egypt the new method now began to run concurrently. The fulfilment had, actually, set in before the prophecy. But only in the following year did it begin in a way to carry conviction; for that year far exceeded the preceding one in richness; and whereas the first had been merely somewhat above the average, the second proved to be a veritable year of marvels, magnificence, and jubilation, fertile past all expectation in every line. The Nile had got very fine and large—not wild and swollen, tearing away the farmer's fields, yet not a single fraction lower than the best year on record. It lay over the expanse of fields and quietly deposited its dung; it made one laugh to see the splendour of the flourishing land toward the end of the sowing season, and the abundant riches gathered in during the third quarter. The next year was not quite so luxuriant, it was more or less average, it was gratifying, it was even commendable, without being at all surprising. But the next one almost equalled the second and was quite as good as the first, while the fourth merited the adjective "capital," if no more. So we can imagine how Joseph's reputation, as the overseer of all that plenty, waxed among the people, and with what zealous, joyful punctuality his ground-rent law, the tax of the fifth, was carried through, not less by the taxed than by the tax officials. "And he gathered up all the food of the seven years which were in the land of Egypt and laid up the food in the cities, the food of the field which was round about every city laid he up in the same." In other words, the grain tribute of all the land round, year in, year out, streamed into the fabulous skittle-shaped granaries which Adon had built in all the cities and their environs; not too many of them, as it turned out, for they got filled and more and more had to be built to meet the incoming tribute. So well did Hapi the Nourisher mean by his land. The heaping up was in truth like the sands of the sea, song and saga are quite correct. But when they add that "they left numbering, for it was without number," that is an exaggeration due to enthusiasm. The children of Egypt never stopped counting, writing down, and book-keeping, it was not in their nature and did not happen. Though the full-ness of the provision was indeed as the sands of the sea, yet these worshippers of the white ape held it to be their first and finest pre-occupation to cover paper with the close-written calculations and detailed accountings which Joseph exacted from his collectors and in-spectors throughout the period.

They counted five years of abundance; some people, even many people, counted seven. It is idle to dispute the point. Observers who stuck to the five may have been thinking of the five extra days in the year and the tax quota based on that figure. On the other hand, five years of fatness one after another are so joyful in themselves that it would be easy to celebrate by calling them seven. Yes, it is possible to make five out of seven; yet after all a bit more human to make seven out of five— the narrator frankly confesses his uncertainty, for it is not his way to pretend to knowledge where he has not got it. The same thing applies to the admission that we do not know exactly how old Joseph was at a certain point during the period of scarcity. He may have been either thirty-seven or thirty-nine. It is certain that he was thirty when he stood before Pharaoh: objectively certain, from our own point of view, for it is doubtful if he himself knew. But what he was at that later, crucial moment, whether only in his latish thirties or already as good as forty, we do not know, and must be reconciled to the uncertainty. He, of course, a child of his time and place, gave the matter little thought, or none at all.

Anyhow, he was now in the prime of life. If as a boy he had been stolen away into Babylonia instead of Egypt, he would long ago have assumed a full black beard, curled and pomaded; an appendage which would have helped him not a little in a certain game he was to play. But we can be grateful to the Egyptian custom that kept the Rachel-face free of beard. Even so, he succeeded in the game, and that shows how much the chiselling hand of time, the change of matter, the sun of his adopted land had worked upon his original characteristics to change them.

Joseph's figure, up till the time when he was drawn up out of his second pit to stand before Pharaoh, had remained quite youthful. After his marriage, during the fat years, when God made him fruitful in Asenath the maid and she bore him first Manasseh and then Ephraim in the women's quarters of his house, he grew a little heavier, perhaps a little too heavy, though not fat. He was tall enough to carry it off; his commanding presence, gentled by the shrewd and humorous glance of his black eyes and the charm of the smiling Rachel-mouth, accounted for the popular verdict that Joseph was an exceptionally handsome man. A thought too full-bodied, possibly, but definitely handsome.

His physical increase chimed with the period of general luxuriance. In fact the amazing increase of production showed itself in every direction: the herds, for instance, so multiplied that it reminded the educated of the words of the old song: "Thy goats shall bear twofold, thy sheep drop twins." And the women of Egypt too, in both city and country, bore—probably in consequence of better food—much oftener than usual. But nature, partly through the negligence of the overburdened mothers, partly through the incidence of new infant diseases, redressed the balance by an increase in infant mortality, so there was no danger of over-population. It was only the birth-rate that so strikingly increased.

Pharaoh too became a father. The mistress of the lands had already been expectant on the day of the interpretation; but there was a tendency to believe that its fulfilment was responsible for her happy delivery. It was the sweet princess Merytaton who now came into the world. The physicians, on æsthetic grounds, lengthened the still plastic skull almost excessively, and rejoicings were loud in the palace and throughout the land—the louder to conceal a disappointment at the failure of an heir to the throne. But not even later did one appear; Pharaoh, his life long, begot only daughters, six in all. Nobody knows the law determining sex: whether it is already present in the sperm or whether the balance after some wavering goes down on one side or the other. We can contribute no information on the subject; and neither could the wise men from Babel and On, not even among themselves. On the other hand, we can scarcely be argued out of the conviction that it was something about young Amenhotep himself which resulted in his exclusively female issue.

Be that as it may, the fact must have been a small, an unacknowledged cloudlet upon the King's wedded happiness, though of course the most tender mutual consideration prevailed at all times. Either of them might have said to the other what Jacob said to impatient Rachel: "Am I in God's stead, who hath withheld from thee thy heart's desire?" On one of the sweet princesses, the fourth, there was conferred out of sheer tenderness the title of the Queen of the Lands, Nefernefruaton, for her own name. But the fifth was given one almost identical, Nefernefrure —which would seem to be due to a flagging of interest. The names of the others, still showing some affectionate ingenuity, I could easily tell you too; but sharing the slight irritation which all this female preponderance is bound to set up, I feel no inclination to put them down.

Considering that Tiy, the great mother, still stood at the head of the house of the sun; that Queen Nefertiti had a sister, Nezemmut; that there was a still living sister of the King, the sweet princess Baketaton, and that to these in the course of the years were added the King's six daughters, we must envisage a regular women's court, where Meni was the only cock among a whole flock of hens; and this was not at all consonant with his phœnix-dream of an immaterial father-spirit of light. One is reminded of Joseph's remark during the famous conversation with Pharaoh—one of the best things he said—that the power which strove from below upwards into the purity of light must be truly power and of a masculine kind not mere tenderness.

A slight shadow, then, lay upon the royal happiness of Amenhotep and his golden pigeon, the sweet lady of the land, because no son was vouchsafed them. Joseph's marriage with Asenath the maid was also happy, happy and harmonious throughout, with a similar limitation: only sons were born to them, one, two, and later others on whom the light of history does not fall. In fact the abducted bride bore only sons and was grievously disappointed and probably her spouse as well, who would gladly have begot a daughter for her, at least one daughter! After all, the fact remains that a man can beget but not create. Asenath was simply possessed with the idea of a daughter: not just one daughter, but several; in fact she would have preferred nothing but daughters.

194

She who had been a virgin of the shield desired nothing more ardently than to raise up the same out of the depth of her own virginity. And she was abetted by her nagging mother, who persisted in the affronted pose she had assumed from the beginning and thus fomented a slight but permanent marital discord, always kept within bounds, of course, by affection and consideration.

This was probably at its height in the beginning, when Joseph's eldest son was born. Asenath's disappointment was acute, one might justly call it exaggerated, and it looks as though something of his annoyance at the reproaches he had to bear slipped into the name Joseph gave the child. "I have forgotten," he may have been trying to say, "all that lies behind me, and my father's house as well; but you and your offended mother, you act not only utterly disappointed but as though I were to blame to boot." Something of this kind may lie at the bottom of the strange choice of the name Manasseh; but it is well to add that we need not take the name or its meaning too seriously. If God had made Joseph forget all his past connections and his father's house, how then did the same Joseph come to give Hebrew names to his Egyptian sons? Was it because he could count on the foreign names being found elegant in the monkey-land of Egypt? No; it was because Jacob's son, however long he had been arrayed in the fleshly garment of an Egyptian, had not forgotten at all but had always in his mind what he said he had forgotten. The name Manasseh was nothing but a polite flourish; a case not of foolishness but the reverse, and an instance of the tact of which Joseph all his life long had been past master. It was a plain statement of the fact that God had snatched him away and transplanted him into the worldly sphere out of two motives, one of them jealousy, the other the comprehensive plan of deliverance. As to the second Joseph could only speculate. The first lay entirely open to his shrewd eyes, that saw far enough even to see through God's design and recognize that it was really the first and that the second only offered the means of uniting suffering and wisdom. The words "to see through" may seem irreverent in such a connection. But is there an activity more religious than studying the soul-life of God? To meet the politic of the Highest with an earthly one is indispensable if one wants to get on in life. If Joseph had been silent like the grave, and as the grave, to his father all these years, it was deliberate policy and understanding insight into the soul-life of the Highest that had enabled him to be so. And his name for his first-born

195

was in the same category. "If I am supposed to forget," the name was meant to say, "then lo, I have forgotten." But he had not.

In the third year of abundance Ephraim came into the world. The maiden-mother would not even look at him at first, and the mother-in-law was more out of temper than ever. But Joseph quite calmly gave him the name that meant: "God has made me to grow in the land of my banishment." He might well say so. He drove in his light car, accompanied by runners, acclaimed by Menfe's people in his name of Adon, to and fro between the splendid residence presided over by Mai-Sachme and his offices in the centre of the city, where three hundred clerks were at work; and gathered in stores until there was an abundance almost beyond keeping account of. He was a great man, the universal friend of a great king, Amenhotep IV, who by that time, to the furious chagrin of the temple of Karnak, had put aside his Amun-name and taken on that of Ikh-n-Aton ("It is pleasing to Aton"). He was also playing with the idea of leaving Thebes altogether and building himself a city dedicated entirely to Aton, where he thought to reside. Pharaoh, of course, wanted to see his shadow-dispenser of the teaching as often as possible to discuss with him about above and below. Likewise it could not fail to happen that Joseph, in pursuance of his great office, travelled several times in the year by land or water to Nowet-Amun to make report to Hor in the palace, when the two would spend hours in intimate talk. And Pharaoh too, on every trip to golden On, or when he drove forth to look for a proper site for his new city, the city of the horizon, would stop at Menfe and stay with Joseph. This of course put a heavy burden upon Mai-Sachme, though he never faltered in his perfect poise.

The friendship between the frail descendant of the pyramid-builders and Jacob's son, the foundations for which had been laid in the Cretan loggia, grew with the years into a warm and intimate bond. Young Pharaoh called Joseph his little uncle, and when he embraced him slapped him on the back. For this god was an enthusiast for informality, and it was Joseph who, out of native reserve, kept the balance in their relations. The King often laughed at the formality which his friend preserved in the midst of their familiar intercourse. They talked of their ill luck as fathers, that the one got only daughters, the other only sons. But the dissatisfaction of Joseph's wife and her nagging mother did little to dampen his joy in the grandsons of Jacob, who were growing up in the strange worldly world so far away from their grandsire. Equally the failure of a male heir could never depress Pharaoh's buoyant spirits for long at a time. Everything was going so wonderfully well in the maternal kingdom of the black earth that his reputation as the teacher of the fatherly light was strengthened mightily thereby, and he might sit in the shade of prosperity, giving witness to the God on whom his soul hung, and in speech as in solitude expending all his parts to think him better and better forth.

Debating thus, defining and comparing the high and holy properties of Pharaoh's father Aton, they might remind us of the religio-diplomatic exchanges which took place at Salem between Abram and Melchizedek the priest of El Elyon, the highest and also the only god; exchanges which ended in the agreement that this El was just the same, or pretty much the same, as Abram's God. It was noticeable, however, that it was always at the point where the discussion seemed to be approaching such an agreement that the courtly reserve which Joseph preserved in his relations with his exalted friend came out most plainly.

_____

Chapter Five

TAMAR

THE FOURTH

A WOMAN sat at the feet of Jacob the rich in tales, in the grove of Mamre at Hebron the city or close by, in the land of Canaan. Often she sat at his feet: either in the "house of hair," near the entrance, on the very spot where once the father had talked with his darling and been beguiled of the many-coloured coat; or else beneath the tree of enlightenment; or at the marge of the well close by, where first we met the subtle lad beneath the moon and watched the father go peering after him, leaning on his staff. How is it the woman sits with him now, in this place or that, her face lifted to his, and hearkens to his words? Whence comes she, this grave young creature so often found at his feet, and what sort of woman is she?

Her name was Tamar.—We look round at the faces of our hearers and see on but few, only here and there, the light of knowledge. Clearly the great majority of those who are here to learn the precise circumstances of this story do not recall, perhaps do not even know, the bare facts. We might be disposed to censure, did not the common ignorance jump with the advantage of the story-teller, by adding to the importance of his task. So you really no longer know, or to your knowledge never have known, who Tamar was? A Canaanite woman, simply a native, and in the first place no more than that. But in the second place Jacob's son's son's wife, daughter-in-law of Jehudah, Jacob's fourth, granddaughter-in-law, so to speak, of the man of the blessing. And in the third place, and finally, she was Jacob's devotee and his pupil in knowledge of the world and of God; who hung on his lips and looked up into his solemn face with such reverent attention that the heart of the bereaved old man opened utterly to her in turn, and he was even just a little in love with her. For Tamar's nature was strangely mingled, in a way even hard and heavy to herself: with a part of her being she was austere and

198

full of spiritual striving (to which later on we must give an even stronger name); but in the other gifted with the soul-and-body charm and mystery of Astarte. We know how receptive to such a combination a man can be, and to what advanced years, when like Jacob he has always yielded to and dignified his own emotions.

Since Joseph's death, or rather because of that lacerating event, which he seemed at first quite unable to accept, Jacob's personal majesty had only increased. Then, when once he got used to the fact and his wrangling with God had worn itself out, the Deity's cruel dispensation having at length worked its way into the mind so desperately shut against it, it became an enrichment of his life, an addition to its weight of history. By virtue of it his musing—when he fell into a musing fit—grew more expressively, more completely and picturesquely "musing" than ever, so that observers were seized with awe and whispered to one another: "Lo, Israel muses on his tales!" True it is, expression makes impression. The two have always gone together, and very likely the one has always had its eye on the other. That is nothing to laugh at, if the expression has behind it not mere humbug but real life experience and a burden of tales. In such a case the furthest we may go is a respectful smile.

Tamar, the native girl, knew naught of even such a smile. She was profoundly impressed by Jacob's majesty, directly she came in touch with him—and that had not come about merely through Judah, Leah's fourth, and his sons, two of whom she married one after the other. All this we know, as well as the sinister and half-equivocal accompanying circumstances, in other words the destruction of both Judah's sons. What is not known, since the chronicle passes it over, is Tamar's connection with Jacob, which after all is the indispensable premise of the whole episode and a remarkable secondary action within our whole history, which we interpolate while at the same time being aware that that history—which one may well call seductive, since it seduces us to such explicitness of detail—the history of Joseph and his brothers, is itself an interpolation in an epos incomparably vaster in scope.

Tamar, the native girl, daughter of quite simple Baal-farmers, moving within this episode of an episode—had she a notion of the fact? The answer is: quite certainly she had. Her own behaviour, which was deadly serious, gallant and offensive both at once, is evidence of the fact. It is not for nothing that the word I used above, the word "interpolation," keeps coming into my mind, as though it had a will of its own. Interpolation, insertion, pushing in: these form the motive of the hour, they were Tamar's watchword and mainspring. She was bent on pushing herself into the great history, and she did it, with amazing strength of purpose. It was the most spacious scene of which she had knowledge, and she would not, at any price whatsoever, be shut out of it. I think I also let fall the word "seduction"? There we have another key word; for it was by seduction that Tamar shoved herself into the great history of which this is an episode. She played the temptress and whored by the way, that she might not be shut out; she abased herself recklessly to be exalted. . . . How did that come about?

When first, or by what prosaic chance, Tamar got access to the friend of God and became his devotee no one precisely knows. Perhaps it happened before Joseph's death, and perhaps it was by Jacob's arrangement that she was taken into the tribe and given for wife to young Er, Judah's eldest. But the relation between her and the old man deepened and became intimacy only after the frightful blow had fallen and after Jacob's slow and unwilling recovery; only when his bereaved heart was unconsciously reaching for new emotional outlets. Then only did he become aware of Tamar, and drew her to himself because of her admiration for him.

By that time the eleven, his sons, were almost all married; the older ones long since, the younger more recently; and had children from their wives. Even Benoni-Benjamin, the little son of death, had come on in his turn—scarcely had he outgrown his urchinhood, become a youth, and then reached man's estate, seven years, perhaps, after the loss of his brother, when Jacob found and wooed for him first Mahalia, daughter of a certain Aram, of whom it was said that he was a "grandson of Terah" and so somehow or other descended from Abraham or from one of his brothers; and then the maid Arbath, daughter of a man named Simron, called quite explicitly a "son of Abram," which might mean that he came of that stock by some concubine. As for the pedigree of Jacob's daughters-in-law, the record has been both toned down and touched up and an effort made to show the blood kinship of the priestly stock, although the case had not a leg to stand on and was not even consistently attempted. Levi's and Issachar's wives were held to be "the granddaughters of Eber"—perhaps they were; even so they might have come from Assur or Elam. Gad and the glib Naphtali had followed their father's example and taken wives from Haran and Mesopotamia, but that these wives were actually great-granddaughters of Nahor, Abraham's uncle, they did not themselves assert, it was asserted of them. Asher the sweet-tooth took a nut-brown maid from the seed of Ishmael. Well, at least that was a relation, if a dubious one. Zebulon, of whom one might have expected a Phœnician marriage, actually went in unto a Midianite. This was correct only in so far as Midian was a son of Keturah, Abram's second wife; but had not big Reuben already gone and incontinently married a Canaanite woman? So too had Judah, as we know, and so Simeon, for his Bunah had been stolen from Shechem. As for Dan, Bilhah's son, whom they called snake and adder, his wife was well known to be a Moabitess, descended from that Moab whom Lot's eldest daughter had borne to her own father—and to herself her own brother. Not particularly wholesome, that; nor had it anything to do with blood kinship, since Lot had not been Abram's brother, but only a proselyte. From Adam, of course, he too descended and equally, of course, from Shem, since he came from the land of the two rivers. Blood kinship is always possible to demonstrate if one takes in enough of the picture.

So all the sons "brought their wives to their father's house," as we are told; in other words, the place of the tribe in the grove of Mamre near Kirjath Arba and the burying-ground, around Jacob's house of hair, grew larger as the days went on and descendants multiplied according to the promise, round Jacob's knees when the majestic greybeard permitted it, and in his goodness he sometimes did and fondled his grandchildren. Particularly Benjamin's he fondled. For Turturra, a stocky little fellow who still had his trustful grey eyes and heavy metallic helmet of hair, also a rather muddy complexion, had become father to five sons in quick succession, borne to him by his Aramaic wife as well as other little ones in between, born of the daughter of Simron; the grandchildren of Rachel were always Jacob's favourites. But despite their presence and Benoni's paternal dignity Jacob still treated his youngest like a child, kept him in leading-strings as though he were not grown up, and gave him very small freedom lest mischance befall him. Scarcely to go into the town, to Hebron, scarcely to the fields, to say nothing of making a trip across country, would he permit his one remaining pledge of Rachel's love; though he was far from loving Benoni as he had loved Joseph and there was no actual reason on his account to fear the jealousy of the Higher Power. Still, since the lovely one had fallen to the tooth of the swine, Benoni had become the only treasure of Jacob's care and concern, wherefore he did not let him out of his sight and would pass no hour without knowing where Benjamin was and what he was doing. Such supervision could not but be painful to Benjamin and wounding to his dignity as husband and father. Yet he bore with it, though it depressed him, and presented himself before his father several times a day in obedience to Jacob's whim; for if he did not, Jacob came himself on his long staff halting from his hip to see after him—although as Benjamin well knew and as was plain enough from the old man's capricious behaviour, Jacob's feelings were actually very divided, being a queer mixture of hidden grudge and sense of property. For at bottom he never ceased to see in Benoni the matricide and the instrument God had used to take Rachel from him.

One important advantage, certainly, besides that of being the youngest-born, Benoni had over all the living brothers; and for Jacob's dreamily associational mentality it made one more reason to keep his youngest always at home. For Benjamin had been at home when Joseph got lost in the world, and as we know Jacob, this equivalence between being at home and being innocent, having quite definitely no share in a crime committed from home, was symbolically well lodged in his mind. Thus Benjamin had always to be on hand as the sign and the permanent token of his guiltlessness and of the fact that he alone, the youngest, did not lie under the abiding, ever silently gnawing suspicion which both rightly and wrongly Jacob cherished and which the others knew that he cherished. It was the suspicion that the boar which had rent Joseph had been a beast with ten heads; and Benjamin had to be "at home" in token that the beast had quite definitely not had eleven.

But perhaps not even ten heads, God only knew, and He might keep it to Himself. Indeed, as the days and years went on, the question lost importance. It did so above all because Jacob, since he had stopped bickering with God, had gradually arrived at the view that it was not God who had by main strength laid upon him the sacrifice of Isaac, but that he himself had done it of his own free will. As long as the first agony lasted, such an idea had been far from him; he had only thought of himself as cruelly misused. But as the pain faded, habit set in, death made his advantage good—namely, that Joseph was safe in His bosom and care, for ever and ever seventeen years old—then this soft, pathetic soul had seriously begun to conceive itself capable of Abraham's deed of sacrifice. To the honour of God this fancy was born—and to Jacob's own. God had not monstrously and craftily robbed him of his dearest. He had but taken what, consciously and in heroic spirit, had been offered, the dearest thing that Jacob owned. Believe it or not, Jacob pretended to himself, and bore himself witness for the sake of his pride, that in the hour when he let Joseph set out on the journey to Shechem he had committed the Isaac-sacrifice and freely out of love of God had surrendered to Him the being he too dearly loved. Jacob did not believe this all the time. Sometimes he confessed to himself with contrition and fresh-flowing tears that he would never have been capable, for the love of God, of tearing the beloved from his heart. But the yearning to believe it sometimes won the day; and when it did, the question who had mangled Joseph became relatively unimportant.

The suspicion—certainly it was none the less there, it gnawed, but more gently, and not at every hour; sometimes in later years it slumbered and slept. The brothers had pictured living under suspicion, under half-wrongful suspicion, as being worse than in fact it proved to be. The father was on good terms with the sons, that is clear. He spoke with them and broke bread with them, he shared their business, their household sorrows and joys; he looked in their faces, and only once in a while, only at intervals already quite far apart, did the gleam come into his old eyes or suspicion and hypocrisy cloud his old gaze, before which they, breaking off in their words, had to cast down their eyes. But how much did that mean? A man casts down his eyes even if he knows no more than that another suspects him. It does not inevitably mean he is guilty. A scrupulous innocence and pity for the man sick of mistrust may equally so express itself. And so at last a man even gets sick of his suspicions. In the end he lets them rest; especially if confirmation, without reference to past events, can change nothing of the future, or the promise, or anything that is to be. The brothers might be the ten-headed Cain, they might be fratricides; but after all they were what they were, Jacob's sons; they were the given conditions that must be reckoned with, they were Israel. For Jacob had deliberately taken to using the name he had wrested at Jabbok (after which he halted upon his thigh), not only for his own person but with a broader and larger meaning. Why not? Since it was his name, hardly won, and not until the dawn, he might deal with it as he would. Israel: thus should not only he personally be called but all that belonged to him, the man of the blessing, from the nearest to the latest-never-last member in all the branchings and collateral branchings, the kin, the stock, the folk, whose numbers should be like the stars and the sands by the sea. The children sometimes permitted to play at Jacob's knee—they were Israel, collectively he called them so, and even fell back on it gratefully when he could not keep all their names in mind. It was particularly the names of the children of the Ishmaelite and definitely Canaanite women that escaped him. But "Iisrael" these women were too, including the Moabites and the slave-woman from Shechem; and Iisrael in the first line and above all were their husbands, the eleven; deprived of their full zodiacal number by early-evident and prolonged fraternal strife and by heroic sacrifice; yet still a goodly rank: Jacob's sons, progenitors of countless generations, to whom they in their turn would bequeath their name—mighty men before the Lord, whatever each single one might be like inside and whatever each one had in his mind when he cast down his eyes. What did it all matter, when through thick and thin they always remained Iisrael? For Jacob knew, long before it stood written—and it only stands written because he knew it—that Iisrael, even when it had sinned, always remained Israel.

But in Israel there was always one head on whom the blessing rested before the others, as Jacob had been before Esau—and Joseph was dead. Upon one rested the promise, or would rest, when Jacob conferred the blessing; from him the salvation should come, for which the father long sought a name and had found one, for the present, which no one knew save only the young female who sat at Jacob's feet. Who was the chosen one among the brothers, from whom it should come? Who was the man of the blessing, now that the choice no longer went by love—for the love was dead? Not Reuben, the eldest, who had shot away like the unstable waterfall and had played the hippopotamus. Not Simeon or Levi, they were personally nothing but unlicked cubs, and had some unforgettable items against them on their score. For they had behaved like heathen savages at Shechem and like satyrs in Hamor's city. This three were accurst, in so far as Israel can be accurst, they fell away. And so it had to be the fourth who came next after them, Judah. He it was.

Did he know it was he? He could count it up on his fingers, and often literally did, but never without shrinking from his election and painfully doubting whether he was worthy; yes, even fearing that the choice might become corrupt in him. We know Jehudah; when Joseph still lay in his father's bosom we sometimes saw in the group of brothers that suffering leonine head and the stag's eyes. We watched him when Joseph suffered his mishap. On the whole Judah did not come so badly out of that affair; not so well, of course, as Benjamin, who had been "at home," but almost as well as Reuben, who had never wanted the boy dead but had procured him the pit in order to steal him out of it. To draw him up out of the pit and give him his life, that had been Judah's idea too; for it was he who had suggested that they sell their brother, because in these times one did not know how to treat him like Lamech in the song. The excuse was trifling, a mere pretext, as most excuses are. Jehudah had acutely realized that to let the boy perish in the pit was no whit better than to shed his blood and had wanted to save him. That he came too late with his proposal, since the Ishmaelites had already done their work and freed Joseph, was not his fault. He could honestly say that his conduct in the accursed business had been comparatively decent, since he had wanted the lad to come out alive.

Still, the crime plagued him more and worse than it did those who could have put up no defence—and why not? Only the thick-witted should commit crimes; they do not mind, they live from day to day and nothing worries them. Evil is for the dull-witted; anyone with even traces of sensibility should avoid it if he possibly can, for he will have to smart for it. That he has a conscience makes him worse off than ever; he will be punished precisely on account of his conscience.

The deed done to Joseph and his father pursued Judah horribly. He suffered, because he was capable of suffering, as one could guess from his stag's eyes and a certain line round the thin nostrils and full lips. The deed lay like a curse upon him and punished him with sore adversity —or rather: whatever evil and adversity he suffered he laid to that cause, regarding it as payment for the committed, the participated-in sin—and this again is evidence of a strangely arrogant conscience. For he saw, of course, that the others—Dan or Gaddiel or Zebulon, to say nothing of the savage twins—went unscathed; that it mattered not at all to them and they had nothing to repent of; which might have taught him that his own plagues, those with himself and those with his sons, were perhaps quite independent of the common crime and came from within him. But no, he would have it that he was suffering punishment, he alone, and looked with contempt on those who, thanks to their thick skins, remained unscathed. Such is the peculiar arrogance of conscience.

Now the torments he suffered all bore the sign of Ashtaroth; and he need not have been surprised that they came from this quarter, because he had always been plagued by the mistress, in other words had been her slave without loving her. Judah believed in the God of his fathers, El Elyon, the Highest, Shaddai, the Mighty One of Jacob, the Rock and the Shepherd, Jahwe, from whose nose, when He was wroth, steam came and consuming fire from His mouth, that it lightened from it. Judah made burnt offerings to Him and brought Him oxen and milch sheep to the altar as often as seemed proper. But he believed also in the Elohim of the people, which was nothing against him if he did not serve them. When one observes how late and how far from their beginnings the people of Jacob still had to be admonished to put away strange gods, Baal and Ashtaroth, and not to hold sacrificial feasts with the Moabites, one is impressed by their obstinate instability and tendency to backslide and fall away, down to the latest generation. Thus one is not surprised to learn that so early a figure, so near to the source as Jehudah ben Jekew, believed in Ashtaroth, who was entirely a folk-goddess, exalted everywhere under various names. She was Judah's mistress and he bore her yoke, that was the harsh reality—harsh to his soul and his election both—and so forsooth how should he not have believed in her? He did not sacrifice to her—not in the strict sense of the word; that is, he did not bring her a sweet savour of oxen and milch sheep. But to sorrier, more passionate sacrifices her cruel spear enforced him, sacrifices which he made not gladly, not with a light heart, but only under the mistress's lash; for his spirit groaned against his lust and he freed himself from no hierodule's arms without hiding his head in shame and doubting with anguish his fitness for election.

Since, then, they had together got Joseph out of the world, Judah had begun to regard the plagues of Astarte as a punishment for his guilt; for they increased, they beleaguered him from without as they laid siege to him from within. One can only say that since that time the man had

206

atoned in hell—in one of the hells there are, the hell of sex. One might think that of all the several hells there are, that cannot be the worst. But he who thinks so knows not the thirst for purity without which indeed there is no hell, neither this one nor any other. Hell is for the pure; that is the law of the moral world. For it is for sinners, and one can sin only against one's own purity. If one is like the beasts of the field one cannot sin, one knows no hell. Thus it is arranged, and hell is quite certainly inhabited only by the better sort; which is not just— but then, what is our justice?

The history of Judah's marriage and that of his sons and their destruction thereby is extremely strange and abnormal and actually incomprehensible, so that it can be spoken of with half-words, and that not merely out of delicacy. We know that Leah's fourth married young—the step was taken out of love of purity, in order to find and restrict himself and thus find peace. But in vain; he reckoned without the goddess and her spear. His wife, whose name tradition has not given us—perhaps she was not much called by it—she was simply the daughter of Shuah, that Canaanite man whose acquaintance Judah had made through his friend and head shepherd Hirah from Adullam. This woman, then, had much to weep over, much to forgive, and it was somewhat easier for her because three times she experienced the joy of motherhood. Yet after all it was a brief joy, for the sons she gave Judah were only nice in the beginning, and grew up nasty. The youngest, however, Shelah, born at quite an interval after the second, was only sickly; but the two elder ones, Er and Onan, were both sickly and evil; sickly in an evil way and evil in a sickly way, though both were pretty to look at, and sprightly in their manners. In short, they were an affliction in Israel. Lads like these, unusual and sickly, yet charming in their own way, are a misfit in time and place, a sign of Nature's rashness, who will sometimes for a moment fall doting and forget where she is. Er and Onan would have fitted into a late and ancient society, into an old-man world of mocking heirs; for instance, into the monkey-land of Egypt. So close to the beginnings of an effort addressed to the future and into space they were an error in time and place and had to be blotted out. Judah, their father, should have recognized the fact and blamed nobody—except perhaps himself for having begot them. But he put off the blame for their badness on their mother, Shuah's daughter, and only on himself in so far as he considered he had committed a folly when he took a born Baal-fool to wife. For their destruction he blamed the woman to whom he gave them in marriage, and whom he accused of being in the likeness of Ishtar, who destroys her beloved so that they die of her love. That was unfair: to his wife, who soon died of her grief; and certainly most unfair to Tamar as well.

TAMAR LEARNS THE WORLD

Tamar, she it was. She sat at Jacob's feet, had sat there a long time now, profoundly moved by the expression on his face, listening to the words of Israel. Never did she lean back, she sat up very straight, on a footstool, on a well-step, on a knot of root beneath the tree of wisdom, with throat outstretched and concave back, two folds of strain between her velvet brows. She came from a little place in the environs of Hebron, where people lived on their vineyards and kept a few cattle. There stood her parents' house, they were small farmers and sent the wench to Jacob with parched corn and fresh cheeses, lentil and grits. And he bought them with copper. So came she to him and first found her way thither on mere pretext, for actually she was moved by a higher compulsion.

She was beautiful in her way; not pretty-beautiful, but beautiful after an austere and forbidding fashion, so that she looked angry at her own beauty, and with some justice too, for it had a compelling power which left the men no rest; and it was precisely their unrest which had graved the furrows in her brows. She was tall and almost thin, but of a thinness more disturbing than any fleshliness however ripe; accordingly the unrest was not of the flesh and so must be called dæmonic. She had wonderfully beautiful and piercingly eloquent brown eyes, nearly round nostrils, and a haughty mouth.

What wonder that Jacob was taken with her, and as a reward for her admiration drew her to himself? He was an old man, loving feeling, only waiting to be able to feel again; and in order to reawaken feeling in us old folk, or at least something which mildly and dimly reminds us of the feelings of our youth, there must come something out of the ordinary to give us strength by its admiration, at once Astartelike and spiritually eager for our wisdom.

Tamar was a seeker. The furrows between her brows signified not alone anger at her beauty but also strain and searching for truth and salvation. Where in the world does one not meet concern with God? It is present on the thrones of kings and in the mountain hut of the poorest peasant. Tamar felt it. The unrest she aroused distressed and exasperated her precisely on account of the higher unrest which she herself felt. One might have supposed that this country girl would have been satisfied by the wood and meadow nature-worship of her tradition. But not so: it had not answered her urgent need even before she met Jacob. She could not feed on the Baalim and fertility deities, for her soul divined that there was something other and higher in the world, and she yearned and strove towards it. There are such souls; there only needs to come something new, some change into the world and their sensibilities are touched and seized on, they must make straight for it. Their unrest is not of the first order, not like that of the wanderer from Ur, which drove him into the void, where nothing was, so that he had to create the new out of himself. Not so these souls. But if the new is there in the world, it disturbs their sensitive feelings from afar off and they must forthwith go faring after it.

Tamar had not far to fare. The wares she brought to Jacob in his tent, receiving their weight in copper in exchange, were certainly only a pretext of her spirit, a device born of unrest. She found her way to Jacob; and now often and often she sat at the feet of the stately old man weighed down by the weight of his tales. She sat very erect, the great penetrating wide-open eyes cast up to him, so fixed and moveless with attention that the silver earrings on either side her sunken cheeks hung down unswaying. And he told her of the world; that is, he told her his tales, which with intent to instruct he boldly presented as the history of the world—the history of the spreading branches of a genealogical tree, a family history grown out of God and presided over by Him.

He taught her the beginning, chaos and old night, and their division by God's word; the work of the six days and how the sea at command had filled with fishes, next space under the firmament where the great lights hang, with many winged fowl, and the greening earth with cattle and reptiles and all manner of beasts. He gave her to hear the vigorous, blithely plural summons of God to Himself, the enterprising proposal: "Let us make man." And to Tamar it was as though it was Jacob who had said it and certainly as though God—who always and ever was called simply God, as nowhere else in the world—as though He must look just like Jacob; and indeed did not God go on to say: "in our image, after our likeness"? She heard of the garden eastwards in Eden and of the trees in it, the tree of life and the tree of knowledge; of the temptation and of God's first attack of jealousy: how he was alarmed lest man, who now indeed knew good and evil, might eat also of the tree of life and be entirely like "us." So then the likes of us made haste, drove out the man, and set the cherub with the flaming sword before the gate. And to the man he gave toil and death that he might be an image like to "us," indeed, but yet not too like, only somewhat liker than the fishes, the birds, and the beasts, and still with the privately assigned task of becoming against our jealous opposition ever as much more like as possible.

So she heard it. Very connected it was not; all pretty puzzling, but also very grand, like Jacob himself who told it. She heard of the brothers who were enemies, and of the slaying on the field. Of the children of Cain and their kinds and how they divided themselves in three on this earth: such as dwell in tents and have cattle; such as are artificers in brass and iron; and such as merely fiddle and whistle. That was a temporary classification. For from Seth, born to replace Abel, came many generations, down to Noah, the exceeding wise one: him God, going back on Himself and His annihilating wrath, permitted to save all creation; he survived the flood with his sons, Shem, Ham and Japheth, after which the world was divided up afresh, for each one of the three produced countless generations and Jacob knew them all—the names of the tribes and their settlements on earth poured forth from his lips into Tamar's ears: wide was the prospect over the swarming brood and the places of their dwellings; then all at once it all came together into the particular and family history. For Shem begot Eber in the third remove, and he Terah in the fifth, and so it came to Abram, one of three, he was the one!

For to him God gave unrest in his heart on His account, so that he laboured tirelessly on God to think Him forth and make Him a name; he made Him unto himself for a benefactor and He repaid with far-reaching promises the creature who created the Creator in the spirit. He made a mutual bond with him: that one should become ever holier in the other; and gave him the right of election, the power of cursing and blessing, that he might bless the blessed and curse the accurst. Far futures he opened out before him wherein the peoples surged, and to them all his name should be a blessing. And promised him boundless fatherhood—since after all Abram was unfruitful in Sarah up till his eighty-sixth year.

Then he took the Egyptian maid and begot upon her and named her son Ishmael. But that was a begetting on a side-line, not on the path of salvation but belonging to the desert, and first-father did not believe God's assurances that he should yet have a son by the true wife, named Isaac; but fell on his face with laughter at God's word, for he was already an hundred years old and with Sarah it had ceased to be after the manner of women. But his laughter was a wrong unto her, for Jizchak appeared, the saved sacrifice, of whom it was said from on high that he should beget twelve princes. That was not strictly accurate; God sometimes misspoke and did not always mean exactly what He said. It was not Isaac who begot the twelve, or only indirectly. Actually it was himself, from whose solemn lips the tale fell on which the simple maid was hanging. It was Jacob, brother of the Red One; with four women he begot the twelve, being servant of the devil Laban at Sinear.

And now Tamar heard once more about brothers who were enemies: the red hunter, the gentle shepherd; she learned of the blessing-deception that put things straight, and the flight of the blessing-thief. A little there was about Eliphaz, son of the deposed son, and the meeting with him by the way; but it was toned down to save Jacob's face. Here and elsewhere the narrator went delicately: for instance, when speaking of Rachel's loveliness and his love of her. He was sparing himself when he softened the account of his humiliation at Eliphaz's hands. But in the case of the dearly beloved he was sparing Tamar; for he was a little in love with her and his feeling told him that in the presence of one woman one does not praise too warmly the charms of another.

On the other hand the great dream of the ladder, which the thief of the blessing dreamed at Luz, that his pupil heard about in all its magnitude and splendour; though such a glorious lifting up of the head perhaps did not sound quite reasonable unless one knew about the deep humiliation that went before. She heard tell of the heir—looking at him the while all eyes and ears—who bought the blessing of Abraham and had power to pass it on to one who should be Lord over his brothers, at whose feet his mother's children must bow down. And again she heard the words: "Through thee and thy seed shall be blessed all the generations on the earth." And did not stir.

Yes, what all did she not hear, and how impressively delivered, in these hours—what tales they were! The fourteen years' service in the land of mud and gold unrolled before her and then the extra years that made them twenty-five, and how the wrong one and the right one and their handmaidens together assembled the eleven, including the charming one. Of the flight together she heard, of Laban's pursuit and search. Of the wrestling with the ox-eyed one till the dawn, from which Jacob all his life limped like a smith. Of Shechem and its abominations, when the savage twins strangled the bridegroom and destroyed the cattle and were cursed—up to a point. Of Rachel's dying a furlong only from the inn, and of the little son of death. Of Reuben's irresponsible shooting away and how he too was cursed, in so far as Israel can be cursed. And then the story of Joseph: how the father had loved him sore, but, strong of soul and heroic in God, had sent him forth and knowingly given the best beloved a sacrifice.

This "once on a time" was still fresh, and Jacob's voice shook, whereas in the earlier ones, already overlaid with years, it had been epically unmoved, solemn and blithe of word and tone, even in the grim and heavy, heavy parts; for these were all God's-stories, sacred in the telling. But it is quite certain now, could not be otherwise and must be conceded, that Tamar's listening soul in the course of instruction was fed not alone on historical, time-overlaid once-on-a-time, the time-honoured "once," but with "one day" as well. And "one day" is a word of scope, it has two faces. It looks back, into solemnly twilit distances, and it looks forwards, far, far forwards, into space, and is not less solemn because it deals with the to-be than that other dealing with the has-been. Many deny this. To them the "one day" of the past is the only holy one; that of the future they account trifling. They are "pious," not pious, fools and clouded souls, Jacob sat not in their church. Who honours not the future "one day," to him the past has had naught to say, and even the present he fronts the wrong way. Such is our creed, if we may interpolate it into the teachings which Jacob ben Jizchak imparted to Tamar: teachings full of the double-faced "one day"—and why not, since he was telling her the "world" and that is "one day" in both senses, of knowledge and of foreknowledge? Well might she gratefully say to him, as she did: "You have paid too little heed, my master and lord, to telling me what has come to pass, but spoken ever to thy handmaiden of the far future." For so he had done, quite unconsciously, since into all his stories of the beginning there came an element of promise, so that one could not tell them without foretelling.

Of what did he speak to her? He spoke of Shiloh.

The assumption would be entirely wrong that it was only upon his death-bed, feeling the promptings of oncoming dissolution, that Jacob spoke of Shiloh the hero. In that moment he had no promptings at all; merely pronouncing the long-known and prepared words, having considered and conned them half his life long, so that his dying hour could only confer on them an added solemnity. I mean the blessing and cursing judgments upon his sons, and the reference to the figure of the promise, whom he called Shiloh. It had occupied Jacob's thoughts even in Tamar's time and even though he spoke of it to nobody but her, and then out of gratitude for her great attentiveness and because with the remnant of his power of feeling he was a little in love with her.

Strange indeed, and extraordinary, how he had mused it all out to himself! For Shiloh was really nothing but a place-name, the name of a walled settlement in the country farther north, where often the children of the land, when they had fought and come off victors, would gather to divide the spoil. Not a particularly sacred place, but it was called place of quiet or rest, for that is what Shiloh means: it signifies peace, signifies drawing a long and relieved breath after bloody feud. It is a blessing-word, as proper for a person as for a place. Sichem, son of the citadel, had had the same name as his city; and in the same way Shiloh might serve for a man and son of man called bearer and bringer of peace. In Jacob's thoughts he was the man of expectation, promised in those earliest and ever renewed vows and precepts: promised to the womb of the woman, promised in Noah's blessing on Shem, promised to Abraham, through whose seed all the breeds on the earth should be blessed. The prince of peace and the anointed, who should reign from sea to sea and from river to river to the end of the world, to whom all kings should bow, and all the peoples cleave to the hero who one day should be awoken out of the chosen seed, and to whom the seed of his kingdom should be confirmed for ever.

Him who would then come he called Shiloh. And now we are challenged to use our imagination as well as we can and picture to ourself how the old man, endowed with such rich gifts of expression and impressiveness, spoke to Tamar of Shiloh in these hours and bound up the earliest beginning with the furthest future. His language was powerful, it was weighty with meaning. Tamar, the female, the single soul deemed worthy to hear it, sat motionless. Even watching very closely you could not be sure of even the slightest swaying of her ear-rings. She heard "the world," which in the early things hid promise of the late: a vast, ever branching eventful history, through which ran the scarlet thread of promise and expectancy from "one day" to "one day," from the earliest "one day" to the furthest future one. On that "one day," in a cosmic catastrophe of salvation, two stars which flamed in wrath against each other, the star of might and the star of right, would rush upon each other in consummating thunder-crash to be henceforward one and shine with mild and mighty radiance for ever on the heads of men: the star of peace. That was Shiloh's star, star of the son of man, the son of the election, who was promised to the seed of the woman, that he should tread the serpent underfoot. Now Tamar was a woman, she was *the* woman, for every woman is *the* woman, instrument of the Fall and womb of salvation, Astarte and the mother of God; and at the feet of the father-man she sat, on whom at a confirming nod the blessing had fallen and who should pass it on in history to one in Israel. Who was it? Above whose brow would the father lift up his horn that he anoint him as his heir? Tamar had fingers whereon to reckon it up. Three of the sons had been cursed, the favoured, son of the true wife, was dead. Not love could guide the course of inheritance, and where love has gone, nothing but justice remains. Justice was the horn out of which the oil of anointing must trickle on the brow of the fourth. Judah, he was the heir.

THE RESOLUTE ONE

From now on, the standing furrows between Tamar's brows took on yet another meaning. Not only of anger against her beauty they spoke, of searching and strain, but also of determination. Here let me impress upon you: Tamar had made up her mind, cost what it might, by dint of her womanhood to squeeze herself into the history of the world. So ambitious she was. In this inexorable and almost sinister resolve—there is about the inexorable always something sinister—her spiritual aspirations had issued. There are natures wherein teaching is straightway converted into resolve; indeed, they only seek instruction in order to feed their will-power and give it an aim. Tamar had needed only to be instructed about the world and its striving toward its goal, to arrive at the unconditional resolve to mingle her womanhood with these strivings and to become historic.

Let me be clear: everybody has a place in the history of the world. Simply to be born into it one must, one way or the other and roughly speaking, contribute by one's little span one's mite to the whole of the world-span. Most of us, however, swarm in the periphery, far off to one side, unaware of the world-history, unsharing in it, modest and at bottom not displeased at not belonging to its illustrious dramatis personæ. For such an attitude Tamar had only contempt. Scarcely had she received instruction when she resolved and willed, or, better put, she had taken instruction to learn what it was she willed and did not will, and she made up her mind to put herself in line, into the line of the promise. She wanted to be of the family, to shove herself and her womb into the course of history, which led, through time, to salvation. *She* was the woman, the dispensation had come to her seed. She would be the foremother of Shiloh, no more and no less. Firm stood the folds between her velvet brows. They already meant three things, they could not fail to mean yet a fourth: they came to mean anger and envious scorn for Shuah's daughter, Jehudah's wife. This jade was already in the line, she had a privileged place, and that without merit, knowledge, or will-power (for Tamar counted these as merits); she was a cipher dignified by history. Tamar bore her ill will, she hated her, quite consciously and most femininely. She would have, equally open-eyed, wished for her death if that had had any sense. But it had none because the woman had already borne three sons to Judah, so that Tamar would have had to wish all three of them dead too to have things put back and a free place made for herself at the side of the inheritor of the blessing. It was in this character that she loved Judah and desired him; her love was ambition. Probably never—or never up till then—did a woman love and desire a man so entirely apart from his own sake and so entirely for the sake of an idea as Tamar loved Judah. It was a new basis for love, for the first time in existence: love which comes not from the flesh but from the idea, so that one might well call it dæmonic, as we did the unrest which Tamar herself evoked in men aside from her fleshly form.

She could have got at Judah with her Astarte side and would probably have been pleased to do so, for she knew him much too well as slave to the mistress not to be sure of success. But it was too late; which always means too late in time. She came too late, her ambition-love was in the wrong time-place. She could no longer shove herself in at this link in the chain and put herself into the line. So she would have to take a step forward or else back in time and the generations: she would have to change her own generation and address her ambitious designs to the point where she would have preferred to be mother. The idea was not a difficult one, for in the highest sphere mother and beloved had always been one. In short, she would have to avert her gaze from Judah and direct it upon his sons, the grandsons of the inheritance, whom under other circumstances she could almost have wished out of the way, in order to bear them again herself to better purpose. And first, of course, she directed it solely upon the boy Er, he being the heir.

Her personal position in time made the descent quite possible. She would not have been much too young for Judah, and for Er not entirely too old. Still, she took the step without joy. She was put off by the sickliness and degeneracy of the brothers, no matter how much charm they had. But her ambition came to her aid, and luckily, for otherwise she would have found it inadequate. Ambition told her that the promise did not always take the promising or even the suitable course; that it might run through a great deal that was dubious or worthless or even depraved without exhausting itself. That disease did not always come of disease, but that it can issue in tested and developed strength and continue on the way of salvation—especially when brought out and developed by dint of such a resolute will as Tamar called her own. Besides, the scions of Judah were just degenerate males, just that. It depended on the female, on the right person coming in at the weak point. The first promise had to do with the womb of the woman. What in fact had the men got to do with it?

So, then, to reach her goal she had to rise in time to the third generation; otherwise the thing was not possible. She did indeed practise her Astarte wiles on the young man but his response was both childish and vicious. Er only wanted to sport with her, and when she set the darkness of her brows against him he fell away and was incapable of being serious. A certain delicacy restrained her from going further up and working on Judah; for it had been he whom she actually wanted or would have wanted, and though he did not know that, yet she did, and was ashamed to beg from him the son whom she would gladly have borne him. Therefore she got behind the head of the tribe, her master, Jacob, and worked on his dignified weakness for her, of which she was fully aware, of course, and more flattered than wounded it by wooing for admission and desiring from him his grandson for her husband. They sat in the tent, on the very spot where Joseph had once talked the old man out of the many-coloured coat. Her task was easier than his.

"Master and lord," she said, "little Father, dear and great, hear now thy handmaid and incline thine ear to her prayer and her earnest and yearning desire. Lo, thou hast made me distinguished and great before the daughters of the land, hast instructed me in the world and in God, the only Highest; hast opened my eyes, and taught me so that I am thy creation. But how has this been vouchsafed to me that I found favour in thine eyes and thou hast comforted me and spoken to thy handmaid with kindness, which may the Lord requite thee and may thy reward be perfect in the God of Israel, to whom I have come by thy hand so that I have safety beneath His wings? For I guard myself and keep well my soul that I forget not the tales which you have made me see, and that they shall not come away from my heart as long as I live. My children and my children's children, if God give me such, them will I tell, that they destroy themselves not, nor make themselves any image like unto man or woman or cattle on earth or birds beneath the sky or reptiles or fishes; nor that they shall lift up their eyes and see the sun, the moon, and the stars, and fall away from me to worship them. Thy people are my people and thy God my God. So if He give me children they shall not come to me from a man of a strange people, it may not be. A man from out of thy house, my lord, perchance may take a daughter of the land, such as I was, and lead her to God. But I as I now am, new-born and thine image, cannot be bride to an uninstructed one and who prays to images of wood and stone from the hand of the artificer, which can neither hear nor see nor smell. Behold now, Father and lord, what thou hast done in shaping me, that thou hast made me fine and delicate of soul so that I cannot live like the hosts of the ignorant and wed the first wooer and give my womanhood to a God-fool as once in my simplicity I should have done. These now are the drawbacks of refinement and the hardships that elevation brings in its train. Therefore reckon it not to thy daughter and handmaid for a naughtiness if she point out the responsibility thou hast taken on thyself when thou didst form her, and how thou standest now in her debt almost as much as she in thine, since thou must now pay for her having been lifted up."

"What thou sayest, my daughter, is boldly conceived and not without sense: one hears it with applause. But show me thine aim, for I see it not yet, and confide in me whither thou thinkest. For it is dark to me."

"Of thy people," she answered, "am I in spirit. Of thy people alone can I be in the flesh and with my womanhood. Thou hast opened mine eyes, let me open thine. A branch grows from thy trunk, Er, eldest son of thy fourth son, and is like a palm tree by the waters and like a slender reed in the fence. Speak then with Judah, thy lion, that he give me to Er for a bride."

Jacob was exceedingly surprised.

"So that was thy meaning," he answered, "and thither went thy thought? Truly, truly, I should not have guessed it. Thou hast spoken to me of the responsibility I have taken on and makest me now concerned precisely on thine account. Verily I can speak with my lion and make my word avail with him. But can I justify it? Welcome art thou to my house, it opens its arms with joy to receive thee. But shall I have trained thee up to God so that thou becomest unblest? Unwillingly do I speak with doubt of anyone in Israel, but the sons of the daughter of Shuah are indeed an unable breed and good-for-nothings before the Lord, from whom I prefer to avert my gaze. Truly I hesitate very much to go along with thy wish, for it is my conviction the lads are no good for wedlock, and anyhow not with thee."

"With me," said she firmly, "if with nobody else. Bethink thee after all, my master and lord! It was irretrievably decreed that Judah have sons. Now they are as they are and at least must be sound at the core, for in them is Israel. And they cannot be passed over, nor can one leave them out save that they themselves fall away and do not stand the test of life. Unavoidable is it that they should in turn have sons, at least one of them, one at least, Er, the first-born, the palm tree by the brook. I love him and I will build him up with my love to a hero in Israel."

"A heroine, at least," he responded, "art thou thyself, my daughter. And I trust in thee to perform it."

So he promised her to make his word good with Judah his lion, and his heart was full of varying and conflicting feelings. For he loved the woman, with what strong feeling was left him, and was glad to present her to a man of his own blood. Still he was sorry and it went against his honour, that it should be no better man. And again, he knew not why, the whole idea made him somewhat to shudder.

Judah did not live with his brothers in the grove of Mamre, "in his father's house"; since he had become good friends with the man Hirah, he pastured farther down towards the plain in the grazing-ground by Adullam, and there his son Er, his eldest, and Tamar celebrated their wedding, provided by Jacob, who had sent for his fourth and made his word avail with him. Why should Judah have kicked against the pricks? He consented not too gracefully, with rather a gloomy air, but he did consent with no ado and so Tamar was given to Er to wife.

It befits us not to look behind the veil of this marriage—even in the beginning no one liked it and humanity has always expressed itself baldly and brusquely as to the facts, finding it too much trouble, as always, to soften them with pity or excuse. The factors of failure were present in it: on one side historic ambition to play a part in history, combined with the gifts of Astarte; on the other enervation, a youth capable of standing no serious test in life. We shall do well to follow the example of tradition and baldly and brusquely state that Judah's Er, quite shortly after the wedding, died; or as tradition has it, the Lord slew him—well, the Lord does all, and all that happens may be regarded as His doing. In Tamar's arms the youth died of a hæmorrhage which would probably have killed him even if he had not choked to death with the blood. Some people may feel relieved that at least he did not die quite alone like an animal but in the arms of his wife, though again it is distressing to picture her dyed with the life-blood of her young husband.

Dark-browed she stood up. She washed herself clean of the blood and straightway demanded for her husband Onan, Judah's second son.

The determination of this woman has always had something staggering about it. She went up to Jacob and lamented to him; in a way she accused God to him, so that the old man was seriously embarrassed for Yah.

"My husband has died and left me," she said. "Er, thy grandson, in a trice and the twinkling of an eye. How is one to understand that? How can God do so?"

"He can do everything," Jacob replied. "Humble thyself! He does, when occasion requires, the most frightful things. For to be able to do everything one wants is, when you come to think of it, a great temptation. There are vestiges of the desert—try to explain it so to thyself. He sometimes falls on a man and slays him whether or no, without rhyme or reason. One must just accept it."

"I accept it," she replied, "so far as God is concerned. But not for my own part, for I do not recognize my widowhood, I cannot and I may not. Since one has fallen away, the next must take his place; that my fire be not quenched which still lives and to my husband no name remain and nothing else upon earth. I speak not for myself alone and for the slain one, I speak generally and for all time. Thou, Father and lord, must make thy word avail in Israel and exalt it into a law, that where there are brothers and one dies childless, his wife shall take no strange man from outside, but her brother-in-law shall step in and wed her. But the first son whom she bears shall he confirm after the name of his deceased brother, that his name shall not be uprooted out of Israel."

"But if it please not the man," Jacob objected, "to take his sister-in-law?"

"In that case," said Tamar firmly, "she shall stand forth before the people and say: 'My brother-in-law refuses to reawaken for his brother a name in Israel and will not marry me.' Then shall one require him and speak with him. But if he stand and speak: 'I like not to take her,' then shall she stand to him before all the people and take one of his shoes from off his foot and spit upon it and answer and say: 'Thus shall one do to every man who will not build up his brother's house.' And his name shall be Barefooter!"

"Then certainly he will bethink himself," said Jacob. "And thou art right, my daughter, in so far as it will be easier for me to make my word avail with Judah that he should give thee Onan for a husband if I make a general law on which I can support myself, which I have proclaimed under the tree of wisdom."

It was the brother-in-law marriage which at Tamar's instigation was thus founded and became a matter of history. This country girl had certainly a flair for the historical. Skipping over the stage of widowhood, she now received the boy Onan as her husband, though Judah showed small desire for the arrangement or the collateral marriage, and the person most concerned even less. Judah, sent for to his father from the grazing-ground of Adullam, rebelled a long time against the father's counsel and denied that it was advisable to repeat with his second what had turned out so unhappily with his first. Besides, Onan was only twenty, and if capable of marriage at all, certainly not yet ripe for it, and neither willing nor disposed thereto.

"But she will take off his shoe and all that if he refuse to build up his brother's house, and will be called Barefooter all his days."

"Thou makest, Israel, as though that were established fact, and it is so only because thou hast but now thyself introduced it—I know well by whose advice."

"God speaks out of the maid," responded Jacob. "He has brought her to me that I make her acquaint with Him, that He may speak out of her."

Then Judah rebelled no more, but ordered the wedding.

It is beneath the dignity of this narrator to pry into the secrets of the bedchamber. So then, baldly and brusquely: Judah's second son, Onan, in his own way quite pleasing—and his way was a dubious one—was, again in his own way, quite a character. He had a deep-seated perversity of disposition, amounting to a judgment upon himself and a denial of life. I do not mean his own personal life, not exactly that; for he possessed much self-love and rouged and adorned himself like any dandy. Yet in the very soul of him he denied life; for in those inmost depths he uttered an emphatic no to any continuation of life after or through him. We are told that he was angry at being forced to become a surrogate husband and raise up seed not to himself but to his brother. That is probably true; so far as words and even thoughts come in question, he might put the thing so to himself. But in reality, for which words and thoughts are only paraphrases, the knowledge was inborn in all the sons of Judah that life was a blind alley; that whatever way it might take, in no case would, should, could, or might it continue further through them, the three sons. Not through us, they said with one voice, and in their way they were right. Life and lustiness might go their ways, the three turned up their noses. Particularly Onan; and his prettiness and charm were merely an expression of the narcissism of a man beyond whom the line does not continue.

Forced into marriage, he resolved to make a fool of the womb. But he reckoned without Tamar's strength of will and her Astarte equipment, which confronted his perversity as one thunder-cloud confronts another; like thunder-clouds they met and lightning followed—the stroke of death.

He was paralysed and died in her arms from one second to the next. His brain stood still and he was dead.

Tamar rose up and straightway demanded that Shelah be given her for husband, he, Judah's youngest-born, being then only sixteen years old. She might be called the most amazing figure in this whole story—few will be found to deny it.

This time she did not prevail. Even Jacob hesitated, if only in anticipation of Judah's emphatic objection, and that was not long in coming. They called him a lion; but like a lioness he stood before his last cub, whatever he might or might not be worth, and would not budge.

"Never!" he said. "What! So he is to die too, in blood like one, without, like the other? God shall prevent it, it shall not be. I have obeyed thy summons, Israel, and hastened up to thee from my wife's kin in the plain where Shuah's daughter bore me this son and where she now lies sickened. For she is ailing and drooping towards death, and if Shelah die too, then I am bare. There is no question of disobedience here, for thou mayst indeed not command me at all, and thou makest only a hesitant suggestion. But I hesitate not only. I say no and never, for thee and for me. What thinks this woman, that I shall give her my ewe lamb that she destroy it? That is an Ishtar, who slays her beloved. A devourer of youth is she, a greed insatiable. Besides, this one is still a boy, still under full years, so that the lamb will avail her nothing in the fold of her arms."

Really nobody could have imagined Shelah, at least not now, in the rôle of married man. He looked more like an angel than a human being, very smug and unserviceable, and had neither beard nor bass.

"It is only on account of the shoe and the rest of it," Jacob reminded him quaveringly, "if the boy refuses to build up his brother's house."

"I will tell thee a thing, my friend," quoth Judah. "If this devourer go not now away and put on widow's garb and continue to do her seemly mourning in her father's house as the bereaved of two husbands and behave quietly, then I myself, as sure as I am thy fourth son, will take off her shoe before all the people and do all the rest of it and accuse her openly of being a vampire that she may be stoned or burned."

"That is going too far," said Jacob in painful agitation, "in thy dislike of my suggestion."

"Going too far? And how far wouldst thou go if they would take Benjamin from thee and try to send him on some very dangerous journey, who after all is not thine only one but merely thy youngest? Thou guardest him with thy staff and keepest him close that he too may not be lost and scarce can he go out on the highroad. Well, Shelah is my Benjamin and I resist, everything in me rises up against yielding him up."

"I will make thee a fair proposal," Jacob said, for this argument had gone home to him. "Just in order to gain time and not grossly to offend the girl, thy daughter-in-law, we will not reject her demand but wean her from it. Go to her and say: 'My son Shelah is still too young and is even unripe for his years. Remain a widow in thy father's house till the lad grow up, then I will give him to thee that he may raise up seed to his brother.' So shall we silence her demand for some years before she can renew it. Then perhaps she will get used to the widow's state and not renew it at all. Or if she do, then we will console her, saying with more or less truth that the lad is still not ripe."

"Be it so," said Judah. "It is the same to me what we tell her if only I do not have to yield that tenderness and pride into the burning embrace of Moloch."

And it came about according to Jacob's instructions. Tamar received dark-browed her father-in-law's verdict, looking deep into his eyes, but she yielded. As a widow and a woman who mourns she remained in her father's house and nothing was heard of her, one year and two years and even a third. After two she would have been justified in renewing her claim; but she expressly waited a third year in order not to be told that Shelah was still too young. The patience of this woman was as remarkable as her resolution. Indeed, resolution and patience are probably the same thing.

But now that Shelah was nineteen and in the bloom of whatever manhood he would ever rejoice in, she came before Judah and spoke:

"The term is up and the time is now ripe for thee to give me to thy son as wife and him to me as husband, that he raise up to his brother name and seed. Remember thy bond."

Now Judah, even before the first year of waiting was out, had become a widower. Shuah's daughter had died, out of affliction over his bondage to Astarte, the loss of her sons, and the blame on her head for their loss. He had now only Shelah left and was less than ever minded to send him on the perilous journey. So he answered:

"Bond? There was never one made, my friend. Do I mean by that that I do not stand by the simple word of my mouth? Not so. But I would not have thought thou wouldst insist after so long a time, for it was a word of delay. Wilt thou have another such? If so, I will give it thee, but it should not be needed, for thou shouldst already have consoled thyself. True, Shelah is older, but only a little, and thou art further forward of him than when my word consoled thee. Thou mightest almost be his mother."

"Oh, might I?" asked she. "Thou showest me my place, I see."

"Thy place," said he, "in my opinion, is in thy father's house, to remain there a widow and a woman who wears mourning for two husbands."

She bowed and went hence. Now comes the sequel.

This woman was not so easy to put off the track and remove from the line of descent. The more we observe her, the more we are amazed. She had dealt very freely with her position in time, moving it down with her to the grandchildren, whom she cursed because they were in the way of those whom she would bring forward. Now she resolved to change generations a second time and climb up again; she would pass over the one remaining member of the generation of grandchildren, whom they would not give her, that he might either die or else bring her and her womb into the line of descent. She would do this, for her flame might not be quenched nor would she suffer them to shut her out of her God-inheritance.

THE SHEEP-SHEARING

Now, these following are the things which happened to Judah, Jacob's son. Not many days after the day when the lion again played lioness and put himself before his cub, the sheep-shearing came round and the feast of the wool-harvest. And the shepherds and herders of the region gathered to eat and drink and offer sacrifice. The feast was held in different places. This time it was in the mountains, called Timnath, and hither came the shepherds and owners of the flock down from above and up from below, to shear their sheep and have a good time. Judah went up together with Hirah of Adullam, his friend and head shepherd, the same through whom he had got to know Shuah's daughter; for they too meant to shear and have a good time—at least Hirah did, for Judah was not inclined for a good time, he never was. He lived in hell, in punishment for former share in evil doings, and the way his sons had lost their lives looked very like this hell. He was afflicted over his election and on account of it would rather have had no feast and no good time, for if one is bond-slave to hell, all gaiety takes on the nature of the hellish and leads to nothing save befouling the election. But what was the use? Only the ill in body are excused from life. If one ails only in spirit, that does not count. No one understands it and one must play one's part in life and keep the seasons with the rest. So Judah stopped three days at the shearing at Timnath, sacrificed and feasted.

The way back to his own place he travelled alone; he liked it better alone. We know that he went on foot for he had a good knobbed staff of some value, a walking-staff, not a cudgel for a beast. With it he strode down the hilly paths between vineyards and villages, in the parting gleams of the day, which went redly to its rest. The roads and bypaths were familiar; there was Enam, the place Enajim at the foot of the heights, which he must pass on his way towards Adullam and the village of his kinfolk. The gate, the mud walls, the very houses shone crimson in the glory of the exulting heavens. By the gate crouched a figure; when he came closer he saw that it was wrapped in a *ketonet paspasîm,* the shrouding garment of those who are temptresses.

His first thought was: "I am alone." His second: "I will go by." The third: "To hell with her! Must the *kedeshe,* the daughter of joy, sit on my peaceful homeward way? So it looks to me. But I will take no heed, for I am twofold, that I am: he of whom it looks likely and he who is bitter, denies himself and goes angrily by. The old song! Must it be sung for ever? So sing the chained galley-slaves from their groaning hearts at the oar. Up above I groaned and sang it with a dancing-girl and should be sated for a while. As though hell were ever sated! Shameful craving and absurd for the hundredfold hateful! What will she say, how behave? He who comes after me may try. I will go past."

And he stopped.

"Greeting to the Mistress."

"May she strengthen thee," she whispered.

The angel of desire had already seized upon him and her whisper made him shiver with lustful curiosity after this woman.

"Whispering wayside one," said he, with trembling lips, "for whom dost thou wait?"

"I wait," she replied, "on a lusty lustling who will share with me the mystery of the goddess."

225

"Then am I half the right man," said he, "for a lustling am I if not a lusty one. I have no lust to lust, yet she to me. In thy calling, methinks, one is not very lusty for lust either, but must be glad if others feel it."

"We are givers," she said, "but if the right one comes we know how to receive as well. Hast thou lust to me?"

He put his hand upon her.

"But what wilt thou give me?" she stopped him.

He laughed. "In sign," he said, "that I am a son of lust with some trace of lustiness I will give thee a he-goat from the flock that thou remember me."

"But thou hast it not by thee."

"I will send it thee."

"A man says that beforehand. Afterwards he is a different man and remembers not his former word. I must have a pledge."

"Name it."

"Give me thy signet from thy finger and thy bracelets and thy staff that is in thy hands."

"Thou knowest how to look out for the Mistress," he said.

"Take them!"

And he sang the song with her by the wayside in the red evening glow and she went away round the wall. But he went on home and next morning he said to Hirah, his shepherd.

"Well, so and so, you know how such things are. At the gate of Enajim, the place of Enam, there was a temple prostitute, and her eyes had something about them under the *ketonet*—in short, why make so much of it between men? Be so good and take her the he-goat I promised so I get back my things I had to leave her, ring, staff, and bracelets. Take her a fine big billy-goat, I won't be shabby with the shabby creature. Maybe she is sitting again by the gate, or ask the people of the place."

Hirah picked out the goat, diabolically ugly and magnificent with ringed horns, cleft nose, and long beard, and took him to the gate by Enajim, where nobody was. "The whore," he asked within, "who sat outside by the road? Where is she? You must know your whores."

But they answered him: "Here was and is no whore. We have none here, we are a decent little place. Look elsewhere for the she-goat for thy he-goat, or stones will be flying."

Hirah told that to Judah, who shrugged his shoulders.

"If she cannot be found, then the fault is hers. We have offered to pay, nobody can reproach us. Of course, I have lost my things. The staff had a crystal knob. Put the goat back to the herd."

With that he forgot it. But three months later it became plain that Tamar was with child.

It was a scandal such as the neighbourhood had not seen for a long time. She had lived a widow, in mourning garments, in her parents' house, and now it came to light and could no longer be hid that she had carried on shamelessly, in a manner worthy death. The men growled in their beards, the women screeched their scorn and curses. For Tamar had always been arrogant and behaved as though she were above them. The hue and cry soon came to Judah's ears: "Hast thou heard, hast thou heard? Tamar, thy daughter-in-law, has so behaved that she cannot hide it longer. She is with child by whoredom."

Judah went pale. His stag-eyes stood out, his nostrils flickered. Sinners can be extremely sensitive to the sins of the world; besides he had bad blood towards the woman because she had consumed his two sons and also because he had broken his promise about his third.

"She is guilty of crime," said he. "Brazen be the sky above her head and iron the earth beneath her! She should be burnt with fire. Long ago she was due to the stake; but now the sin is open, she has committed an abomination in Israel and besmirched her mourning garment. They shall set her out before the door of her father's house and burn her to ashes. Her blood be on her own head!"

With long strides he outpaced the informers, who flourished switches, and on the way were increased by other flourishers from the villages round, so that it was an eager crowd who came up before the widow's house in Judah's train, whistling and jeering. Inside one could hear Tamar's parents sobbing and lamenting, but from herself no sound.

Then three men were told off to go in and produce the courtesan. They squared their shoulders and went in, stiff-armed, chins drawn in, fists ready, to fetch out Tamar, first to be pilloried and then to be burnt. After a while they came out again without Tamar, bearing certain things with them. One had a ring between two fingers, the others splayed out. The second held a staff out in front of him by the middle. The third had a purple cord dangling from his hand. They brought the things to Judah, standing there foremost, and said:

"We were to say this to thee from Tamar thy daughter-in-law: 'From the man whose pledges these are I carry my pawn. Dost thou know them? Then hearken: I am not the woman to let herself be destroyed together with her son from the heir of God.' "

Judah the lion looked at the things while the crowd pressed round him and peered in his face. White as he had been all the time with anger, so slowly now he grew red as fire, up into the roots of his hair and even into his very eyes, and was dumb. And then a woman began to laugh and then another and then a man and then several men and women and at length the whole place rang with their laughter going on and on; they bent over with laughing and their mouths gaped up towards the sky and they cried: "Judah, 'twas thou! Ho, ho, ho! Judah hath got his son an heir from his whore! Ha, ha, ho, ho, ho!"

And Leah's fourth? He spoke very low, standing there in the crowd: "She is more justified than I." And went with bowed head out of their midst.

But when six months later Tamar's hour came she gave birth to twins and they became mighty men. Two sons she had destroyed out of Israel when she descended in time, and for them she gave back two others incomparably better when she climbed up again. The first-come, Pharez, was in particular a most doughty man and in the seventh remove he begot one who was doughtiness itself, named Boaz, husband of a lovely one. They waxed great in Ephratha and were praised in Bethlehem, for their grandson was Isaiah the Bethlehemite, father of seven sons and of a little one who kept the sheep, brown, with beautiful eyes. He could play on the lute and with the sling he brought the giant low—by then he had been secretly anointed king.

All that lies far hence in the open future and belongs to the great history of which the history of Joseph is only an interlude. But into this history has been interpolated and there for ever remains the story of the woman who would not at any price let herself be put aside, but with astounding tenacity wormed herself into a place in the line of descent. There she stands, tall and almost sinister, on the slope of her native hills; one hand on her body, the other shading her eyes, she looks out upon the fruitful plains where the light breaks from towering clouds to radiate in waves of glory across the land.

Chapter Six

THE GOD-STORY

OF WATERS AND WINDS

THE children of Egypt, even the wisest and best-instructed of them, had in general the most childish ideas about the nature of their nourisher-god, that aspect and manifestation of divinity which the Abram-people called El Shaddei, the god of feeding, and the children of the black earth Hapi: the onswelling, surging one, the stream which had built up their marvellous oasis between the deserts and fed their existence and their comfortable, pious life-and-death philosophy—in other words, the river Nile. They believed, and from generation to generation taught their children, that the river—God knew where and how—arose out of the underworld, on its way to the "Great Green"—that is to say, the immeasurable ocean, as which they envisaged the Mediterranean—and that its subsidence, after its fructifying rise, was in the nature of a return to the lower world. . . . In short, there reigned among them the most utterly superstitious ignorance on this whole subject; and only the fact that there was no more enlightenment, indeed rather less, in the rest of the world, got them through life at all in such a darkened state. True, in spite of it they built up a mighty and magnificent king-dom, admired on all hands and holding out for many millennia; pro-duced many beautiful things and in particular were geniuses at dealing with the object of their uninstructedness: namely, the river that fed them. Still, we who know so much more, in fact know everything, can-not but regret that none of us was on the spot at that time, to lighten the darkness within their souls and give them real understanding of the nature of Egypt's great river. What a buzz it would have made in the seminaries and academies, to be told that Hapi, far from having his source in the lower world (the lower world itself having been rejected as a baseless superstition) is merely the outlet of the great lakes in tropical Africa; and that the food-god, to become what he is, has first to be fed himself, by taking in all the rivers that flow down westwards from the Ethiopian Alps. In the rainy season, mountain brooks, full of fine detritus, rush and tumble down from the heights and flow together to form the two watercourses which are, so to speak, the prehistory of the future river: the Blue Nile and the Atbara. These, then, at a later locality, namely at Khartum and Berber, go together to bed and turn into the creative stream, the river Nile. For this, their common bed, about the middle of the summer, gradually becomes so full with the volume of water and liquid mud that the river spreads out widely over its banks—so widely, indeed, that the common epithet for it is the Overflowing One. The flood lasts for months, then just as gradually it subsides within its bounds. But the crust of mud, the deposit left by its overflowing, forms, as the seminarists well knew too, the fertile soil of Kemt.

But they would probably have been amazed, and even embittered against the harbingers of truth, when they heard that the Nile comes not from below but from above—in the last analysis from heights as high as the rain that in other less exceptional countries plays the fertilizing rôle. There, they used to say, meaning in the wretched foreign countries, the Nile is set in heaven, meaning by that the rain. And it must be confessed that a surprising intuition, almost approaching enlightenment, expresses itself in the florid phraseology: an insight, that is, into the relations existing between all the watercourses and watersources in the world. The rise of the Nile depends on the amount of rainfall in the high mountains of Abyssinia; but the rains in turn are actually cloud-bursts from clouds formed over the Mediterranean and driven by the wind into those regions. The well-being of Egypt depends on how high the Nile rises; and in the same way the well-being of Canaan, the land Kenana, the Upper Retenu, as it was once called, or Palestine as we in our enlightenment designate Joseph's homeland and his fathers', is conditioned by the rains which, in the rule, fall twice in the year: the early rain in the late autumn, the latter rain in the early part of the year. For the country is poor in springs, and not much can be done with the water of the rivers that run in the deep gorges. So everything depends on the rains, especially on the latter ones, and from the earliest times the rainfall has been collected. If the rains do not come, if instead of the moisture-bearing west wind it blows regularly from the south and east, from off the desert, then there is no hope of a harvest;

aridity, crop failure, and famine follow—and not only here. For if it does not rain in Canaan, then there are no downpours in the Ethiopian hills, the mountain torrents do not tumble down from the heights, the two nourishers of the nourisher are not nourished—at least not enough for him to become "great," as the children of Egypt always put it; not great enough to fill the canals which carry the water to the higher levels. Then crop failure and want ensue, even here in the country where the Nile is not in heaven but on earth. And thus we see the connection between all the waters of the earth, in their sources and courses.

Though we ourselves are enlightened only in a general way on these matters, we see nothing strange (though much that is unfortunate) in the phenomenon that hard times come at the same time "in all lands"; not only in the land of mud but also in Syria, the land of the Philistines, Canaan, even the countries on the Red Sea, probably even in Mesopotamia and Babylonia; and that "the dearth was great in all lands." Yes, things can go from bad to worse, one year of irregularity, failure, and want can follow on another in ill-tempered succession; the strands of misfortune may spin themselves out over a number of years, until even the fabulous number of seven is reached—or perhaps not quite seven, but then even five is bad enough.

JOSEPH ENJOYS LIFE

For five whole years now the winds and the waters had behaved their best, and the harvest been so rich that in sheer gratitude people made a seven out of the five—and the five fully deserved it. But now the page turned. Pharaoh, maternally concerned for the kingdom of the black earth, had unclearly dreamed, and Joseph had boldly interpreted: the Nile failed to rise, because in Canaan the winter—that is, the latter—rain did not fall. It failed once; that was a misfortune. It failed twice, and that was ground for lamentation. It failed three times; there was blanching and blenching and wringing of hands. After that it might as well keep right on failing and go down in the records as a seven years' drought.

We human beings, when so unnaturally visited by nature, always behave the same way. At first we deceive ourselves, in our day-by-day minds, about the nature of the event: we do not understand what it means. We good-naturedly take it for an ordinary, average episode. After we have gradually learned that it is extraordinary, a first-class calamity such as we could never have dreamed could attack us in our lifetime, we look back in amazement on our former blindness. Thus the children of Egypt. It was long before they grasped the fact that this which they were enduring was the phenomenon called the "seven lean years." It had probably come to pass before now: in earlier times, in their legendary history, it had played a gruesome rôle; but they had never thought of it as affecting themselves. Their dullness of comprehension was not even as excusable as short-sightedness sometimes is. For Pharaoh had dreamed, and Joseph had interpreted. That they had really experienced the seven fat years might have been enough evidence that the seven lean ones would come along in their turn. But during the fat years the children of Egypt had put the lean ones out of their minds, as the man in the legend forgets the devil's bookkeeping. Now the day of reckoning was at hand. When the nourisher had been pitiably low once, twice, and thrice, they had to admit it; and a patent result of the admission was a vast enlargement of Joseph's reputation.

Of course that too had steadily waxed in the years of fatness. How much more now must his fame have increased when the incidence of the lean ones proved that the measures he had taken were inspired by the profoundest wisdom!

In times of crop failure and hunger a minister of agriculture is in a bad position. The dull-witted population, never at the best very reasonable, always tending to make their feelings their guide, lay the blame for disaster on the shoulders of the highest responsible official. But if that official have acted in time to erect a magic barrier against evil, so that even if it work great changes, it is at least robbed of its character of a major catastrophe; if the official have done this, then he is a glorious and awe-inspiring leader of men.

Men living in a land which is theirs merely by adoption sometimes display the national traits more strongly than even the native-born. During the twenty years of Joseph's adoption into the land of Egypt, the typically Egyptian idea of careful, preventive preservation had got into his flesh and bones. He put it into practice; it was the motive for his acts. But it was a conscious motive, for he preserved enough distance from his guiding principle to keep in mind the truth that it was also popular with the Egyptians, and to deal accordingly. And this was a

232

combination of sincerity and a sense of humour which goes down better than sincerity by itself.

And now his harvest time had come, and he reaped as he had sown. The sowing was his tax-economy during the good years; the harvest time was the distribution, a crown business of proportions never son of Re had known since the time of that god. For as it is set down, and told in song and story, "the dearth was in all lands; but in all the land of Egypt there was bread." Which of course does not mean that there was not scarcity in Egypt too. What the price of corn rose to in response to frenzied demand, anyone can imagine who has even a vague idea of the working of economic laws. He may grow pale at the realization, but at the same time he will also see that this scarcity was controlled, as the plenty had been before, by the same shrewd and kindly man; that the scarcity lay in his hand and he could wield it as he would. For Pharaoh he got out of it all that he could, but he did the same for those least able to cope with it, the little people. He did this by a combination of liberality and exploitation; of government usury and fiscal measures such as had never been seen before. His mingling of severity and mildness impressed everyone, even the hardest hit, as superhuman and godlike—for the gods do behave in just this ambivalent way and one never knows whether to call it cruel or kind.

The situation was fantastic. Agriculture was in a state that made the dream of the seven singed ears not even a parable but the bare bald truth. The dream-ears were burnt by the east wind, namely Khamsin, a scorching south-easter, and now Khamsin blew all summer long and throughout the harvest time, called Shemu, from February to June, almost without cease. Often it was a tempest like an oven, filling the air with a dust like ashes that coated the young growth. Whatever feeble green the unnourished nourisher had bred was charred by this desert breath. Seven ears? Yes, actually and literally—there were no more. In other words, the ears were not there, the harvest was not. But what was there, in quantity most scrupulously dealt out, was corn: every kind of grain and cereal, in the royal magazines and pits up and down the river in all the cities and towns and their vicinage. Throughout the length and breadth of Egypt—but only Egypt. Elsewhere there had been no provision, no building of bins, no foresight before the flood. Yes, in all Egypt, and only there, was bread; in the hand of the state, in the hand of Joseph, the superintendent of all that the heavens had given;

233

and now he himself became like the heavens which gave and the river Nile which provides. He opened his chambers—not wide open, but with circumspection—and gave bread and grain to all who needed, and that was everybody; Egyptians as well as strangers from afar travelled hither to get food from Pharaoh's land, which now more correctly than ever was called a granary, the granary of the world. He gave, that is, he sold, to them that had, at prices not they but he fixed, corresponding to the extraordinary economic situation; so that he made Pharaoh gold and silver and still could give in more literal sense to the little lean-ribbed. To them he distributed, in measure, what they clamoured for: to the small farmers and the dwellers in the little guttered alleys of the big towns; gave them bread and grain, that they might not die.

That was godlike; but it was a praiseworthy human pattern too. There had always been good officials, who with justice had had written in their tombs that they had fed the King's subjects in time of need, given to the widow, not favoured the great before the small; and afterwards, when the Nile had once more grown, "had not taken the peasant's arrears"—that is, had not pressed for advance payment or a fixed date. The people thought of these tomb inscriptions as they saw Joseph's business methods. But "since the days of Set" no official had shown such benevolence, or was equipped with such plenary powers and such a truly godlike manipulation of them. The grain business, superintended by a staff of ten thousand scribes and under-scribes, reached out all over Egypt, but all the threads ran back to Menfe, into the palace of the King's shadow-dispenser and universal friend; there was not one final decision upon sale, loan, or gift which he had not reserved to himself. The rich man, the landed proprietor, came before him and cried for grain. To him he sold for his silver and gold, making the sale conditional upon the modernization of the man's irrigation system, so that he should stop muddling along in feudal inefficiency. Thus he kept faith with the highest, with Pharaoh, into whose treasuries flowed the rich man's silver and gold. The cry of the poor came before him too; and to them he distributed from the stores for nothing and again for nothing, that they might not hunger but eat. Herein he was true to his fundamental characteristic of human sympathy, to which we have already done justice and need not dwell longer upon it. Though we might just say once more that it has to do with mother-wit; for truly there was something deserving the adjective "witty" in Joseph's technique of combined largesse and exploitation; despite hard work and heavy cares he was always in high spirits, and at home would say to Asenath, his wife and daughter of the sun: "My girl, I am enjoying life!"

He sold abroad too, at high prices, as we know, and studied lists of the cereals delivered to the "nobles of the wretched Retenu." For many city kings of Canaan, among them the kings of Megiddo and Shahuren, sent to him for grain; the envoy from Ascalon came and cried before Joseph on behalf of his city and was given—at a price. But here too Joseph struck a balance between strict interest and friendliness, and starving sand-rabbits, shepherd stock from Syria and Lebanon—"barbarians, who do not know how to live," as his scribes said—he allowed to enter with their flocks, past the well-guarded gates of the land and east of the river, toward stony Arabia, to find a living on the fat pastures of Zoan, on the Tanitic arm of the Nile, if they promised not to trespass beyond their allotted territory.

Thus he would get from the frontier reports which ran like this: "We have passed Bedouins from Edom through the fortress of Merneptah and toward the lakes of Merneptah, to pasture their flocks on the great meadows of Pharaoh, the exalted sun of the lands."

He read very carefully. He read all the frontier reports with the utmost care and by his orders they had to be precise. He ordered a tightening of the regulations governing the entry of all persons through the eastern border fortresses into that rich land which now had become so uniquely rich. There had to be a list of names of every person coming out of the lands of wretchedness to fetch food from Pharaoh's cornbins. Frontier officials like that Lieutenant Hor-waz of Thel, scribe of the great gate, who had once passed Joseph himself with his Ishmaelites into the land, had to take great pains with such lists, and to record all immigrants not only according to their names, trades, and places of origin, but also by their fathers' and grandfathers' names. The lists then had to be sent daily by fast messenger down to Menfe, to the offices of the King's shadow-dispenser.

There they were copied out fair on extra good paper with red and black ink and laid before the provider. And he, though quite busy enough without that, read them through every day from beginning to end, as carefully as they had been compiled.

It was in the second year of the lean kine, on a day in the middle of Epiph, May by our reckoning and frightfully hot, as it is anyhow in Egypt in their summer season, but even hotter than usual. The sun was like fire from heaven, we should have measured it at well over one hundred degrees in the shade. The wind was blowing and driving the hot sand into the red-lidded eyes of the little people in Menfe's narrow streets. There were hosts of flies, and they and the human beings were alike sluggish. The rich would have given large sums for half an hour of a breeze from the north-west; they would even have been willing that the poor should benefit as well.

Joseph too, the King's first mouthpiece, had a perspiring face caked with sand. But as he went home at noon from his office he seemed to be in high spirits and very lively—if the word be applicable to a man borne in state in a litter. Followed by the equipages of some of his upper officials, who were to lunch with him, according to a custom which the vice-god even today did not fail to observe, he soon turned off from the wide boulevard and was carried through some of the mean alleys of the poorer quarters, where he was hailed with cordial and confident familiarity. "Dgepnuteefonech!" the little lean-ribbed ones shouted, throwing kisses. "Hapi! Hapi! Ten thousand years to you, our provider, beyond the end of your destiny!" And they, who would simply be rolled in a mat when they were taken out to the desert, wished him: "Four excellent jugs for your entrails, and for your mummy an alabaster coffin!" Such was the form their sympathy took, in response to his for them.

At length the litter bore him through the painted gate in the wall of his gracious villa, into the front garden, where olive, pepper, and fig trees, the shadowy cypress and the spreading fanlike palm were grouped about the gay papyrus columns of the terrace before the house, and mirrored in the square walled-in lotus pool. A broad gravelled drive ran round the pond; the bearers followed it and came to a halt, whereupon the runners offered Joseph knee and neck, so that he stepped first upon them and then to the ground. Mai-Sachme was quietly awaiting him on the terrace or rather at the top of the flight of steps at one side, as were Hepi and Hezes, two greyhounds from Punt, most aristocratic beasts in gold collars, a-quiver with nerves. Pharaoh's friend sprang up the shallow steps, more precipitately than usual; indeed, more briskly than an Egyptian noble should move before spectators. He did not look at his retinue.

"Mai," said he hurriedly, in a low tone, as he patted the animals' heads and they put their fore-paws on his chest to greet him, "I must talk to you at once, alone. Come into my room. Let them wait, there is no hurry about the meal, and I could not eat a mouthful. This is much more pressing business, about the roll here in my hand—or rather the roll is about the pressing business—I will explain it all to you if you will come with me where we can be alone."

"But steady," expostulated Mai-Sachme. "What is the matter with you, Adon? You are shaking. And I am sorry to hear you cannot eat, you who make so many to eat. Will you not have water poured to cleanse your sweat? It is not good to let it dry in the pores and hollows of the body. It itches and inflames, especially when mixed with grit."

"I'll do that later, Mai. Washing and eating are not urgent, by comparison; for you must hear at once what I have heard, the roll here tells me, that was brought to my office just before I left and here it is: it has come, I mean they have come, which is the same thing; and the question is what will happen and how I am to receive them—and what shall I do, for I am fearfully excited!"

"Why, Adon? Just be calm. You say it has come. That means you expected it; and what you were expecting cannot surprise you. Kindly tell me what is, or who are, come; then I will prove to you that there is no reason to be upset; on the contrary calmness is the one thing needful."

They were talking as they went through the peristyle to the fountain court, moving with a rapid gait which the man of poise tried to slow down. But Joseph turned, and Mai-Sachme followed with Hepi and Hezes into a room on the right, with a coloured ceiling, a malachite lintel and gay friezes along the walls. It served him as a library and lay between his sleeping-chamber and the great reception-hall. It was furnished with true Egyptian charm. There was an inlaid day-bed covered with skins and cushions, delightful little carved chests on legs, inlaid and inscribed, for the protection of the book-rolls; lion-footed chairs with rush seats and backs of stamped and gilded leather; flower-stands and tables with faïence vases and vessels of iridescent glass. Joseph

237

squeezed his steward's arm as he balanced up and down on the balls of his feet; his eyes were wet.

"Mai," he cried, and there was something like suppressed exultation, a choked off rapture in his voice, "they are coming, they are here, they have passed the fortress of Thel—I knew it. I have been waiting for it, and yet I can't believe it has come. My heart is in my mouth, I am so excited that I don't know where I am—"

"Be so good, Adon, as to stop dancing up and down in front of me. I am a man of peace and quiet; pray make it clear to me who has come."

"My brothers, Mai, my brothers!" Joseph cried, and bounced up and down the more.

"Your brothers? The ones who rent your garments and threw you into the well and sold you into slavery?" asked the captain, who had long since learned the whole story by heart.

"Yes, yes! To whom I owe all my good luck and my glory down here!"

"But, Adon, that is certainly putting things too much in their favour."

"God has put it that way, O my steward! God has turned all to good, to everyone's good, and we must look at the results which He had in mind. Before we could see how it turned out, and had only the fact but not the result, I agree that it had a bad look. But now we must judge the fact according to the result."

"That is a question, after all, my good lord. Imhotep the wise might have had a different view. And they showed your father the blood of an animal for yours."

"Yes, that was beastly. He must certainly have fallen on his back. But that probably had to be, because things could not go on as they were. For my father, great-hearted and soft-hearted as he was—and then I myself, what a young peacock I was in those days, a regular young cock of the walk, full of really vicious vanity and self-importance! It is a shame how long some people take to grow up. Even supposing I am grown up even now. Perhaps it takes you your whole life to grow up."

"It may be, Adon, that there is still a good deal of the boy about you. So you are convinced it is really your brothers?"

"Convinced? There cannot be the slightest doubt. Why else did I give such strict orders for records and reports? All that was not for nothing, be sure; and as for giving Manasseh, my eldest, the name I gave him, that was just for form's sake—I have not forgotten my father's house, oh, not in the very least; I have thought of it daily, hourly, all these years, and how I promised my little brother Ben in the hiding-place of the mangled one that I would have them all come after me when I had been lifted up and had the power of binding and loosing! Convinced! Here, look, it is written down, it came by running messenger and is a day or so ahead of them: the sons of Jacob, son of Yitzschak from the grove of Mamre which is at Hebron: Reuben, Simeon, Levi, Judah, Dan, Naphtali, and so on . . . to buy corn—and you talk as though there were any doubt! It is the brothers, all ten of them. They entered with a troop of buyers. The scribes never dreamed, when they wrote it down. Nor did they, they have not the least idea before whom they will be brought, nor who it is sells in the King's name, as his first mouthpiece. Mai, Mai, if you only knew how I feel! But I do not know myself, it is all Tohu and Bohu within me—if you know what that means. And yet I knew and have been expecting it for years. I knew when I stood before Pharaoh and when I interpreted to him I was doing it to myself too, reading the purposes of God and how He guides our history. What a history, Mai, is this we are in! One of the very best. And now it depends on us, it is our affair to give it a fine form and make something perfectly beautiful of it, putting all our wits at the service of God. How shall we begin, in order to do justice to such a story? That is what excites me so much. . . . Do you think they will recognize me?"

"How should I know, Adon? No, I should think not. You are considerably matured since the time they pulled you to pieces. And anyhow they could never dream of such a thing, and that will make them blind, so they will never think of it or even trust their own eyes. To recognize and to know that you recognize are two very different things."

"Right, right. But I fear they will, I fear it so much that my heart is pounding in my chest."

"You mean you do not want them to?"

"Not first off, Mai, not on any account! They must only grasp it by degrees; the thing must draw itself out before I speak the words and say I am I. In the first place, that is required for the shaping and adorning of the tale; and secondly, there is so much to be gone through and so many tests to make, and there will be a great deal of beating about the bush, first of all in the business about Benjamin—"

"Is Benjamin with them?"

"That is just the thing of it: he is not. I tell you there are ten, not

239

eleven of them. And we are twelve, all together. It is the red-eyed ones and the sons of the maids; but not my mother's son, not the little one. Do you know what that means? You are so calm, your wits move slowly. Ben not being here might mean one of two things. It may mean—I hope it does—that my father is still alive—think of it, that he still lives, that old, old man!—and keeps guard over his youngest, so that he forbade him the journey and did not want him to take it, for fear harm might come. His Rachel died on a journey, I died on a journey—why should he not be prejudiced against them and keep at home with him the last pledge of his lovely one? This may be the meaning. But it might mean too that he is gone, my father, and that they have behaved badly to Ben because he is alone and unprotected; and thrust him out as though he were not their brother, and would not let him come with them because he is a son of the true wife, poor little soul—"

"You keep calling him little, Adon; you do not take into account that he must have grown up too, in the meantime, this only real brother of yours. When you think of it, he must be a man in the prime of life."

"Quite right, it is quite possible. But he remains the youngest, my friend, the youngest of twelve, why should I not call him the little one? And there is always something sweet about the youngest in the family; all over the world the youngest is the favourite and leads a charmed life; it is almost as much in the picture for the older ones to conspire against him."

"Hearing your story, my lord, it almost seems as though you had been the youngest."

"Just so, just so. I will not deny it, there may be some truth in what you say. Maybe history here repeats itself with a difference. But it is on my conscience; I am determined the little one shall have his due as the youngest; and if the ten have thrust him out or treated him badly—if they have played fast and loose, which I do not like to think, as they did with me—then may the Elohim have mercy on them, for they will come up against me. I will not reveal myself to them at all; the beautiful speech to tell them who I am will just not be made; if they recognize me I will deny it and say: 'No, I am not he, ye evil-doers'; and they will find in me only a harsh and stranger judge."

"There, you see, Adon. Now you put on a different face and sing a new tune. No more sentimental tenderness in your heart. You are re-

240

membering how they played fast and loose with you, and you seem perfectly able to distinguish between the fact and the result."

"I don't know, Mai, what sort of man I am. One does not know beforehand how one will behave in one's story; but when the time comes it is clear enough and then a man gets acquainted with himself. I am curious myself to see how I shall act and how talk to them—at this moment I have no idea. That is what makes me tremble so. When I had to stand before Pharaoh I was not a thousandth part so excited. And yet they are my own brothers. But that is just it. Everything is upside-down inside me: it is a perfect muddle of joy and dread and suspense and quite indescribable, just as I tell you. How startled I was when I came to the names on the list, though I had known and definitely expected to see them—you cannot imagine it, of course not, because you cannot be startled. Was I startled on their account or my own? I do not know. But they would have good ground to be startled themselves— to be frightened down to the very soles of their shoes, I do not deny that. For it was no small thing then; and long ago as it all was, it has not got any smaller with the years. I said I went to them to see that every-thing was in order; that was cheeky, I agree—I admit it all, especially that I ought not to have told them my dreams. Besides, it is true that if they had granted me my life I would have told the whole thing to my father—so they had to leave me where I was. And still and all—that they were deaf when I cried out of the depths, lying there in my bonds, covered with welts, and wailed and begged them not to do this to my father, to let me perish in the hole and show him the blood of a beast for mine—yes, my friend, it was all pretty bad. Not so much to me, I am not talking about that; it was bad towards my father. If he is dead now of his grief and has gone down in sorrow to Sheol, shall I be able to be friendly to them? I do not know, I do not know how I am under such conditions; but I very much fear I could not be friendly. If they have brought down his grey hairs with sorrow to the grave, that also would belong to the result, Mai, even first and foremost; and would very much obscure the light shed by the result upon the fact. In any case, it remains a fact, and it must be set over against the result. Eye to eye with it, so that confronted by its goodness it may be ashamed of its badness."

"What do you mean to do with them?"

"How do I know? I am asking you for advice and counsel just be-cause I don't know what to do: you, my steward, whom I took into this story for you to give me of your steadiness when I get excited. You can afford to give me some, for you've got too much, you are far too phlegmatic, you just stand there and raise your eyebrows and put your lips together, and just because you are like that you do not have any ideas. But we need ideas, we owe it to the kind of story it is. For the meeting of the act and the result is a feast of no common sort, it must be celebrated and adorned with all sorts of solemn flourishes and pious manœuvres so that the world will have to laugh and cry over it five thousand years and more."

"Excitement and fear are less productive than peace and quiet, Adon. I will mix you a soothing drink now. I will shake a powder into water and it will sink and be still. But if I shake another kind into the cup, then the two will seethe up together, and if you drink it foaming it will act as a sedative."

"I will gladly drink it later, Mai, at the right moment, when I need it most. Now hearken to what I have done so far: I have sent running messengers with orders to segregate them from the other travellers and not to give them corn in the border cities but to send them on to Menfe, to the head office. I have arranged to have an eye kept on them so that they are sent to good rest-houses with their animals and are cared for without their knowing it in the strange land, as new and strange to them as it was to me when I died up above there and was brought down here, at seventeen years old. I was flexible then, but they, I realize, are all getting to the end of the forties, except Benjamin, and he is not with them, and all I know is that he must be fetched; in the first place so I can see him and in the second place because if he is here the father will come too. In short, I have laid upon our people to make smooth the way under their feet so that they strike not against a stone—if the figure means anything to you. And they shall be brought before me in the ministry, in the hall of audience."

"Not in your house?"

"No, not yet. At first quite formally at the office. Between you and me, the hall there is much bigger and more impressive."

"And what will you do with them there?"

"Yes, of course that will be the moment for me to drink your foaming draught. Because I have not the least idea in the world what I shall do, when they do not know me, nor what when I tell them who I am— but one thing I do know: I will not be so clumsy as to spoil the beautiful

242

story and burst out headlong with the climax like an inexperienced story-teller. No, I will sit tight when they come in and treat them like strangers."

"You mean you will be unfriendly?"

"I mean formal to the point of unfriendliness. For I think, Mai, I shall hardly succeed in being strange unless I force myself to be unfriendly. That will be easier. I must think of some reason why I have to speak harshly and can go at them properly. I must act as though their case was suspicious and strict investigations had to be made and all the circumstances cleared up, whether or no."

"Will you speak with them in their tongue?"

"That is the first useful word your stolidity has managed to utter," cried Joseph, striking his brow. "I certainly needed to be reminded of that, for the fact is I am always speaking Canaanitish with them in my mind, like the fool that I am. How should I come to know Canaanitish? That would be a frightful *faux pas*. I do speak it with the children; I suppose I am giving them an Egyptian accent. Well, that is the least of my troubles. I seem to be talking at random, saying things that might be important under less exciting circumstances but not now. Of course, I cannot know any Canaanitish, I must speak through an interpreter, we must have one here, I will give orders in the ministry, a good one, who knows both languages about equally so that he can render what I say exactly without making it any weaker or stronger. For what they say themselves, for instance big Reuben—oh, Reuben, my God, he was at the empty pit to save me, I know it from the watchman, I don't know if I told you about that, some time I will—what they say themselves of course I shall understand, but I must not show that I do or forget and answer what they say before the long-winded interpreter has translated."

"When you have taken it in, Adon, you will do it all right. And then perhaps you might pretend you take them for scouts come to spy out the weakness of the land."

"I beg of you, Mai, spare me your ideas! How do you come to make big eyes and suggest things to me?"

"I thought I was supposed to, my lord."

"I thought so at first myself, my friend. But I see after all that nobody can or should advise me in this most solemn business. I must shape its course all by myself. Remember how you are using your ingenuity in the story of the three love-affairs to make it as exciting and delightful as possible, and let me use mine on my own. Who told you I had not got the idea of pretending I took them for spies?"

"So we both have the same idea."

"Of course, because it is the only right one and as good as written down already. In fact, this whole story is written down already in God's book, Mai, and we shall read it together between laughing and tears. For you will be there, won't you, and come to the office when they are here, tomorrow or day after, and are brought into the great hall of the Nourisher with himself painted over and over on the walls? Of course you will be among my train. I must have a stately retinue when I receive them. . . . Ah, Mai," he burst out, and buried his face in his hands —those hands at which the little urchin Benoni had looked in the grove of the Lord Adon, as they wove the myrtle garland; now one of them wore Pharaoh's sky-blue lapis lazuli ring inscribed: "Be as myself"— "I shall see them, my own folk, my own, for they were always that however much we quarrelled through the fault of all of us. I shall speak with them, Jacob's sons, my brothers, to whom I have kept so long the silence of death and learn whether he can still hear that I am alive and that God accepted the beast instead of the son! I shall hear everything, I shall learn all that has happened, how Benjamin lives and whether they treat him brotherly. And I must get him down here and my father too! Oh, my task-master, now my house-master, it is all too exciting and solemn for words! And just because it is so solemn it must be treated with a light touch. For lightness, my friend, flippancy, the artful jest, that is God's very best gift to man, the profoundest knowledge we have of that complex, questionable thing we call life. God gave it to humanity, that life's terribly serious face might be forced to wear a smile. My brothers rent my garment and flung me into the pit; now they are to stand before my stool—and that is life. And the question whether we are to judge the act by the result and approve the bad act because it was needed for the good result—that is life too. Life puts such questions as these and they cannot be answered with a long face. Only in lightness can the spirit of man rise above them: with a laugh at being faced with the unanswerable, perhaps he can make even God Himself, the great Unanswering, to laugh."

Joseph was indeed as Pharaoh when he sat in his seat on his raised dais in the hall of the Nourisher beneath white ostrich-feather fans thrust into chased gold shields, held above him by pages in aprons, with bobbed hair. About him were his chief scribes from the ministry, an austere group of magistrates; along the dais to right and left lance-bearers of his household guard stood in a row. Two double lines of orange columns covered with ornamental inscriptions, on white bases, with green lotus capitals and over-pieces in coloured enamel, ran from his dais to the farthest entrance doors and on the long and high side-walls above the dado, Hapi, the overflowing, was repeatedly pictured: in human form, with covered sex, one breast male, the other female, the royal beard on his chin, reeds on his head, bearing on his palms the presentation tray with wild jungle flowers and slender water-jugs. Between these repeated representations of the god came other forms of life in flowing lines and bright colours, gleaming in the rays of light that fell through the stone gratings of the high windows. There were scenes of sowing and threshing, Pharaoh himself ploughed with oxen and cut the first swath with the sickle into the golden grain; there were the seven kine of Osiris, with the bull whose name he knew, pacing in a row, with exquisite inscriptions, such as: "Oh, may the Nile give me food and nourishment and every green thing according to its time!"

Such was the hall of audience where every cry for bread came before the Vice-Horus, for he reserved to himself each decision. Here now he sat, on the third day after his talk with his steward; Mai-Sachme now stood behind his seat and had actually mingled him a foaming draught; and Joseph had just dismissed a pigtailed and bearded delegation wearing shoes turned up at the toes, from the land of the great King Murshili, in other words Hatti, where too famine reigned. He had been absent-minded and heedless, as everyone had remarked; for he had dictated to his "actual scribe" a figure of more wheat, spelt, rice, and millet and at a lower price than the delegates from Hatti had themselves offered. Some of those present thought there might be diplomatic reasons for this: perhaps, who knew, the moment had come in the world political sphere to show King Murshili some attention. Others ascribed it to the physical condition of the universal friend, as he had remarked before the sitting that he had a catarrh from the dust, and he kept a handker-chief before his mouth.

Above the handkerchief his eyes looked out into the great hall when the men from Hatti had left and the group of Asiatics were brought in in their turn. One of their number was tall like a tower; another had a melancholy leonine head; one was solid and marrowy, another had long nimble legs; two others did not dissemble their natively belligerent air; one kept giving piercing glances round about him, another was striking because of his very bony joints, and still another because his eyes and lips were so bright and humid. One had curly hair, a round beard, and much red and blue dye of the purple snail about his garment. Each, in short, had something to distinguish him. In the middle of the hall they found it good to fall on their faces, and the universal friend had to wait till they stood up again to beckon them near him with his fan. They came closer and then again fell on their faces.

"So many?" he asked in a muffled voice which, oddly enough, he had pitched almost in a growl. "Ten all at once? Why not eleven? Interpreter, ask them why there are not eleven of them or even twelve—or do you men understand Egyptian?"

"Not so well as we should like to, O lord, our refuge," answered one of them in his own tongue. It was he on the runner's legs, whose tongue, it seemed, was nimble too. "You are as Pharaoh, you are as the moon, the merciful father, who comes forth in majestic garment. You are as a first-born steer in his adornment, Moshel, ruler! Our hearts praise with one voice him who here holds market, nourisher of the lands, food of the world, without whom no one has breath, and we wish for you as many years of life as the year has days. But your tongue, O Adon, we understand not enough to deal with you, be merciful unto us."

"You are as Pharaoh," they all repeated in chorus.

While the interpreter rapidly and monotonously translated Naphtali's words, Joseph devoured with his eyes the men standing before him. He knew them every one and had no trouble in marking in each the work the hand of time had done upon them too. O God of dispensations, they were all there, the hate-hungry wolf-pack that had flung itself on him with cries of "Down with him, down with him!" How he had begged: "Do not tear it, do not tear it!" But all the furious pack had dragged him to the pit with shoutings and hallooings, the while he questioned the heavens in a daze: "What is this that has come upon me?" They

246

had sold him as a criminal to the Ishmaelites for twenty silver pieces and before his eyes had dabbled the ruins of his garment in blood. Here they were now, his brothers in Jacob, come up out of long-ago time, his murderers because of dreams, led to him by dreams—and the whole past was like one dream. There were the red-eyed ones, all six of them, and the four of the maids: Bilhah's adder and snake and her prattler of news; Zilpah's sturdy eldest in his tunic, the forthright Gad, and his brother the sweet-tooth. He was one of the youngest next to Issachar the beast of burden and the tarry Zebulon, and he had wrinkles already and lines in his face and much silver in his beard and his smooth oiled hair. Good God, how old they had got! It was very moving—as all life is moving. But he shrank back at sight of them, for with them so old it was unbelievable that the father was still alive.

With his heart full of laughing and weeping and dismay he looked at them, recognized every single one despite the beards, which some of them in his time had not yet worn. But they, looking at him in their turn, had no such thoughts; for their seeing eyes were wrapped in blindness against the possibility that it could be he. They had once sold a blood-brother and shameless brat away into the world, out into far horizons and misty distances. That they never ceased to know, they knew it now. But that the aristocratic heathen there in his throned chair under the feather fans, in brilliant white that blazed against the perfectly Egyptian brownness of his brow and arms—that the potentate and provider here to whom they had come in their need; he who had about his neck the collar of favour, an amazing piece of goldsmith's work and an equally marvellous breastpiece with falcons, sun-beetles, and life-crosses arranged with the utmost art—that he there, under the waving fly-fans, the silver ceremonial hatchet in his belt, his headcloth wound in the manner of the country, with stiff lappets falling on the shoulders—that this could be the one-time outcast, mourned by the father till he mourned himself out; the dreamer of dreams—to such a thought they were immune, they were shut and bolted against it. Besides, the man kept his handkerchief to his face all the time and made even the barely possible impossible.

He spoke again, and every time, directly he paused, the interpreter beside him rattled off what he had said in monotonous Canaanitish.

"Whether there can be any dealing here at all, or any delivery of grain," he said crossly, "is still a question. We must consider it. It may

247

easily turn out otherwise. That you do not speak the language of men is the least of your troubles. I pity you, if you thought you could hold speech in your jargon with Pharaoh's first mouthpiece. A man like me speaks the tongue of Babylon, and Chetitish; but he can hardly let himself in for Khabirish and such-like gibberish; and if he had ever known it he would make haste to forget it."

Pause for translation.

"You look at me," he went on, not waiting for an answer, "you stare at me, like men without culture, and take private note that I keep a handkerchief before my face—from which you conclude that I am not feeling well. Well, I am not—what is there in that to remark and take down and draw conclusions from? I have a catarrh from the dust—even a man like me can suffer from catarrh. My physicians will cure me. Medical science is far advanced in Egypt. My own house steward, the overseer of my private palace, is a physician himself. So you see, he will treat me. But people, however remote from me, who had to undertake a journey, and furthermore a journey through desert lands, under these abnormal and unfavourable meteorological conditions, have my sincere sympathy. I feel keenly what they must have had to endure on the journey. Whence do you come?"

"From Hebron, great Adon, from Kirjath Arba, the four-square town, and from the terebinths of Mamre in the land of Canaan, to buy food in Egypt. We are all—"

"Stop! Who is that speaking? Who is the little man with the shining lips? Why is it he speaks—why not that tall tower over there? He is built like one, at least. He seems to be the oldest and most intelligent amongst your crew."

"It is Asher, by your favour; Asher, so is your servant's name, a brother among brothers. For we are all brothers and sons of one man, in the bond of brotherhood, and when a thing concerns all of us it is Asher, your humble servant, who is accustomed to take the word."

"Oh, so you are the common mouth for commonplaces. Good. But now I come to look at you all, it does not escape my penetration that although you are supposed to be brothers, you are very different among yourselves, some belonging in one group and some in another. This common mouth here looks like the man over there in a short coat with bits of bronze sewed on it; the one beyond with eyes like a snake has something or other in common with the man next him, standing first on one leg and

248

then on the other. But several of you seem to belong together by virtue of the red eyes you have in common."

It was Reuben who took upon himself to reply.

"Verily you see all, lord," Joseph heard him say. "Likenesses and differences are due to our being from different mothers, four from two and six from one. But we are one man's sons, Jacob your servant, who begot us and who sent us to you to buy bread."

"He sent you to me?" repeated Joseph, and lifted the handkerchief until it almost covered his whole face. He looked at them over it.

"Man, you surprise me by the thinness of your voice, coming from such a tower of a body; but I am still more surprised at your words. Time has silvered all your hair and beards, and the eldest of you, who has no beard, has more silver hair to make up for it. Your looks contradict your words; for you do not look like people whose father is still alive."

"By your favour, he lives, O lord," Judah took up the tale. "Let me bear witness to my brother's words. We deal in truth. Our father, your servant, lives in his state—and really he is not so old after all, maybe eighty or ninety, which is not unusual in our stock. For our ancestor was a hundred years old when he begot the true and right son, our father's father."

"How uncivilized!" said Joseph, his voice breaking. He turned round to his steward, then back, and for a while said nothing, to the unease of his audience.

"You might," he said at length, "answer my questions more precisely, without going off into unessentials. What I asked was how you stood the journey under such hard conditions, whether you suffered much from the drought, whether your water supply held out, whether you were attacked by roving bands or a dust-abubu, whether anybody was overcome by the heat—that was what I asked."

"We got on reasonably well, Adon, thank you for the kind inquiry. Our train was strong against roving bands, we were well supplied with water, we scarcely lost even an ass, and we were all in good health. Just one dust-abubu, of medium severity, was the most we had to bear."

"So much the better. My inquiry was not kind, it was strictly practical. A journey like yours is after all not so uncommon. There is much travel in the world; seventeen days' journeys, even seven times seventeen, are no rarity, and they have to be put behind the traveller step by step, for seldom does the earth spring to meet him. Merchants take the road from Gilead, leading from the town of Beisan through Yenin and the valley of—wait, I knew it once, it will come back to me—the valley of Dothan; whence they meet the great caravan route from Damascus to Leyun and Ramleh and the port of Khadati. You had it better, you simply came down from Hebron to Gaza and then along the coast down towards our land."

"As you say, O lord. You know all."

"I know a great deal. Partly because of my natural shrewdness, partly by other means which a man like me knows how to command. But at Gaza, where you probably joined the caravan, begins the worst part of the trip. You have to survive an iron city and an accursed sea-bottom covered with skeletons."

"We did not look round, and with God's help we came safe through the horrors."

"I am glad to hear it. Perhaps you had a column of fire to guide you?"

"There was one, once, that went on in front of us. It collapsed, and then came the dust-abubu, of moderate severity."

"You refrain from boasting of its terrors, but it might easily have been the death of you. It concerns me that travellers are exposed to such hardship on the way down to Egypt. I say that quite objectively. But you thought yourselves lucky when you got into the regions of our watch-towers and bastions?"

"Yes, we counted ourselves fortunate and praised God aloud for our being spared."

"Were you afraid at the fortress of Thel and its armed troops?"

"We feared only in the sense of awe."

"And what happened to you there?"

"They did not forbid us to pass when we told them we were buyers come to buy corn from this granary that our wives and children may live and not die. But they separated us from the others."

"I wanted to hear about that. Were you surprised at the measure? It had not happened before, to your knowledge, to say nothing of your being the object? At least they had provision put up for you in full number, all ten of you, if ten can be called a full number. They did not separate any of you from each other, but only from the others that entered with you?"

"So was it, lord. They told us we could not buy bread for our money except at Menfe, balance of the lands, and from yourself, lord of bread and friend of the harvest of God."

"Correct. They put you on the road? You had good journey from the frontier to the city of the swaddled one?"

"Very good, Adon. They kept an eye on us. Men who came and went directed us to lodgement and rest-houses with our animals, and in the morning when we offered pay the host would not take it."

"Two kinds of people receive free lodgement and board: the guest of honour and the prisoner.—How do you like Egypt?"

"It is a land of marvels, great vizier. Like Nimrod's is its might and magnificence, it is splendid in form and adornment, whether towering or extended flat, its temples are overpowering and its tombs touch the skies. Often our eyes ran over."

"Not so much, I hope, that you neglected to ply your trade and task, or were prevented from spying and reconnoitring and drawing your conclusions."

"Your word, O lord, is dark to us."

"So you pretend not to know why you were set apart and why people kept an eye on you and brought you before my face?"

"Gladly would we know, great lord, but we know not."

"You put on a face as though you never dreamed—does not your conscience whisper to you that you are under a cloud, that a suspicion rests upon you, a sinister one, and that your villainy is open to my eyes?"

"What say you, lord? You are as Pharaoh—what suspicion?"

"That you are spies," Joseph cried out. He struck the arm of his lion-footed chair with his hand and stood up. He had said *daialu,* spy, a heavily offensive Akkadian word; and he pointed at them, in their faces, with his fan.

"*Daialu,*" the interpreter hollowly repeated.

They started back as one man, thunderstruck, indignant.

"What say you?" they repeated, in a growling chorus.

"I said what I said. Spies you are, come to spy out the secret bareness of the land that you may discover it and reveal the way for invasion and plunder. That is my conviction. If you can gainsay it, do so."

Reuben spoke, all the others frantically gesturing to him to set them right. He shook his head slowly and said:

"What is there, sovereign lord, to gainsay? Only because it is you

251

who say it is it worth a word, but otherwise only a shrug of the shoulders. Even the great err. Your suspicion is false. We do not cast down our eyes before it, but as you see we look up freely and honestly to your face, and even in polite reproof that you can so misread us. For we know you in your greatness, but you know us not in our good faith. Look at us, and let your eyes be opened at the sight. We are all sons of one man, an excellent man in the land of Canaan, a king of herds and a friend of God. We are true men. We came in amongst others coming to buy food, for good silver rings which you can weigh on exact scales: food for our women and children. That is our aim. Spies, by the God of gods, have your servants never been."

"But you are!" answered Joseph, and stamped with his sandalled foot. "What a man like me has in his mind he sticks to. You are come to discover the shame of the land, that it may be harmed with the sickle. It is my belief you have this commission from wicked kings of the east; to disprove it rests with you. But far from doing so, what that tall tower there has said is merely to assert baldly that it is not true. That is no evidence to satisfy a man like me."

"But consider in mercy, lord," said one of them, "that it rather rests with you to give evidence for such an accusation than for us to disprove it."

"Who is that speaking so subtly out of your midst and piercing me with his eyes? For some time I have remarked your darting eye like a snake's. How are you called?"

"Dan, by your good favour, Adon. Dan I am called, born of a maid upon the knees of the mistress."

"I am pleased to hear it. And so, Master Dan, to judge by the subtlety of your words, you set yourself up for a judge and in your own case to boot? But here it is myself who sit as judge and the accused must make himself clean before me. Have you sand-dwellers and sons of misery any notion of the parlous balance of this pearl of great price among all the lands, over which I am set and must render account of its safety before god's son in his palace? It is ever threatened by the lustful covetousness of the desert-born who spy after its weakness, Bedu, Mentiu, and Peztiu. Shall the Khabirites deal here as they have dealt time and again beyond the borders in Pharaoh's provinces? I know of cities they have fallen upon like mad bulls and in their fury strangled the man and slain the oxen in savage wantonness. You see, I know more than you thought. Two or three of you, I will not say all, look to me quite capable of such games. And shall I take your bare word that you mean no ill and were not aiming at the secret parts of our land?"

They shifted about among themselves and took counsel with excited gesturings. In the end it was Judah to whom they beckoned to answer and represent them. He did it with the dignity of the tried and tested man.

"Lord," said he, "let me speak before you and set forth our state according to the exact truth, that you may know we are true men. Lo, we your servants are twelve brothers, sons of one father, in the land—"

"Stop!" cried Joseph, who had sat down but now stood up again. "What? So now all of a sudden you are twelve men? So then you have not dealt in truth when you said you were ten?"

"—in the land of Canaan," finished Judah firmly. His face wore a look which seemed to say that he found it uncalled for and premature to interrupt him when he was about to launch out into a full explanation. "Twelve sons are we, your servants, or we were—we have never said this was all of us as we stood before you, we only bore witness that all ten of us were one man's sons. At home we were originally twelve, but the youngest brother, not born of any of our mothers but from a fourth, who has been dead as many years as he is old, has stopped at home with our father, and one of us is no longer with us."

"What do you mean by 'no longer with us'?"

"Gone, lord, in his early years, lost to our father and to us, lost in the world."

"He must have been an adventurous fellow. But what have I got to do with him? Now the little one, your youngest brother: he is not lost—not got out of hand—"

"He is at home, lord, always at home and at our father's hand."

"From which I conclude that this old father of yours is alive and well?"

"You have asked that before, Adon, by your leave, and we told you yes."

"Not at all! It may well be that I asked you once about your father's life, but about his well-being I am now asking you for the first time."

"Things are very well," answered Judah, "with your servant, our father, under all the circumstances. But there has been hardship in the world for some time now, as my lord well knows. For since the heavens denied their watery blessings, once and then twice, the scarcity presses the harder the longer it goes on, in all the lands, and so in ours. Even to speak of scarcity is to make small the evil, for there is no grain for love or money, for either seed or bread. Our father is rich, he lives on an easy footing—"

"How rich and how easy? Has he for instance an ancestral tomb?"

"As you say, lord, Machpelach, the double hollow. There sleep our forefathers."

"For instance, does he live on such a footing that he has an oldest servant, a steward, as I have, who is a doctor as well?"

"So is it, Highness. He had a wise and much-travelled first servant, Eliezer by name. Sheol hides him; he bowed his head and died. But he left two sons, Damasek and Elinos, and the elder, Damasek, has taken the place of the deceased; he is now called Eliezer."

"You don't say," said Joseph, "you don't say." And his eyes were brimming for some while as his gaze travelled above their heads into space. Then he asked: "Why do you interrupt yourself, lion-head, in your attempted justification? Do you not know how to go on?"

Judah smiled forbearingly. He did not say that it was not he who kept interrupting.

"Your servant was in act and remains ready to tell you all our circumstances and the kind of journey we had in order and faithfully, that you may see we deal in truthfulness. Numerous is our house—not precisely as the sands of the sea, but very numerous. We number in the seventies, for we are all heads under our father's headship, we are all married and blessed with—"

"All ten of you married?"

"All eleven of us, Lord, and blessed—"

"What, your youngest too is married and the head of a family?"

"Lord, as you say it. From two women he has eight children."

"Impossible!" cried Joseph, without waiting for the man to translate. He struck his palm on the arm of his chair and burst out laughing. The Egyptian officials behind him laughed too, out of the purest sycophancy. The brothers smiled anxiously. Mai-Sachme, Joseph's steward, gave him a private nudge in the back.

"You nodded your head," said Joseph, drying his eyes. "So I understood that your youngest is married and a father too. That is fine. I am only laughing because it is really very good and something to laugh at.

Because one always thinks of the youngest as a little chap, not as a husband and father. That is what made me laugh; but you see I have stopped already. This business is much too serious and suspicious to be a laughing matter and that you, lion-head, have got stuck again in your defence seems to me a most suspicious thing."

"With your permission," answered Judah, "I will go on with it without stopping, and connectedly. For the dearness of all things, which one might better call a dearth because there is no food at all at any price, this catastrophe weighs upon the country, the herds perish, and on our ears strikes the cry of our children for bread, which, lord, is the bitterest of all sounds to a human ear and hardest to bear, save it may be the complaint of venerable age that he misses his due and daily comfort; for we heard our father say that he was not far from having his lamp go out so that he must sleep in the dark."

"Unheard of," said Joseph; "that is a vexation, not to say an abomination. Have you people let it come to that? No provision, no looking ahead, no measures against calamity, which after all does exist in the world and can take on presentness at any moment! No imagination, no fear, no sense of the past! Living like the beasts of the field from day to day, mindful of nothing that is not before your face and eyes—until the father in his old age must go without his habitual comforts! Shame! Have you, then, no education, no history? Do you not know that under some circumstances the blade cannot shoot and all blossoming things lie in bonds, because the fields bring forth only salt and no herb grows, nor any smallest sprout of grain? That life is numb with grief, the bull leaps not on the cow nor does the ass cover the she-ass? Have you never heard of floods that cover the earth so that only the exceeding wise man survives because he has made himself to swim upon the return primeval flood? Must, then, before you heed, everything be before your eyes and face presentwards to you, which was merely turned away, until your dearest-loved old age must want oil for its lamp?"

They hung their heads.

"Go on," he said. "That man who was speaking, let him continue! But let me hear no more of your father sleeping in the dark!"

"That is only a figure, Adon, it means that he too suffers from the hard times and has no bread for the offering. We saw many folk gird themselves up and set out for this country, to buy from Pharaoh's granaries, and they brought back food, for only in Egypt is there corn and a grain-

255

market. But for long we would not come before our father with the suggestion that we too gird our loins and come down likewise to do business and buy."

"Why would you not?"

"He has the fixed ideas of his old age, lord, all sorts of opinions about everything, and so about the land of your gods—he thinks his own thoughts about Mizraim and has a prejudice against its customs and ways."

"One must just shut one's eyes to that and not notice."

"He probably would not have let us come, if we had asked him. So we thought it better counsel to wait until he noticed the scarcity himself."

"Perhaps that ought not to be either, that you put your heads together about the father; it looks as if you were playing fast and loose with him."

"There was nothing else to do. And of course we saw his side-glances and how he would open his mouth to speak and then shut it again. Finally he said to us: 'Why do you look at each other with side-glances? Lo, I hear, and the rumour reached me, that in the south-land grain is cheap and there is a market there. Up with you, and sit not on your backsides till all of us are lost! Choose out one or two of you by lot and on whom it falls, Simeon or Dan, he may gird his loins and travel down with the travellers and buy food for your wives and children, that we may live and not die.' 'Good,' we brothers answered him, 'but it is not enough that two should go, for the question of need will arise. We must all go and show the number of our heads, that the children of Egypt may see we need corn not by the ephah but the homer!' So he said: 'Then all ten of you go.' We told him it would be better if we all went and showed that we are eleven households under his headship, otherwise we should be given too little. But he answered and said: 'Are you out of your wits? I see you want to make me childless. Do you not know that Benjamin must be at home and at hand? Suppose an accident were to befall him on the way? Ten of you go, or else we sleep in the dark.' So we came."

"Is that your justification?" Joseph asked.

"My lord," answered Judah, "if my faithful testimony overcome not your suspicion and if you do not recognize that we are innocent folk and deal in truth, then we must despair of any justification."

"I fear it will come to that," Joseph said, "for about your innocence I have my own ideas. But as for the suspicion you are under and my yet unshaken accusation that you are naught else but spies—very good, I will test you. You say I ought to know by the good faith of your deposition that you deal in honesty and are not rogues. I say: Good. Bring then your youngest brother here, of whom you speak. Set him here with yourselves before my face, that I may convince myself that your details all hang together and have weight; then I shall begin to doubt my suspicions and be slowly shaken in my accusation. But if not, by Pharaoh's life—and I hope you know one can take no higher oath in this country—there can be no talk of dealing by the homer nor yet by the ephah and it will be finally proven that you are *daialu,* and you should have realized how such people are treated before you took to this way of life."

They were all pale and mottled in the face and stood there helpless.

"You mean, lord," they asked through the interpreter, "that we are to put our way behind us again, nine or seventeen days long (for the earth does not spring to meet us) and then repeat the journey hither to bring our youngest brother before your face?"

"That would be wonderful," he retorted. "No, certainly not. Do you think a man like me catches spies and then just lets them go again? You are prisoners. I will put you apart in a separate wing of this house and guard you for three days, by which I mean today, tomorrow, and some part of the day after. During that time you may choose one of you by lot or by consent to make the journey and fetch the subject of the test. But the others shall remain prisoners, until he stands before me; for by Pharaoh's life, without him you shall not see my face again."

They looked down at their feet and bit their lips.

"Lord," said the eldest, "what you command is possible, up to the point where the messenger reaches home and confesses before our father that before we can have bread we must fetch down his youngest to you. You have no idea how he will go on at that, for our father's mind is very wilful and most of all on this very point, that the young one must always be at home and never go on journeys. You see, he is the youngest fledgling—"

"That is absurd," cried Joseph. "Who would nurse such fairy-tale prejudices about a youngest son? A man with eight children is old and sensible enough to leave home, even if he were twelve times the youngest.

257

Do you think your father will leave you all here in jail for spying rather than to let his youngest go a journey?"

They took counsel together awhile with looks and shoulder-shrugs, and at last Reuben said:

"We think that possible, lord."

"Well, then," said Joseph, and got to his feet, "I think it is not possible. You can't make that wash with a man like me, and as for what I said, by that we shall abide. Set your youngest before me, I charge you strictly. For by Pharaoh's life, if you cannot do it, you shall be convicted as spies."

He nodded to the officer of the guard, who uttered a word; whereat lance-bearers stepped to the side of the frightened men and led them out of the room.

IT IS EXACTED

It was no prison and no pit into which they were thrown. They were only subject to house arrest in a separate part of the palace, a hall with flower-twined columns, to which some steps led down, and which seemed like an unused writing-room or archive for old documents. It afforded sufficient room for ten people and had benches running round it. For tent-dwelling shepherds it was accommodation bordering on the sumptuous. That the apertures for light had gratings over them meant nothing, for such openings always had some kind of lattice. True, guards paced up and down outside the door.

Jacob's sons squatted on their ankle-bones and considered matters. They had plenty of time to choose the man for the return journey to make the proposal to the father; time until day after tomorrow. So first they discussed the situation as a whole and the trouble they were all in. Full of distress, they unanimously voted it to be very evil and threatening. What a diabolical mischance to have fallen under suspicion—nobody knew how or why! They reproached each other for not having seen misfortune coming; their segregation on the frontier, the dispatch to Menfe, the watchful eye during the passage thither, all that, they now saw and said, had been in itself suspicious, in the sense that they themselves had been suspected, while all the time they had taken it for friendliness. All together, there had been a mixture of friendliness and alarmingness that was very puzzling; it upset them and at the same time

258

they still had an odd feeling of pleasure in the midst of all their heavy care and vexation. They could not make out the man before whom they had stood, who had this unhappy suspicion about perfectly sincere and innocent men and put off upon them the burden of proving their innocence. Absurd, unbelievably capricious the suspicion was, from the point of view of their tenfold innocence and business good faith: to call them spies, come to spy out the shame of the land! But he had got it into his head, and quite aside from the life-and-death seriousness of the charge, it really pained the brothers as well; for this man, this keeper of the market and great lord of Egypt, somehow they liked him; it hurt their feelings that it was just this very man who thought so ill of them.

A man good to look at. You might call him handsome and well-favoured. You could, without going too far, compare him to a first-born bull in his adornment. And he was friendly too, in a sort of way. That was just it: the mixture of pleasure and exasperation in the whole thing was concentrated in his person. He was *"tam"*; the brothers concurred in the epithet. He was equivocal, double-faced, a man of both this and that, beautiful and beshadowed, stimulating and disturbing, kindly and dangerous. You could not make him out, just as you could not quite explain the quality *"tam"* in which the upper- and the under-world meet. He could be sympathetic; he had concerned himself about the hardships of their journey. He had found it worth while to ask about the life and well-being of their father, and he had laughed aloud when he heard that the little one was married. But then as though he had only wanted to lull them in friendly security, he flew in their faces with his utterly arbitrary and capricious accusation and ruthlessly flung them into the condition of hostages until they should produce the eleventh son as evidence of good faith—as though that could seriously be considered a refutation! *"Tam"*—there was no other word for it. A man of the solstice, of chopping and changing, at home above and below. He was a business man too, and there was always a trace of trickery about business which belonged to the rest of it.

But of what avail to have noticed these things, what use to lament because the man they liked so much had been so harsh with them? It did not mend matters or help the plight they were in, and that, they confessed to each other, was the worst thing that had ever happened to them. And then came the moment when they put together the unreasonable suspicion they were under with another most reasonable one:

259

perhaps this that was happening had some connection with the suspicion they were used to living under at home—in short, that this visitation was a punishment for long past guilt.

It would be a mistake to conclude, or to gather from the text, that they first mentioned the suspicion in front of Joseph, at their second confrontation with him. No, it had occurred to them before that. Here in the place of their first arrest it mounted to their lips and they spoke of Joseph. That was strange. They were capable of not even the faintest mental association between this lord of the corn and their sold and buried brother, yet—they spoke of him. It was not a merely moral association; they did not at first come on to it by such a route, one suspicion leading back to the other. At first it was not a matter of guilt and punishment, it was a matter of contact.

Mai-Sachme had been right when he remarked in his imperturbable way that it was a far cry between knowing and knowing that you knew. A man cannot come into contact with his blood-brother without knowing it, especially if he has once spilled that blood. But confessing it to oneself is a different pair of shoes. To assert that the sons had at this point in the story recognized the keeper of the market as their brother would be a clumsy way to put it and could only be denied forthwith; for why then their boundless amazement when he revealed himself? No, they had not the faintest idea. And quite specifically they had no idea either why Joseph's image and their ancient guilt came to their minds after or even during their first contact with this attractive and alarming potentate.

This time it was not Asher who out of pure relish put into words the unexpressed feelings that united them. It was Judah, the man with a conscience. For Asher realized that he did not carry enough weight, whereas Judah knew that it was his fitting task.

"Brothers in Jacob," said he, "we are in great peril. Strangers in a foreign land, we are in a trap, we have fallen into a pit of incomprehensible but ruinous suspicion. If Israel refuses Benjamin to our messenger, as I fear he will, either we are dead men, and they will lead us into the house of martyrdom and execution, as the children of Egypt say; or we shall be sold into bondage, either building tombs or washing gold in some horrible place, and never see our children again and the lash of the Egyptian house of bondage will make weals on our backs. How is it that this is happening to us? Bethink yourselves, brothers, why

260

this comes upon us and learn to know God. For God our Father is a God of vengeance, and He forgets not. Neither has He allowed us to forget, but least of all does He Himself forget. Why He did not, at once and straightway, in the long ago, consume us with fire out of His nostrils, but let whole lifetimes pass and coolly postponed the judgment until now it comes upon us, this ask of Him and not of me. For we were young when we did it and he a little lad, and we are not the same people on whom punishment now falls. But I say to you: we have been guilty towards our brother, when we saw the anguish of his soul when he cried up to us from below and we would not hearken. Therefore this calamity comes upon us."

They all nodded heavily, for he had uttered the thought of each; and they murmured:

"Shaddei, Yehu, Eloah."

But Reuben, his grey head between his fists, red in the face with distress, the veins swollen on his forehead, burst out through drawn lips:

"Yes, yes, remember now, grumble and groan! Did I not say so? Did I not tell you when I warned you and said: Lay not your hand on the boy? But who would not hear but you? So now you have it—his blood is exacted of us!"

Precisely that the good Reuben had not really said. Yet he had prevented something: he had prevented Joseph's blood from being shed, at least not more than from the superficial marring of his beauty, and it was not accurate to say that his blood was exacted from them. Or did Reuben mean the blood of the beast which had stood to the father for Joseph's blood? But at least the others did agree that he had warned them of repayment to come; they nodded their heads again and said:

"True, true, it is exacted."

They were given food, and very good food it was, white bread and beer—here again, they felt, was that odd mixture of kindliness and threat. They slept at night on the benches, which even had supports for the lifting up of their heads. Next day they had to choose the messenger who according to the will of this man should travel back to fetch their youngest—and who perhaps might never come again, if Jacob said no. It took them actually the whole day; for they would not leave it to the drawing of lots, but took their reason to their guide in this weighty case, which had to be considered in all its various lights.

261

Who amongst them had most influence with the father to prevail with him? Whom could they themselves best spare in their grave peril? Who was the most indispensable for the seed, that it might survive after they perished? All that had to be weighed and sifted, and the varying answers reconciled; by evening they had not got to the end. Those among them already accurst—in so far as Israel could be accurst—were not the men. So there was much in favour of sending Judah. True, they would be loath to spare him; but he might be the right one to win the father over, and they united in seeing in him the most indispensable for the seed. But he himself took exception. He shook his leonine head and said he was a sinner and bondman, neither worthy nor willing to survive.

So whom should they designate, to whom should the finger point? To Dan, because of his shrewdness? To Gaddiel, on account of his forthright way? To Asher because he liked to move his moist lips to represent them all? Zebulon and Issachar both felt there was nothing to be said in their favour. The lot would probably have fallen upon Naphtali, Bilhah's son, in the end. His talebearing zeal urged him to be gone, his long legs twitched, his tongue already ran; though to the others, and even to himself, he seemed not weighty or considerable enough, either spiritually or mentally, in any but a superficially mythical sense. So up till the third morning the finger did not point decisively at any one of them; but it would probably have pointed to Naphtali if the next audience had not shown all their brain-racking to be vain, since it turned out that the stern keeper of the market had thought of another plan.

THE MONEY IN THE SACKS

Joseph was scarcely once more alone with Mai-Sachme, after receiving and dismissing his train of notables, when with still glowing face, rapt and exulting, he said:

"Mai, did you hear? He still lives, Jacob is alive, he can still hear that I am alive and not dead—and Benjamin is a married man, with a host of children!"

"That was a bad slip you made, Adon, when you burst out laughing before it was repeated to you."

"No matter! I patched it up all right. In such an exciting moment one cannot think of everything. But aside from that, how was it? How did

I do? Did I manage well? Did I adorn the God-story properly? Did I give it some impressive detail?"

"You did it very well, Adon. Wonderful. Very pretty. It was a rewarding situation too."

"Yes, rewarding. But what is not rewarding is you. You take everything for granted, you only make big eyes. When I stood up and accused them, wasn't that pretty telling? I had led up to it, you could see it coming; but when it came it was impressive. And when big Reuben said: 'We recognize you in your greatness, but you not us in our innocence'—wasn't that silver and gold?"

"You had nothing to do with his saying it, Adon."

"But I had led up to it! And, after all, the details of the feast are all my affair. No, Mai, you are ungrateful, and I cannot get at you, and you cannot be surprised. But now I will tell you something: I am not at all as satisfied as I seem, because I was stupid."

"How so, Adon? You did it charmingly."

"One important thing I did badly, and I saw it directly, but it was too late to alter it then. Keeping nine of them as hostages and sending one back was clumsy—a much worse blunder than my laughing was. I must correct it. What should I do with nine of them here, since I can do nothing to hasten the action of the God-story until Benjamin is here, and I cannot even see them, since they are forbidden my countenance until they set him before me? That was badly botched. Are they just to sit here in pawn, while at home there is no food and my father has no bread for the offering? No, it must be arranged just the other way: one stops on here as guarantee, one by whom the father sets least store, say one of the twins (just between ourselves, they were the ones who behaved the most savagely when they all fell upon me); the rest shall go and take home the needful for their hunger—for which they must pay, of course; if I gave it to them it would look too suspicious. I do not for a moment think they would leave the hostage to his fate and confess themselves guilty to the charge, by sacrificing him and not coming back with the little one."

"But that may take a long time, my dear lord. My mind misgives me lest your father refuse to let the little married man go, until the bread is all gone and the lamp again threatens to go out. You are taking a long time for your tale."

"Well, yes, Mai. And why should not such a God-story take time, and we not patiently work on its careful embellishment? If it is a whole year before they come back with Benjamin, it will not be too long for me. What is a year, anyhow, in this story? After all, I have taken you into it expressly because you are patience itself and can lend me some when I get fidgety."

"With pleasure, Adon. It is an honour to be present in it. I can see ahead and guess some of the things you will do to give it form. I think you mean to have them pay for the food you give them to take with them, but secretly, before they leave, you will have the money put in the top of their sacks, so that they will find it at their first stage. That will give them something to puzzle over."

Joseph looked at him big-eyed.

"Mai," said he, "that is capital. That is silver and gold. You remind me of a detail I should probably have come on by myself, because of course it belongs to the story, yet I might have overlooked it. I should never have thought that one who could not be astonished could think up anything so astonishing as that."

"I should not be astonished, my lord, but they will be."

"Yes, they will; they will be bewildered, and they will guess—but not yet know that they guess. And they will feel they are dealing with a man who means well by them and plays tricks on them. I leave it to you to arrange; it is as good as set down in the tale. I charge you to slip the money into the fodder-bags so that everyone finds his own as soon as they feed. Aside from the hostage, they will feel even more bound to come back. And now till day after tomorrow. We must just wait till then, and then I will tell them the new arrangement. But what are a year and a day in a tale like this!"

So on the third day the brothers stood again in the hall of audience before the chair of Joseph the provider—or rather they lay, they pressed their foreheads to the pavement, they rose half-way, lifting their arms palms upwards, then they fell down again, murmuring in chorus:

"You are as Pharaoh. Your servants are without guilt before you."

"Yes, yes, you think you can get round me with bendings and bow-ings; but you are just a sheaf of hollow ears—interpreter, tell them what I said, that they have ears but they hear not. And by hollow I mean hypocritical, dishonest. But you cannot pull the wool over the ears of a man like me with shows of that kind; my suspicions are not to be put to sleep by your bobbing up and down. So long as you have not brought

264

up the evidence and set it here before me, I mean your youngest brother you talk about, just so long you are rascals in my eyes, and fear not God. But I fear Him. Therefore I will tell you how it is ordained. I do not want your children to suffer hunger or your old father to sleep in the dark. You will be given provision according to your numbers at the price fixed by the market. Even you could not imagine that I would give you bread because you are this or that, all sons of one man, and twelve of you in all. That is no reason why a man like me should not deal with you in a businesslike way; especially when I am in all probability dealing with spies. You shall receive for ten families if you can pay for it; but I will let only nine of you carry it home. One of you must remain as hostage and be held here until you get back and wash yourselves clean by setting all eleven of you before me, who once were twelve. And the pawn shall be the one on whom my eye first lights, in other words he!"

And he pointed with his fan to Simeon, who looked defiantly straight ahead as though it did not concern him at all.

They laid him in bonds. While the soldiers put them on, the brothers pressed round and spoke to him. Then it was they came back to what they had already said in private, speaking what was not meant for Joseph's ears; but he heard and understood it.

"Simeon," they said, "courage, man! So it is to be you, he has picked you out. Bear it like the man you are, a stout man and brave, a Lamech! We will do everything to get back and set you free. But you need not fear: it will not be too bad in the meantime, not anything beyond your considerable powers to endure. The man is only half hostile—he is half friendly too. He will not send you to the mines unconvicted. Remember he sent us roast goose into our prison. He is perfectly unaccountable; but he is by no means a bad sort. Maybe you will not be kept in bonds all that time; but if you are, even that is better than washing gold. We do pity you; but the lot has fallen upon you by the man's whim, so what can you do? It might have been any one of us, and indeed it is all of us, God knows. But at least you do get out of one thing, you do not have to stand before Jacob and tell him we have left one of us in pawn and have to take back the youngest-born with us. The whole thing is a calamity, an affliction sent upon us by avenging powers. For remember what Judah said, when he spoke to us all from the depths of his heart and reminded us how our brother cried to us out of the depths of the well and we were deaf to his weeping when he pleaded with us for our father's sake, that he might not fall on his back. And you cannot deny that you two, you and Levi, were the most savage of all in your treatment of him!"

And Reuben added:

"Courage, twin, your children shall have what to eat. All this has come upon us because none of you would listen when I warned you and said: 'Do not lay hands on the boy!' But no, you would not be checked, and when I came back to the pit the boy was gone. Now God is asking us: 'Where is your brother Abel!'"

Joseph heard it. His nose began to prickle inside, he sniffed a little, and his eyes all at once ran over, so that he had to turn round as he sat, and Mai-Sachme had to thump him on the back. It did not help him at once. Even when he turned round, he was blinking his eyes and his speech was halting and thick.

"I will not," said he, "charge you the highest price which the market permits. You shall not be able to say that Pharaoh's friend exploited you when you came to the father of the famine. What you can carry and your sacks can hold will be given, I assign it to you. I am granting you wheat and barley; I recommend you the kind that comes from Uto, the land of the serpent, it is the best sort. What I further advise is that you use the corn for bread and not risk much on the sowing. The drought may continue—in fact it certainly will—and the seed would be wasted. Farewell! I bid you farewell like honest people, for after all you are not yet convicted, however sorely suspect, and in case you set the eleventh brother before me I will believe you, and not take you for monsters of the prime but eleven sacred signs of the zodiac. Yet where is your twelfth sign? It is hidden by the sun. Shall it be so, men? Good luck on the journey. You are a strange, riddling folk. Take heedful way now that ye go, and very heedful when you come back. For now only necessity is your guide, and that is hard enough; but when you return you will be bringing your youngest. The god of your fathers be your shield and buckler! And forget not Egypt, where Usir was lured into the chest and mangled, but became the first in the kingdom of the dead and lighted the under-earthly sheepfold."

So then he broke off the audience and rose from his seat beneath the feather fans. The brothers received their vouchers in an office in the building, whither they were led; and the price was fixed by bushel and measure and load and their animals and beasts of burden were fetched from the courtyard, and the purchase price was weighed out to the sworn officers presiding over the scales: from each of them ten silver rings, so there was a just balance between rings and weights, and the wheat and the barley poured forth out of the bins and filled their sacks to bursting—great double sacks they were, bulging out over the flanks of the heavy-laden beasts. The fodder-sacks, however, were hung on the riding-animals, in front of the saddles. Now they would have set off, to lose no time but get a good piece from Menfe towards the frontier on their first day. But the officials first spread them a meal for their strengthening, while the caravan waited in the court: beer soup with raisins, and legs of mutton. Likewise they were given food for the first days of the journey, packed in gay packages to keep it fresh—that was the custom, they were told; the provisions were included in the purchase price, for this was Egypt, the land of the gods, a land that could well afford to be generous.

It was Mai-Sachme, steward of the lord's house, who said this to them. He had supervised all these arrangements with the greatest care, lifting his heavy black brows above his round brown eyes. They very much liked him and his easy ways; especially when he comforted them about Simeon, and said that he thought his lot would be fairly tolerable. The business of putting him in bonds had been mostly symbolic, it would probably not last. Only if they decamped and left him in the lurch and did not come back with the youngest-born by a year from now at the latest, then, of course, he, Mai, would answer for nothing. For his master—well, of course, he was a potentate: friendly, yes, certainly, very pleasant; but on the other hand quite relentless once he had got a thing into his head. He thought it quite possible things would go very hard with Simeon if they did not follow out what his master had said. Then there would be two gone instead of one—which surely would not please the old man their father any better.

"Oh no," they said. And they would do all they could. But it was hard to live between two fires. Spoken in all honour, of course, so far as his master was concerned; for he was *tam,* a man of the solstice, and had something godlike in his goodness and his awfulness.

"That you may well say," he responded. "Have you had enough? Then good journey to you! And remember my words!"

So then they pulled out from the city; silent at first, for they were depressed about Simeon and also about the problem of bringing home

267

to the father that they had forfeited him, and breaking to him the only way there was to redeem the forfeit. But it was a long way yet to the father, and they talked among themselves too, after a while. They said how much they liked the Egyptian beer soup; and how indeed trouble had overtaken them, but yet they had had easy bargaining and come out well—after all, the father ought to be pleased at that. They spoke of the stocky steward and what a pleasant, composed man he was, not *tam* but quite simply friendly and without any sharp corners. But who knew how he would have behaved if he had been not just an eldest servant, but the master and keeper of the market? Simple people are less tempted, they can easily be kind-hearted; whereas greatness without bounds inevitably made people capricious and unaccountable. The All-Highest Himself was an instance; often He was hard to understand with His uncanny ways. Anyhow, the Moshel had been almost entirely friendly today—up to the point where he had put Simeon in bonds. He had given them good advice, blessed them, and almost solemnly compared them with the signs of the zodiac, of which one was hidden. Probably he was an astrologer, besides being a reader and interpreter of signs. Indeed, he had let fall a hint that he was not without higher means of increasing his own perceptions. It would not surprise them to hear that he could read the stars. But if the stars had told him this about the brothers being spies, then it was sheer nonsense he read in them.

They talked over all these matters; and on the same day got a good piece on in the direction of the Bitter Lakes. But when it began to grow dark they chose a camping-ground for the night, a pleasant, convenient spot, half surrounded by lime cliffs, from which in one place a crooked palm tree grew out and then straightened itself to make a shade. There was a well, and a shelter-hut, and the blackened earth showed that other people had camped here and made fire. The locality has a further rôle to play in the rest of the story; we shall know it again by the palm tree, the well, and the hut.

The nine brothers made themselves comfortable there. Some unloaded the asses and put the packs together. Others drew water and piled branches for a fire. But one of them, Issachar, at once set about feeding his animal—for his nickname of the "bony ass" gave him special sympathy with the wants of his beast, and the animal had several times brayed piteously for its food.

The son of Leah opened his feed-bag. He gave a shout.

"Halloo!" he cried. "Look here! See what I have here, brothers in Jacob! Come hither, all of you!"

They come up from all sides, stretch their necks, and look. Right at the top of the feed-bag Issachar had found his ten silver rings, the price of his load of corn.

They stand and are amazed, they shake their heads and make signs to ward off evil. "Well, bony one," they cry, "what has happened to you?"

Suddenly they rush each to his own bag. Each one looks, and needs not to search: at the top of each man's bag lies his purchase money.

They sit down where they are on the ground. What does it mean? The money had been fairly counted out against the weights; now they have it back again. Their hearts sink under the sheer incomprehensibility of it. What in all the world could it mean? Certainly it is good, it makes the face light up, to get one's money back along with the goods. But yet it was uncanny—particularly because they were under suspicion as it was. There was the mutual good feeling—that in itself was suspicious, and cast a distorted light in both directions. It still remained warming and satisfying—but again, there was a screw loose somewhere, for why, oh, why had God done this?

"Do you know why God does this to us?" asked big Reuben, and nodded at them with the muscles of his face all drawn.

They understood well what he meant. He referred to the old story, and connected this crazy good luck with the crazy bad luck in which they were involved; because once, against his warning (if he *had* actually warned them), they had laid hands on the boy. That they brought God into the thing, asking each other why He did this, showed that they had the same thoughts. But thinking of it, they felt, was going far enough; Reuben need not wag his head at them. Now that this had happened, it would be harder than ever to stand before the father; it gave them still another confession to make. Simeon, Benjamin—and now this queer, this altogether crazy business into the bargain; no, they were not exactly going home with their heads high. Perhaps it might please Jacob to hear that they had got the corn gratis; on the other hand his business honour might be touched, and more than ever they should stand in a bad light before him.

Once they all jumped up at the same time to run to their asses and return the purchase price. But then they all saw the futility of that and sat down again. No sense in that, they said. And truly there was as little

269

sense in returning the money as there was in their having it back in the first place.

They shook their heads. They even kept on shaking their heads in their sleep, often several at a time. And they sighed, too, as they slept—probably not one of them but unconsciously heaved a sigh twice or thrice in the night. Yet anon a smile would play on the lips of this or that sleeper; yes, several of them smiled happily in their sleep.

THE MISSING NUMBER

Good news! The return of his sons was announced to Jacob, and their approach towards the paternal tent, with their asses moving heavily under the burden of Mizraim's corn. At first it was not noticed that there were only nine of them, instead of the ten who had gone forth. Nine makes a sizable group, and with all their animals, nine was almost like ten to the eye. Only a very sharp eye will notice that it is not one more. Benjamin, standing with his father before the house of hair (the old man had him by the hand, the husband of Mahalia and Arbath, like a little lad), did not notice anything wrong. He saw neither nine nor ten—just the brothers, moving up in their goodly numbers. But Jacob saw at once.

Astonishing. After all, the patriarch was close to ninety; one would not expect keenness of vision from those brown eyes, faded and blinking from age, with the flabby sacs beneath them. For unimportant things—and how much has not become unimportant?—they were not keen. But the deficiencies of age are more mental than physical: the senses have seen and heard and felt enough—let them grow dull. But there are things for which they can surprisingly regain the keen ear of the hunter, the quick eye of the sheep-counting shepherd; and the integrality of Israel was a subject on which Jacob saw better than anybody else.

"There are only nine," he said in a decisive though somewhat quavering tone, and pointed. After a very brief space he added:

"Simeon is not there."

"Yes, Simeon is missing," replied Benjamin after a careful look. "I don't see him either. He must be coming after them."

"We will hope so," said the old man very firmly, and clasped the hand

270

of his youngest in his. Thus he let them come up. He did not smile, he said not a word of greeting. He only asked:

"Where is Simeon?"

There they had it. Obviously he was minded, as before, to make things as hard as he could for them.

"Of Simeon later," answered Judah. "Greeting, Father! Of him presently; for the moment only this much: that you have no cause for worry about him. Look, we are back from our journey and once more with the head of our house."

"But not all," said he immovably. "To you too greetings, but where is Simeon?"

"Well, yes, he is missing for the moment," they told him. "He is not here just now. That is because of the business we did and the way the man down there—"

"Perhaps you have sold my son for bread?"

"Of course not. But we bring corn, as our lord sees, plenty of corn, at least plenty for a while and very good quality, wheat and prime barley from Lower Egypt, and you will have your little white loaves for the offerings. That is the first thing we have to tell you."

"And the second?"

"The second may sound somewhat strange, one might even say more than strange; if you like, even abnormal. But we did think it would please you. We have all this good corn for nothing. That is, it was not for nothing at first; we paid for it, and our money faithfully balanced the weights of the land. But when we camped the first night, Issachar found his money in his feed-bag and, lo and behold, we all found ours too, so that we are bringing home the goods and the money too, for which we count on your approval."

"But my son Simeon you do not bring home. It is as good as settled that you have traded him for common bread."

"Again! What can our dear lord be thinking of! We are not the men for that kind of trade. Shall we sit down here with you and reassure you about your son our brother? But first shall we let a little golden grain run into your hand and show you the money we brought back that you may see how gold and silver are present both at once?"

"What I desire first of all is to be informed about my son Simeon," he said.

They sat down in a circle with him and Benjamin and made their

271

report: how they had been segregated on the frontier and sent to Menfe, a great noisy bustling city. How they were led through rows of crouching men-beasts to the great official palace and into a room of overwhelming splendour, and before the seat of the great lord who was as Pharaoh, and was the keeper of the market to whom all the world came for bread. He was a strange kind of man, spoiled by greatness, erratic and charming. They had bowed and bent before the man, Pharaoh's friend, the provider, and thought to deal with him in the way of business; but he showed a double face, both friendly and grim. In part he spoke them very friendly, in part and suddenly very harsh; he had asserted what they could scarcely bear to repeat; namely, that they were spies, who wanted to search out the secret shame of the land—they, the ten true men! Their hearts had misgiven them; they had told him precisely who they were, ten men dealing in truth, all of them sons of one man, the friend of God, in the land of Canaan, and in their full number not ten but twelve, since the youngest was at home with the father and one had been lost in the world at an early age. But the man there, the lord of the land, did not and would not believe that their father was still alive, seeing that they themselves were no longer of the youngest. He had to be told twice, for in the land of Egypt they probably knew no such length of days as our dear lord owns, they probably die off early of their apelike excesses.

"Enough," he said. "Where is my son Simeon?"

They were just coming to that, they said, or at least without long delay. But first for good or ill they must speak of somebody else, and it was a pity he had not gone with them in the first place as they had wished and suggested. If he had they would probably all be back again in full numbers by now; for then the proof would have been forthcoming which the man, not trusting them, had required. For he had never given up the notion that they were spies, or believed their solemn word as to their honourable origins; but had demanded as proof of their innocence that they send the youngest-born of them all before his seat. If they did not, then, he had said, they were proven spies.

Benjamin laughed.

"Lead me to him!" he said. "I am curious to see this curious man."

"You will be silent, Benoni," Jacob sternly admonished him, "and cease your childish prattle. Does an urchin like you mix in such counsels as this?—I have still to hear about my son Simeon."

"Yes," said they, "you would hear if you would listen, dear father, and did not expect us to tell you all the details at once." It had been clear that, lying under such a suspicion and enforced by such a demand, they would not have been allowed to leave—to say nothing of buying bread. There had to be a guarantee. The man had first proposed to keep them all and only send one to bring back the evidence; but by skilful talk and persuasion they succeeded in changing his mind, so that he only kept one, Simeon, and let the rest of them leave, provided with grain.

"And so your brother, my son Simeon, has been sold for debt into the Egyptian house of bondage," said Jacob with terrifying self-control.

The steward of the lord of the land, they answered, a good, steady-going man, had assured them that Simeon would be well treated, everything considered, and that his bonds would soon be loosed.

"Better and better," he said, "do I understand why I was loath to give you leave for the journey. You keep for ever at me with your itch to go down to Egypt, and when I finally consent you make such use of my weakness that only some of you come back, leaving the best of you in the clutch of the oppressor."

"You did not always speak so well of Simeon."

"Lord of Heaven," he said with face upraised, "they accuse me of having no heart for Leah's second, the war-like hero. They act as though it was I had sold him away for a measure of meal and given him to the jaws of leviathan for food for their children—I, not they! How must I thank Thee that Thou hast at least strengthened my heart against their assault and kept me firm against their naughtiness when they wanted to go in their full numbers, taking the youngest as well! They would have been quite capable of coming back without him and telling me: 'You did not set any great store by him'!"

"On the contrary, Father! If all eleven of us had gone and the youngest had been with us, so that we could have set him before the man, the lord of the land, who required his presence, then we should all have come back together. But there is nothing lost, for we need only take Benjamin down and set him before the man, Pharaoh's keeper of the market, there in the hall of the provider, and Simeon will be free and you will have them both back again, your hero and your child."

"In other words, since you have squandered away Simeon you want to tear Benjamin out of my arms and take him to where Simeon is."

"We want that because of the man's whim, to cleanse ourselves and with the proof redeem the pledge."

"You hearts of wolves! You rob me of my children and all your thought is how to decimate Israel. Joseph is no more, Simeon is no more, and now you would take Benjamin away. As you have brewed, so I must drink, and everything goes on over my head."

"No, you describe it not as it is, Father and lord. Benjamin is not to be given up in addition to Simeon, rather both shall come back to you, if only we first set our youngest before the man's eyes that he may see we go about with truth. We humbly beg you to give us Benjamin for the journey that we may free Simeon and Israel may be once more his full number as of yore."

"Full number? And where is Joseph? In plain words you demand from me that I shall send this last remaining one to join his brother Joseph. Well, you are refused."

Then Reuben, the oldest brother, grew hot and gushed forth like boiling water and said:

"Father, hear me now! Listen to me alone who am the head of all this! For not to them shall you give the boy for the journey, but only to me. If I do not bring him back, then may it happen to me thus and thus. If I do not bring him back, then shall you strangle my two sons, Hanoch and Pallu. Strangle them, I say, before my eyes with your own hands and I will not stir an eyelash if I broke my word to you and did not free the pledge."

"Yes, yes, there you go headlong like a waterfall," Jacob answered; "where were you when the swine trod down my lovely son? Did you know how to protect Joseph? What should I have from your sons? And am I an avenging angel to strangle them and decimate Israel with my own hands? I reject you all and your demand, my son shall not go down with you, for his brother is dead and he alone remains to me. If aught happen to him on the way, then the world would see the sight of my grey hairs brought down in sorrow to the grave."

They looked at each other and compressed their lips. It was wonderful, the way he called Benjamin "my son" and not their brother and said that he alone was left to him!

"And Simeon, your hero?" they asked.

He answered: "I will sit here alone and mourn for him. Disperse!"

274

"Our duty and thanks to you," said they, and left him. Benjamin went with them and patted the arm of one or two of the brothers with his short-fingered hand.

"Don't be annoyed," he begged, "and be not bitter that he stands on his dignity. Do you think it flatters me to be called his only son or that I brag because he said I am all that is left him and he refuses to let me go with you? I always know he never forgets how Rachel died to give me my life, and this tutelage I suffer under he practises in bitterness. Think how long it took for him to let you go down, without me; and see how dear you are to him. Now it will only take a little time till he will yield and send me down with you to the land, for he will not leave our brother in the hands of the heathen, he cannot; and besides, how long will the bread last which you were so clever as to get for nothing? So be of good cheer! The little one will have his journey yet. But now tell me a bit more about this keeper of the market, the stern lord who accused you so outrageously and asked such outlandish questions about the youngest of the family! I might almost boast about that—that he wants to see me at all and use me for a witness. Tell me about him. The highest, you said, among all those lower than the highest? And lifted up above all? How did he look to you, how does he speak? It is no wonder I am curious about a man who is so curious about me."

JACOB WRESTLES AT JABBOK

Yes, what is a year compared with this tale; and who would be miserly with time or patience on its account? Joseph practised patience; he had to live and be a statesman and a business man in the meantime. The brothers practised patience, well or ill, with Jacob's self-will, and Benjamin did too, restraining his curiosity about the journey and the curious keeper of the market. We are better off than they, and that not because we already know how it all turned out. That, indeed, is a disadvantage compared with the position of those who lived in the story and experienced it in their own persons; for we must summon up a lively feeling of suspense where by rights there can be none. But yet we do have a certain advantage, because we have power over the whole quantum of time to stretch or shrink it at will. We do not have to pay for the year of waiting in all its daily ups and downs as Jacob had to pay with his seven years in Mesopotamia. We may simply open our lips and say: A year passed—and lo, it has passed. It has passed, and Jacob is ripe.

It is a well-known fact, of course, that meteorological conditions in this quarter of the globe remained erratic for a considerable time. The drought continued to oppress the lands in which our story moves. Misfortunes, they say, never come singly; one leads to another and then to another, until instead of the hit-or-miss pattern usually obtaining in this world of chance and change, it seems as though fate took a diabolic delight in making the same bad luck come to pass time after time with infuriating repetition. Of course, there simply has to come a turn sooner or later; otherwise it would end by nullifying itself. But it can go on and on for years, without rhyme or reason; that it should repeat itself as many as seven times is not, generally speaking, anything extraordinary.

In our explanations of the cloud movements between the sea and the African Alps in the land of the Moors where the waters of the Nile take their rise, we have, indeed, considered the how but not the why of this situation. For once you begin with the why you can never get to the end. It is like the dunes by the sea, where behind each foreland lies still another and the space of time where you might come to final rest is somewhere in dim infinity. The Nourisher did not grow great and overflow its banks, because in the land of the Moors it did not rain. It did not rain because no rain fell in Canaan; and that was because the sea manufactured no clouds for seven, or certainly at least for five years on end. Why not? Here too there are overarching reasons reaching into cosmic matters and to the heavenly bodies which doubtless control our wind and weather. There are the sun-spots; they are a sufficiently remote cause perhaps; yet since every child knows that the sun is not the last and highest, and since Abram, in his time, refused to worship it as the final cause, we ourselves should be ashamed to stop at it. There are higher orders in the All, which compelled even the sun's fixed regal status to subordinate its motions; and the sun-spots on its disk are in their turn, so to speak, a subordinate why; but even from this you must not conclude that the final and ultimate resting-place lies in those super-systems or in still superior systems. The ultimate obviously lies or has its seat in a remoteness which is at the same time a nearness, since in it farness and nearness, cause and effect are all one; it is where we find ourselves by losing ourselves and where we suspect a design which for the sake of its ends renounces even the bread for the offering.

The drought and the scarcity were sore and oppressive indeed. It did not take even a whole year for Jacob to be ripe. The provisions which his sons had so luckily and uncannily got for nothing had all been consumed; they had not been much among so many, and more were not to be had anywhere in the land at any price. So, a few moons earlier than the year before, Israel brought up the subject the brothers had been waiting for.

"Tell me what you think," he said. "For to me it seems that there is a preposterous contradiction yawning between the riches which I own and which have increased since I broke the dusty bolts of Laban's kingdom, and the present bad state of things; for we have neither seed-corn nor bake-stuff and our children cry for bread."

Yes, they told him; that was due to the bad times.

"They are strange times," said he. "A man has a whole troop of grown sons whom with God's help he did not fail to raise up to his aid; and they sit here on their backsides and lift not a finger against the want that consumes us."

"Yes, that is easy to say; but what can we do?"

"Do? In Egypt, as I hear on all sides, there is grain market. How would it be if you gird yourselves for the journey and go down and buy a little bread?"

"That would be splendid, Father, and we would have gone already. But you forget what the harsh ruler down there said about Benjamin: that we should not see his face unless our youngest brother were with us, and we could show him on the spot in token of our good faith. It appears the man is an astrologer. He says that of the twelve one is hidden behind the sun; but it must not be two at once that are hidden, and the eleventh must be set before him before he will even see us again. Give us Benjamin and we will go."

Jacob sighed.

"I knew that would come," he said, "and that you would only torment me again about the child."

And he chided them loudly.

"Unhappy that ye are, and unheeding! Why did you have to prattle and tattle and in your folly turn out all your affairs before the man so that he heard you had another brother, my son, and could demand him from me? If you had been dignified and stuck to business without prattling, he would know nothing about Benjamin and could not ask my

277

heart's blood as the price of flour for bread! Richly you deserve that I should curse you one and all!"

"Do not, lord," said Judah; "for what would become of Israel? Consider in what straits we were and how we were forced to tell truth when he set about us with his suspicion and examined us about our kindred. For he questioned us so narrowly: 'Does your father yet live?' 'Have you another brother?' 'Is your father well?' And when we told him it was not so well with you as it should be, he scolded us loudly and railed at us for letting it come to that."

"H'm," went Jacob, and stroked his beard.

"We were frightened," Judah went on, "by his severity, yet drawn to him by his interest. For after all it is no small thing when such a great man of the world, at whose mercy we then were, shows such concern." And how, Judah went on, could they have foreseen that the man would demand their brother's presence and lay upon them so bindingly to fetch Benjamin down?

Thus Judah, the tried and tested man, who today took the word. For they had so planned it among them, in case Jacob showed signs of being ripe. Reuben was already out of the field, after he had impulsively made the clumsy and offensive suggestion that Jacob should strangle his two sons. Levi, though much upset by the loss of his twin, and only half a man since then, could not be put forward on account of Shechem. But Judah spoke very well, with manly persuasiveness and warmth of feeling.

"Israel," he said, "overcome yourself, even though you wrestle with yourself until the dawn, as once before you did with another. This is a Jabbok hour, would you go out of it like a hero of God! Lo, the man's mind down there is unchangeable. We shall not see him, and Leah's third son remains fallen to the house of bondage, and there is not even a thought of bread, unless Benjamin is with us. I, your lion, know how bitter it is for you to yield up Rachel's last pledge to take a journey, on account of the 'being always at home'; and worse than that, a journey down to the land of mud and dead gods. And you probably do not trust this man, the lord in the land, suspecting that he is laying a trap for us and will give back neither the pledge nor the youngest—or perhaps not any of us at all. But I say to you, I who know men and expect not much good from high or low: the man is not such a man; so far I know him and know that, and would put my hand in the fire for it: to lure us into a trap is not in his mind. He may be strange and not quite canny, but

278

he is also very winning, and though full of error yet not false. I, Judah, go bail for him, as also I go bail for your youngest son, our brother. Let him go down at my side, and I will be father and mother to him, like you; both on the road and in the land, that he strike not his foot against a stone nor is besmirched in his soul by the vices of Egypt. Give him into my hand, that we may journey at length, and live and not die: we, you, and the little children of us all. For at my hand shall you require him, and if I bring him not and set him before your face I will bear the blame all my life long. As you have him now, so shall you have him again—and could have had him long since as now you have him, for had we not delayed we could have been there and back twice over with the pledge, the witness, and the bread."

"Until the dawn," answered Jacob, "give me time."

And by next morning he had surrendered and acquiesced, he would give Benjamin to go a journey—not a journey to Shechem, a few days distant, but some seventeen days down into the underworld. Jacob had red eyes and failed not to express how hard the enforced resolve had borne upon his soul. But as he had not only honourably and sorely wrestled with necessity and come off conqueror, but expressed his pain with such great-hearted dignity, they were all much edified, and all those round about him said with feeling: "Lo, Israel has this night overcome himself!"

His head drooped upon his shoulder as he said:

"If it must be so, and stands written in bronze that everything shall go out from me, then take it and do it and go forth, for I consent. Take of the choicest things in your packs, for which our land is praised through-out the world, to present to the man to soften his heart: oil of balsam, gum of tragacanth from the goat's-thorn, grape honey cooked to a thick-ness, to drink in water or sweeten the dessert, also pistache nuts and fruit of the terebinth—and call it little in his eyes. Furthermore take double the money, for the new grain and for the earlier time as well, for I recall that the money was found in your sacks and there may have been a mistake. And take Benjamin—yes, yes, you hear me aright— take him and lead him down to the man that he may stand before him. I give my consent. I see on your faces consternation painted at my words; but my decision is final, Israel girds himself up to be as a man who is bereft of his children. But may El Shaddei," he broke out, his hands raised to heaven, "give you pity in the man's eyes that he yield you your other brother back, and Benjamin. Lord, only as a loan and to be returned give I him to you; for the journey only, let no misunderstanding be between me and you, for I offer him not to be devoured like my other son, I will have him back! Remember, O Lord, the bond, that the heart of man become fine and holy in You and You in it. Fall not below the feeling human heart, O mighty One, and defraud me not of the boy on the journey and fling him to the devourer, but be moderate, I implore You, and honourably return me the loan; then I will serve You in the dust and burn before You what shall ravish Your nostrils, the very best parts!"

So he sent up his prayers. Then he arranged with Eliezer, whose name was Damasek, to make ready the little son of death for the journey and to provide him in all ways like a mother; for at the next dawning the brothers should set out, in order not to miss the caravan from Gaza. And hearing this, Benoni's eager cup overflowed with joy, seeing that at last he should be released out of his symbolic durance and go to see the world. He did not jump for joy before Jacob and the brothers, nor kick his heels together, because he was not seventeen, as Joseph had been, but nearly thirty; and he would not wound that soft pathetic heart with showing his gladness. Besides, his darkened existence as a mother-slayer did not suit with much jumping for joy, and he might not fall out of his rôle. But before his wives and children he plumed himself not a little over his freedom of action and the fact that he was going down to Mizraim to set Simeon free, he and he alone having such power over the lord of the land.

They were able to shorten their preparations because they could supply in Gaza all their wants for the trip through the desert. For the present their packs chiefly consisted of presents for Simeon's jailer, the Egyptian keeper of the market, which young Eliezer had taken out of the stores: the aromatic distillations, the grape syrup, the gums and myrrh, the nuts and fruit. A single donkey was reserved for these gifts, for which the country was renowned.

In the light of early dawn the brothers set forth on their second journey, in the same strength as before, one less and one more. The families and servants stood about, and within the group the ten with their beasts on halters. But at the heart of it stood Jacob, and held all that he had left of the beloved of his youth. That was what the audience came for: to see how Jacob took leave of his dearest possession and to be edified by his pangs and his stately expression of them. Long he held his youngest to him; hung round him the phylactery from his own neck and murmured at his cheek with eyes upraised. But the brothers bent theirs on the ground, with bitter, forbearing smiles.

"Judah, it was you," he said at last; all of them heard him. "You have given your bond for this child, that I may require him at your hand. But now hearken: you are released from your bond. For can a man give his bond for God? Not upon you will I build my trust, for what could you avail against God's anger? I will build upon Him alone, who is the Rock and the Shepherd, that He grant me back this pledge that I have entrusted to Him in good faith. Hear, all of you: He is no monster who mocks at human hearts and treads them like a savage in the dust. He is a great God, purified and enlightened, a God of the bond and of good faith; if any man is to vouch for Him, I need you not, my lion, for I myself will vouch for His faith and He will not so injure Himself as to make His guarantee a mock. Go!" he said, and put Benjamin from him, "go in the name of God, the true and the merciful. But all the same, take care of him!" he added in a breaking voice, and turned away to his dwelling.

THE SILVER CUP

And so, in due course, Joseph the provider came from his office to his house, and the news was in his heart that the ten travellers from Canaan had passed the frontier. Mai-Sachme took it in at once, and asked:

"Well, Adon, so we are for it, the waiting time is over?"

"We are," answered Joseph, "and it is. It has turned out as it ought to, they have come. The third day from today they should be here— with the little one," said he, "with the little one. This God-story of ours made a pause for a while and we had to wait. But time does not stand still, and it only seems to have no burden, and the shadow of the sun moves slowly on. One must steadfastly trust himself to time and trouble about it hardly at all—the Ishmaelites taught me that, with whom I travelled—for it continues to ripen and brings everything in its train."

"So now," said Mai-Sachme, "there is much to think of, and the course of the plot has to be carefully thought out. Shall I make suggestions?"

"Ah, Mai, as though I had not long ago thought out and composed everything and had in my composing spared any care! It will run off as though it were already written down and was being played according to the script. There are no surprises, only the thrill of seeing the familiar of long ago become the present. And I am not nearly so excited this time either, I only feel solemn as we go on to the next scene; at most my heart gives a jump at the thought of the 'It is I'; I mean it jumps on their account—you would better have a draught ready for them."

"It shall be done, Adon. But even though you want no advice I will just give you some: take care for the little one! He is not merely half of your blood, he is your blood brother, and besides, as I know you, you will not be able to leave things alone, you will put him on the scent. The youngest of the family is always the cleverest; he might easily get ahead of your 'It is I' by saying 'It is you' and spoil your whole plan."

"Well, and what then, Mai? I shouldn't mind much. There would be a great laugh, as when children build a sand-castle and knock it down again and shout for joy. But I don't think so. A little chap like that, and tells Pharaoh's friend and Vice-Horus, the great man of business, right to his face: 'Pooh! You are nobody but my brother Joseph!' That would be impertinent. No, the rôle of saying who I am will fall to me."

"Will you receive them again in the hall of audience?"

"No, this time it shall be here. I will have luncheon with them, they shall eat with us. Slay and provide for eleven more guests than you had down the third day from today. Who are invited for that day?"

"Some city dignitaries," said Mai-Sachme, consulting his memorandum. "Their worships Ptah-hotpe, reader from the house of Ptah; the god's Champion, Colonel Entef-oker, of the god's household troops; the chief surveyor and boundary-inspector Pa-neshe, who has a tomb where the Lord lies; and from the main commissariat a couple of scribes."

"Good. They will find it strange to sit down with the foreigners."

"Strange indeed, I am afraid, Adon. There are difficulties about the food laws and customs, I must warn you, and certain prohibitions. To some it may seem an offence to eat with the Ibrim."

"Go along with you, Mai, you talk like Dudu, a dwarf I once knew, who worshipped all the old saws. Trying to teach me my Egyptians—as though they still had a horror of such things! They would have to have a horror of eating with me; everybody knows I was not brought up on Nile water. Here is Pharaoh's ring: Be as myself; that will silence all objections. Whoever I eat with must obey that injunction at table too, and then there is Pharaoh's teaching which everybody professes who wants to stand well at court: that all men are the beloved children of his father. But of course you can serve us separately to preserve the forms. The Egyptians by themselves, the brothers by themselves, and me by myself. But you must seat my brothers together according to age, big Reuben first and Benoni last. Be careful to make no mistake, I will tell you the order again and you can write it down."

"Very well, Adon. But it is a risk. How do you come to know their ages so well without their being surprised at it?"

"And you must put my cup at my place, my silver cup that I look into."

"Yes, your cup. Will you tell them their ages out of it?"

"I could use it for that too."

"I wish, Adon, I could use it for prophesying too. I wish I could read, the way gold pieces and gems look in clear water, what you planned for the story and how you build it up to the point where you make yourself known. If I do not know, I fear I shall be able to serve you but poorly; but I must serve you and be useful to you in order not merely to stand about in this story into which you have so kindly taken me."

"That you certainly shall not. It would not be right. In the first place you are to put the cup at my place out of which I sometimes read, just for fun."

"The cup—very good, the cup," said Mai-Sachme, widening his eyes as though in an effort to remember. "They bring you Benjamin and you see your little brother again among his brothers. And when you have eaten with them and filled their sacks a second time they will take the youngest-born away with them again and go home to your father and there you will be!"

"Look again into the cup, Mai, see how it looks in the water! They go away again, of course; but perhaps they have forgotten something, so they have to come back again?"

The captain shook his head.

"Or they have taken something with them and we miss it, and go after them on account of it and fetch them back again?"

Mai-Sachme looked at him round-eyed, his brows drawn up; slowly his small mouth widened in a smile. When a man has a little mouth, no matter how square and strongly he may be built, when he smiles it is like a woman smiling. Thus Mai-Sachme smiled and despite his growth

283

of black beard his smile was sweet and almost feminine. He must have been pleased with what he read in the cup, for he nodded to Joseph with a twinkle in his eye and Joseph nodded too. He lifted his hand and clapped his steward on the back. And Mai-Sachme—despite the fact that Joseph had once been a convict in his prison—lifted his hand too and patted the other's shoulder. Thus they stood, nodding and clapping; it was clear that both fully understood how the story was to run off.

THE MEAL WITH THE BROTHERS:
FRAGRANCE OF MYRTLE

And here is how it ran off, in its appointed hour. Jacob's sons made their entry into Menfe, the house of Ptah, and alighted at the same inn as before. They were relieved to have brought Benjamin safely so far; during the nearly seventeen days of the journey they had handled him like a basket of eggs; partly out of fear of Jacob, partly because he was the most important member of their party, the indispensable evidence to convince the two-faced keeper of the market. Without Benjamin they would neither see the man's face nor get Simeon back. These would have been reasons enough to treat the little one like the apple of their eye, to give him of the best in food and lodgement and guard him as they did their precious water supply. Fear of the man stood in the foreground and behind it fear of the father. But behind those was still a third motive for their assiduity: namely, that they wanted to make good in Benjamin what they had sinned in Joseph. For the memory of him and of their evil deed was astir in them now after all these years, owing to the events of their first journey; it had risen up out of the drift of the years, till now it seemed only yesterday that they had sold their brother and uprooted a stem out of Israel. Retribution was in the air, they felt it like a hand drawing them to an accounting; a zealous care for Rachel's second child seemed to them the best means of making the hand relax its grip.

They dressed Benjamin in a fine gay smock with fringes and draperies, to introduce him to the lord of the land; his furry thatch of hair they anointed till it truly looked like a shiny helmet; they lengthened his eyes with a pointed pencil. But when they announced themselves at the great office where tickets were issued and grain delivered, they were sent on to the provider's own house. That alarmed them as everything alarmed them that did not go as it had before and seemed to involve them in fresh complications. Why were they set apart and sent to the man's private house? Did it portend good or ill? Possibly it had to do with the money returned to them in so strange a way. Perhaps the trick was now being used against them in a new trick and because of the money they had carried off all eleven of them were now to be enslaved. They had the wretched money with them as well as more for fresh supplies; but the fact did little to reassure them. They were strongly tempted to turn round, not to show themselves to the man but to take refuge in flight—and particularly because they feared for Benjamin. But the little brother spoke up boldly and insisted on being brought before the keeper of the market. He was adorned and anointed, he said, and he had no reason to hide from the man; as a matter of fact, neither had they, for it was only a mistake that the money had been returned and innocent men must not behave as though they were guilty.

Yes, guilty, they said. A little guilty in general they always did feel: not in this particular case, of course, it was only that they never did feel quite comfortable. He, Benjamin, could say what he liked; he was always at home, he had never been exposed, he never found unexplained money in his feed-bag, whereas they had had to be out in the world, where it was hard to keep oneself entirely pure.

Benoni tried to cheer them. The man, he said, was a man of the world, he would understand that kind of sense of guilt. About the money: it was certainly a puzzle, but probably perfectly all right—and had they not come, among other reasons, in order to give it back? But they knew as well as he did that Simeon must be released and that they had to have more provisions. There could be no talk of running away; that was to be called spies and thieves and brother-murderers to boot.

They knew it all as well as he did. They knew they had to face the music at the risk of being made slaves all round. The delicacies they had brought with them, Jacob's presents and bribes, the pride of their native land, gave them a little hope; and they felt something might be gained by trying to speak first with that pleasant and equable steward, if they could get hold of him.

This they succeeded in doing. They reached the gracious villa which Pharaoh had given his friend in the best quarter of the town, dismounted from their asses at the gate, and led them round the lotus pond to the house. And there he was, the man who had inspired their confidence; he came towards them down the terrace, greeted them, and thanked them for keeping their word even after this lapse of time. They presented their youngest brother, at whom he looked round-eyed and said "Bravo!" The animals were led round to the courtyard, where the servants unloaded them and carried into the house the bales containing Canaan's pride. Mai-Sachme led the brothers up the steps, and as they went they consulted anxiously with him about the money. Some of them had already begun as soon as they saw him, almost from afar, so eager they were:

"Worthy house-steward, head superintendent," said they, "thus and so it was; incredible as it seems, so it was." But here was double the money, for they were honest men. They had found the previously paid-out silver, first one of them and then all of them, in their feed-bags at the first camp, and the mysterious treasure-trove had greatly troubled them. Here it was again full weight, along with more money for the new purchases. His master, Pharaoh's friend, would not lay it up against them and condemn them?

They all talked at once, they tugged his arm in their distress and vowed they would not enter under the beautiful doors of the house unless he swore that his master was playing them no trick nor laying the mysterious chance to their charge.

But he was calmness itself; he quieted them and said:

"Calm yourself, my friends, do not be afraid, for everything is in order. Or even if out of the natural order, it is a benign miracle. We got our money and that must content us, it is no reason why we should play tricks on you. After all you have told me I can only assume that your God and the God of your fathers amused Himself by putting the treasure in your sacks. No other explanation suggests itself to me. Probably you are His good and faithful servants and He would show you His awareness once in a way—that one can understand. But you seem to me very much excited, and that is not good. I will have some foot-baths prepared for you, first for hospitality's sake, for you are our guests and are to take the meal with Pharaoh's friend; but also they draw the blood from the head and will have a soothing effect. Now go inside and see who is waiting for you in the hall!"

And lo, inside there stood their brother Simeon, quite unattended and not in the least hollow-eyed or wasted, but as bouncing and heroic as ever. He had fared very well, he told his brothers as they crowded round him; he had lived in a room in the office building and been very comfortable for a hostage, though he had not seen the Moshel's face again and had lived in fear lest they come not back. But the excellent food and drink had kept him up. They asked Leah's second to forgive them for taking so long, on account of Jacob's obstinacy—of course he would know how it was, and of course he did, and he rejoiced with them, especially with his brother Levi, for the two ruffians had missed each other sorely. There was no kissing and embracing, but they could scarcely leave off punching each other in the ribs.

The brothers all sat down together and washed their feet. Then the steward led them into the hall where the meal was laid out, magnificent with flowers and fruit and beautiful tableware. And he helped them arrange their gifts on a long buffet: spices, honey, fruits, and nuts, to make a fine display for the master's eye. But presently Mai-Sachme had to hurry away, for people were arriving, and Joseph came home with the Egyptian gentlemen whom he had invited as his guests of the day: the prophet of Ptah, the Champion of the god, the chief surveyor, and the masters of the books. He came in with them and said: "Greetings!" They fell on their faces as if they had been mown down.

He stood a little while, rubbing his fingers across his forehead. Then he repeated:

"Greetings, friends. Stand up and let me see your faces that I may recognize them. For you recognize me, I see, as the keeper of the market of Egypt who had to behave sternly to you because of this priceless land. But now you have appeased me and reassured me by your return in your proper numbers so that all the brothers are assembled in one room and under one roof. That is capital. Do you notice that I am speaking to you in your own tongue? Yes, I can speak it now. The other time you were here made me aware that I knew no Hebrew and it annoyed me. So since then I learned it. A man like me can do such things in a twinkling. But how are you all anyhow? And first of all, is your old father still alive about whom you told me, and is he well?"

"Your servant, our father," they said, "is very well and keeps his usual state. He would be much touched by the kind inquiry."

And they fell down again with their faces to the pavement.

"Enough of this bowing and bending," he said; "too much in fact. Let me see. Is that your youngest brother you told me about?" he asked in

287

rather clumsy Canaanitish, for he was really out of practice, and he went up to Benjamin. The benedict, standing there in his fine garb, respectfully raised his clear grey eyes, with their usual expression of gentle sadness, to Joseph's face.

"God be gracious to you, my son," Joseph said, and laid his hand on the other's shoulder. "Have you always had such good eyes, and such a fine shining helmet of hair even when you were a little urchin and ran about in the meadows?"

He swallowed.

"I will come back in a moment," he said. "I will just—" and went out quickly, probably to his own sleeping-chamber. He came back presently, with his eyes fresh-washed.

"I am neglecting all my duties," he said, "and not making my guests acquainted with each other. Gentlemen, these are merchants from Canaan, of distinguished parentage, all sons of one remarkable man."

And he told the Egyptians the names of Jacob's sons, in the order of their age, very fluently and rhythmically: after every third name he dropped his voice, omitted his own, of course, making a little pause after Zebulon, and then finished: "and Benjamin." The brothers, certainly, were vastly surprised to have him know all this, and they marvelled among themselves.

Then he named the names of the Egyptian dignitaries, who behaved so stiffly that it made Joseph smile. Then he commanded the meal to be served, rubbing his hands as one who goes to table. But his steward pointed to the presents spread out on the buffet, and he praised and admired them warmly.

"From the old man your father?" he asked. "That is a touching attention. You must take him my best thanks."

It was a trifle, they told him: a few of the good things their country boasted.

"It is not a trifle, it is a great deal," he demurred. "And more than that, the quality is very fine. I have never seen such fine tragacanth. Or such pistache nuts. You can tell the wonderful taste of the oil from here. Only in your home do they grow like that. I can hardly keep my eyes off them. But now we must sit down."

Mai-Sachme showed them all to their places; and the brothers found fresh matter for wonder; for they were seated exactly in order of age, only in reverse, for the youngest sat next the master of the house, then

288

Zebulon, Issachar, and Asher and so on to big Reuben. The feast was laid so that the dishes stood in an open triangle between the columns running round the hall; and the apex of the triangle was the host's seat. On his right were the Egyptian notables, on his left the Asiatic foreigners, so that he presided over both, with Benjamin on his left hand and the prophet of Ptah on his right. In hearty and hospitable spirit he exhorted them all to fall to and not to spare the food and drink.

The meal that followed is world-famous for being "merry." The early stiffness of the Egyptian guests was put to rout; they soon thawed out and forgot that it was an abomination to break bread with the Hebrews. The King's Champion, Colonel Entef-oker, was the first to relax, after several deep draughts of Syrian wine. He picked out the forthright Gad as the most likeable of the sand-dwellers, and made the room ring by shouting across the table to him.

We must not be put off by the fact that tradition makes no mention of the presence of Joseph's wife, the daughter of the sun-priest; but represents the banquet as being entirely masculine—though it was Egyptian practice for married couples to eat together and the mistress of the house was regularly present at banquets. But the description that has been handed down is correct: Asenath was not present at the meal. That might be explained by recalling the terms of the marriage contract and concluding that the maiden was visiting her parents at the time. However, the true explanation lies in the routine of Joseph's days, which seldom permitted the exalted one to eat with his wife and children. This meal with the brothers and the resident honourables, however lively and enjoyable it was, was not a social but a business function, and Pharaoh's friend had to perform it nearly every day. Thus he usually took only the evening meal with his wife, in the women's wing of the house, after spending a little time playing with his charming half-breed sons, Manasseh and Ephraim. At midday, then, he took his meal in male society, either with the ranking and upper officials of the office or with important travelling dignitaries or emissaries or plenipotentiaries of foreign powers; the present feast was no exception in the house of the friend of the harvest of God. That is, it was outwardly no exception; for its actual significance, its place in the structure and development of a marvellous God-story and recurrent feast; or the reason why the exalted host was so uncommonly and infectiously hilarious—none of the guests knew aught of all this at the time.

None of the guests? Can we bear out that comprehensive statement? Mai-Sachme, standing stockily in the open side of the triangle and pointing the nimble cup-bearers and dapifers hither and thither with a white pointer, he knew; but he was not a guest. Was there any other for whom the disguise had a disturbing, delicious, uncanny, unconfessed semi-transparence? The question must certainly refer to little Turturra-Benoni, sitting at the left of the host; but it must as certainly remain unanswered. Benjamin's feelings were indescribable, they have never been described, and this narrative will not attempt what has never been attempted: will not put into words the faint intuition, with its accompanying mingled sweetness and terror, for a long time not even daring to be a conscious intuition but always stopping short at a sudden brief dreamlike attack of memory, which made the heart beat fast, but was after all only a recognition of this or that point of likeness between two quite different and remote phenomena: one of them from childhood days long gone and one here present in the flesh. Let us try to imagine what it was like.

They sat at ease in comfortable chairs with footstools, each had a table at his side, laden with delights for the eye and the appetite: fruit, cakes, vegetables, pastries, cucumbers and melons, cornucopias with flowers and spun-sugar ornaments. At the other side of each chair was a dainty washing-stand with amphora and copper refuse basin. Each person had the same. Aproned servants supervised by the wine steward kept the beakers full; others received the main dishes, veal, mutton, fish, fowl, and game, from the steward of the buffet and brought them to the guests, who, because of the high rank of the host, did not have precedence over him. For Adon not only was served first but also received the best and in greater quantity than the rest—to the end, indeed, that he could share with others; it is written: "Food was given them from his own dish." In other words, he sent with his compliments to various guests now a roast duck, now a quince jelly or a gilded bone trimmed with delicious ringlets of crust. He sent to the Egyptians, he sent to the stranger guests. But to the youngest of the Asiatics, his neighbour on the left, he gave over and over from his own plate. Such proofs of favour meant a great deal and were watched and counted by the Egyptians. They reckoned it up to each other and related it afterwards, so that it has come down to us, that the young Bedouin actually had five times as much as anyone else at the master's table.

Benjamin was embarrassed; he begged to be excused from all these gifts and looked round apologetically at the Egyptians as well as at his own brothers. He could not have eaten all he got even if he had felt like eating. He was possessed by a dazed and uneasy feeling; it sought, found, lost, and then so suddenly and unmistakably found again that his heart would give a quick, heavy, irregular throb. He looked into the beardless face of his host, framed in the hieratic winged cap, this man who had demanded him in evidence, this great Egyptian, a somewhat heavy figure, in the white garment with glittering jewels on his breast. He looked at the mouth moving after its own fashion as it smiled and spoke. He looked into the black eyes, which met his own sparkling with fun but then grew veiled as though in retreat; they looked most grave and forbidding at just those moments when Benjamin's own had widened with terror and incredulous joy. He looked at the hand as it gave him something or lifted the cup to drink: at its articulation and at the sky-blue stone that adorned it. And he was pervaded by an old, familiar, childhood air: pungent, sun-warmed, spicy, the essential aroma of all the love and trust, security and adoration, all the childlike bewildered sympathy, intuition, and half-knowledge Benoni had ever known. It was the scent of myrtle. The memory-fragrance was identical with what went on inside him as he faithfully, anxiously, trustingly tried to explore this bewitching riddle, this alarming and blissful possibility of a point where two things met: the jolly, friendly present and something far higher, something of the divine—ah, that was why Turturra's blunt little nose sniffed the spicy scent of childhood! For it was now as it had been then, only the other way on—but what did that matter?—and in the high and unknown presence here the familiar tried to make itself known in flashes that brought his heart into his mouth.

The lord of the grain chatted delightfully with him during the meal—five times as much with him as with the Egyptian dignitaries on his right. He asked Benoni about his life at home, his father, wives, and children; the oldest was named Belah, the youngest—youngest for the present—Muppim. "Muppim," said the lord of the grain. "Give him a kiss from me when you get home. I find it exquisite that the youngest son should have a youngest son. But what is the one next youngest? He is called Rosh? Bravo! Has he the same mother as the other—yes? And do they ramble about together through a green and flowery world? I hope the older lad does not frighten the little urchin with all sorts of God-stories

291

and far-flung fancies unsuitable for small ears. You must look out for that, Father Benjamin!" Then he talked about Manasseh and Ephraim, his own sons, borne to him by the daughter of the sun. How did Benjamin like the names? "Very much," said Benjamin and was on the point of asking why he had chosen such significant ones; but hesitated and just sat there, wide-eyed. So the prince in the land of Egypt began to tell anecdotes about Manasseh and Ephraim, the funny things they said and the mischief they did. Benjamin was reminded of some nursery tale of his own; and the two were seen to be rocking with laughter over their stories.

As they talked and laughed Benjamin took heart to say:

"Would Your Excellency perhaps answer a question which puzzles me?"

"To the best of my ability," the other replied.

"It is only," said the little man, "that you should gratify my curiosity about the knowledge of us which you show in your arrangements. You have our names by heart, my brothers' and mine, also our ages in their right order, so you could reel them off—the way our father says all the children in the world will have to know them, because we are a chosen people of God. How do you know and how is it your steward could seat us in order of age from first-born to last?"

"Ah," answered the keeper of the market, "you are surprised at that? It is quite simple. Do you see this cup here? Silver, with a cuneiform inscription. I drink out of it, but I can see things in it too. Of course, I have a good intelligence; it may be above the average, for I am what I am, and Pharaoh himself wished to be higher than I only by the height of the royal throne. But even so I could scarcely get on without my cup. The King of Babylon presented it to Pharaoh's father—I do not mean myself, though you might think so because of my title, Father of Pharaoh (Pharaoh by the bye calls me uncle), I mean his real earthly father— not divine—Pharaoh's predecessor, King Neb-ma-re. The King of Babylon sent the cup to him as a present and so it came to my lord and master, who deigned to pleasure me with it. It is a thing I can really use; its properties are most helpful to me. I can read the past and future in it, penetrate the mysteries of the world, and lay open the relationships between them. Take for instance the order of your birth: I read it out of my cup with no trouble at all. A good part of my cleverness, pretty much all that is above the average, comes from this cup. I don't give this away to all and sundry, of course; but as you are my guest and my neighbour at table I don't mind telling you. You would not believe it; but when I hold the cup in the right way I can see pictures of distant places and things that happened there. Shall I describe your mother's grave to you?"

"You know she is dead?"

"Your brothers told me that she had gone westwards early in life; a lovely one whose cheeks smelled like rose leaves. I do not pretend to have got this knowledge by supernatural means. But now I need only put the magic cup to my forehead, like this, and I see your mother's grave, so clearly that it surprises even me. The clearness of the picture comes from the brightness of the morning sun; there are mountains; there is your own town on a slope, not far away at all, not more than a furlong. There are small ploughed fields in among the shingle, vineyards on the right and a dry masonry wall in the foreground. And there is a mulberry tree growing on the wall, old and partly hollow; the trunk leans over and is propped up with stones. No one has ever seen a tree more clearly than I see that mulberry tree with the morning breeze playing in its leaves. Near the tree is the grave with a stone marker. And lo, some one is kneeling at the spot; he has brought food and water and un- leavened bread—he must be the rider of the ass waiting under the tree— what a nice animal, white with sensitive ears and a curly forelock grow- ing down into its friendly eyes. I would never have thought the cup could make me see all that so plainly. Is that your mother's grave?"

"Yes, it is hers," said Benjamin. "But tell me, my lord, can you see the ass so clearly and not the rider?"

"Him I see, if possible, even more clearly. But there is not much to see. He is just a young chap, seventeen at most, kneeling with his offer- ing. He has got some kind of bright-coloured finery draped round him, the silly youth, with figures woven in it. He must be foolish in his head, for he thinks he is just going a ride, but actually he is riding to his destruc- tion. Only a day or so away from this grave his own awaits him."

"That is my brother Joseph," said Benjamin, and his grey eyes brimmed over with tears.

"Oh, forgive me," his neighbour begged in dismay and put down the cup. "I would not have spoken so lightly if I had known it was your lost brother. And what I said about the grave, I mean his grave, you must not take that too seriously. I mean do not exaggerate. Certainly the grave is serious enough, a deep dark pit; but its power to hold fast is not so great after all. Its nature is to be empty, you must know that—empty is the hollow when it awaits the prey, and if you come when it has taken it in, lo, it is empty again—the stone is rolled away. I do not say it is worth no weeping, the grave; one must even wail shrilly in its honour, for it is there, a fact, a profoundly melancholy dispensation throughout the world; and part of the story of the feast in all its hours. I would go so far as to say that out of reverence for the grave one should not betray one's knowledge of its inherent emptiness and impotence. That would be treating a serious matter far too lightly. So shall we weep and wail, aloud and shrilly; but privately we may tell ourselves that there is no descent whatever upon which a rising does not follow. The two belong together, else how fragmentary would everything be: the feast would be only half a feast which got as far as the grave and knew no more to follow. No, the world is not half but whole; the feast too is a whole, and in the whole lies comfort that cannot be taken away. So do not let your heart be troubled by what I said about your brother's grave, but be of good cheer."

And he took Benjamin's hand by the wrist and waved it in the air like a little fan.

Benoni was aghast. His situation had reached a pitch of singularity impossible to describe. His breath left him, his brows were fiercely drawn, tears stood in his eyes, and through them he looked into the face of the master of the corn—the mixture making an impossible conflict of expressions. His mouth stood open as though he would cry out, but he did not; for instead his head drooped somewhat to one side, the mouth closed, and the whole expression of his tearful face became one heartfelt, urgent prayer. Before it the other's eyes went on the defensive, they shrouded themselves once more; it would be a bold man who dared to say there might be something like assent in the drooping lid.

Ah, yes, let anyone try to think or say what was now going on in Benjamin's breast, the breast of a man near to belief.

"Let us get up now," he heard his neighbour say. "I hope you have all eaten well and enjoyed yourselves. Unfortunately I must now go to the office and be there until the evening. Your brothers will probably set out for home early tomorrow morning, after picking up the grain I will assign to you: food for twelve houses this time, yours and your father's. And I will gladly take pay for it for Pharaoh's treasury—what would you have? I am the god's man of business. Farewell, in case I do not see you again. But by the bye and in all friendliness, why do you not take heart and exchange your own country for this one: migrate into Egypt, father, sons, wives, and children, all seventy of you, or however many there are, and graze on Pharaoh's land? That is a proposal from me to you; think it over, it would not be the most foolish thing you could do! They would show you the most suitable grazing-ground, it would take only a word from me, for whatever I say here goes. I know that Canaan means a good deal to you, but after all, Egypt is the great world and Canaan a provincial hole, where they do not know how to live. You are a migrant folk, not a people of walled dwellings. Here there is a good living, you could trade and make profit freely through the country. Well, there is my advice to you, take it or not as you see fit. I must be off to hear the pleas of the improvident."

A servant had poured water on his hands as he talked in this man-of-the-world vein with the brothers. He got up, said good-bye to all the guests, and broke up the table. The tradition suggests that his brothers were drunken with Joseph at this meal. But that is a mistake, they were no more than merry. No one would have dared to get actually drunk, not even the wild twins. Only Benjamin was drunk—but not even he with wine.

THE CRY KEPT BACK

In definitely better spirits, this time, did the brothers take the road from Menfe towards the Bitter Lakes and the fortified frontier. Everything had gone off so well that it could not have gone better. The lord of the land had been unequivocally charming. Benjamin was safe, Simeon freed, and they were honourably acquitted of the charge of espionage; so honourably, indeed, that they had even broken bread with the all-powerful lord and his courtiers. It put them in a jovial frame, made their hearts light and prideful. For so is man: when he has been found innocent and pronounced blameless in some one connection, he straightway thinks he is innocent in all, oblivious of anything else he might have on his conscience. We can easily pardon the brothers. They had been wrongfully accused, and involuntarily they had associated the accusation with their ancient guilt. No wonder, then, that when they

295

were cleared they promptly assumed that their former guilt was of no importance whatever.

They were soon to learn that they would not get off so cheaply or blithely, their sacks full to bursting with food for twelve houses, all duly paid for. Too soon they would learn that they were dragging a chain which would pull them back to fresh disaster. At first their spirits were so high they could have shouted and sung for joy in their new-found innocence. When the grain was given out they had been feasted again; Mai-Sachme had quietly supervised everything, and made them all presents as they took their leave. All that could give them credit in the father's eyes they had as they moved off: Benjamin, Simeon, provisions for twelve houses, even though Joseph was no longer there. They were still only eleven; but thanks to their proven innocence, they were still that.

Such was the colour of the brothers' minds—at least the minds of Leah's sons and the sons of the maids. No trouble to describe. But the mental state of Rachel's second son remains quite indescribable. Enough, the little man had scarcely slept, that night at the inn, or else with wild, confused, anomalous dreams—anomalous yet not nameless, for they did have a name, a dear and precious name, impossible and mad, for they were called Joseph. Benoni had seen a man in whom was Joseph. How could that possibly be described? It has happened that men have encountered gods who have chosen to assume a familiar human form and behaved accordingly though not willing to be so addressed. Here it was the other way round: the humanly familiar was not semi-transparent for the divine, but the high and divine semi-transparent for the long-familiar childhood, the memory being metamorphosed into this unknown, exalted shape. It would not let itself be addressed, it kept withdrawing behind its eyelids. Yet the disguised is not that behind which he disguises himself and from behind which he looks. They remain two. To recognize the one in the other does not mean to make one out of two, to relieve one's breast with the cry: "It is he!" It is impossible to produce the one out of the other, however desperately the mind struggles to do it. The cry was dammed back in Benjamin's breast though his heart nearly burst to contain it. Or rather it is not quite right to say it was dammed back, for it was not yet there, it had no voice or body—and therein precisely lay the indescribable thing. Its only refuge was in mad, dissolving dreams, which in the morning melted into pure

296

distress which was not existence at all and had no other relation to outward circumstances than just this: that Benjamin could not understand how the brothers could now do their business and go, leaving the situation as it was behind them. "By the Eternal!" he swore to himself, "it is impossible for us to go! We must stay here and watch this, this man and vice-god, Pharaoh's great keeper of the market. There is still a cry due that is not yet: with it still in our breasts we cannot just leave and go home to our father and live as though nothing had happened. This cry is just on the point of bursting out and filling the whole world with the sound of it. For indeed it is so great a cry that it will crack my heart!"

In his distress Benjamin turned to big Reuben. Large-eyed he put the question: did Reuben think they should now leave for home, or did it seem to him, perhaps, that they were not quite finished here, or rather not finished at all; that there were good and sound reasons for stopping?

"What do you mean?" Reuben asked in his turn. "What are the good and sound reasons? Everything has been done and accomplished and the man dismissed us graciously when we produced you. Now the thing is to get back with all speed to the father, waiting and fearing there on your account, that we may bring him what we have bought and he can have bread again for the offering. Do you remember how angry the man was when he heard Jacob's complaint that his lamp went out and he had to sleep in the dark?"

"Yes," Benjamin said, "I remember." And he looked up urgently into the big brother's beardless, muscular face. Suddenly he saw—or was it an illusion?—that the red Leah-eyes retreated before his gaze behind the blinking lids. Only yesterday he had had that same defensive, half-assenting motion from other eyes. He said no more. Perhaps he only thought he saw it because he had seen it yesterday, and by night in his dreams. The plans were not changed, they took their leave—there being no words in which to suggest that they should stay. But Benjamin's distress was great. Their gracious dismissal by the keeper of the market was the sorest point of all. They could not go—not at any price—but on the other hand, if he himself sent them, then what else could they do? They set out.

Benjamin rode beside Reuben. In one way they made a pair: not only as the oldest and the youngest of a family, the big boy and the little boy; but also because they had something like the same relation to him that was gone and to the reason why he was gone. We remember

Reuben's weakness—rather grumpy, to be sure—for the father's lamb, and his behaviour at the time of the mangling and burial. To all appearance he had shared in the brothers' feelings and their deed; and with them he had taken the frightful oath the ten had bound themselves by, never by word or deed, by sign or sound to betray that it had not been Joseph's blood but the blood of an animal or the remnants of his clothing which they had brought to the father. But Reuben had had no part in the sale, he had not been present, and his ideas about what had become of Joseph were vaguer than the brothers'—and theirs were hazy enough, though even so not hazy enough for their own comfort. They knew they had sold the boy to the Ishmaelites; even that was too much. Reuben had the advantage of not knowing it: while they were selling Joseph he had been at the pit; and the feelings of one standing by an empty grave must be quite different from those the brothers had, who had sold the sacrifice out into the wide, wide world.

In short, big Reuben, whether he knew it or not, had nourished the seed of expectation all these years; and by this measure he was closer than any of the others to Benjamin the blameless, who had shared not at all, and by whom the absence of his adored brother had never been accepted as final. It is long, long ago, but we can still hear his childish words to the broken old man: "He will come back. Or he will send for us to come." A good twenty years ago, that was; but the sound is still in our ears, and the hope still in Benjamin's heart. He had not the brothers' knowledge of the sale, nor yet Reuben's knowledge of the pit. Like the father, he knew only that Joseph had died, a fact which left no ground for either hope or faith. But faith actually seems to find lodgement best where there is no room for it.

Benjamin rode with Reuben; and on the way Reuben asked him what the man had talked about during the meal, he himself as the eldest having sat at the other end of the table.

"All sorts of things," answered the youngest. "We told each other funny stories about our children."

"Yes, and you laughed," said Reuben. "We all saw you rocking with laughter. I think the Egyptians were surprised."

"Of course, you know he is charming," went on the little man. "He knows how to talk with everybody to put them at their ease."

"But he can be otherwise too," replied Reuben. "He can be very awkward, we know that."

"Of course," said Benjamin, "you know all about that. And yet he wishes us well, I am certain of it. The last thing he said to me was that we should come and settle in Egypt, no matter how many of us; he invited us to migrate down here with the father and pasture our flocks."

"Did he say that?" asked Reuben. "Yes, a man like that knows a lot about us and our father, doesn't he! Especially about the father! And he always knows just what to say, does he? First he makes him send you on a journey to clear us and to fetch bread; then he invites Jacob himself to come down into the land of mud! A lot he knows about Jacob!"

"Are you mocking at him," asked Benjamin, "or at the father? I don't care for either, Reuben, for I am very sad. Reuben, listen to me, for my heart is heavy because we are leaving."

"Yes," said Reuben, "one cannot break bread every day with the lord of Egypt and jest with him. That is a treat, of course. But now you must remember that you are no longer a child but the head of a house and your children are crying for bread."

BENJAMIN HAS IT

Soon they came to the spot where they thought to take their midday rest and wait till it was cooler. On their first return journey they had reached the place at night; but now it was only midday. We recognize the spot by the palm tree, the spring, and the hut; and see it as clearly as the man, thanks to his magic cup, had seen Rachel's grave. They rejoiced to have reached the pleasant spot. It had indeed some unpleasant memories, but that ghost was laid; it had dissolved in harmony and peace; they might enjoy their rest without a care.

They were still standing, looking about them; they had not put hand to their packs. There came a noise from the direction from which they had come; it grew and spread, they heard shouting and hallooing. Was it for them? They stood rooted to the spot to listen, so surprised that they did not even turn round. Only Benjamin did; then he flung up his arms and his stumpy hands and gave a cry, a single cry. After that he was silent—silent for a long time.

It was Mai-Sachme, approaching with chariot and steed, attended by several wagons full of armed men. They jumped out and barred off the opening in the rocky circle. The steward stolidly advanced.

His face was grim. He had drawn his heavy brows together and was biting one corner of his mouth, only one corner, which gave him an unusual, sinister look. He said:

"So I have found you and overtaken you. I rushed after you with all speed at my master's command and caught you where you thought you would camp and hide yourself. How do you feel now that you see me?"

The dazed group answered that they did not know. They saw that everything was beginning all over again. That the hand had once more reached out to drag them to judgment; that all the sweet harmony had turned into discord.

"We do not know how," they said. "We rejoice to see you again so soon but we had not hoped to see you."

"You may not have hoped, but you must have feared. Why have you repaid good with evil, so that we had to come after you and stop you? Your position is very serious, my man."

"Explain yourself," said they. "What are you talking about?"

"Do you need to ask?" he answered. "I am talking about my master's drinking-cup out of which he divines. It has been missed. The master had it yesterday at table. It has been taken."

"You are speaking of a winecup?"

"I am. Of Pharaoh's silvered beaker, my master's own. He drank out of it yesterday noon. It is gone. Clearly it has been filched. Somebody has got away with it. Who? Unfortunately there can be no doubt. Men, you have done very ill."

They were silent.

"You are suggesting," asked Judah, Leah's son, in a slightly unsteady voice, "your words mean that we have taken a dish from your master's table and made off with it like thieves?"

"Unfortunately there is no other name for your behaviour. The thing is gone since yesterday; obviously it has been bagged. Who can have done it? There is only one answer, alas. I can only repeat that you men have done very ill and are in a very serious case."

They were silent again, with their arms akimbo, puffing and blowing.

"Listen, my dear sir," said Judah. "How would it be if you gave heed to your words and considered before you spoke? The thing is un-

300

heard of. We ask you in all politeness but in all seriousness as well, what do you take us for? Do we look to you like vagabonds and thieves? Or what sort of impression may you have of us that you try to make it appear that we have taken a valuable piece from your master's table, a cup, apparently, and been light-fingered with it? That is what I mean when I say unheard of, speaking in the name of all eleven of us. For we are all faithfully sons of one man and our whole number was twelve. One is no longer with us, otherwise I would call it unheard of in his name as well. You say we have done ill. Well, I do not claim that we brothers are saints, having never done ill, but come through the rough and tumble of life without ever taking a fall. I do not say we are innocents, that would be sacrilege. But there is guilt and guilt; and maybe guilt is prouder than innocence is; anyhow, to nab silver cups is not in our line. We have cleared ourselves before your master and showed him that we walk in truth, by bringing our eleventh brother to witness. We have cleared ourselves before you, for the purchase money we found in our feed-bags we brought back out of the land of Canaan and offered it to you again but you would not take it. After these experiences will you not stop and consider before you accuse us of taking silver or gold from your master's table?"

But Reuben was boiling over; he spurted out:

"Why do you not answer, steward, this convincing speech of my brother Jehudah? And why do you bite deeper in the corner of your mouth in that offensive way? Here we are. Search us! And with whomever it is found, your wretched silver cup, let him die! Search! If you find it, the rest of us, all of us, will be your slaves for life!"

"Reuben," said Judah, "do not burst out like that. Our complete innocence needs not such oaths."

And Mai-Sachme spoke: "You are right, there is no need of hasty words. We too know how to be moderate. He in whose sack we find the cup, he becomes our slave and remains in our hands. The rest of you will go free. Be pleased to open your sacks."

They were already at it. They had run to their sacks, they could not take them down fast enough from their asses and tear them open. "Laban!" they cried with laughter. "Laban, searching on the Mount of Gilead! Ha, ha! Let him sweat and swear! Here, master steward, come and search mine first!"

"Quietly, quietly," said Mai-Sachme. "Everything in order and in

301

turn, the way my master knew your names. We will begin with the big hothead."

As he searched they mocked, their triumph mounting as he went on. They called him Laban and jeered at him for a sweating clod, as he moved from sack to sack, stooped and looked with his hands on his hips, shook his head and shrugged his shoulders, then went on to the next. He searched Asher and Issachar and came to Zebulon. Nothing there. He was almost at the end of his search, only Benjamin was left. They jeered yet more loudly.

"Now he is looking in Benjamin's," they cried. "What luck with the most innocent of all—not only in this but in all other respects, for he has never done ill in his life! Watch how he searches in the last bag, listen to what he will say next to justify—"

All at once they were still. They saw it shining in the steward's hand. Out of Benjamin's feed-bag, from not very far down, he had drawn the silver cup.

"Here it is," he said. "Found in the youngest's sack. I should have begun at the other end and spared myself trouble and abuse. So young and already so thievish! Of course, I am glad to have found the cup; but my pleasure is marred by the knowledge of such early corruption and ingratitude. Young one, you are in a bad fix."

And the others? They held their heads, staring at the cup till their eyes bulged out. They whistled through lips so puffed out that they could not speak but only whistle.

"Benoni!" they cried, their voices shrill to breaking. "Defend yourself! Open your mouth. How did you come by the cup?"

But Benjamin was silent. He dropped his chin on his chest so that no one could see his eyes, and was dumb. They tore their clothing. Some of them actually seized the hem of their smocks and with one pull rent them from bottom to top.

"We are shamed!" they wailed. "Shamed by our youngest! Benjamin, for the last time open your mouth and justify yourself!"

But Benjamin was silent. He did not lift his head, he spoke no word. His silence was quite impossible to describe.

"He did cry out at first," shouted Bilhah's Dan. "Now I remember he gave a great cry when this man came up. Terror tore the shriek out of him, he knew why the man came after us!"

Then they fell on Benjamin with loud railing and reviling **and called** him a thief and the son of a thief, reminding him how his mother had stolen her father's teraphim. "It is inherited, he has it in his blood. Oh, thief's blood, did you have to apply your inheritance just here, to bring us all to shame with you, us and our whole stock, the father and all of us and our children?"

"Now you are exaggerating," said Mai-Sachme. "That is not our way. The rest of you are all cleared and free. We do not assume your guilt, but rather that your youngest stole on his own account. You can freely go home to your honourable father. Only he who took the cup, he falls to us."

But Judah answered him: "There can be no talk of that, steward, for I will speak with your master, he shall hear the words of Judah, I am resolved upon it. We all go back with you before his face and he shall judge us all. For we are all liable in this matter and are as one with respect to what has happened. Lo, our youngest was innocent all his years, for he was at home. But we others were out in the world and became guilty. We are not minded to play the guiltless and leave him in the lurch because he became guilty on his travels while we in this one respect are innocent. Up with us all, lead us together with him before the throne of the keeper of the market!"

"Be it so," said Mai-Sachme. "As you will."

So they went back to the city, surrounded with the troop of lancers, taking the road they had lately covered so free from care. But Benjamin said no word.

I AM HE

It was already the latter part of the afternoon when they came before Joseph's house, for the steward led them thither and not to the great office where they had first bowed and bent their knees. Joseph was not there, he was in his own house.

"He was yet there," the story says, and it is correct. After the merry meeting of the day before, Pharaoh's friend had gone back to his office, but today he could not have left his house. He knew that his steward was at his task; and he waited with extreme impatience. The feast was nearing its climax and it rested with the ten whether they would be on the scene or only hear what happened at second hand. Would they make the youngest come back alone with Mai-Sachme? Or would they all stick together? Joseph's suspense was great: on this point depended his future relations with the brothers. We, of course, are in no suspense: in the first place we know all the phases of the story by heart; moreover we have just been present at the search for the cup and have seen that the brothers did not forsake Benjamin in his guilt, whereas the fact was still hidden from Joseph. So in our wisdom we may smile at him as he wandered up and down and to and fro, from the book-room to the reception-hall, thence to the banqueting-hall, back through all the rooms into his sleeping-chamber, where he feverishly gave this or that last touch to his toilette, like an actor nervously adjusting his make-up before the curtain goes up.

He went to see his wife Asenath, in the women's quarters; they sat together watching Manasseh and Ephraim at their play, and he could not disguise his stage fright.

"My husband and dear lord," said she, "what is the matter? You are nervous, you keep shuffling your feet and listening for something. What have you on your mind? Shall we have a game to divert you, or shall some of my women dance before you?"

"No, my girl," he replied. "Thank you, not now. I have other moves in my head from those in the game, and I cannot watch the dancing, I have too much jigging and juggling to do myself, while God and the world look on. I must get back nearer to the hall, that is the theatre. But for your maids I know a better task than dancing; for I came to tell them to make you beautiful even beyond your beauty, and dress and adorn you; and the nurses must wash Manasseh's and Ephraim's hands and put on their embroidered smocks, for I am expecting very special guests and will present you all as my family so soon as the word has been spoken and they know who I am and whose you are. Yes, you are making big eyes, my shield-maid with the tiny waist! But just do as I say and make yourselves fine, and you shall hear from me!"

With that he was off again into the other part of the house. He would gladly have luxuriated in pure waiting and the pleasure of suspense; but as always there was business to transact: officials to see, accounts and papers to examine and sign, brought to him in his book-room by his reader and his acting scribe. He cursed them mentally, yet welcomed them for their company too.

The sun declined as he sat over his papers, with one ear cocked. At last he heard a confusion of sounds in front of the house: the hour had come, the brothers were here. Mai-Sachme entered, the corner of his mouth drawn tighter than ever, the cup in his hand. He handed it to his master. "The youngest had it," said he. "After a long search. They are in the hall, awaiting your sentence."

"All of them?" Joseph asked.

"All of them," Mai-Sachme replied.

"You see that I am busy," said Joseph. "These gentlemen here are not here for fun, we are occupied with the business of the crown. You have been my steward long enough to know whether I can take time from pressing official business for such petty matters. You and your men can wait."

And he bent again over the roll held open for him by an official. But as he could see nothing that was written there, he said after a pause:

"We might as well get that little matter over with first. It is a case of criminal ingratitude, and I must pass judgment. Gentlemen, follow me to the hall, where the evil-doers are awaiting sentence."

They attended him as he went up three steps and through a hanging out on to the raised dais of the hall, where stood his chair. With the cup in his hand he sat down. Servants straightway held fans over his head, for he was always thus protected the moment he sat down.

A slanting ray full of dancing motes shone from one of the left-hand upper openings between the columns and the sphinxes and the red sandstone crouching lions with Pharaoh-heads. It fell upon the group of sinners who had flung themselves down a few paces from Joseph's chair with their foreheads to the ground. Spears guarded them on either side. A host of the curious, cooks and waiting-boys, sprinklers and flower-table stewards, crowded round the doors.

"Brothers, stand up," said Joseph. "I should not have thought to see you again, and on such an occasion. But there are many things I should not have thought. I should not have thought you could do as you have done, when I had treated you like gentlemen. I am glad, of course, to have my cup back again, out of which I drink and from which I divine. But I am greatly cast down by your gross behaviour. It is incomprehensible to me. How could you bring yourselves so crudely to repay good with evil, to offend a man like me by taking away something he is fond of and which is useful to him? The deed was as stupid as it was hateful, for you might have guessed that a man like me would miss so valuable a piece at once and know everything. Did you imagine that when I saw I had been robbed I could not divine where it had gone? And now I assume that you have admitted your guilt?"

It was Judah who answered. He became the spokesman for them all this day, for he had passed through trials in life which they had been spared; he had familiar knowledge of sin and guilt, and therefore he could fitly represent the brothers. On their way back to Menfe this had been settled among them and he had considered what to say. Now, with his garments rent, he stood among his brothers and spoke:

"What shall we say unto my lord, and what sense would there be in trying to clear ourselves before him? We are guilty before you, O lord, guilty in the sense that your cup was found among us, with one of us and that means with all. How the cup came into the sack of the youngest and most innocent of us all, who was always safe at home, I do not know. We do not know. We are powerless to speculate about it before your seat. You are a mighty one of earth, you are good and evil, you raise up and cast down. We are your servants. No defence of ours has any worth before you, and foolish is the sinner who presumes upon present innocence when the avenger demands pay for all misdeeds. Not for nothing did our old father lament that we would make him childless in his old age. Lo, he was right. We and he with whom the cup was found are fallen to my lord as slaves."

In this opening speech of Judah's, which was not yet the one for which he is famous, there were points which Joseph preferred to ignore. He therefore answered only the one touching on their slavery, to reject it.

"No, not so," he said. "Far from it. There is no behaviour so bad that it can make a man like me behave inhumanly. You have bought food for the old man your father in the land of Egypt and he is waiting for it. I am Pharaoh's great man of business: no one shall say I took advantage of your crime to keep the money, the goods, and the buyers too. Whether only one of you sinned or all of you together I will not inquire. To your youngest I talked familiarly at table, we were merry together and I told him the virtues of my beloved cup and by its means showed him his mother's grave. It may be he prattled to you about it and all of you concerted the ungrateful plot of stealing the treasure. I assume it was not for the sake of the silver you took it. You wanted to use its magic for yourselves, perhaps to find out what became of your missing

306

brother, the one who left home—how can I tell? But again, maybe your youngest committed the crime on his own, told you nothing and took the cup. I do not wish to hear. The booty was found with the thief. He shall be my servant. But the rest of you may go home in peace to your father, the old man, that he may not be childless and may have food to eat."

Thus the exalted; and for a while there was silence. Then Judah, the man of afflictions, to whom they had given the word, strode out of the group. He trod before the throne, close up to Joseph, took a long breath, and spoke:

"Hear me now, my lord, for I will hold speech before your ears and relate how it all came about and what you did and how it stands with these and with me, with us brothers all. My words will make clear beyond peradventure that you cannot and may not separate our youngest from us and you may not keep him to belong to you. And further, that we others, and in particular I, Judah, fourth among us, cannot possibly ever return home to our father without our youngest. And thirdly I will make my lord an offer and propose to you how you will receive your due in a possible and not in an impossible way. This will be the order of my speech. Therefore let not your anger burn against your servant and stop him not, I beg you, in the speech which I shall make as the spirit gives it to me, and my own guilt. You are as Pharaoh. Now I begin at the beginning and as you began it, for it was thus:

"When we came down hither, sent by our father that we might get us bread from this granary like thousands of others, we did not fare like the other thousands, but were segregated and specially dealt with and led down to your city and before my lord's face. And even there we were unusually treated, for my lord too was strange, I mean he was rough and smooth, soft and hard, in other words he showed two faces. He questioned us particularly about our family. Have you, asked my lord, a father at home or a brother? We have, we replied, a father, he is old, and we have certainly a young brother too, the youngest, late born to him and whom he cherishes as the apple of his eye and keeps him by the hand because his brother fell away untimely and is gone. Only this one son of his mother remains to our father, so that he clings to him beyond measure. Answered my lord: bring him down here to me. Not a hair of his head shall be harmed. It cannot be, we said, for the reason we have given. To snatch away his youngest from the father will be his death. But you replied harshly to your servants: By the life of Pharaoh!

307

if ye come not with your youngest brother, surviving from the lovely mother, so shall you not see my face again."

And Judah continued and said:

"I ask my lord whether it was so and so begun or whether it was not so but began otherwise than that my lord asked after the boy and insisted on his coming, despite our warning. For it pleased my lord to put it that we should clear ourselves from the accusation of spying by bringing him down and thereby showing evidence that we deal in truth. But what sort of clearing is that and what sort of accusation? No man can take us for spies, we brothers in Jacob do not look like spies and it does not clear us to produce our youngest, it is only an arbitrary decision and only because my lord happens to be bent on seeing our brother with his own eyes—why? On that point I may not speak, it rests with God." And Jehudah went on in his speech, flung up his leonine head, put out his hand and spoke:

"Lo, this your servant believes in the God of his fathers and that all knowledge is with Him. But what he does not believe is that our God smuggles valuables into the packs of his servants, so that they have their purchase money back as well as the goods—that has never been, and we have no tradition whatever of this kind. Not Abram nor Isaac nor Jacob, our father, has ever found God-silver in his pack that the Lord slipped him. What is not is not; all that happened was from arbitrary choice and has its source in one single mystery.

"But can you now, my lord—can you, after we worked on our father with the famine to our aid and got him to lend us his little one for this journey—can you, who relentlessly forced his coming, for without that extraordinary demand he would never have set foot in the land, can you, who said: No harm shall come to him here below—can you hold him as a bondsman because they found your cup in his bag?

"That you cannot!

"But we on our side and especially your servant Judah who here holds speech, we cannot come before our father's face without his youngest—nevermore. We can do it as little as without him we could have come before yours—and not on grounds of personal whim but on grounds most potent and compelling. Your servant, our father, had spoken to us again and said: Go yet once more and buy us a little food; and we answered him: We cannot go down unless you give us our youngest brother, for the man down there who is lord in the land said we must bring him or we shall not see his face. Then the grey-haired one set up his lament, a song well known and which cut us to the heart, like the flute that sobs in the gorges, for he launched into song and said:

" 'Rachel, the lovely and willing, for whom my young years served Laban, the black moon, seven years; heart of my heart, who died on the way and left me, only a furlong from the inn; she was my wife and she gave me to my loving desire two sons, one in life and one in death, Dumuzi-Absu, the lamb, Joseph, the brilliant one, who knew how to get round me so that I gave him all that I had; and Benoni, the little son of death, whom I still have at hand. For the other went out from me, as I willed him to, and all the universe was filled with the cry: Mangled is he, the lovely one mangled! Then fell I on my back, and ever since I have been stiff. But with my stiffened hand I hold this little one who is all I have left, for mangled, mangled and torn in pieces, was the true son. If now you take from me my only one, that the boar mayhap may tread him down, then you will bring down my grey hairs to the grave in such sorrow that it would be too much for the world and it could not bear it. Full to the outermost rim is the world with the cry: Mangled, mangled is the beloved; and were this one given too, the world must be rent asunder and be naught.'

"Has my lord heard this cry of the flutes, this father-lament? Then let him judge after his own understanding if we brothers can come before the old man without our youngest, the little man, and confess: We have lost him, he is missing; whether we could hold out before the soul that hangs on Benjamin's soul, and before the world which is full of affliction and cannot bear more, for it would receive its death-blow in this blow. And above all whether I, Judah, his fourth son who speak, can so come before my father, that you shall judge. For not yet all does my lord know, but far from all; the heart of your servant feels that his word must mount to quite another theme at this hour of our need: it must deal with this mystery here, and can only do so through the revelation of another mystery."

A murmuring rose from among the troop of brothers. They stirred uneasily. But Judah the lion raised his voice against it, spoke on and said:

"I took the responsibility before my father and made myself surety for the little one. Just as now I came close up to your seat to hold this speech, so then I went close up to the father and took my oath before him in these words: Give him into my hand, I vouch for him; if I bring

309

him not again I will bear the blame before you for ever. Such my vow; now judge, O strange man, whether I can go back to my father without the little one, lest peradventure I see an evil too great for me and for the world to bear. Accept my offer! Me shall you keep for your bondman instead of the lad, that you may receive your due in a possible and not an impossible way. I myself will expiate for us all. Here before you, strange man, I take the frightful oath we brothers swore—with both hands I take that oath and I break it in two across my knee. Our eleventh brother, the father's ewe lamb, first son of the true wife, him the beast did not rend; but we his brothers sold him into the world."

Thus did Judah end his famous speech, thus and not otherwise. He stood there weaving to and fro. The brothers had gone pale; yet they were deeply relieved that the secret was out at last. For it is not impossible to go pale and yet feel relieved at the same time. But two of them cried out, and they were the oldest and the youngest. Reuben shouted: "What do I hear?" And Benjamin did just as he had done before when the steward overtook them: he flung up his arms and gave an indescribable cry. And Joseph? He had got up from his seat and glittering tears ran down his cheeks. For it happened that the shaft of light which had been falling aslant upon the group of brothers had now moved round and was coming through an opening at the end of the hall. It fell directly on Joseph's face and in it his tears glittered like jewels.

"All that is Egyptian go out from me!" said he. "Out with you, go! For I invited God and the world to this play, but now shall God alone be witness."

Reluctantly they obeyed. Mai-Sachme put his hands on the backs of the scribes on the platform, urged them towards the door with nods and gestures, and helped them out. The crowds vanished from the entrance—though it is not likely they moved very far; they all stood in and out of the book-room with their heads cocked in the direction of the hall. Some even held their hands to their ears.

And Joseph, heedless of the tears on his face, stretched out his arms and made himself known. Often before now he had done the same and made people stare, giving them to think that some higher power moved in him other than what he was himself and mingled in his single person with a dreamy and seductive charm. But now quite simply—and despite the outstretched arms with a deprecating little laugh—he said:

"Children, here I am, I am your brother Joseph!"

"Of course he is, of course he is!" shouted Benjamin, almost choking with joy. He stumbled forwards and up the steps, fell on his knees, and stormily embraced the new-found brother's knees.

"Jashup, Joseph-el, Jehosiph!" he sobbed, with his head tipped back to look up in his brother's face. "You are, you are, of course you are! You are not dead, you have overturned the great abode of the shadow of death, you have risen up to the seventh threshold, you are set as Metatron and inner prince—I knew it, I knew it, you are lifted up on high, the Lord has made you a seat like to his own! But me you know still, your mother's son, and you fanned the air with my hand!"

"Little one!" said Joseph. "Little one!" He raised Benjamin up and put their heads together. "Do not talk, it is none of it so great nor so remote and I have no such glory and the great thing of all is that we are twelve once more."

WRANGLE NOT

He put his arm around Benoni's shoulders and went down with him to the brothers—ah yes, the brothers: how was it with them as they stood there? Some stood with legs apart and arms dangling awkwardly down almost to their knees. They stared open-mouthed into space. Some held their clenched fists upon breasts that heaved up and down with the fury of their panting. All of them had gone pale at Judah's confession; now they were crimson, a deep dark red like the colour of pine-trunks, red as that time when squatting on their hands they had seen Joseph coming towards them in the coat of many colours. Without Benoni's rapturous cry they would not have believed or even grasped what the man said. But now the sons of Rachel came with their arms about each other to stand among them; and a mere association—for all of them had long since felt that this man had something or other to do with Joseph—swelled and changed into an identification, and what wonder that their brains felt as though they would burst? At one moment they would succeed in putting together the sacrificed lamb yonder and the lord here in his glory; the next moment the two ideas fell apart again. They had work to hold them together, and that was because their chagrin and horror were so great.

"Come here to me," said Joseph as he approached. "Yes, yes, I am

311

your brother Joseph whom you sold down into Egypt; but never mind about that, for you did me no harm. Tell me, my father is truly alive? —Speak to me, don't be afraid. Judah, that was a great speech you made. You made it for ever and ever. I dearly embrace and congratulate you, I greet you and kiss your lion's head. See, it is the kiss you gave me in front of the Minæans; today I give it back, my brother, and it is all blotted out. I kiss you all in one; never think I am angry that you sold me down here. That all had to be. God did it, not you. El Shaddei estranged me early from my father's house, He separated me according to His plan. He sent me on ahead of you to be your provider—and in His beautiful providence He brought it about that I should feed Israel together with all strangers in time of dearth. That was a perfectly simple, practical matter—though physically important, of course; but nothing to make a shout about. For your brother is no god-hero, no harbinger of spiritual salvation. He is just a farmer and manager. Remember how your sheaves bowed down to mine in the dream I prattled about when I was a young brat, and the stars that made curtsies? Well, that has turned out to mean nothing so very extraordinary: just that my fathers and brothers would thank me for what I could give them. When a man receives bread, he says, not 'Hosanna in the highest,' but just 'Thank you very much.' However, bread there has to be. Bread comes first, before all the hosannas. Now do you understand how simple the thing was that the Lord meant, and will you not believe that I am alive? You know yourselves that I did not stay in the pit, because the children of Ishmael drew me up out of it and you sold me to them. Put your hands on me, take hold of me, feel and see that I am your brother Joseph and I am alive!"

Two or three of them actually did touch him. They cautiously ran their hands down his garment and timidly grinned.

"Then it was only a joke and you just behaved like a prince?" asked Issachar. "And you are really only our brother Joseph?"

"Only?" he answered. "That is the best that I am. But you must try to understand that I am both. I am Joseph, whom the Lord Pharaoh has set as father and prince in all Egypt. Joseph I am, arrayed in the splendour of this world."

"Then," said Zebulon, "we must not say you are only the one and not the other, for actually you are both in one. We had a glimmering of it all along. And it is good that you are not the lord of the market all

312

the way through, else it would go hard with us. But under your fine raiment you are our brother Joseph, who will protect us from the wrath of the keeper of the market. But you must understand, my lord—"

"Will you drop it, stupid? Just leave off this lord business, once and for all—"

"You must see that we have to seek the protection of the keeper of the market against our brother, for in time past we did him ill."

"That you did," said Reuben, with the muscles of his jaw standing out. "It is unheard of, Jehosiph, what I have been ignorant of up till now! They sold you behind my back and never gave me a hint and all these years I did not know that they got rid of you and took money for you—"

"That will do, Reuben," said Bilhah's Dan. "You did this and that behind our backs too and went secretly to the pit meaning to steal the boy. As for the purchase price, it was no great sum, as Joseph's grace well knows. Twenty shekels Phœnician, that was all, thanks to the old man's bargaining powers, and we can settle it any time and you can get your due."

"Wrangle not, men," said Joseph; "don't dispute about what one of you did without the other knowing. For God has put all right. I thank you, Reuben, my big brother, that you came to the pit with your rope to pull me out and give me back to the father. But I was not there. And that was good, for it was not to be so and would not have been right. But now it is right. Now we must all of us think of nothing but the father—"

"Yes, yes," nodded Naphtali, and his tongue went like a clapper and his legs twitched. "What our exalted brother said is quite right, for it must not be that Jacob sits far away in his house of hair or outside it without the dimmest idea of what has happened here: that Joseph is alive and has got high up in the world and has a glittering post among the heathen. Only think, there he sits, Jacob, wrapped in ignorance that we stand here talking face to face with the lost one and touch his garment to convince ourselves. Everything was misunderstanding and wrong information and the father's high-flown lament is as naught and as naught the worm that has gnawn us all our lives. All that is so thrilling it is enough to make a man jump out of his skin—everything in the world is so unbearably awry that we are here and know and he does not know only because he is there and great and foolish distances divide his knowledge from ours; so that the truth can only get a few paces ahead and then lies still and can no more. Oh, if I could just put my hands to my mouth and shout across seventeen days' distance and say: 'Father, halloo! Joseph is alive and he is as Pharaoh in the land of Egypt, that is the latest news.' But however loud one might shout, there he sits unhearing and unmoved. Or if one could loose a dove whose wings had the speed of lightning, with a screed under its wing: 'Know all men by these presents!'—that the awryness might be gone out of the world and everybody here and there know the same thing! No, I can stay here no longer, I cannot stand it. Send me, send me! I will do it; I will run, defying the fleet stag, to give him good account. For could any account be better than that which tells the latest news?"

Joseph applauded his zeal, but he said: "Let well alone, Naphtali, do not be precipitate, for you may not run off alone and no one has a right to say to our father what I will have said to him and what I planned to say long ago when I lay at night and mused on this story. You shall all stay with me seven days and share all my honours and I will set you before my wife the sun-maid and my sons shall bow before you. After that you shall load your animals and go up together with Benjamin and tell him: Joseph your son is not dead but lives, and speaks to you with his living voice and says: 'God gave me rank among strangers, and folk I know not are subject to me. Come down here to me, delay not nor fear, dear Father, fear not the land of tombs whither Abram too came in time of famine. As for the scarcity, and that for two years now there is no ploughing nor harvest in the world, that will certainly go on either three or five years more. But I will look out for you, and you shall settle here in rich pasture. If you ask me whether Pharaoh permits it, I answer you: him your son twists round his finger. And if His Majesty desire that you should settle in the land of Goshen and on the plains of Zoan, towards Arabia, I will see to it, you and your children and your children's children, your flocks and herds and fowl and all that is yours. For the land of Goshen, also called Gosem, or Gosen, is the place I had long since chosen for you when you should be sent for, because it is not yet quite Egypt, not quite so Egyptian, and you could live there on the fish of the delta and the fat of the land and you need not have much to do with the children of Egypt, and their old-man cleverness and your own native ways need not clash. And you would be near to me.' You must speak so to my father in my name and do it cleverly and skilfully

314

to bring it home to him in his rigid old age, first that I am alive and then that you are all to come down here. Oh, if I could only go up with you all and coax him into it, I certainly would. But I cannot, I cannot get away for a day. So you must do it for me: very lovingly and with great guile, and break these things to him about my being alive and his coming down. Don't say to him all at once: 'Joseph is alive'; begin by asking: 'Suppose it were true that Joseph had not died, how would our lord and father feel?' So he could come on to it gradually. And then do not blurt out that you are all to come down and settle down below in the land of the corpse gods; say in the neighbourhood of Goshen. Can you do it like that without me, sly and loving at once? In these next days we can talk about how it should be done. Now I will show you my wife, the sun-maid, and my boys, Manasseh and Ephraim. And we shall eat and drink all twelve of us together and be merry. And recall old times, yet forgetting much. But while I think of it: when you get home to our father, tell him all that you have seen and stint not your description of my glory here below. For his heart has been sorely bruised, and it must be healed by the sweet music of his son's magnificence."

PHARAOH WRITES TO JOSEPH

It would be a pity if now, having heard all these things, our audience were to disperse, or to turn away its ears, thinking: Well, that was that; the great revelation has been made, the climax reached, nothing better can be coming, there is only the end of the tale, and we know how it turned out already, we cannot get excited. Take my word for it, you are wrong. The author of this tale, by whom I mean Him who has made all tales, has given it many climaxes, and He knows how to get its effects one through the other. With Him it is always: "The best is still to come"; He always gives us something to look forward to. That was a lovely place where Joseph heard that his father was alive. But where Jacob, the old man, rigid with suffering in body and brain, slowly opens his senses to the song of spring and resurrection and girds himself to go down and embrace his living son—there is nothing thrilling in that? Some who still stay to listen might tell the others how thrilling it was; then they will be sorry all their lives for not having been there when Jacob blessed his Egyptian grandchildren with his hands crossed, and when the venerable man encountered his last hour. We know already! But that is a foolish thought. Anybody can know the story. To have been there is the thing. But it seems the injunction was needless: nobody has stirred.

So, then, when Joseph had thus spoken with the eleven, they went out thence together from where he had revealed himself, to Asenath the maiden, his wife, to bow before her. And they saw their nephews Manasseh and Ephraim with the Egyptian youth-lock on their heads. Through the whole great house there was a bustling and much joyous laughter, for all the household staff had listened at the doors and Joseph needed to make no announcement, no, for everybody knew and one shouted to another that the provider's brothers were come and the sons of his father had found their way hither from Zahi-land. It was the greatest fun for them all, especially because they could count on cakes and ale being given out to celebrate the event. But the scribes from the office had also listened and spread the news throughout the city, and it would have rejoiced the nimble Naphtali's heart to see it run like a forest fire throughout all Menfe so that everybody was quickly on an equal footing of knowledge; they all knew something at the same time: that the troop of brothers of Pharaoh's universal friend had arrived at his house. There was much jumping for joy in the streets and a crowd in front of Joseph's house in the best suburb of Menfe shouting hurrahs and demanding the sight of him surrounded by his Asiatic kin. They were finally gratified: the twelve showed themselves on the terrace. What a pity Menfe's folk knew not how to manipulate light-rays as we do, so that the group could be perpetuated in a photograph! They were satisfied with their own natural lenses and did not miss anything, because they could not even conceive of such an idea.

The titillating news did not long stop within the walls of the metropolis of tombs. It flew like a dove out into the land, and first to get wind of it was Pharaoh, who, and his whole court with him, was, of course, greatly delighted. Pharaoh was now called Ikhnaton, having laid aside the harsh Amun name and assumed one which contained that of his Father in heaven. Some years before, he had moved nearer to the city of his minister and favourite. He had ceased to reside in Thebes, the house of Amun-Re and gone down further north into the Upper Egyptian hare district. There after long search he had found a spot suitable for the erection of a new city entirely dedicated to his beloved deity. The site was a little south of Khnunu, the house of Thoth, at a place where a little island rose from the stream that simply cried out for the erection of elegant little pleasure-pavilions. The rocks on the left bank retreated in a curve affording space for laying out temples, palaces, and terraces, adequate to a thinker on God who had a hard time in life and ought also to have an easy one. The lord of the sweet breath had found a place after his own heart, needing no counsel save his own thoughts and him who dwelt therein, to whom alone in this sweet spot the songs of praise should swell. The gracious command of His Majesty went forth to his artists and stone-masons to build here with the greatest speed a city, the city of his father, the city of the horizon Akhetaton. It was a severe blow for Nowet-Amun, hundred-gated Thebes, for with the departure of the court it ran the risk of sinking to the level of a provincial city; moreover the move boldly served notice on the God of the empire at Karnak, with whose domineering priesthood Pharaoh's tender enthusiasm for the beloved all-in-one had during the fat years come into ever increasing conflict.

Pharaoh's delicate constitution could not stand these recurrent bouts with the might of the warlike national god, armed in the full panoply of tradition. He suffered more and more from the contradiction between the placability of his own soul and the necessity of doing offensive battle for his own higher God-concept. To flee from this necessity was fortunately also the means of doing the enemy the most harm. Thus he resolved for his own consecrated person to shake Wese's dust from off his sandals, even though his little Mama, partly for the sake of keeping watch of Amun, partly out of loyalty towards the residence of King Neb-ma-re, her deceased husband, might stop behind in her old palace. For two years Ikhnaton had had to control his impatience to escape from Amun's jurisdiction, for it took that long to build the city despite ruthless drafting of flogged slave labour. And even when the King shifted thither with great pomp and ceremony and offerings of bread and beer, of horned and hornless cattle, fowl, birds, wine, incense, and all fine herbs, it was as yet no city, only an improvised residence of half-finished luxury, consisting of a palace for him and the great consort Nefernefruaton-Nefertiti and the royal princesses, wherein they might sleep but not properly live, because painters and decorators were still everywhere at work. There was further a temple for God the Lord, very bright and gay and flower-scented, with floating and flapping red streamers, with seven courts, splendid pylons, and magnificent pillared halls; and simply marvellous parks and ingenious sheltered nooks, artificial ponds, trees and shrubbery transplanted into the desert in clumps of earth from their habitat in the fertile region of the Nile. White quays shimmered along the shore and there were a dozen brand-new dwelling-houses for the Aton-worshipping royal retinue; as well as a whole row of conveniently placed rock tombs in the surrounding hills. Of the whole, these were the most nearly ready for occupation.

This, for the moment, was all there was of Akhetaton, but it was expected that the court would quickly draw hither in its train a growing population and the embellishment of the city would go zealously on, since Pharaoh was already there on his throne, serving his Father in heaven, holding feasts of tribute, and getting daughters to enlarge the state of his women's quarters; the third, Ankhsenpaaton, had already arrived.

Joseph had sent a special messenger to make formal announcement to the god of the arrival of his brothers, from whom he had been separated since early youth. But even before the messenger reached the new-smelling palace, the news had spread thither by word of mouth and been much and excitedly discussed by Pharaoh, his queen Nefertiti, her sister Nezemmut, his own sister Baketaton, and his courtiers and staff of artists. He answered the letter straightway. It was superscribed:

Command to the administrator of that which the heavens give, actual overseer of operations, vice-spender of the King and his universal friend; my Uncle:

Know that My Majesty regards your letter as one which he reads with sincere joy. Lo, Pharaoh has shed many joyful tears over the news which he has received from you; the great consort Nefernefruaton, also the sweet princesses Baketaton and Nezemut, have mingled their tears with those of the beloved son of my Father in heaven. All that you tell me is extraordinarily splendid and what you announce makes my heart to leap up. As for what you write, that your brothers have come to you, and your father is still alive, at this news the heavens are joyful, the earth exults, and the hearts of good men frolic, while even those of evil folk are doubtless softened thereby. Know herewith that the lovely child of Aton, Nefer-Kheperu-Re, lord of the two lands, in consequence of your letter finds himself in extraordinarily gracious mood. The wishes which you link with your enclosures were granted beforehand, even before you set them

318

down. It is my beautiful will, and I give my gracious consent, that all of yours, however many, should come to Egypt where you are as myself, and you may allot them room wherein to settle according to your best opinion, whose richness shall nourish them. Say to your brothers: Thus shall you do and thus Pharaoh commands, in whose heart is the love of his father Aton. Lade your beasts and take wagons with you out of the stores of the king for your little ones and your wives and your father and come. Look not to your household goods, for you shall be provided in the land with all that you need. Pharaoh knows indeed that your culture does not stand very high and your wants are easy to satisfy. And when you come into your land, take your father and his people and his whole house and bring them down to me that you graze near your brother, the steward of the whole land, for the land shall lie open to you. Thus far the direction of Pharaoh to your brothers, given amid tears. Did not many and important affairs keep me at Akhetaton, the only capital of the lands, my residential city, I would mount my great car, made of electrum, and hasten to Men-nefru-Mire that I might see you among your brothers and you would set your brothers before me. But when they are returned you must bring some of them before me. Not all of them, for that would be too fatiguing for Pharaoh; but a chosen group, that I may question them; and also the old man your father shall you bring before me that I may show him favour by my words and he shall live in honour for that Pharaoh has spoken with him. Farewell!

This letter Joseph received by running messenger in his house at Menfe and showed it to the eleven, who kissed their fingertips. One quarter of the moon they stayed in his house. It was twenty years that the father had believed him mangled; a day or so more did not matter, nor the exact moment when he should learn that Joseph was alive. And Joseph's servants served them, and his wife the daughter of the sun spoke them friendly words and they talked with their aristocratic little nephews in the youth-lock, Manasseh and Ephraim, who could speak to them in their tongue. The younger, Ephraim, looked more like Joseph and Rachel than did Manasseh, who took after the mother's, the Egyptian side, so that Judah said: "You will see, Jacob will favour Ephraim and in his mouth it will be not Manasseh and Ephraim but Ephraim and Manasseh." And he advised his brother to cut off the Egyptian youth-lock above the boys' ears before Jacob came, as it would be an offence to him.

Then, at the end of the week, they packed up and girded themselves

319

for the journey. For there was to be a trade caravan from the kingdom, from Menfe, balance of the lands, up through the land of Canaan to Mitanniland, and the brothers were to join it, with wagons from the royal stores, two- and four-wheeled carts, given them with mules and drivers. Considering the ten asses, laden with all sorts of luxurious specialities of Egypt, exclusive and costly specimens of a lofty culture and fastidious taste, presented by Joseph to Jacob; and the ten she-asses, likewise for Jacob, whose loads consisted of grain, wine, preserves, smoked meats, and unguents—considering all this, it is clear that the brothers' own train was a stately one even by itself, swollen as their possessions were in addition by presents from their brother. It is well known that he gave to each man a change of raiment; but to Benjamin he gave three hundred silver deben and no less than five feast-day garments, one for each of the five extra days in the year. That might have been the reason why he said to them as they took their leave: "Do not fall out on the way!" but he really meant that they should not dwell on old times and reproach each other for what one had done behind each other's back. For it never entered his head or theirs that they could be jealous of Benjamin because he had given so much more lavishly to his own little brother. They were like lambs, they found everything in the best of order. When they were young and unruly they had rebelled against injustice; now it had turned out that they had come to terms with injustice and nevermore had aught to object to in the great "I favour whom I favour and show mercy to whom I show mercy."

HOW SHALL WE TELL HIM?

The mind dwells pleasantly upon the marvellous correspondencies which history shows: it loves to contemplate the way in which one part is balanced by another part and one scene has its pendant in the next. As once the brothers, seven days after Jacob had received the sign of Joseph's death, had returned from Dothan to mourn with their father and they had been sick with dread, how they should find him and how dwell with him under the half false yet partly true suspicion that they were the lad's slayers: so now, with white hairs among their dark, they were returning again to Hebron, with the news that Joseph had not died at all, was not dead now, but living in great glory; and they were almost as weighed down with the task of telling the old man. For uncanny is uncanny and overwhelming overwhelming—whether the content be life or death. They were sore afraid that Jacob would fall on his back as before; and this time, since he had got twenty years older in the meantime, he might quite simply "die of joy," in other words of shock, so that Joseph's life would be the cause of his death and he would no longer see the living with his eyes nor the living him with his. Besides, the truth must now almost inevitably come out that they had not indeed slain the lad as Jacob all the time had half believed, but yet that they had half slain him and only by chance not quite, thanks to the enterprise of the Ishmaelites who had taken him down to Egypt. The thought added to their pangs of conflicting joy and dread. But they drew some comfort from the thought that Jacob would be impressed, seeing they had been saved from murder by His messengers, the Midianites; this favour which God had shown the brothers would prevent Jacob from quarrelling with or cursing them.

They discussed all this during the whole seventeen-day journey; with all their impatience to bring it to an end they even found it too short a time in which to decide how to tell Jacob in the least dangerous way and how they would stand in his eyes once they had done so.

"Children," they said to each other—for since Joseph had said, "Children, I am your brother," they often used the word to each other, though it could never have been their habit before—"children, you will see, we shall have him falling on his back when we tell him, unless we go about it very tactfully and cautiously. But whether well or ill told, do you think he will believe what we say? The chances are he will not. For in so many years the idea of death fixes itself firmly in head and heart and is not easily dislodged or exchanged for the thought of life—it is not welcome to the mind, for the mind clings to habit. Brother Joseph thinks it will be a great joy to the old man and so, of course, it will be, a tremendous joy, but let us hope not too tremendous for his strength. But does a man know how to take hold of a joy straight off, when sorrow was his portion for years on end, and does he want to be told that he spent his life in a delusion and his days in error? For his affliction was all his life and now it is all bitterness. It is passing strange that we shall have to talk him out of something we once talked him into by means of the blood-stained garment, so that he clings to it now. And in the end we shall suffer more because we take it away than because we did it to him in the first place. Certainly he will close his mind and not believe us, and that is all for the best. For some time he must and may not believe us, for if he grasped it all at once it would lay him out. The question is, how to tell him so that the joy shall not be too abrupt and we do not suddenly thwart his settled sorrow. The best thing would be if we did not need to say anything, but could just take him down to Egypt and set him before Joseph his son, so he could see him with his own eyes and make all words superfluous. But it will be hard enough to get him down to Mizraim on to the fat feeding-grounds even when he knows that Joseph lives there; he has to know it beforehand or he surely will not go. But truth has not only words, it has also signs, such as the presents of the exalted ones and Pharaoh's wagons at our disposal. We will show him them, perhaps first of all before we say anything, and then explain the signs. But by the signs he will see how kindly the exalted one means by us and how we are one heart and soul with him we sold; so when it comes out, the old man will not be able to scold us for long, neither curse us—for can he then curse Israel, ten out of twelve? That he cannot, for it would be to kick against God's plan, who sent Joseph down thither before us as quartermaster in Egypt. Therefore, children, let us not be too fearful. The hour will come, and the moment whisper us how we shall use it. First we will spread out the gifts before him, the pride of Egypt, and ask: Where do you suppose they come from, Father, and from whom? Guess! Well, they come from the great keeper of the market down yonder, he sent them to you. But then it must be he loves you very much? He must love you almost as a son loves his father? But when we have got as far as the little word 'son,' then we are more than half-way, we are past the worst. And then we play for a while on the word and finally, instead of saying the keeper of the market sent it, we say: Your son sent it, Joseph sent it to you, for he is still alive and is a lord over all Egypt."

Thus the eleven planned and took counsel together under their nightly tent, and almost too swiftly for their misgivings the now familiar road lay behind them: from Menfe up to the frontier fortress, through the wilderness, and then towards the land of the Philistines and Gaza the seaport Khadati, where they separated from the merchant caravan they had marched with and struck inland into the hills towards Hebron in short day-marches and mainly by night; for it was flowery spring when they came and the nights were beautiful, silvered by an almost full moon. Moreover, they found very troublesome the curiosity they excited everywhere by reason of their train, swollen as it was by the Egyptian wagons, the mules and mule-boys, and a herd of almost fifty asses. So they regularly rested by day and by nightly stages pushed nearer home to the terebinths of the grove of Mamre, where stood the father's house of hair and the huts of nearly all the tribe.

But the last day they set out early in the morning and by five in the afternoon were close to the goal, though it was still hidden by the familiar hills as they climbed the last slope. They had left the luggage a little distance back and they rode on before it, eleven silent donkey-riders who had left off talking, for their hearts were pounding in their chests, and despite all their previous planning none of them was clear how to begin to break the news to the father without upsetting him. Now they had come to the point, all the plans misliked them, they found them stupid and unsuitable; in particular such foolishness as "Just guess!" and "Who could it be?" seemed to them frightfully out of place. Each one of them privately rejected it with scorn, and some at the very last minute tried to think of another idea. Perhaps they ought to send one of them on ahead, for instance Naphtali the runner, to tell Jacob they were all close at hand with Benjamin and brought great, incredible news: incredible partly in the sense that one could not believe it, partly because it went so counter to all their habits of thought that perhaps one could not even wish to believe it—and yet it was the living truth of God. So, thought some of them, the father's heart would best be attuned to receive the news and be best prepared for it by a forerunner before the others came up. They rode at a foot pace.

TELLING THE NEWS

It was a rough, stony slope where their animals were picking their way, but strewn thickly with spring flowers. There was larger-sized rubble as well as small; but wherever there was any soil, or even, it seemed, out of the stones themselves, wild flowers gushed, blossoms far and wide, white, yellow, sky-blue, purple, and rose; low bushes, mats and tussocks of bloom, a riot of gaiety and charm. The spring had summoned them and they had blossomed at their due hour. Even in the absence of the winter rains, it seemed they drew moisture enough from

323

the morning dew if only for a fleeting, soon fading splendour. Even the bushes here and there bloomed in their season, rose-coloured and white. Only the merest flaky cloudlets gathered high up in the heavenly blue.

On a little rock, against which a foam of blossoms beat like surf on a cliff, sat a figure almost, as seen from afar, like a flower itself. Soon they could tell it was a little maid, alone under the wide sky, in red smock with daisies in her hair. On her arm she held a zither and her slender brown fingers travelled up and down the strings. It was Serah, Asher's child; her father was the first to recognize her and with fatherly pride he said:

"That is my little Serah, sitting there on a stone, playing herself a little tune on her zither. The little wench is like that, she loves to sit alone and practise herself in psalmody. She belongs to the tribe of whistlers and fiddlers. God knows where she gets it, but she has had it ever since she was born; she has to make psalter and psalm; she can play on the strings till they ring and mingle her voice in songs of praise, clearer and stronger than you could believe, seeing her wisp of a body. Some day she will be famous in Israel, the little monkey. Look, she sees us, she flings up her arms and runs toward us. Halloo, Serah! Here is your father Asher coming with your uncles."

The child was already there; she ran barefoot through blossoms and rubble till the silver rings on wrists and ankles clashed and the yellow and white wreath bobbed up and down on her head. She laughed for pleasure and panted out breathless words of greetings; but even the gasping sounds she made had something sonorous about them, though one would not have known whence it came, her body being so frail.

She was a proper little maid; no longer a child and not yet a maiden, at most twelve years old. Asher's wife was supposed to be a great-grand-child of Ishmael. Had Serah something in her of Isaac's wild and beautiful half-brother that made her sing? Or—since men's traits do undergo the strangest transformations in their posterity—did Father Asher's moist and sensual lips and eyes, his greedy love of sensation and feeling combine become a musical quality in little Serah? Perhaps it is too bold and far-fetched to trace back to the father's sweet-tooth the child's love of the art of song. But some explanation there must be—so why not that?—for little Serah's strange gift.

The eleven looked down from their long-legged asses upon the little maid, gave her greeting, caressed her, and their eyes grew speculative. Most of them dismounted and stood round Serah, their hands on their back, nodding and wagging their heads, saying "Well, well!" and "Now, now!" and "So, little music-lips, have you run out to meet us and be the first to greet us, sitting here and playing on your zither like this?" But finally Dan, nicknamed snake and adder, said:

"Listen, children, I see by your eyes that we all have the same idea and it is Asher who should be saying what I now say; but being her father he does not think of it. Now, I have often shown that I am a good judge, and my native shrewdness tells me this is not just chance that the little monkey, Serah the song-maker, should meet us here before any of the others. God has sent her as a sign, to show what we should do. For the things we were planning about how to tell the father and hint to him so as not to harm him—that was all nonsense. Serah shall tell him, in her own way, so that the truth speaks to him in song, which is always the gentlest, whether sweet or bitter or bitter-sweet in one. Serah shall go on before us and sing to him, and even if he does not believe it, at least we shall have softened the soil of his soul and shall find it prepared for the seed of truth when we follow it up with chapter and verse and he will be forced to believe that song and truth are the same; just as we had to believe, however hard, that Pharaoh's keeper of the market was the same as our brother Joseph. Now have I spoken truly and put on solid ground what hung in the air in front of all your eyes when you saw Serah's childish little head dreaming into space?"

Yes, they said, he had, and he judged correctly. So it should be, it was the hand of heaven and a great relief. And then they took the child to instruct her and to stamp the truth on her mind. It was not easy, for they all talked at once and one would not let another speak, and Serah looked with darting, delighted eyes at their excited faces and their waving hands.

"Serah," said they, "it is thus and so. Believe it or not, just sing it and then we will come and prove it. But it would be better if you believed it, for you would sing the better, and it is true, however unlikely it sounds; after all, you will believe your father and all your uncles together? Look now, you did not know your uncle Jehosiph who was lost and gone, the son of the true wife, Rachel's son, who was called the star-virgin, but he was called Dumuzi. Well, he was lost to your grandfather long before you were born, and the world swallowed him up so that he was no more here, and in Jacob's heart was he dead all these years. But now it turns out, though hard to believe, that the truth is quite different—"

> "Oh wondrous strange, for now the truth is plain
> That quite, quite otherwise it came to pass,"

Serah began, going off half-cocked, singing and laughing so loud and musically that the gruff voices of her uncles were drowned out.

"Be quiet, little prodigy!" they cried. "You can't start singing until you know what to say. Listen and learn before you warble: your uncle Joseph has arisen, in other words he was never dead, he is alive, and not only alive but lives in this and this way. He lives in Mizraim and is this and this person. It was all a mistake, you see, the bloody garment was a mistake. God has turned all to good in ways we knew not of. Have you got that? We were with him in Egypt, and he made himself known to us beyond the shadow of a doubt, saying: 'I am he, I am your brother.' And spoke after such fashion to us that he would have us all come down there, and you too, little Serah. Have you taken all that in, so you could give it out again in song? Then you are to sing it to Jacob. Our Serah is a clever maid, she will do it. Take your zither and go on ahead of us, and sing loud and resoundingly that Joseph lives. Go in among the hills straight to Israel's camp, look neither right nor left, but just keep on singing. If anyone meets you and asks what you mean and what you are playing and singing, make no reply, just run and sing and sing and ring: 'He is alive!' And when you get to where Jacob your grandfather is, sit down at his feet and sing as sweetly as you know how: 'Joseph is not dead, he is alive.' He too will ask you what that means and what you are so rash as to say in your singing. But you must not answer him either; just keep on twanging your zither and singing away. Then all of us will come up and explain it to him in proper words. Will you be our good clever song-bird and do all this?"

"Gladly will I," answered Serah in her ringing tones. "Never before have I had such words to string on my strings; perhaps now I can show what they can do. Many sing, in tribe and town, but now I have better matter than they and will sing them out of the field."

So saying she took her instrument from the stone where she had sat and held it on one arm and spread her tapering brown fingers across the strings, the thumb here, the four fingers there. She began to move

326

steadily through the flowers, now fast, now slow according to the
measure of her song:

> "Oh let my soul sing a new song as it goeth,
> For a fine chant on eight strings my heart knoweth.
> Of what it is full let it run over in rhyme
> More precious than gold and fine gold from the mine,
> Sweeter than purest honey in the comb,
> For the spring's message I bring home.

> "Hearken all people to my harp-tone sweet,
> Listen and mark what I may here repeat,
> For upon me the lovely lot doth fall,
> And I am chosen out among the daughters all,
> For given am I the strangest matter yet
> Singer ever fell on to his harp to set,
> Now on my eight my little fingers string
> To Grandfather old the golden news to bring.

> "Lovely notes in order ringing,
> Balsam to all worldly woes,
> Sweeter when to lofty silence bringing
> Singing voice in words the meaning shows.
> How all that is then exalted,
> Full of sense the sweetest sound,
> Over all is praise allotted
> To song and psalter in combined round."

Thus she sang as she went on across pastures toward the hills and
the opening between the hills; struck till they rang at the strings and
picked them till they thrilled and sang:

> "Burden worthy of the music,
> Tone and word together strive,
> Each combining other's beauty,
> For they sing: the lad's alive!

"Yea, O Beneficent, what has here been wrought,
And what have the ears of me little one caught,
And what open-mouthed just now have I learned
From men who were in Egypt and returned,
From Father dear and high uncles mine
Who show me words to make a song so fine.
And they gave me matter of splendour unmeasured,
For who was it in Egypt they discovered?
Little Grandfather dear at first you will not follow,
But in the end you will have it to swallow.
Lovely as a dream yet true withal,
And just as real as it is wonderful.

"Rarest wonder past believing
That in one should be the two,
That all poesy is living
And the beautiful the true.
Now for once is here achieved
That for which the soul doth strive,
Let my burden be believed,
True and beautiful, thy son's alive.

"Still 'twere better if you think it
Beautiful awhile but yet not true,
Lest the cup if suddenly you drink it
Fling you on your back and lay you low.
As when once the worthless bloody token,
Lying in their throats, they brought you home,
Night fell on your soul for ever unbroken,
Straight a pillar of salt you would become.

"Ah, what pangs you bore in thinking
Nevermore to see him with your eyes,
Dead he lay within your heart and buried,
Now therein he sweetly doth arise."

Here a man sought to question her, a shepherd in a shady hat standing on the hill. He had been watching her for a long time, listening in wonder to her song. Now he came down to her, set his pace to hers, and asked:

"Maiden, what is it you sing as you go? It sounds so strange. I have often heard you praising and psaltering and I know you can play right soundingly on the strings, but never before so teasingly and riddlingly as this. And then the way you keep the time and set the pace as you go! Are you going to Jacob the master, and has what you sing to do with him? It seems to me so. But what do you mean by beautiful and true, and what with your refrain: 'the lad's alive'?"

But Serah as she walked looked not at him, she only smilingly shook her head. She took her hand a moment from the strings to lay her finger on her lips, then she went on:

> "Sing, Serah, Asher's child, what thou hast learned
> From the eleven now out of Egypt returned.
> Sing how that God in His mercy has blessed them
> That to the man down below they addressed them.
> Who then the man, who but Joseph is he,
> My uncle as tall and as fine as can be.
> Old one, look up, it is thy dear son,
> Greater is Pharaoh only by his throne.
> Lord of the lands his name they call,
> The state's first servant they name him all,
> Kings of the earth his praises sing,
> Stranger folk kneeling to him tribute bring.
> Over uncounted lands is he set,
> To all the people he giveth their meat,
> From thousands of barns he spendeth them bread
> To carry them over their hunger and need.
> For he it was in foresight wisely hoarded
> And therefore is his name o'er all belauded.
> His garments in myrrh and in aloes are pressed,
> In ivory palaces he sets up his rest,
> Forth from them like a bridegroom doth he come—
> Lo, old one, behold what has come of thy lamb!"

The man went along with her and listened with growing amazement to the words of her song. Seeing other folk at a distance, man or maid, he beckoned them up, to listen with him. Serah was soon the centre of a little troop of men, women, and children, which grew as they came nearer the camp. The children danced to the rhythm, the elders walked in the time of it; all their faces were turned to her, and she went on singing:

> "Whiles thou believedst him mangled and dead,
>   And with tears hast watered thy daily bread,
>   Twenty measured years have sped,
>   Mourning him with ashes on thy head—
>   Lo, now, old one, behold and see,
>   God He can scourge and can heal;
>   How marvellous all His Ways can be
>   For human children's weal!
>
> "Past understanding is His rule,
>   Great all the work of His hands;
>   He dealt with His servant as a fool
>   And laid thee under bands.
>   Creation laughs at the lordly jest,
>   Tabor and Hermon leap:
>   He snatched away thy dearest and best,
>   But now thou shalt have him to keep.
>   Thou has writhen, old man, in thy pain,
>   And found thyself in it again;
>   But now he is returned to you,
>   Still lovely, though rather stouter to view.
>
> "Thou knowest not his face,
>   Nor yet his name canst guess;
>   Stammering you will greet
>   Nor know who shall fall at whose feet.
>   Thus God went about at His ease
>   My dear little grandfather to tease."

By this time she had drawn with her train quite close to her home under Mamre's terebinths. She saw Jacob, the man of the blessing, sitting stately on his mat before the curtains of his dwelling. Now she lifted her instrument and held it higher and more firmly in her arm; up till then she had been picking and twanging the strings in well-tried scherzos and dissonances; but now she drew from it sounding chords of sweeping harmony, to which she sang in her full-throated voice:

> "For a word of beauteous rareness
>   In my music interweaves,
>   Matching all it hath of fairness,
>   And it says: Thy darling lives!
>   Match, O soul, in exultation
>   Golden music of the strings;
>   For the grave no longer hath him—
>   Heart, he is arisen—sing!
> Heart, it is the sorely missed,
> For whom the earth its anguish bore,
> Whom they lured into the coffin,
> Whom the boar's vile tushes tore.
>   Ah, he was no longer present,
>   Desolate the barren earth,
>   Till we heard: He is arisen—
>   Dear old Father, pray have faith!
> Godlike in his steps he paces,
> Round his head bright summer birds do reel,
> As across the flowery spaces
> Lo, he greets thee with a smile!
>   Wintry grief and deathly anguish
>   From his kiss away have flown;
>   On his lips and cheeks and forehead
>   Hath the Eternal favour strewn.
>
> "Read it in his laughing features
>   All was but a godlike jest;
>   And in late-believing raptures
>   Take him to thy father-breast!"

Jacob had long since seen his grandchild, his little music-lips, coming towards him, and listened well pleased to her voice. He even clapped his hands benevolently, just like the audience at a play. When she reached him the maid, without other greeting than her song, sat down on the mat at his feet; her troop of followers stayed at some distance away. The old man listened, and his applauding hands slowly fell; his nodding as slowly turned into a doubtful head-shaking. When she came to an end of her verse he said:

"Good and charming, my granddaughter, so far. It is sweet of you, Serah, and thoughtful, to come and give a little pleasure to the lonely old man. You see, I know you well by name, as I do not all of my grandchildren, for there are too many. But you stand out for your gift of song; it makes a real person of you, so that one remembers your name. But listen now, my gifted one, while I say I have heard with pleasure the music and the poetry, but yet not without some misgiving the sense. For poesy, dear little one, poesy is always an alluring, seductive, dangerous thing. Sense and senses lie close together, and song rhymes all too easily with wrong; grace and charm are prone to gracelessness and harm, if they are not bridled by concern with God. Lovely is the play of thought; but holy the spirit alone. Poesy is play of heart and mind; willingly I applaud it, so long as it loses not sight of spirit but remains in the end concern with God. Now what was it you were saying in your warbling and trilling; and what can I make of a man like a god tripping across the fields with birds flitting about him and laughing at his own jest? He sounds to me like one of these nature-gods hereabouts, whom I hold in great suspicion: the folk of the countryside call him lord, and darken the counsels of the children of Abraham with their folly. We too speak of the Lord, of course; but our meaning is altogether different. Never can I be sufficiently concerned for Israel's soul, nor preach enough under the tree of wisdom, that this 'lord' is not the Lord; our people are always on the point of confusing the two and relapsing into idolatry. For God is a high and difficult task; but 'the gods' are a pleasant sin. Can I then, dear child, applaud, when you lend your gift to pleasant psaltery after the loose ways of the land?"

But Serah only shook her head with a smile, plucked her strings anew, and sang:

> "Who then do I sing, O Grandfather mine,
> Who but my uncle so tall and so fine?
> Look up, old man, it is thy dear son,
> Greater is Pharaoh only by his throne.

Grandfather, at first you cannot follow,
But in the end you will have it to swallow.
  For a word of wonder-rareness
  In my music interweaves,
  Matching all it hath of fairness,
  And it says: Thy darling lives!"

"Child," said Jacob, greatly moved, "truly it is lovely and pleasant that you come before me and sing of my son Joseph, whom you never knew, and devote your gift to divert me. But your song is riddling: the rhymes are well enough but not the reason, and so it hath neither rhyme nor reason. I cannot let it pass; for how can you sing 'The lad's alive'? Such words can give me no joy, they are but lying flourishes, for Joseph died long since. Mangled is he, mangled and dead."

But Serah answered him in ringing chords:

  "Match, O soul, with exaltation
  Golden music of the strings,
  For the grave no longer hath him,
  Heart, he is arisen—sing!
    Ah, he was no longer present,
    Desolate the barren earth—
    Till we heard: He is arisen.
    Dear old Father, pray have faith!
  From thousands of barns he spendeth them bread
  To carry them over their hunger and need;
  For he like Noah wisely hath provided,
    And therefore is his name o'er all beloved.
    His garments in myrrh and in aloes are pressed,
    In ivory palaces he sets up his rest,
    And issueth like bridegroom forth from them—
    Old one, behold what hath come of thy lamb!"

"Serah, my grandchild, reckless little one," said Jacob impressively, "what shall I think of your loose-mouthed song? I have let much pass as poetic licence, though I find it little respectful that you address me as 'old man.' But poetic licence is not the only licence in your song, it is altogether a string of disrespectful and cheating make-believe. You may

333

think to please me by it; but pleasure founded on falseness is no true pleasure, nor can it profit the soul. Dare poesy lend itself to such, is that its province? Are you not abusing your gift from God to dress in it such untrue and unreasonable things? Verily there must be some reason allied to the beauty, else it only mocks the heart."

"Rarest wonder,"

sang Serah, unheeding

> "Rarest wonder, past believing,
> That in one should be the two:
> That all poesy is living,
> And the beautiful the true.
>> Here for once is now achieved
>> That for which the soul doth strive,
>> Let my burden be believed,
>> True and beautiful, thy son's alive!"

"Child," said Jacob, and his head was shaking on his shoulders, "dearest child . . ."

But her voice soared and revelled, borne on the leaping, exulting music of the strings:

> "Lo, now, old one, behold and see,
> God He can scourge and can heal,
> How marvellous all His ways can be
> For His human children's weal!
> He snatched away thy dearest and best,
> But thou shalt take him again to thy breast
> Thou hast writhen, old one, in thy pain,
> Yet found thyself in it again;
> But now he returneth to you,
> Still lovely, though rather stouter to view.
> So God goes about as He pleases
> And dear little Grandfather teases."

Jacob, with his head turned away, for the brown eyes were full of tears, put out one hand as though to stop her. "Child!" he said again, and only that. He seemed not to hear the sudden bustle and movement among the tents; nor paid any heed to the joyous announcement now

334

made him. For the group who had come up with Serah was increased by others approaching to bring glad tidings; servants and other folk came round Jacob from all sides and two of them addressed him:

"Israel, the eleven are back from Egypt, your sons with men and carts and many more asses than they set out with!"

But even as the men spoke, here were the brothers already. They dismounted and came up, with Benjamin in their midst and the rest pulling and pushing him forward, each one zealous to be the one to bring him before the father.

"Peace and good health," they said, "to our father and dear lord! Here is Benjamin. We have kept him safe for you, though he was at one time in some danger. But now you can have him once more at your apron-strings. And here is your hero Simeon. Furthermore, we bring abundance of food and rich presents from the giver of bread. Lo, we are all well and happily returned—happily, in truth, is a word nowhere near strong enough for it."

"Boys," answered Jacob, who had got to his feet, "boys—yes, of course, I am glad to see you."

He put his hand possessively on Benjamin's arm, yet half absently too, and his gaze was bewildered. "You are here again," said he, "safe home again after perilous journey—under other circumstances this would be a great moment and quite fill my soul if it were not taken up with other matters. Yes, you find me greatly taken up, I mean by this little maid here—Asher, she is your child—who came and sat by me and played on her zither, singing so sweetly, yet harping upon such folly about my son Joseph that I know not how to defend my reason from her. I am tempted to welcome your coming solely because I count on you to protect me from this child and the lying tongue her music has, since I know you would not allow my grey hairs to be mocked."

"Never will we do so," responded Judah, "so far as we can prevent it. But in the opinion of all of us, Father, and it is a well-founded opinion, you would do better—even though at first afar off—to consider whether there might not be some truth in her harping."

"Some truth," repeated the old man. He stood up very straight. "You dare come to me with such cowardly advice and speak to Israel of half-measures and half-truths? Where should we be, and where God, if we had ever let ourselves in to be half and half? For the truth is one and indivisible. Three times this child has sung to me: 'Thy son's alive!'

335

There can be nothing true in her words unless it were the truth. So what is it?"

"The truth!" said the eleven in chorus, raising their palms to the sky. And:

"The truth!" came back the amazed and exultant chorus from the gathered host. Men's, women's, and children's voices echoed triumphantly: "She sang the truth!"

"Dear little Father," said Benjamin, embracing Jacob, "as now you hear, so believe, for we too had to, first one of us and then another. The man down there who asked about me, and kept on asking: 'Does your father still live?'—that is Joseph, he and Joseph are one. Never was he dead, my mother's son. Roving men tore him from the claws of the ravening beast and took him down to Egypt, where he has flourished as by a spring and become the first among the men of the land below. The sons of strangers flatter him, for without him they would pine and die. Would you have tokens of this miracle? Look at our train! Twenty asses he sent you, whose load is the food and the riches of Egypt, and the wagons out of Pharaoh's stores shall carry us all down to your son. For from the beginning it was his plan that you should come and I guessed that it was so. He would have us to feed on fat pastures, not far from him, but where it is not too Egyptian, in the land of Goshen."

Jacob had preserved complete, almost severe composure.

"God will dispose," he said in a firm voice. "Only from Him does Israel take instructions and not from the great ones of this earth.—My Damu, my child!" broke from his lips. He had clasped his hands on his breast and stood with his brow raised to the clouds, slowly shaking his old head. Then he dropped it again.

"Boys," said he, "this little maid, whom I now bless and who shall not taste death but go living into the kingdom of heaven if God shall hear me—she sang to me that the Lord vouchsafes me Rachel's first-born back again, still handsome but somewhat heavy. That probably means he is already quite fat with the years and the flesh-pots of Egypt?"

"Not really fat, dear Father, not very," answered Judah soothingly. "Only within the bounds of dignity. You must consider that not death gives him back to you, but life. Death, if that were thinkable, would give him back to you as he was; but since it is life at whose hand you receive him back, he is no more the faun of other days but a royal stag of four points. And you must be prepared to find him a little strange and worldly

336

in his ways and wearing a pleated byssus, like Hermon's driven snow."

"I will go down and see him before I die," said Jacob. "If he had not lived he would not be living. Blessed be the name of the Lord!"

"Blessed!" cried they all, and rushed forward in a wave to congratulate him and the brothers and kiss the hem of Jacob's garment. He did not look down on their heads; his eyes were raised again and he kept shaking his head as he held it turned up to the sky. But Serah, the songlips, sat on the mat and sang:

> "Read it in his laughing features,
> All was but a Godlike jest;
> And in late-believing raptures
> Take him to thy father-breast!"

Chapter Seven

THE LOST IS FOUND

AND so the refractory cow heard the voice of her calf when the crafty farmer brought it to the field that was to be ploughed, so that the cow would be contented there; and the cow yielded her neck to the yoke and ploughed. Hard enough it was for her still, with her considerable dislike of the field, which she thought of as a death-acre. Jacob's deliberate and declared intention was not easier to him than submission was to the cow; indeed, he was glad that at least he had time to think it over. Actually to carry it out, to part from all that was his by ingrained habit, to transport the tribe bag and baggage to the lowland, that took much time; and by the same token it gave him time. The Bene Yisrael were not the people to take literally Pharaoh's words, not to regard their stuff, for that they should be provided withal in the land of Goshen, and they were simply to leave everything where it was. "Not to regard their stuff," that meant at most not to take everything they had—which was impossible anyhow. Not all their tools and equipment and not all the cattle and fowl. On the other hand it certainly did not mean that they were to travel light and leave everything behind for the first comer. They sold off quantities of goods, and certainly not in unseemly haste or without very stiff bargaining. But Jacob let them go ahead and sell. Which proves that he kept to his resolve in its main lines although the way he talked about it might be open to various interpretations.

"I will go down thither and see him," he would say. That might mean: "I will visit him to see his face before I die and then come back." But it was clear to all of them, even to Jacob himself, that it really could not mean that. If it had been a matter of just a visit to behold his face, then certainly it would be his high-and-mightiness Joseph who owed his little father the visit in order to spare him the great inconvenience of a

338

journey to Mizraim. But on the other hand such a thought ran counter to the motif of the sending after, and Jacob perfectly understood that the stars in their courses had so ruled in the matter. Joseph had not been separated and snatched away for that; Jacob's face had not to that end been swollen with weeping, only in order that they should now visit each other. No, the high purpose was that Joseph should have Israel come after him; and Jacob was far too much of an expert in God-knowledge not to know that the snatching away of the lovely one, his magnification down below, the obstinate famine which had driven the brothers down to Egypt—that all these were arrangements in a comprehensive plan, to ignore which would have been the crassest stupidity. One might find Jacob self-centred and arrogant in that a calamity like the present prolonged drought, so wide-spread, affecting so many people and causing such wholesale economic changes, was seen by him merely in the light of a plan for the furtherance of his own tribal history. Quite obviously it was his idea that where he and his house were in question the rest of the world would have to like it or lump it. But arrogance and egoism are only negative words for a highly positive and fruitful attitude which we might call by the more sympathetic name of piety. There are probably no virtues which cannot be called by unsympathetic names; none without inward contradictions, such as, in the present case, humility and arrogance. Piety is the subjectivation of the outer world, its concentration upon the self and its salvation; without the conviction, exaggerated to the point of offensiveness, of God's especial, yes, all-embracing concern, without the fixation of the self and its salvation in the very centre of all things, there is no piety. Piety, in short, is the name we give to that great virtue. Its opposite is the low esteem of the self and its relegation to the unimportant periphery, out of which nothing good can come. He who does not take himself seriously is soon lost, but he who thinks of himself as Abraham did when he resolved that he, and in him man, might serve only the highest, he does, of course, behave presumptuously. But this presumption will be a blessing to many. For here is manifest the connection between the dignity of the self and the dignity of humanity. The claim of the human ego to central importance was the precondition for the discovery of God; and only together, with the consequence of the utter destruction of a humanity which does not take itself seriously, can both discoveries be lost sight of again.

But we must go on from here: for subjectivation does not mean subjection, nor esteem of self disesteem of others. It does not mean isolation or a callous disregard of the general, the exterior and supra-personal; in short, of all that reaches beyond the self. On the contrary it therein solemnly recognizes itself. In other words, if piety is the being penetrated with the importance of the self, then worship is piety's extension and assimilation into the eternalness of being, which returns in it and wherein it recognizes itself. That is to depart from all singleness and limitation, yet with no violence to its own dignity, which it even enhances to the point of consecration.

In such a light, then, we may consider Jacob's mood at this time of the break-up; and we can scarcely think of it as more solemn than it actually was. He was about to carry out quite literally what he had dreamed of at the peak of his affliction and feverishly prattled in Eliezer's ear: he was going down to his dead son in the underworld. That was a cosmic procedure; and where the ego opens its borders to the cosmic and loses itself therein, even until its own identity is blurred, can there be any thought of narrowness or isolation? The very thought of the break-up was full of contrary-tending factors: the factor of abiding, the factor of the return—they elevated the moment above and beyond the episodic and atomic. Jacob the greybeard was Jacob the youth again; he who, after the deception that put things right, had departed from Beersheba to Naharaim. He was Jacob the man who with wives and flocks had got free from Harran after a stay of twenty-five years. But he was not only Jacob, the man in whose life-spiral the break-up repeated itself. He was also Isaac, who went to Gerar, to Abimelech in the land of the Philistines. Again and still further back, he was seeing repeat itself the primeval break-up, Abram the wanderer's exodus from Ur of the Chaldees—and even that was not the first form, but only the earthly reflection and imitation of a celestial wandering: the wandering of the moon, who took her way and freed herself from one station to the next: Bel Harran, the Lord of the Way. But Abram, the first earthly wanderer, had made pause at Harran; so it was plain that Beersheba was to represent it and that Jacob would there make his first moon-station.

He took comfort in the thought of Abram: how during a famine he too had gone to Egypt, to dwell there as a stranger. And Jacob had need of comfort. True, he was looking forward to a joy so keen that it was almost pain; after that he might depart in peace, since nothing to compare with it remained to look for. True, the migration to Egypt, there by Pharaoh's consent to pasture on fat land, was an enviable lot, and so esteemed by many. But when all was said and done, the decision was hard for Jacob. It was hard for him to adapt himself to God's command to void the land of his fathers and exchange it for the offensive land of the animal gods, the land of mud, the land of the children of Ham. He had settled in the land whither Abraham had wandered; had done it provisionally, as it were, and like his forefathers had always been half a stranger there. Still he had thought to die as they had in this spot. He had always considered to refer to this land where he was born and where his dead rested the prophecy made to Abram that his seed would be strange in the land. But now it turned out that the prophecy which, not for nothing, was bound up with thoughts of terror and great darkness actually pointed to the land whither he was now going: to Mizraim, the Egyptian house of bondage. That, we know, had always been Jacob's mistrustful name for the strictly administered land down south. Certainly he had never contemplated its becoming a house of bondage for his own seed—as now became painfully clear to him. His leave-taking was burdened with the insight that God's pronouncement: "And they shall afflict them four hundred years," referred to the country whither he was going. It was in all probability the forced labour of many generations to which he was leading his people. The plan of salvation might be altogether good; or good and bad might be wholly cancelled out in the great concept of destiny and the future. But notwithstanding all that, this was uncontestably a break-up fraught with destiny, to which Jacob now committed himself in God, and as such he felt it.

Yes, they were going to the land of tombs, and that was bad enough. But actually it was the tombs he was leaving behind that he thought of with the keenest pain. Rachel's wayside grave, and Machpelach, the double hollow, which Abram had bought as a burial place with the field it stood in from Ephron the Hittite for four hundred silver shekels by weight according to custom. Israel like all shepherds was free-footed; still he did possess that much real estate, the field with the cave; and his it should remain. The emigrants disposed of many movables, but just this immovable, the field with the tomb, that was inalienable. To Jacob it was the guarantee of his return. For however many generations were to rot in Egypt's soil while his house increased, he was resolved to lay it upon God and man that when the remnant of his own days was lived out, he himself was to be brought back to the permanent home which he, the shepherd and wanderer, possessed on earth: that he might lie where lay his father and the mothers of his sons, all save only the beloved and untimely cut off, who lay by the wayside, mother of his darling taken hence, who summoned him now.

So it was good that Jacob had time to consider his departure down thither to the snatched one. For it was a heavy task, this of understanding God's purposes in the strange destiny of the set-apart darling. Jacob's conclusion on this subject can best be heard from himself. When he spoke of Joseph now he spoke of him not otherwise than as "his lordship my son." "I intend," he would say, "to travel down to his lordship my son in Egypt. He holds high office there." People to whom he said that probably smiled behind the old man's back and made merry over the paternal vanity. They did not know how much deadly serious effort after objectivity, how much renunciation and stern resolve lay behind Jacob's turn of phrase.

SEVENTY OF THEM

The flowery spring had become late summer before Israel had his affairs wound up and the train got under way from the grove of Mamre by Hebron. Beersheba was their nearest goal and some days of ceremonial sojourn were to be spent in this border place where Jacob and his father were born and where the resolute mother Rebecca had once readied the thief of the blessing for the journey into Mesopotamia.

Jacob departed from his own place and set forth with flocks and possessions, with sons and sons' sons, with daughters and daughters' sons. Or, as the story also says: with their little ones and their wives, a limited reckoning since by wives was meant the wives of the sons and by daughters the same thing with addition of the daughters of the sons, for instance the singing Serah. They left seventy strong—that is, they reckoned themselves seventy, but it was not by actual count, merely a feeling of a count, a sort of mental conclusion, in which there prevailed that lunar degree of exactness of which we well know that it was not like our own yet entirely right and justifiable in its time and place.

Seventy was the number of the peoples of the earth listed in the tables of God. Consequently nothing in black and white was required in order to prove that seventy was the number of descendants from forefather's loins. But when it came to Jacob's loins, surely the wives of the sons ought not to have been counted in? And accordingly they were not. For where there is no counting at all there can be no counting in; the sum arrived at was not a matter of counting at all, resting as it did on a foregone conclusion; thus it is idle to ask what was counted and what not. We do not even know whether Jacob himself was one of the seventy, or whether they reckoned him separately as the seventy-first. We must be content to think that the age permitted both possibilities at the same time. Much later, for instance, a descendant of Judah, or more precisely of his son Perez, with whom Tamar had deliberately presented him—this descendant, a man named Isaiah, had seven sons, *and* a youngest son who tended the sheep, upon whom the horn of anointing was lifted up. What does this *and* mean? Was he included as the youngest of seven or did Isaiah have eight sons? The former is more likely, for it is much finer and more orthodox to have seven sons than eight. But it is more than likely, in fact it is certain, that the figure seven as the number of Isaiah's sons did not change to eight when the youngest came along and that the youngest succeeded in being included in the seven even though he was actually one over the count. And once there was another man who had full seventy sons, for he had many wives. One son of these mothers killed all his brothers, the whole seventy sons on one same stone. By our prosaic reckoning he can only, being their brother, have killed sixty-nine. Or rather sixty-eight, since another brother, whose name is given, Jotham, remained alive. The statement is hard to swallow. Yet here one of seventy did kill all seventy and yet left himself and another brother alive—a striking and instructive instance of "counting in" and "not counting in" at the same time.

Jacob, then, actually was the seventy-first among the seventy wanderers—in so far as this figure itself can stand the light of day. For in prosaic truth the number was less rather than more—a fresh contradiction, but unfortunately an unavoidable one. Jacob the father was the seventieth and not the seventy-first on the basis of the fact that the males of the seed came to sixty-nine. However, it did so by including Joseph, who was in Egypt, and his two sons who were even born there. These three males of the stock were certainly not in the train that

343

went down; accordingly we must subtract them even although they belong in the figure seventy. Again, even this deduction leaves too many; for the figure seventy reckoned in a number of souls as yet unborn. We might let pass the case of Jochebed, a daughter of Levi, whose mother was already heavy with her at the time of the journey, she being born "between the walls," probably the walls of the border fortress on their entry into Egypt. But there is more to it than that. For the sum total counts in grandchildren who are neither born nor begot, not present but only foreseen. They came to Egypt, as pious scholars put it, *in lumbis patrum* and took part in the journey only in a metaphysical sense.

So much for the necessary subtractions. But there are equally compelling reasons for increasing the sum total. The male seed of Jacob came to that sum by itself; but if—or rather since—all his immediate descendants must be counted in, then, if certainly not the sons' wives, yet their daughters must be included, for example Serah, quite decidedly, to mention only one. It would be entirely wrong not to count the little maid who brought the good news about Joseph. Her fame was great in Israel and there was never any doubt about the fulfilment of the blessing which Jacob had gratefully conferred on her, that she should not taste death but go up living into heaven. Nobody in fact knows when she died: her life-story has every appearance of continuing on and on. There is the tale that generations later the man Moses, going about hunting for Joseph's grave, had the spot—in the middle of the Nile— pointed out to him by Serah. Vastly later than that even, she seems to have pursued her existence among the people of Abram, under the name of the "wise woman." However that may be, whether it was the same Serah all the time or whether other little maids assumed the name and nature of the first little herald and harbinger, in any event she must be included. No objecting voice will be raised, no matter how her inclusion affects the count.

But we cannot be so thoroughgoing about the wives of the sons—in other words, the mothers of Jacob's grandchildren. The word "mothers" is better than "wives" in this connection, on account of Tamar, who, conformably to the "whither thou goest I will go" made one in the train with her two stout Judah sons. Mostly she went on foot, leaning on a long staff, taking for a woman very long strides; tall and dark, with round nostrils and proud mouth, and that strange distant-dwelling look of hers. This resolute woman, who would not at any price be counted

344

out, should she not be counted in? As for her two husbands, Er and Onan, they could not be counted—neither by moon nor by daylight reckoning, for they were dead; and even if Israel counted unborn souls, surely he did not count dead ones! Shelah, on the other hand, the husband whom she did not get, but whom she no longer needed, since she had given him two fine stout half-brothers, went along, being one among Leah's thirty-two grandchildren.

CARRY HIM

To the agreed number, then, of seventy, Israel pulled out of the grove of Mamre the Amorite. Counting everything not counted in, shepherds, drovers, drivers, baggage men, and slaves, the train was all of a hundred persons and more—a highly-coloured, noisy caterpillar of a migrating tribe, slow-moving, enveloped in clouds of dust raised by the trotting flocks. Its members got forward by various means—and between ourselves, the host of Egyptian conveyances sent by Joseph were of very little use. This does not apply to the so-called *agolt,* whose value should be acknowledged. These were heavy two-wheeled ox-carts, wonderful for household goods, leather water-bottles, and forage, as well as for the women and children. But the actual travelling carriages, such as the light *merkobt,* some of them very luxuriously equipped and drawn by a team of horses or mules, with the shapely wagon-box covered with stamped purple leather; open behind and often consisting simply of a curved wooden railing, gilded in every possible place: these elegant toys, however well-meaning Joseph and his royal master had been in sending them, proved impracticable and went back to Egypt mostly as empty as they had come. Nobody had any good of the fact that some of them were covered inside and out with linen and stucco and in the stucco delightful little reliefs of court and peasant life; or that the nails on the wheels were in the form of Moors' heads, exquisitely modelled. Only two persons could stand in these chariots, or three if they were crowded; they had no springs and were tiring in the long run, over ungentle roads. Or if you sat down you had to sit backwards on the floor with your legs dangling out. Some, like Tamar, chose the time-honoured way of the pilgrim and went on foot with a staff. Most of them, however, rode: on splay-footed camels, bony mules, white or grey asses,

345

all of them decorated with big glass beads, embroidered saddlecloths, and dangling mullen-stalks. Those were the saddle animals, who stirred up the dust in the roads. On them rode Jacob's people, whom Joseph had sent for: a gay, high-coloured tribe, in garments of woven wool, the bearded men in their heavy desert cloaks, with head-cloths often held in place by a felt ring on top. The women had black braids hanging on their shoulders, silver and bronze bracelets on their wrists, their foreheads were hung with coins, their nails reddened with henna, they carried sucklings in their arms, swaddled in great soft wrappings with brocaded borders. They all munched as they rode along: roasted onions, sour bread, and olives. They mostly took the ridge road going down from Jerusalem and the heights of Hebron to the deeper southland, called Negeb, the arid land to Kirjath Sepher, the book city, and to Beersheba.

Our chief concern, of course, is the comfort of Jacob the father. How was he accommodated? Had Joseph, when he sent his wagons, thought that the venerable man would make the journey standing in one of those decorated chariots, behind a gilt railing? Not he. Not even Pharaoh his master thought that. The directions issued by the beautiful child of Aton from his new-smelling palace had said: "Take your father and carry him." The patriarch was to be borne as though in triumph, that was the word used; and among the mostly useless vehicles sent by Joseph was a single conveyance of a different kind, destined for precisely this solemn service, the carrying of Jacob. It was an Egyptian litter, such as the upper classes of Keme used on the streets and when they travelled: an exceptionally elegant specimen too, with a woven reed back-rest, the sides adorned with fine writings, with rich hangings and bronze carrying-poles; it was even provided with a light gaily painted wooden hood at the back for protection against dust and wind. This chair could be carried by boys or on the back of animals by means of cross-poles. Jacob was very comfortable in it, once he had made up his mind to use it. He did so only from Beersheba on, that being in his mind the boundary-line between home and foreign land. Up to that point he was carried by a dromedary, a wise, slow-gazing beast, on a saddle with a sunshade fastened to it.

The old man was a very fine and dignified sight, and he knew it too, as surrounded by his sons he swayed along on his high perch at the rocking gait of his clever beast. The fine wool of his *kofia* was fringed unevenly across his forehead; it lay in folds about neck and shoulder and fell softly on the dark red garment open at the front to reveal the embroidered under-garment. The breezes played in his silver beard. The inward gaze of his gentle shepherd eyes showed that he was musing on his tales, both past and future, and nobody ventured to disturb him; at most they inquired respectfully now and again after his comfort. Foremost in his mind was the expected sight of the sacred tree at Beersheba, planted by Abram, beneath which he meant to sacrifice, to give instruction, and to sleep.

JACOB TEACHES AND DREAMS

The giant tamarisk stood on a hill of medium height near the populated settlement of Beersheba, which our travellers passed by on one side. Beneath its shade stood a primitive stone table and an upright stone column or *massebe*. The tree had, strictly speaking, probably not been planted by Jacob's father's father, but taken over by him from the children of the land and changed from a Baal shrine into a tree of God and *êlôn môreh* or oracle tree, the central point of a shrine and cult of the highest and only God. Jacob might easily know this without being shaken in his belief that the tree was planted by Abram. In a symbolic sense it was, and the mental processes of the father were broader and gentler than ours, which know only one thing or else the other, and are prone to shout, banging on the table: "If that had been a Baal tree, then Abram did not plant it!" Such zeal for the truth is more peppery and thickheaded than wise, and there is far more dignity in the quiet reconciliation of both points of view, as Jacob achieved it.

But the forms in which Israel worshipped the eternal God under the tree did not after all differ much from the cult of the children of Canaan —aside from all the offensive sporting and unseemliness in which the worship of those children used inevitably to wind up. At the foot of the sacred hill, round about, the rest-tents were set up and preparations for the slaughtering got under way at once, to be performed on the dolmen, the primitive stone table, and afterwards partaken of in common, the sacrificial meal. Had the children of Baal done otherwise? Had not they too let the blood of sheep and goats run down upon the altar and struck the caked side-posts with the blood? Surely they had. But the children of Israel did it in a different spirit and in more enlightened wise, as is clear from the fact that after the sacred meal they did not sport with each other in pairs, at least not publicly.

And Jacob instructed them in God, too, under the tree. And it did not bore them; even the young found his words most interesting and important, because they were all more or less gifted in that way and eagerly seized even on the subtleties of his remarks. He showed them the difference between the many-namedness of Baal and that of their Father the highest and only. The many-named Baal was a true plurality; there was no one Baal but many—the occupants, possessors, and patrons of cult sites, groves, shrines, springs, trees: a host of gods of dwelling and soil who worked singly and locally, had in their collectivity no face, no person, no proper name, and at most were called Melkart, city king, if they were that sort of deity, as for instance him of Tyre. One was called Baal Peor after his site, or Baal Hermon or Baal Meon; one was Baal of the Bond, of course, which had been useful in Abram's work on God. There was even one called, quite absurdly, Dance-Baal. There was not much dignity about this and very little collective majesty. Quite otherwise was it with the many names of God the Father, which did no violence whatsoever to his personal oneness. He was called El-Elyon, the highest; El ro'i, the God that sees one; El Olam, God of the æons, or, after Jacob's great vision sprung from his humiliation, El Bethel, the God of Luz. But all these were only interchangeable designations for one and the same highest existing personal God; not localized, existing in everything, like the labelled multiplicity of the Baal gods of town and country, the single proprietorship of which was ascribed to them, the fertility they bestowed, the springs they guarded, the trees wherein they dwelt and murmured, the tempest they raged in, the burgeoning spring, the parching east wind—He was all this that they singly were, to Him it all belonged. He was the All-God of all of it, for from Him it came, in Himself He comprehended it, saying I, the Being of all being, Elohim, the many as one.

On the subject of this name Jacob exhausted himself. He spoke most engrossingly for his audience and not without subtlety. It was clear whence Dan, his fifth son, got his type of mind, though it was only a poor second-generation derivative from his father's much higher qualities. The question Jacob discussed was whether one was to regard Elohim as singular or plural: to say "Elohim wills it" or "the Elohim will it." If you admitted the importance of correct syntax, you must

348

make the distinction, and Jacob seemed to make it correctly in deciding for the singular. God was One, and he who thought that Elohim was the plural of El or God involved himself in grave error. The plural of God would be Elim. Elohim was something quite different. It did not mean a multiplicity any more than the name Abram. The man from Ur had been named Abram and then had the honour of having his name expanded into Abraham. The same was true of Elohim. It was an honorific expansion, nothing else—certainly it had no taint of what one condemned as polytheism. The teacher stressed the point. Elohim was One. But then again it transpired that there were several of Him, some three. Three men came to Abraham in the grove of Mamre, as he sat at the door of his house in the heat of the day. And the three men were, as the hasting Abraham soon saw, God the Lord. "Lord," he had said, bowing to the earth; "Lord," and "thou." But also now and then "Lords" and "you." And had prayed them to sit down in the shade and strengthen themselves with milk and the flesh of cows. And they ate. And then they said: "I will come to you in a year." That was God. He was One, but He was explicitly threefold. He practised manifoldness, but always and on principle said "I," whereas Abraham had addressed him by turns in the singular and the plural. The use of the name Elohim as a plural, his audience heard Jacob further say, had, despite all the above stress to the contrary, something in its favour after all. Yes, as they heard him go on, they got a glimmer of an idea that his experience of God, like Abram's, had been threefold, and comprised three men. Three independent and yet again coincident persons. He spoke, that is, first of all of the Father-God, or God the Father, second of a Good Shepherd who fed His flocks, and third of one whom he called the Angel, of whom the seventy got the impression that He overshadowed as with the wings of doves. All together they were Elohim, the threefold unity.

I cannot tell whether all that goes home to you; but for Jacob's hearers under the tree it was vastly interesting and exciting—they had taste and gifts for such things. As they dispersed, and afterwards in their tents before they slept, they discussed what they had heard, long and eagerly. The honorific expansion and Abram's threefold guest, the avoidance of polytheism enjoined upon them in view of a God out of whose manifold existence there yet went a certain temptation in that direction—all that being like a test of their capacity for God-thoughts: a test to which all of Jacob's people, even the youngest, felt blithely adequate.

349

Their head and chief had his place spread under the sacred tree all the three nights he spent at Beersheba. The first two nights he did not dream, but the third brought him the vision to receive which he slept and which he needed for consolement and strength. He was afraid of Egypt, he urgently needed the assurance that he need not fear to go down thither, since the God of his fathers was not a local deity and would be with him in the lower world as he had been with him in Laban's land. He had need to his heart's depths of the confirmation that God did not only go down with him but after he had made them a multitude would lead him (or at least his seed) back into the land of his fathers. That was the land between Nimrod's kingdoms; an ignorant land indeed, and full of foolish aborigines, but yet no Nimrod kingdom: there better than anywhere else one might serve a spiritual God. In short, what he so thirsted for was the assurance that the promise of the great dream of the ladder that had come to him in Gilgal of Bethel should not be cancelled by his going hence, but that God the King stood by His word which He had sung to the sound of harps. It was to hear this that he slept and in sleep he heard it. God spoke to him in a solemn voice and promised that of which his soul had need. But sweetest of all was the promise that Joseph should "put his hands upon thine eyes"—a profound and meaningful expression which might signify that the all-powerful son would protect him and care for his old age among the heathen; but also that his darling would one day close his eyes—a dream in which for so long now Jacob had not let himself indulge.

Now he let himself dream both this and the other and his sleeping eyes were wet beneath their lids. But when he woke he was strengthened and reassured, and anxious to proceed onwards with all the seventy. He mounted the fine Egyptian carrying-chair, which was slung across the backs of two white asses adorned with mullen stalks; in it he looked even finer and more stately than on the camel.

OF WITHHOLDING LOVE

A trade route ran from the north-east of the delta through the arid southland of Canaan via Beersheba to Hebron. The children of Israel travelled on it, thus taking a somewhat different route from the one the brothers had used on their trips to buy corn. The region was at first

350

well peopled, with many settlements large and small. Then as the days increased, the road ran through stretches where not a grass-blade grew, places accurst, quite empty save for flitting figures afar off, assuredly bent on no good—the armed men of the train scarce let their bows from their hands. Yet even at the very worst, civilization did not quite forsake them. It went with them as God went with them, though with some dreadful gaps where it seemed there was no more trust save in God alone. Most of the time, however, it was visible in the shape of protected desert springs, signposts, spy-towers, and rest-places set up and kept in repair by the spirit of commerce, up to their goal—that is to say, to the region where the priceless land of Egypt had already pushed its guards and wards a good piece into the wilderness. After that came the actual border and the definite place of entry, the walls of the fortress Thel.

They reached it in seventeen days or perhaps a few more. Anyhow they considered it to be seventeen and would have scorned to reckon it up. Certainly it was something resembling seventeen, maybe less, maybe more—it might easily have been a bit more, at least if one counted in the days at Beersheba; for the summer sun still had power and for the sake of sparing the father they only got forward morning and evening. Yes, it was fully seventeen days since they had left Mamre and set out, in other words given themselves over for some time to a life of wandering and tenting. And now the days in their hours had brought them to Thel, the fortress, through which their way led to Joseph's kingdom.

Lest anyone be concerned about the difficulties of our travellers at the forbidding border stronghold, let him be reassured. For good heavens! They had passes, papers, and official escort; certainly no people of the wretched lands, knocking at the gates of Egypt, had ever travelled so accompanied. For them there were no gates, no walls, no gratings; the outworks and towers of Thel were thin air, there was nothing but smiling politeness in lieu of the usual control. Pharaoh's officers had their orders, of course, touching these travellers, orders to which they bowed. The children of Israel were invited into the land by no less a person than Menfe's lord of bread, the shadow-dispenser of the King, Djepnuteefonech, Pharaoh's universal friend; invited to pasture and settle! Difficulties? Trouble? The very litter in which they carried their old chieftain within the walls spoke for itself and its occupant, for it bore the uræus, it came from Pharaoh's storehouses. And he who sat in it, the gentle, solemn, tired old man, they were bearing him to the near-by rendezvous with his son, a pretty highly placed personage, who could put in corpse-colour anyone who even asked these children of Israel any questions, however politely.

It is impossible to picture the officer's bearing as more flattering and obsequious than it was. The bronze gratings swung open, the Jacob people passed through rows of upstretched hands across the drawbridge with luggage and trotting flocks, into a swampy marshy pastureland with scattered clumps of trees, dams, ditches, and hamlets. This was Pharaoh's land, this was Gosen, also called Kosen, Kesem, Gosem, and Goshen.

Thus varied were the pronunciations of the little people working on a strip of land beside the towing-path, bordered by ditches and reeds. The travellers' route led them along this path and they inquired of the cultivators whether they were on the right road. If they went on westwards for one short day's travel, they were told, they would reach the Per-Bastet arm of the Nile and the city of that name, the abode of the she-cat. But nearer still lay the substantial little city of Pa-Kos, market and county seat, which probably gave its name to the district. For looking abroad over the land with its meadows and marshes, its mirrorlike ponds, its islets of shrubbery and soggy flatlands, they saw the pylon of Pa-Koses temple against the morning sky. It was early when Israel entered into Egypt, having camped before the fort the night before. And they went on for a couple of hours towards the monument on the horizon. Then they halted and Jacob's litter was let down from the asses' backs; for somewhere near the market of Pa-Kos, not far from here, was the place Joseph had appointed for the meeting, whither he had said he would come to greet his family.

There is no doubt that this was a definite arrangement. The story says: "He sent Judah on before him to Joseph, to direct his face unto Goshen." But it would be a mistake to conclude that Judah went on to the house of the swaddled one and only thereupon did Joseph make ready his escort and set out to meet his father at Goshen. No, the exalted one was already close at hand and had been for a couple of days. Judah was merely sent out into the neighbourhood to seek him and take him to their father. "Here will Israel wait on his lordship and son," said Jacob. "Put me down. And thou, Jehudah, my son, take three servants and ride hence and find me out thy brother, Rachel's first-born, and tell him where we are." And Judah obeyed.

Certainly he was not long gone, only an hour or so, and came back after he had found Joseph. That he did not come with Joseph is clear from the question which Jacob, as we shall hear, asked as Joseph approached.

It was a charming spot where Jacob waited: three palm trees, growing, it seemed, from one root, shaded his seat, and coolness came from a little pool with tall papyrus and blue- and rose-coloured lotus blossoms. There he sat, surrounded by his sons, the ten, who were eleven as soon as Judah got back. In front of Jacob lay the open meadow and pastureland, with birds flying across and across. His old eyes could look far out to where the twelfth should appear.

Now he saw Judah posting up with his three servants; they nodded and motioned behind them across the land, without saying a word. So he looked where they pointed; and out there afar off something was stirring. There was a glittering and a flashing, a shimmer of colour; it rolled on swiftly and turned into chariots with prancing steeds and shining harness, gay with feathers. Runners were in front and rear and at the sides. They all fixed their eyes on the foremost car, above which were poles with fans. On it came, it grew to full size, and they could see distinct figures in it. Jacob gazed too, his old hands shading his eyes. Now he said to one of his sons who stood beside him:

"Judah!"

"Here am I, Father," he answered.

"Who is the fairly thickset man," asked Jacob, "arrayed in all the splendour of this world, just getting down from his car and the gilded basket of his car, and his neck-ornament is like the rainbow and his garment altogether like the brightness of heaven?"

"That is your son Joseph, Father," replied Judah.

"If it is indeed he," said Jacob, "then I will get up and go to meet him."

And although Benjamin and the others at first tried to prevent him, he rose from the litter with their help in laboured stateliness, limping from the hip more than ever, for he purposely exaggerated his lameness. Alone he went up to the other, who hastened his steps to shorten the distance between them. The man's smiling lips shaped the word "Father" and he held his arms open before him. But Jacob had his own stretched out like a blind man groping; his hands moved as though beckoning, yet partly too as though to protect himself. For as they came close he did not allow Joseph to fall on his neck and hide his face on his shoulder as his son would have done. Instead he peered and searched with his tired old eyes, his head laid back and sideways; peered long and urgently into the Egyptian's face with love and sorrow painted on his own, and did not recognize his son. But it came to pass that Joseph's eyes slowly filled with tears under Jacob's gaze. Their blackness swam in moisture, they overflowed; and lo, they were Rachel's eyes, Rachel's dewy cheeks where Jacob in life's dreamy long-ago had kissed away the tears. Now he knew his son. He let his head fall on the stranger's shoulder and wept bitter tears.

They stood there alone, for the brothers kept back and so did Joseph's train, his marshal, his écuyer, his runners and fan-bearers. And likewise all the curious from the near-by little city held aloof.

"Father, do you forgive me?" asked the son. And in that question he begged forgiveness for much: for playing fast and loose and for deceit; for childish arrogance and incorrigible naughtiness, for self-esteem and blind conceit, for a hundred follies, for which he had atoned with the silence of the dead, living behind the back of the old man who suffered with him. "Father, can you forgive me?"

Jacob straightened himself and stood erect, his self-control restored.

"God has forgiven us," he answered. "You see He has, for He has given you back to me, and Israel can die happy since you have come back."

"And you to me," Joseph said. "Little Father—may I call you that again?"

"If it is agreeable to you, my son," answered Jacob with formality— and old and dignified as he was, he bowed a little before the young man—"I should prefer to have you call me just Father. That the heart may compose itself in seriousness and not jest."

Joseph understood perfectly.

"I hear and obey," said he, and bowed in his turn. "But no more nonsense about dying," he added gaily. "Live, Father! We shall live together. the penance being performed and the long lack made good."

"It was bitterly long," the old man nodded, "for His anger is mighty and His wrath the wrath of a great and mighty God. He is so great and mighty that He can have no other kind of anger, no lesser kind, and He punishes us weaklings that our cries pour out like water."

"It would be understandable," said Joseph conversably, "if He could not in His greatness quite measure, and could not, He who has not His like, quite put Himself in the place of the likes of us. It may be He has a somewhat heavy hand, so that the weight of it is almost crushing even though He does not mean it so and would only prick us and stroke us."

Jacob could not forbear to smile.

"I see," he rejoined, "my son still has his old delightful keenness of perception in God-matters, even of stranger gods. What it has pleased you to say may have some truth in it. Even Abraham in his time often reproached Him for His intemperance, and I know I myself once spoke to Him in the same sense: 'Gently, gently, Lord, not so hasty!' But He is as He is and cannot make Himself more moderate for the sake of our weak hearts."

"A friendly restraining hand," Joseph responded, "as of one whom He loves, can do no harm. But now we will praise His mercy and His forgiving spirit, even though it has taken Him such a long time! For His greatness is like only to His wisdom, I mean the fullness of His thought and the rich meaning of His acts. Always there is added manifold action to His decrees, that is the admirable thing. When He punishes, He indeed means punishment, and this serious purpose is both for His own sake and as means to the furtherance of great events. You, my father, and me he had seized upon roughly and torn us apart so that I died to you. He meant it and He did it so. But at the same time He meant to bring me hither before you in order to save you, that I should provide for your needs, yours and the brothers' and your whole house in the famine, which He designed in manifold meaning and which in its turn was a means to much, but above all that we should come together again. All that is highly admirable in all its interweavings. We blow hot or cold, but His passion is providence and His anger far-seeing goodness. Has your son come somewhere near to fit expression about God the Father?"

"Somewhere near," Jacob confirmed him. "He is the God of life, and life, of course, one only gets somewhere near. This to praise and excuse you. But you need no praise of mine, for you are praised of kings. May your life which you have led in the place whither you were snatched be not all too much in need of excuse."

355

He said this while his mistrustful gaze travelled down the figure of the Egyptian Joseph, from the striped green and yellow head-dress, the gleaming ornaments, the costly fashionable costume, the rich jewelled tools in his girdle and his hand, on down to the gold buckles of his sandal-shoes.

"Child," he said earnestly, "have you kept your purity among a people whose lust is like the lust of the ass and the stallion?"

"Oh, dear little Father—I mean Father," answered Joseph in some embarrassment, "why does my dear lord trouble so? Let be: the children of Egypt are as other children, not essentially better or worse. Believe me, only Sodom in its time was especially distinguished in evil. Since it was swallowed up in fire and brimstone, things are pretty much the same everywhere in this respect, in other words they are so-so. You yourself once warned God and said to him: 'Not so hasty.' So it will not be a sin if now I, your child, warn you and would like in my love to advise you that since you are here, do not let the people of this country see what you think of them. Do not sit in judgment on their behaviour in the light of your own spirit; rather forget not that we are strangers and Gerim here and Pharaoh has made me great among these children; therefore take a position among them according to God's will."

"I know, my son, I know," answered Jacob and again he made a little bow. "Do not doubt of my respect for the world.—You say you have sons?" he added.

"Yes indeed, Father. From my maiden, the daughter of the sun, a very aristocratic woman. Their names—"

"Maiden? Daughter of the sun? That does not put me off. I have grandchildren from Shechem, and grandchildren from Moab, and have grandchildren from Midian. Why not grandchildren from a daughter of On? After all, it is myself from whom they descend. What are the boys called?"

"Manasseh, Father, and Ephraim."

"Ephraim and Manasseh. Good, my son, my lamb, it is very good that you have sons, two of them, and have given them such names. I will see them. As soon as possible you will bring them before me, if you will."

"At your command, Father," said Joseph.

"And do you know, dear child," Jacob went on softly and wet-eyed, "why it is so good and so fitting before the Lord?"

356

He laid his arm about Joseph's neck and spoke in his ear, which the son bent to his mouth by turning his face aside.

"Jehosiph, once I let you have the coat of many colours and gave it to you when you begged for it. You know that it did not mean the first-born and the inheritance?"

"I know," answered Joseph as softly.

"But I meant it so, I suppose, or more or less, in my heart," Jacob said; "for my heart loved you and will always love you, whether you live or are dead, more than your brothers. But God tore your garment and admonished me with mighty hand, against which is no rebelling. He separated you and sent you away from my house; the branch He took away from the trunk and planted it out in the world—there is only submission left. Submission of purpose and deed, for the heart knows not submission. He cannot take my heart from me or its election without taking my life. But if this heart neither purposes nor acts according to its love, that is submission. You understand?"

Joseph turned his head towards his father and nodded. He saw tears in the old brown eyes and his own too were wet.

"I hear and know," he whispered, and again turned his ear to listen.

"God has given and has taken you," murmured Jacob, "and He has given you back, but yet not quite, for He has kept you too. He did let the blood of the beast count for that of the son; yet you are not like Isaac, a saved sacrifice. You have spoken of the fullness of His thought and the high double meaning of His counsel and you have spoken wisely. For wisdom is His, but shrewdness is man's, to think himself carefully into the knowledge of wisdom. He has elevated and rejected you both in one, I say it in your ear, beloved child, and you are wise enough to be able to hear it. He has raised you above your brothers just as in your dream—and I have, my darling, ever held your dreams in my heart. But He has raised you in a worldly way, not in the sense of salvation and the inheritance of the blessing. You know that?"

"I hear and know," repeated Joseph, as for a moment he took his ear away and turned his whispering mouth instead.

"You are blessed, my dear one," went on Jacob, "blessed from the heavens above downward and from the depths that lie beneath, blessed with blitheness and with destiny, with wit and with dreams. Still, it is a worldly blessing, not a spiritual one. Have you ever heard the voice of self-denying love? Then you hear it now in your ear, in all submissive-

357

ness. God too loves you, child, though at the same time he denies you the inheritance and has punished me because secretly I wanted you to have it. The first-born you are, in earthly things, and a benefactor, as to strangers, so to your own. But through you salvation is not to reach the peoples and the leadership is denied you. You know it?"

"I know," answered Joseph.

"It is well," said Jacob. "It is well to look at fate with cheerful admiring eyes, one's own as well. But I will do as did God, who granted to you in denying to you. You are the set-apart, severed from your stem, you are and shall be no stem. But I will exalt you in the father-rank so that your sons, the first-born, shall be as my sons. Those you are still to get shall be yours, but these mine, for I will take them as sons. You are not like the fathers, my child, for you are no spiritual prince, but a worldly one. Yet you shall sit at my side, at the side of the progenitor, as a father of tribes. Are you content?"

"I thank you as low as your feet," answered Joseph softly, as once more he turned his ear away and put his mouth to Jacob's ear. Then Israel loosed him from his embrace.

THE RECEPTION

The bystanders, Joseph's train at a distance on one side and the Jacob-people on the other, had respectfully looked on at the intimate converse between the two. Now they saw that it was over and that Pharaoh's friend was inviting his father to drive on. He turned towards the brothers and went to greet them. They on their side hastened to greet him and all bowed before him and he took to his heart Benjamin, his mother's son.

"Now I will see your wives and children, Turturra," he said to the little man. "The wives and children of all of you I will see and get acquainted with. You must present them before the father and me and I will sit at his side. I have had a tent set up near by to receive you; it was there my brother Judah found me and I came hither from there. Take our father again and carry him, and mount, all of you, and follow me. I will go ahead in my car, but if one of you will drive with me, for instance Judah, who was so kind as to come and meet me,

358

there is room enough for us both and the driver. Judah, it is you whom I invite. Will you come with me?"

And Judah thanked him and mounted into the car that Joseph beckoned up; he drove in the car of the exalted one and stood with him in the gilded basket of the car with the prancing steeds in front with their gay feathers and purple leather harness. Joseph's people followed and then the children of Israel, at their head Jacob in his swaying sedan. The people from the market-place of Pa-Kos ran alongside, for they were eager to see all that went on.

So they came to a fine and spacious tent gaily painted and carpeted, with servants inside; along the walls were garlanded wine-jugs in reed holders; there were cushions and mats, drinking-vessels and water-basins and all sorts of cakes and fruits. Joseph ushered his father and brothers inside, welcomed them again, and offered them refreshments, assisted by his steward, Mai-Sachme, who was already known to the brothers. They were all very merry. He drank with them from golden beakers into which servants strained the wine. Afterwards he sat down with Jacob his father on two campstools at the door of the tent and Jacob's "wives, daughters, and sons and the wives of his sons" passed before him—that is to say, the wives of Joseph's brothers and their children, in short Israel—that he might see them and make their acquaintance. Reuben, his eldest brother, named their names and he spoke cordially to them all. But Jacob was recalling another such scene out of the depth of the past: the day after the night of the wrestling at Peni-el, when he presented his family to Esau, the hairy one: the maids first with their children, then Leah with her six, and last Rachel, together with him who now sat beside him, whose head had been so lifted up in the world.

"They are seventy," he said proudly to Joseph. His son did not ask whether he meant seventy with or without Jacob and with or without himself; he did not ask for a count, just looked blithely at them as they walked before him, drew Benjamin's youngest sons, Muppim and Rosh, to his knee to stand beside him, and was most interested and pleased when Serah, Asher's child, was set before him and he learned that it was she who had first sung to Jacob the news that Joseph was alive. He thanked the little maid and said as soon as possible, as soon as he had time, she must sing the song to him too upon her eight strings, so that he might hear it. Among the brother's wives Tamar passed over with

359

her two sons from Judah. Reuben, naming their names, forbore to tell
her story; it was too long and would have to go over to a more suitable
time. Tall and dark, Tamar strode past, a son on either hand, and bowed
haughtily to the shadow-dispenser. For to herself she was saying: "I am
in the line of descent and you are not, no matter how much you glitter."

When they had all been introduced, the wives and the sons of the
daughters and the daughters of the wives were all served to refreshments
in the tent. But Joseph gathered the heads of houses about him and his
father and with worldly foresight and circumspection instructed them
in the details of his arrangements.

"You are now in the land of Goshen, Pharaoh's beautiful pastureland," he said. "And I will so arrange that you will stay here, where
things are still not too Egyptian, and you shall live here as Gerim, free-
footed and at will as you did in Canaan. Graze your flocks only on these
meadows, build huts and sustain yourselves. Father, for you I have
already set up a house, carefully copied from yours at Mamre, so that
you may find everything as you are used to it—a little distance from
here, nearer the market-place of Pa-Kos, for it is best to live in the
country but yet not too far from a town. So did our fathers do, they lived
under trees and not between walls but near to Beersheba and Hebron.
At Pa-Kos, Per-Sopd, and Per-Bastet on this branch of the Nile you can
market your wares; it will be pleasing to Pharaoh my master that you
graze, trade, and transact your business. For I will petition His Majesty
for an audience and speak before him about you. I will tell him that you
are in Goshen and your staying here is clearly desirable, since you have
always been shepherds of sheep and goats as were your fathers before
you. I must explain to you that keepers of sheep have always been
looked at a little askance by the children of Egypt—not so much as
swineherds, not that; but they have a slight distaste, which you must
not mind, on the contrary we must take advantage of it, so that you
can stay here, somewhat apart from the Egyptians, for shepherds belong
in the land of Goshen. After all, Pharaoh's flocks graze here, the god's
own sheep and goats. So, as you brothers are experienced shepherds and breeders, it is a natural thought and I will suggest it to
His Majesty so that he comes upon it by himself, as it were, that he
should appoint you, or some of you, as overseers over his flocks. He is
very charming and easy to get on with, and you know he has already
given orders that I introduce some of you—a few of you, for the whole

family would be too many—before him, so he can ask you questions and you can answer. But when he asks about your living and your occupation you will know that that is just for form's sake and that he already knows from me what you do, and I have already hinted at the idea of putting you over his flocks. That will be the idea behind his formal question. So you must back up what I have told him, saying: 'Your servants are people having to do with flocks from our youth up, and our fathers before us.' Then he will arrange that your abode shall be Goshen, the lowland region, and then he will come on the idea that I shall do well to set the most capable of you over his flocks. Which of you it shall be you must decide amongst yourselves, or perhaps our father and dear lord will decide. When all this has been seen to, I will also arrange a private audience for you, my dear father, with the son of the god; for it is fitting he should see you in all the dignity and weightiness of your God-stories and you should see him, who is so tenderly concerned and very much on the right way if not quite the right one for the way. He has himself already commanded in a letter to me that he will see and talk to you. I cannot say how much I look forward to presenting you to him, that he may behold Abram's grandson, the man of the blessing, in all his solemn greatness. He already knows something about you, for instance the story of the peeled wands. But when you stand before him, you will for my sake remember that I have a position among the children of Egypt and you will not criticize these children before Pharaoh their King because of the way their customs appear to you; for that would be a mistake."

"Certainly not, have no fear, my lord son and dear child," answered Jacob. "Your old father knows how to have consideration before the greatness of the world, for it too is from God. Our thanks for the house and dwelling you have made ready in the land of Goshen. Thither will Israel now go and muse upon all this to embody it into his tales."

ISRAEL STANDS BEFORE PHARAOH

With amazement we note that this story nears its end. Who would have thought that it would ever be finished or the well run dry? The truth is, it is ending just as little as it ever began. It is only that it cannot go on for ever; at some point it must make its adieux and the lips of the teller must close. It must in all common sense set a limit to itself, since end it has none. Faced by the infinite it is the part of reason to yield—indeed, it is proverbial that the more reasonable party always does.

The story, then, despite certain previously made statements about its immoderate character, does preserve a sound sense of proportion; and hence begins to fix its eye on its last little hour, just as Jacob did, when the seventeen years he had still to live were coming to an end and he set about putting his house in order. Seventeen years, that is the limit which is likewise fixed for our story, or rather the story fixes for itself by reason of its innate sense of proportion. Never, in its most expansive days, did it contemplate living longer than Jacob did—or at least only so much longer as would take to recount his death. Its proportions in space and time are patriarchal enough already. Old and satiated with life, satisfied that there should be a limit to all things, it will then set its feet together and be still.

But as long as it lasts it will not falter or tire but fill out its time and sturdily record what everybody already knows, that Joseph kept his word and brought before Pharaoh's face a group of his brothers, five in number. After that he formally presented Jacob, his father, to the lovely son of Aton, and the patriarch conducted himself with great dignity, if by worldly standards a thought too condescendingly. Of that anon. Joseph himself personally asked for the audience with the lord of the breath of sweetness, and it is worth while to notice how familiar tradition shows itself with the usage concerning the conceptions "up" and "down." One went down to Egypt: the children of Israel had come down to Goshen's meadows. But if you went down farther in the same direction you went up, that is to say upstream, towards Upper Egypt, and the story says quite correctly that Joseph betook himself up to Akhetaton, the city of the horizon in the hare district, the only capital of the land, to show Hor in the Palace that the brothers and the family of his father had come to him and to suggest that one could not do a cleverer thing than to set these experienced shepherds over the royal flocks in the land of Goshen. Pharaoh took pleasure in the thought which had come to him, and when the five brothers stood before him he talked of it to them and appointed them for his shepherds.

This happened not many days after Israel's arrival in Egypt, as soon as Pharaoh next visited On, his beloved city, and gleamed in the horizon

362

of his palace as he had done when Joseph was first brought before him to interpret his dreams. This little pause had been made for Jacob's sake, the man of many days, that he need not have a long journey to Pharaoh's seat. At this time he was in Joseph's house at Menfe together with the five selected brothers, the two sons of Leah, Reuben and Judah; one of Bilhah, Naphtali; one of Zilpah's, Gaddiel; and Benoni-Benjamin, Rachel's son. They had come up with their father to the city of the swaddled one on the west bank and were at the house of their exalted brother. There Asenath the maid greeted the father of her abductor and the Egyptian grandsons were brought before him, that he might try them and bless them. The old man was deeply moved. "The Lord's kindness is overpowering," said he; "He has let me to see your face, my son which I had not thought to see, and lo, God has showed me also your seed." And he asked the bigger boy his name.

"Manasseh," he replied.

"And what is your name?" he next asked the smaller one.

"Ephraim," was the reply.

"Ephraim and Manasseh," repeated the old man, naming first the name he had last heard. Then he held Ephraim at his right knee and Manasseh at the other, caressed them, and corrected their Hebrew pronunciation.

"How often have I told you both," Joseph chid them, "to say it like that?"

"Ephraim and Manasseh cannot help it," said the old man. "Your own mouth, my son, is already a little wry. Do you want to grow into a multitude in the name of your father?" he asked the two.

"We should like to," answered Ephraim, who had remarked that he was the favourite. And Jacob blessed them both for the time being.

Next it was reported that Pharaoh had come to the dwelling of Re-Horakhte at On, and Joseph drove down to him, followed by the five chosen brethren. But Jacob was "carried." Should anyone ask why he, the man of years and stateliness, was not the first to be received in audience by Pharaoh, instead of the brothers, as we are told was the case, the answer is: for the sake of heightening the interest. In the ordering of any festal occasion, the best feature is seldom put first. It begins as a rule with some minor attraction, then comes something a bit better, and only at the end does true excellence and honour come swaying up, while the crescendo of applause and shouting rises to its climax. That is an old dispute, the struggle for precedence. But from the ceremonial point of view it was always an idle one. The poorer attraction has the *pas;* when it insists, its betters will always give way with a smile.

Furthermore, the audience with the brothers had something practical in view; it was a business appointment, with a certain matter to discuss and settle. Whereas Jacob's presentation to the young god was merely a graceful formality, with so little content indeed that Pharaoh was gravelled for lack of subject-matter and hit on nothing better than to ask the patriarch how old he was. His talk with the sons had more sense; on the other hand it was quite stereotyped, being like all the King's audiences, arranged beforehand by his ministers.

The five brothers were ushered by the mincing chamberlain into the council- and audience-chamber; young Pharaoh sat there surrounded by a ring of standing palace officials. He bore the crook, the scourge, and a life-symbol and sat under a beribboned baldachin, on a carved chair of the ancient and traditional uncomfortableness, yet he somehow contrived to relax and sit at ease in it, for he did not approve of the hieratic posture of the limbs, the stiffness of which he felt was out of harmony with the lovely naturalness of his god. His first mouthpiece, the lord of the bread, Djepnuteefonech, the provider, stood at the right forepost and saw to it that the interview, which was conducted through an interpreter, ran off according to plan. The newcomers duly brought their foreheads into contact with the pavement of the hall; then they mumbled a pæan of adulation, not too long a one, having been drilled by Joseph, who had so composed it that it answered the court requirements without offending their own beliefs. It was not translated, being a mere introductory flourish; Pharaoh thanked them for it at once, in his shy treble, and added that His Majesty was sincerely glad to welcome before his throne the worthy relatives of his faithful shadow-dispenser and uncle. "What is your occupation?" he next inquired.

It was Judah who answered, saying that they were shepherds, both they and also their fathers, and they understood every sort of cattle-breeding from the ground up. They had come hither to this country because there was no longer pasture for their flocks, the famine being sore in the land of Canaan. If they might venture a request before Pharaoh's countenance, it was this: that they might dwell in the land of Goshen, where they had for the time pitched their tent.

Ikhnaton's sensitive face betrayed a faint distaste when the interpreter pronounced the word for shepherd. He turned to Joseph, with the prescribed words: "Your kin have come unto you. The land of Egypt is before you and before them; in the best of the land make your father and your brethren to dwell; in the land of Goshen they can dwell, it will be very agreeable to My Majesty." Joseph prompted him by a glance, and he added: "My Father who is in heaven has also given My Majesty an idea which the heart of Pharaoh rejoices in: you, my friend, know your brothers and their activities better than anyone else; you shall set them according to their activities over my flocks and make them rulers over my cattle. My Majesty graciously and cordially commands that the indentures be written out. I have been very much gratified."

And next it was Jacob's turn. His entrance was most stately and labouring. He deliberately exaggerated his age and infirmities, that they might weigh down the balance against any Nimrod impressiveness and strengthen his God not to give ground. He was perfectly aware that his courtier son was uneasy lest the father behave with condescension to Pharaoh or begin talking about the ram Bindidi; with filial concern he had explicitly warned him against it. Jacob had no idea of doing so; on the other hand he was determined to give no ground, and so set up as a defence this overpowering impression of great age. He had been dispensed from any genuflections, being presumably too stiff; and also it had been decided to make the audience very brief to spare the old man long standing.

They looked at each other for a while in silence: the luxurious young modern and dreamer of dreams about God, curiously rising a little out of his gilt and adorned little box and his over-easy posture, and Yitzchak's son, the father of twelve. They looked at each other, all lapped in together as they were in this single hour, yet ages apart: the sickly boy, heir to an immemorial crown, striving with his feeble might to distil from millennial accumulations of religious thought the attar of a tender and sentimental religion of love; and the wise, experienced old man, whose position in time was at the very source and fount of widely developing being. Pharaoh soon became embarrassed. He was used to begin with the greeting hymn, according to protocol, and not to addressing the person who stood before him. But neither, we are told, was Jacob wholly unmindful of the opening formula; for on entering as on leaving he solemnly "blessed" Pharaoh. This must be taken quite literally: the patriarch substituted the blessing for the routine jingle of adulation; not lifting both hands, as he always did before his God, but only the right, stretching it straight out towards Pharaoh—it shook in the most impressive manner as he did it—as though from this distance he was putting a fatherly hand upon the young man's head.

"May the Lord bless you, King over Egypt," he said, in the voice of advanced old age. Pharaoh was greatly impressed.

"And how old might you be, little grandfather?" he inquired in amazement.

And here again Jacob exaggerated. We are told that he reckoned his age at a hundred and thirty years—an entirely arbitrary figure, for in the first place he did not know with any exactness; even today, in his part of the world, people are not very clear on the point of age, and aside from that, we know that he was to live a hundred and six years in all, an age within the bounds of the possible, if close to its extreme limit. And according to this reckoning he had by now not yet reached ninety, though very well preserved for so considerable an age. But the question gave him a chance to clothe himself in the uttermost solemnity before Pharaoh. His gesture was that of a blind prophet, his speech deliberately measured: "The days of the years of my pilgrimage are an hundred and thirty years," he said, and added: "few and evil have the days of the years of my life been and have not attained unto the days of the years of the life of my fathers in the days of their pilgrimage."

Pharaoh shuddered. He was destined to die young, and his sensitive nature was attuned to the idea; so that the mere thought of all that mass of life seemed to horrify him.

"Ye heavenly powers!" said he, in something like alarm. "And have you always lived at Hebron, little grandfather, in the wretched Retenu?"

"Mostly, my child," answered Jacob, so that it went through the pleated one at the side of the canopy like a stroke. And Joseph shook his head warningly at his father. Jacob saw him but pretended not to see. Obstinately continuing to bear down with all the oppressive evidence of age, he added:

"Two thousand and three hundred, according to the wise men, are the years of Hebron, and even Menfe, the city of tombs, does not go back so far."

Again Joseph hastily shook his head. But the old man paid not the least heed, and Pharaoh behaved with great compliance.

"It may be so, grandfather, it may be so," he hastened to say. "But how can you call your lifetime evil when you begot a son whom Pharaoh loves as the apple of his eye, so that none is greater in the two lands save only the lord of the double crown?"

"I begot twelve sons," answered Jacob, "and he was one of their number. Among them is cursing as well as blessing, and blessing as well as cursing. Some have been rejected and remain the chosen. But as one has been chosen, he remains rejected in love. As I lost him, so should I find him, and as I found him, so was he lost to me. Upon a pedestal was he lifted up, and withdrew from among the number of those I begot; but in his stead there come in those whom he raised up to me, before the one the other."

Pharaoh listened with his mouth open to these sibylline remarks, which had become even more obscure by the time the interpreter finished with them. He looked imploringly at Joseph, but the latter kept his eyes cast down.

"Yes, yes," said he. "Of course, little grandfather, that is quite clear. Well and wisely said, as Pharaoh loves to have it. But now you must not tire yourself with standing longer before My Majesty. Go in peace, and live, so long as you have joy of it, years without number added to your hundred and thirty!"

And Jacob blessed Pharaoh again with lifted hand and then, having given ground by not even the thickness of a hair, he went hence out of his presence, with the same majestic formality and the same labouring gait as before.

OF THE TWINKLING EYE

It may be in place here to set down a faithful account of Joseph's stewardship, in order once for all to take the ground from under the feet of the half-instructed chatterers whom we have always with us, very ready with their harsh judgment and abuse. The responsibility for these censures, which several times went so far as to use the word "atrocious" to describe Joseph's conduct of his office, must rest—the statement may not be shirked—first of all upon the earliest narration of the story, whose laconic style so little approaches the way in which it first told itself, I mean in the happening realism of "once upon a time."

They are hard dry facts, to which the first written account of the activities of Pharaoh's great man of business goes back; they give neither an idea of the general admiration which his measures originally called forth, nor any explanation of it, though it often came close to idolatry. Some of Joseph's titles—such as Provider and Lord of Bread —were taken quite literally by great masses of the people; who hazily thought of him as a sort of Nile deity, yes, an incarnation of Hapi himself, the preserver and life-giver.

This legendary popularity which Joseph achieved—he had probably counted on it from the beginning—rested most of all on the mixed and changeable character of his technique; which operated as it were on two planes, and in a way quite peculiar to him. In short, he used the magic of his wit to reconcile conflicting aims. I use the word "wit" because this principle has its place in the little cosmos of our tale, and quite early on it was said that wit is of the nature of a messenger to and fro and of a go-between betwixt opposed spheres and influences: for instance between the power of the sun and of the moon, between father- and mother-inheritance, between the blessing of the day and the blessing of the night, yes, to put it directly and succinctly, between life and death. This spirit of mediation, brisk, blithe, and nimble at its reconciling task, was not represented by any deity in the pantheon of Joseph's adopted country, the land of the black earth. Thoth, the scribe and guide of the dead, inventor of manifold skills, comes closest to it. Pharaoh only, before whom information about the divine was borne from distant lands, Pharaoh had inklings of a more consummate development of this god-nature. In fact the favour Joseph found in his eyes was due preponderantly to the circumstance that Pharaoh had recognized in him traits of the adroit child of the cave, the master of pranks, and rightly said to himself that no king could wish better for himself than to have as his minister a manifestation and incarnation of this most happy god-nature.

It was in the form of Joseph himself that the children of Egypt got acquainted with the winged figure; if they did not take it into their pantheon it was only because the place was occupied by Djehuti, the white ape. However, the experience meant for them an enrichment of their religion in a certain field and a highly diverting experience as well: I mean in the field of magic, and the change their legendary conception of it underwent to their own great amazement. To the children

368

of Egypt magic was a serious and solemn business and gave them much concern. Its office was to build up walls against the dragon of evil, walls as thick as possible in order to fend it off and prevent its penetration. That was all the meaning the word had for them, and in that light they saw Joseph's preparations against famine, his hoarding of grain, the host of bins he built. But now for the first time they were seeing magic as a conjunction of evil and foresight. I mean this: that the shadow-dispenser, thanks to his foresight, led the dragon by the nose, made it serve their profit and advantage in purposes which the dragon, bent only on destruction, could never have thought of. This was magic married to enlightenment and good cheer, it made the children of Egypt laugh instead of cry.

In fact there was much laughter among the people, admiring laughter, at the way in which Joseph coolly exploited the price situation in dealing with the rich and great to the advantage of his master, Hor in the Palace, making him gold and silver by pouring vast sums into Pharaoh's treasury in exchange for the corn he gave the property-owners. He was displaying therein a shrewd loyalty to the divine, which is the essence of all dutiful, devoted, and rewarding service. But hand in hand with this service went the free distribution of grain among the hungry little people of the cities, in the name of young Pharaoh, the god-dreamer, to whom thus accrued as much and even more profit than to Joseph by his gilding. It was a combination of crown politics and concern for the little man, a novel, ingenious, and invigorating policy, the attractiveness of which can be gathered from the original narrator only by those who study his style with some care and know how to read between the lines. The relation of our source to its own original (I mean the self-narrating events themselves) is betrayed by certain crude phrases of comic relief, which seem like survivals of a popular farce; through these the character of the original events faintly glimmers. For instance, when the famished folk cried before Joseph: "Give us bread; for why should we die in your presence for that the money faileth?" A very poor way of talking, which does not occur elsewhere in the Pentateuch. But Joseph answered in the same style: namely, with the words: "Give your cattle and I will give you for your cattle, if money fail." Of course the needy folk and Pharaoh's great keeper of the market did not treat in this key, rather the style is reminiscent of the mood in which the people experienced the actual event—a farcical mood quite devoid of moral self-pity.

Still, the venerable document has not been able to stand aloof from the reproach of exploitation and harshness in Joseph's proceedings; indeed, it has evoked the moral condemnation of serious minds, and quite naturally. We learn that Joseph, in the course of the years of the lean ears, first gathered all the money in the country unto himself—that is, into Pharaoh's treasury—then took the people's cattle in pawn and then their lands; and finally drove them from hearth and home, sent them to work on strange soil as servants of the state. It is an unpleasant hearing. But the actual situation was quite different, as we can glean from certain remarkable turns of phrase. One reads: "He gave them bread in exchange for horses and for the flocks and for the cattle of the herds and for the asses; and he fed them with bread for all the cattle of that year." But the translation is inexact and makes us miss a certain reference which the original does not neglect to give. For instead of "fed" there is a word which means led: "and led them," it says, "with bread for all their cattle for that year." It is an odd expression and was deliberately chosen. For it is taken from shepherd's language and means protect or pasture, the gentle and careful tendance of helpless creatures, especially of an easily frightened flock of sheep. For an ear practised in mythology, the rôle and quality of the good shepherd is ascribed to the son of Jacob in these striking and traditional words: the shepherd who guards the sheep and leads them upon green meadows and to fresh waters. Here, as in the conventional comedy phrase quoted above, the colour of the original happening strikes through; this strange word, "led," which has as it were slipped out of reality into the narrative text, betrays the light in which the people saw Pharaoh's great favourite. Their judgment is quite distinct from that which state moralists think today to pass upon him; for cherishing, feeding, and leading are the activities of a god known as "lord of the under-earthly sheepfold."

There is no shaking the factual statements of the text. Joseph sold to those who had property, that is to the haughty district barons and owners of large estates, at the highest price the market would bear; and "put money," that is to say exchange, into the royal treasury; so that soon there was no money in the narrower sense of the word, that is to say precious metal in any form, among the people. Money in the sense of coin there was none; and all sorts of cattle had always been among the exchange values given for corn. That was not cause and effect, nor was it any rise of prices; any picture suggesting that Joseph used the scarcity of currency to take away the inhabitants' horses, oxen, and sheep is only a partial picture. Cattle are money too; they are money in the most definite sense, as is clear from our modern word "pecuniary"; and even before the well-to-do paid with their gold and silver vessels they paid with their flocks and herds. There is, however, no mention of their passing over the last cow to Pharaoh's stables and pens. It was not stalls and sheepfolds that Joseph had built for seven years on end, but granaries; and he would not have had space or use for all that cattle-money. If one is ignorant of the methods of money-lenders certainly one cannot follow a story like this. The cattle were loaned—or pawned, whichever you prefer. They remained for the most part on the estates and farmyards, but they ceased to belong to the occupants in the old sense of the word. That is, they were their property and yet they were not; it was only conditionally and as a lien on the property; and if our first authority fails us anywhere, it is here: it does not give the clear impression, which nevertheless it is so important to get, that Joseph's proceedings had as their consistent goal the dislocation of the property concept and its transformation into a state which was neither ownership nor not-ownership, but a conditioned feudal tenure.

For as one year of drought and low water was added to another; as the face of the harvest queen remained averted, no grass grew nor any grain; as the womb of mother earth was closed and she let no child of hers to prosper; then great parts of the black earth which up till now had been in private hands passed to the crown. For the text has it: "And Joseph bought all the land of Egypt for Pharaoh, for the Egyptians sold every man his field." For what? For seed-corn. Scholars agree that this must have been towards the end of the succession of hungry years, when the bonds of infertility began to loosen, the rainfall returned to more or less normal, and the fields would have been capable of yield if one could have sown them. Hence the words of the petitioners: "Wherefore shall we die before your eyes, both we and our land? Buy us and our land for bread and we and our land will be servants unto Pharaoh; and give us seed that we may live and not die, that the land be not desolate." Who is it speaking? These are spoken words, not a cry from the people. It is a proposal, an offer, made by individuals, a group, a class of men up till then very untractable and antagonistic, the great estate-owners and district princes, on whom Pharaoh Akhmose, at the beginning of the dynasty, had had to confer great titles, like First King's Son of the Goddess Nekhbet, and great independent landed possessions as well. They were old-fashioned, recalcitrant feudal lords, whose out-of-date methods, injurious to the general weal, had long been a thorn in the flesh of the modern state. Joseph the statesman exploited the crisis to force these arrogant gentlemen into compliance with the spirit of the times. It was they with whom in the first instance the exploitations and migrations we hear of had to do; what happened under this wise and resolute minister was the breaking up of the still existing large estates and the settling of peasant owners on the smaller ones, farmers who became responsible to the state for an up-to-date management, improvement of the canals, and irrigation of the soil. The result was a more even distribution of the land among the people and an improvement of agriculture under crown supervision. Many "first sons of the king" became such tenant peasants or moved into the town, many a farmer was taken from the soil he had worked and put on one of the newly divided small properties, while his own passed into stranger hands. And if these shifts were practised in other cases, if one hears that the lord of bread parcelled out the people "by cities," that is to say in districts lying roundabout cities, and from one soil to another, Joseph did this in accordance with a deliberate policy of education involving that very remodelling of the property concept into something which was both preservation and abrogation.

The essential condition for all state requisition of state property was the continuation of the levy of the fifth part, the same tax by means of which, during the fat years, Joseph had amassed the magic store into which he now dipped; it was the promulgation of this tax in permanence, its confirmation to everlasting time. Note that this imposition, without the shifting of populations, would have been the only form in which the "sale" of the lands, together with their occupants—for the occupants were included in the bargain—could have expressed itself. It has never been sufficiently emphasized that Joseph made only nominal use of this feature (the sale of themselves by the small farmers, to which they had consented in order not to be ruined). Nobody has pointed out that for his own part Joseph never used the word "slavery" or "villeinage," which for easily understood reasons he did not like. The imposition of the tax meant in itself that land and people were no longer free in the old sense; it received no stronger emphasis, but in actual practice it meant that those who were provided with seed-corn no longer worked exclusively for themselves, but partly for Pharaoh, in other words for the state, the public land. To this extent their labour was the forced labour of serfs—every friend of humanity is free to use the word if at the same time he is ready to apply it to himself as well.

And yet if we observe the measure of serfdom which Joseph laid upon those who submitted to it, we shall feel that it can scarcely be called by that name without exaggeration. If he had forced them to surrender three quarters or even a half of their crops, that would have made them more sensible of the fact that they themselves and their fields no longer belonged to them. But twenty out of a hundred—malice itself must concede that that was keeping the exploitation within bounds. Four fifths of their harvest remained to the people for the new sowing and their own and their children's food. In view of this it is allowable to speak of the serfdom as nominal. Down the centuries ring the words of gratitude with which those under the yoke greeted their oppressor: "Thou hast saved our lives; let us find grace in the sight of my lord and we will be Pharaoh's servants." What more do we want? But if anyone does want more, let me tell him that Jacob himself, with whom Joseph repeatedly discussed the matter, expressly approved the tax, that is as to its amount if not as to its destination. If, said he, he had now increased to a multitude of people, for whom a constitution was to be laid down, then the people ought to regard themselves only as factors of their soil, and would have to pay the tax of the fifth—but not to any Hor-in-the-Palace, rather to Jahwe, the only King and Lord, to whom all fields belong and who grants all possession. But of course he understood that his lord son, the set-apart one, governing a heathen world, must deal in these things after his own way. And Joseph smiled.

But there was little realization of the actual state of things among those submitting to the tax, so long as they remained in the dwelling-places which were no longer theirs. Probably the imposition was too mild for that. Hence the measures of migration: they were the necessary complement to the tribute, which was not enough by itself to make the farmers realize the "sale" of their lands and establish the fact of their new relation to it. A husbandman who stopped on the same soil he had farmed for years would easily remain confused by obsolete conceptions and some day, out of forgetfulness, might lift his head against the claims of the crown. But if he was obliged to leave his own place and receive another from Pharaoh's hand, the lien character of his ownership was made much more perceptible to him.

But the remarkable thing was that the ownership still remained ownership. The criterion of free and personal property is the right of sale and inheritance; and these Joseph permitted to continue. In the whole of Egypt from that time on, all the land belonged to Pharaoh; at the same time it could be sold and inherited. Not idly have we spoken of the way Joseph dealt with the property concept, spiriting it away and putting in its place an equivocal, double-faced picture; so that when the average man tried to fix it in his eye, it turned into a dissolving view. Nothing had been destroyed or cancelled; but there was a general feeling of neither here nor there, exceedingly confusing until one got used to it. Joseph's economic system, in short, was an astonishing mixture of socialization and freehold occupancy by the individual—a mixture which the children of Egypt thought of as "magic," a manifestation of a divinity benign and cunning at once.

The tradition emphasizes that the reform did not extend to the landed possessions of the church: the priesthoods of the numerous shrines endowed by the state, especially the landed property of Amun-Re, remain unmolested and tax-free. "Only the land of the priests bought he not." That too was wise—if wisdom is a shrewdness amounting to guile, which knows how to disarm its antagonist while yielding him all outward respect. This consideration for Amun and the lesser local *lumina* was certainly not to Pharaoh's mind. He would have liked to see the god of Karnak cropped and plundered, and grumbled boyishly to his shadow-dispenser. But little Mama, the mother of the god, agreed with Joseph; with her backing he stood out for sparing the belief of the little man in the old gods of the country, though Pharaoh would gladly have destroyed them root and branch in favour of the doctrine of his Father in heaven. He tried to gain his end by other means with which Joseph could not cope; for he was too jealous to understand that the people would be much more accessible to the new if they were allowed to keep their traditional habits of faith and form. And as for Amun himself, Joseph considered it altogether a mistake to give the ram-headed one the impression that the whole agrarian reform was directed against him and intended as a means to diminish his power. That would only have made him stir up the people against it. It was better to keep him quiet with a polite gesture. The events of all these years, the plenty, the abundance,

374

the preparation, and the saving of the people from famine, were quite enough to weigh down the scale for Pharaoh and the prestige of his teaching; while the riches his sale of corn got and went on getting for the great house meant indirectly such a heavy loss to the state god that the bowing before his anciently sacred right of freedom from taxation looked like sheer irony. It was another case of the same kind of blithe double-dealing which the children of Israel were so ready to admire in their good shepherd.

Pharaoh's pacifism, his unwillingness to wage war, put a tool in the hands of him of Karnak. But it was taken away again, at least deprived of much of its keenness, by Joseph's system of grants and mortgages, which, at least for a time, could restrain the arrogance aroused in our common humanity by a rule grown fastidious and unwilling to use force. Great were the dangers invoked upon the realm of Thutmose the conqueror by the amiable nature of his successor far on in time. The word had everywhere gone round, and was known in all the chancelleries, that in Egypt the key was no longer set by the iron-hearted Amun-Re but by a temperamental deity of flowery spring and twittering birds: a god who at no price whatever would dye his sword in blood. Not to make a fool of such a god would have been asking too much of any ordinary common sense. A tendency to disrespect, to defection and betrayal, gained ground. The tributary eastern provinces from Seir to Karmel were in a state of ferment. There was an unmistakable movement towards independence among the Syrian princes, in which they were supported by the warlike Hatti, pressing southwards. At the same time the desert Bedouins of the east and south had also heard of the reign of sweetness and light. They set fire to Pharaoh's cities and even to some extent took possession of them. Amun's daily summons to vigorous measures, though probably chiefly domestic politics directed against the "teaching," were in foreign affairs only too well justified. The heroic old here aligned itself effectively and convincingly against the effeminate new; and Pharaoh felt greatly stressed, on account of his Father in heaven. But the famine and Joseph together came to his rescue; they deprived Amun's war-cry of much of its force, by putting the wavering little kings of Asia under economic bonds. True, the mildness of Aton was not literally preserved in the process; but what harshness there was amounted to little compared to the fact that it saved Pharaoh from fleshing his sword. The outcry from those thus bound with golden chains to Pharaoh's throne was often so shrill that we can still hear it today; but we are not likely to dissolve in pity at the sound. It is true that to get grain not only silver and wood had to be delivered; actually the youth had to be sent down to Egypt as hostages and pledges. That was a hardship no doubt; but it need not break our hearts, for we know that the children of Asiatic princes were wonderfully well taken care of in elegant pensions at Thebes and Menfe and enjoyed a better upbringing than they would have had at home. "Hence," we hear, "are their sons, their daughters and the wooden furniture of their houses," but of whom is that said? Of Milkili, for instance, the city King of Ashdod; and of him it is hinted that his love for Pharaoh was not of the most reliable, and might very well need strengthening by the presence of his wife and children in Egypt.

In short, I cannot bring myself to see in all this any truthworthy evidence of signal cruelty, which moreover was not in Joseph's character. I am more inclined to agree with the people whom he "led," and to see in it a little trick performed with a twinkle in the eye by a shrewd and skilful servant deity. This was the general view of Joseph's conduct of business far beyond the confines of Egypt. It aroused laughter and admiration—and what is there better that a man can get among men than the kind of admiration which, while it binds hearts together, at the same time lightens them, so that they may laugh.

SUBMISSION

In what remains of our narrative it will be well to turn a realistic eye upon the ages of the characters involved in it; for there has been much confusion and error on the subject, and the arts of painting and poetry have not helped to clear it up, but rather the reverse. I am not referring to Jacob. He is always represented, in his last period, as weighed down with years and almost blind (in fact his eyesight got much worse at the end and he exploited the weakness, taking as his model Isaac, the blind giver of the blessing, in order to heighten the impression of solemnity). But in the case of Joseph and his brothers and sons, tradition has inclined to keep them all more or less at a fixed age and perennially youthful, so that there is a great gap between them and the weight of years on the father's head.

376

It is necessary to correct this legendary vagueness and the resulting false impression, and to point out that it is only death—that is to say, the opposite of all happenings—which can arrest the flow of time and preserve a character as in amber. Life, on the contrary, that is to say a living character in a story, cannot stop as it is, the man must grow older as the story goes on. We ourselves have all got older as we told and listened to this tale; and that is another reason why we should be clear in the matter. I myself confess that I have found it more enjoyable to talk about the charming seventeen-year-old lad or even about the thirty-year-old man than about one hovering round fifty-five. But still we all owe it to life and the processes of life to accept and even insist upon the truth. Jacob, living in the land of Goshen, honoured and cherished by his children and his children's children, was increasing his age by another seventeen years to round them out to the venerable but still possible limit of one hundred and six; the while his set-apart darling, Pharaoh's universal friend, changed from a mature man to an elderly one, whose hair and beard—if the one had not been shorn and covered with an elaborate wig, the other kept smooth-shaven by the custom of the country—would have shown much white among the dark. True, the black Rachel-eyes preserved the friendly sparkle which had always made them a joy to mankind. All in all, despite natural change, the Tammuz-attribute of beauty remained to him, thanks to the double blessing whose child he had ever been and which was a blessing not only from above and in the nature of wit, but also a blessing of the deep which lies under and imparts maternal favour to the bodily form. Not seldom such a nature even experiences a second youth, which gives back to the figure something of its youthful lines. There are some misleading representations which depict Joseph standing by Jacob's death-bed; the violence they do to the truth is the less in that Rachel's first-born, some lustrums earlier, had grown heavier and more fleshy but by this time had got distinctly thinner again and looked more like his twenty-year-old than his forty-year-old self.

But it is certainly quite irresponsible and fantastic to depict the young Egyptian gentlemen Ephraim and Manasseh as curly haired children of seven or eight at the scene of their blessing by their departing grandfather. It is clear that they were then princely young cavaliers at the beginning of the twenties, in dandified belaced and beribboned court-costumes, with buckled sandals and chamberlains' fans; and the otherwise incomprehensible thoughtlessness of these portrayals can only be explained by a few unrealistic phrases in the early text, which says that Jacob put his grandsons on his knees, or rather that Joseph "brought them out from between his knees" after the old man had "kissed them and embraced them." Such treatment would have been most offensive to the young people; it is regrettable that the tradition countenances such nonsense; it can only be due to the desire to make time stand still for most of the people in the story and let Jacob alone grow old, out of all reason, even to a hundred and forty-seven years!

Let us see what actually happened on the visit in question, the second of three visits which Joseph paid his father in the latter end of his life. But first it will be well to cast a brief glance upon the foregoing seventeen years, during which the children of Israel settled down in the land of Goshen, grazed and sheared and milked, transacted their affairs, presented Jacob with great-grandsons, and addressed themselves to becoming a multitude of folk. It can never be said quite definitely how many of these seventeen years fell in the famine time, because it is not clear whether there were seven or "only" five of these (the quotation-marks are ironical, for the figure five is just as rich in associations as the figure seven). As I have pointed out before, the uncertainty was due to the variation in the degree of the affliction from year to year. In the sixth year the provider swelled at Menfe not less than fifteen ells in the season of increase. It went red and green by turns, as is its way when things are going well, and deposited a plenty of fertilizer. But in the next year it was under-nourished and under-nourishing past all belief. So it was a matter of opinion whether these two years were to be counted with the five lean-ribbed ones, as the sixth and seventh, or not. In any case, round the time that this question was being discussed in all the temples and on all the street corners, Joseph's work of agrarian reform was finished and he continued to govern on its foundation as Pharaoh's first mouthpiece and to feed his sheep while shearing them of a fifth.

It cannot be said that he saw his father and brothers very often. They had their tents close by compared with the distance that had once been between them; but even so it was a good journey between their place and Joseph's residence in the city of the swaddled one; and moreover, between his administrative duties and his court functions he was overworked. They saw much less of him than one would have gathered from the last three visits he made to his father in quick succession. But

378

Jacob and his people took no offence, their silence was not only consent but also recognition of the existing obstacles. We, who overheard that murmured conversation between Jacob and Rachel's first-born at their meeting, as they stood alone with the seventy on one side and Joseph's train on the other, we know how to give to that mutual reserve—for it was mutual—its true and somewhat melancholy meaning. It meant submission and renunciation. Joseph was the one set apart, at once lifted up and withdrawn. He was severed from the tribe and was not to be a tribe. The fate of his lovely mother, "rejected despite goodwill," was, with appropriate variation, also her son's fate; its individual formula being "denying love." The truth was understood and accepted; far more than distance or preoccupation it was the reason for the reserve.

And how clearly, how chillingly the reserve is expressed in the phrase used by Jacob when he made a certain request of his son; I mean the rhetorical flourish: "if now I have found grace in thy sight." It is proof, it is almost shamefaced evidence of the distance between father and son, between Joseph and Israel. It reminds us, as it reminded Jacob, of that early dream, the dream of the threshing-floor, when the eleven Kokabim together with sun and moon had bowed down before the dreamer. Joseph's dream had stirred the brothers up to a fiery mortal hatred and ravished them to the evil deed for which they had suffered. How strange it is to think—as they too thought among themselves without saying so —that their misdeed had achieved its purpose and brought them to their desired goal! True, it had turned out, contrary to all reasonable expectation, that they had actually lain on their bellies before him. Yet they had not sold him in vain into the world and also to the world; for he had lost and they had won. The inheritance which the man of feeling had in his wilfulness wanted to give to Joseph was lost to him forever; from Rachel the beloved it had passed to Leah the rejected. Was that not worth a little bowing and scraping?

"If now I have found grace in thy sight." It was on the first of the three visits that Jacob so spoke to the beloved and lost one; at the time when he felt his life fast waning and knew that it was far on in its last quarter, rising low and late and red and wearily over the horizon before the final darkness. He was not ill; he could tell that there was no question of a sudden decline. For he had good control over his life and his powers, he reckoned shrewdly what was left and knew that the end was not quite yet. Still it was fully time to impress on him who alone had power to

379

fulfil it a wish he had at heart, a wish which quite personally concerned him, Jacob.

So he sent to Joseph and begged him to come. Whom did he send? Naphtali, of course, Bilhah's son, the nimble one, for Naphtali was still nimble of limbs and tongue, despite his years. We must speak of this matter of the brothers' ages because here too the tradition is careless and blurred. If we stop to consider we must conclude that the whole span covered a period between forty-seven and seventy-eight years. For Benjamin, the little man, was not less than twenty-one years younger than Zebulon, who was the third youngest before Joseph, and he was sixty-eight years old. I speak of this in order that when Jacob gathers his sons about him in his last hours for cursing and blessing, we shall not picture the tent as full of young men in the prime of life. I repeat that Naphtali despite his five-and-seventy years still rejoiced in the same sinewy long legs and the same tongue like a bell-clapper; nor had he abated in his craving to equalize a state of knowledge among the kingdoms of the earth.

"Boy," said Jacob to this sinewy old man, "go down from here to the great city where my son lives, Pharaoh's friend, and speak before him and say: 'Jacob, our father, would speak to your grace on an important matter.' You must not alarm him or make him think I am dying. You are to tell him: 'Our father, the old man, finds himself in good health at Goshen considering his years and thinks not now to depart hence. But he judges the hour is come to speak with you concerning himself, though the matter reaches out beyond his own life. Therefore in your kindness come to his dwelling-place, which he mostly keeps, although not yet bedridden, in the house which you made for him.' Go, boy, go, step out and tell him that!"

Naphtali glibly repeated the message and betook himself to his heels. He went afoot and took several days for the journey, otherwise Joseph would have been there at once, for he travelled in his chariot with a small retinue, among them Mai-Sachme, his steward, who laid too great stress on being in this story to stop at home when Joseph went abroad. But Mai-Sachme waited outside with the others of Joseph's house while the exalted one was alone with his father in the tent, that well-garnished living- and sleeping-room which is the theatre to which our far-flung scene has now shrunk. For there on his bed in the background or not far from it Jacob spent the last days of his life, waited on by Damasek,

Eliezer's son, himself now called Eliezer, a man in a white-belted smock, still youthful in the face, though bald on top with a fringe of grey hair.

In reality the man was a nephew of Jacob; for Eliezer, Joseph's teacher, was the half-brother of the man of the blessing, born of a maid. His position, however, was that of a servant, though higher than the others round the house. Like his father he called himself Jacob's eldest servant and was over his house as Joseph was over Pharaoh's house and Captain Mai-Sachme over Joseph's. He went out to the captain after announcing Joseph and conversed with him on an equal footing.

The Regent of Egypt knelt down when he entered the chamber and touched with his forehead the felt and the carpet of the floor.

"Not so, not so, my son," Jacob demurred. He sat on his bed at the back of the room, a skin drawn over his knees; on either side of him were earthenware lamps on wooden consoles. "We are in the world and the man of years and religion too much respects its greatness to acquiesce in your action. Welcome, welcome to me in my weakness and age, on account of which I may be pardoned for not coming in respect and fatherly feeling to greet you, my lifted-up lamb! Take a stool here beside me, my dear one; Eliezer, my eldest servant, might have drawn one up when he let you in—he is not what his father was, the wooer of the bride, towards whom the earth sprang; nor would he have been to me what his father was in the time of my shedding tears of blood. What time do I mean? The time when you were lost. He wiped my face with a damp cloth and tenderly reproved me for some refractory feeling that burst out of me against my God. But you were alive. Thank you for asking, I am well. Bilhah's boy, Naphtali, was to tell you that I was not calling you to my death-bed. Or rather this will of course be my death-bed, it is beginning by degrees to take on that character, but does not yet possess it in fullness, for there is yet some life in me. I do not think to die at once and you will return hence twice or thrice to your Egyptian house and your affairs of state before I depart. Indeed, I am minded and resolved to economize the strength I yet have with measure and caution, for I shall still need them for various occasions, especially at the very end, and I must save my strength and my words. Therefore, my son, this our talk will be brief and confine itself to the necessary and important matter in hand, for it were against God to exhaust myself in a

381

superfluity of words. It may even be that I have already talked more than is necessary. When I have said what is needful and put it to you in the form of an urgent plea, you may, if you have time, sit with me a little while in silence on my future death-bed, only for the sake of our being together without making me use my strength in speaking. I will silently lean my head on your shoulder and remember that it is you who are here and how my one true wife bore you to me in Mesopotamia with more than natural pangs; how I lost you and then to some extent got you back through the extraordinary goodness of God. But when you were born with the sun at his height and you lay in your swinging cradle beside the maid who sang and gasped her weariness in song, there was something like a dazzling sweetness about you and I knew, of course, how to recognize it for what it was; and your eyes, as you opened them when I touched you, were as blue as heaven's light and only later got black with a twinkle of mischief in their blackness, which is why I turned over to you the pictured bride-veil here in the house, out at the front. I will perhaps come to speak about it at the very last, but now it is probably unnecessary and does violence to economy. It is very hard for the heart to distinguish between necessary and unnecessary talk. See, you stroke me soothingly in sign of your love and your good faith. There will I begin—on your love and good faith I will base the plea I have to make to you and I will build upon it in the practical request I wish to make while avoiding unnecessary words. For, Joseph-el, my uplifted lamb, the time has come that I am to die, and though I am by no means yet at the final stage, Jacob has come to the time of his departing and to the time of the last will and testament. But when I do put my feet together and am gathered to my fathers, I would like not to be buried in the land of Egypt, take it not amiss of me, I would like it not at all. And also to lie in the land of Goshen where we now are, even though it is not all too Egyptian, would be against my wishes. I know full well that a man when he is dead has no more wishes and it is all the same to him where he lies. But so long as he lives and has wishes it does matter to him that it shall happen to the dead according to the wishes of the living. Again I well know that very many of us, thousands in their number, will be buried in Egypt whether they were born here or in the land of the fathers. But I, the father of them all and of you, I cannot bring myself to give them an example in this matter. With them I came into your kingdom and into the country of your King for that God sent you on ahead as the opener of the way. But in death it is my wish to part from them. If now I have found grace in your sight, put your hand under my thigh, as Eliezer did to Abram, and swear to deal kindly and truly with me and not to bury me in the land of the dead. For I will lie with my fathers and be gathered unto them. Therefore you shall carry my bones out of Egypt and lay them in their tomb, which is called Machpelach or the double cave at Hebron in the land of Canaan. Abraham lies there, whose seed has been multiplied in honour; who in the cave of his birth was suckled by an angel in the form of a goat; he lies there by Sarai, the heroine and heaven-highest queen. Yitzchak lies there, the late-conceived, with Rebecca, the wise and resolute mother of Jacob and Esau, who put all things to rights. And Leah lies there too, whom I first knew, the mother of six. Beside them all will I lie and well see that you are meeting my wish with filial respect and readiness to obey, even though a shadow of doubt and silent questioning may cross your brow. My eyes are no more of the best, for I have entered upon my time of death and my gaze is shrouded in darkness. But the shadow that crosses your face, that I see clearly; because I knew that it would come, for why should it not? There is a grave by the way, only a little piece towards Ephrath, which now they call Bethlehem, where I put to her last sleep that which was dearest to me on God's earth. Will I not lie by her side when you bring me home as I command and lie with her, set apart, by the way? No, my son, I will not. I loved her, I loved her too dearly; but things do not go according to feeling and the luxurious softness of the heart but according to their importance and according to duty. It is not suitable that I lie by the way, rather with his fathers will Jacob lie and by Leah his first wife, from whom came the heir. Lo, now your black eyes are full of tears, that too I clearly see. They look so much like the eyes of the dearly beloved as to make me not believe my own. It is lovely, my son, that you are so like her, when you now in your mercy put your hand under my thigh in token that according to importance and duty you will bury me in Machpelach, the double cave."

Joseph swore the oath. And when he had done so, Israel bowed himself upon the bed's head and gave thanks. Then the set-apart one sat awhile in silence beside his father's couch, and the old man leaned his head on his shoulder and saved his strength for what should come.

A few weeks later he fell ill. His old cheeks were flushed with a slight fever, his breath came short, and he kept his bed, half sitting, propped up in cushions to ease his breathing. It was not necessary for Naphtali to run and tell Joseph, for Joseph had set up a messenger service between Goshen and Menfe, and daily or twice daily had news of the old man. Now he was told: "Your father is ill, with slight fever," and he called his two sons and said in the Canaanitish tongue:

"Get ready, we shall be going down into the lowlands to visit your grandfather on my side."

They answered: "But we have an engagement, Father and lord, to hunt gazelles in the desert."

"Have you heard what I said," he asked in Egyptian, "or have you not?"

"We rejoice greatly to make our grandfather a visit," they answered, and sent word to their friends, the rich young exquisites of Menfe, that for family reasons they could not join in the gazelle-hunt. They were exquisites themselves, products of the highest culture, manicured, curled, perfumed, and touched up, with mother-of-pearl toenails, corseted waists, and coloured ribbons flowing down their aprons at front, back, and sides. They were not bad, either of them, and their dandyism was a result of the society they lived in, they cannot be blamed for it. Manasseh, the elder, was very supercilious, of course; he prided himself less on his father's renown than on his sun-priest blood from his mother's side. Ephraim, on the other hand, with his Rachel-eyes, we may picture as harmless, jolly, and rather modest—on the theory that a modest nature is more prone to jollity than a supercilious one.

They stood behind their father in the bouncing car, steadying themselves with their bebanded arms around each other's shoulders, and drove northwards towards the delta region. Mai-Sachme was with them, in the hope that his physicianly skill might be of some service to the ailing one.

Jacob was dozing in his cushions when Damasek-Eliezer announced the approach of his son Joseph. The old man pulled himself together, had his ever present servant lift him up in bed, and showed extraordinary presence of mind. "If we have found grace," he said, "in the eyes of his

384

lordship, my son, that he visits us, then we must not relax on account of a slight degree of fever." And he took up his silver beard and spread it out on his chest.

"The young gentlemen are with him too," said Eliezer.

"Good, good, that is right," said Jacob, and sat erect, ready to receive them.

Joseph presently entered with his young heirs. Manasseh and Ephraim greeted their grandfather gracefully and remained at the door while Joseph approached the bed and tenderly took the wan hands in his.

"Dear and sainted Father," said he, "I have come with my sons because I was told you were slightly ailing."

"It is only slight," answered Jacob, "as the illnesses of the aged are. Severe illness and high fever belong to youth and vigorous manhood. They attack with violence and dance recklessly with their victims to the grave—that would not be fitting for age. The man of full years has but a light finger laid upon him, the fever itself is weak that comes to quench his fire. But I am not yet quenched, my son. This fever is weaker than I, it has been deceived by my great years and it is not strong enough. You will go home again from this, your second visit to my dying bed, which has not yet become my death-bed. The first time I had you sent for; I begged you to come. This time you came of yourself, but yet once more will I summon you, for the third and last time and to the service for the dead."

"May it be far distant from my lord—yet many a jubilee!"

"How could it, child? Enough that its hour has not yet come, the hour of gathering together. It is courtly politeness that speaks in your words; but I am nigh my day of death, to which no flowers of speech are suited, only sternness and truth. And when we come to the hour of assembly they will be the only subject-matter. I tell you so beforehand."

Joseph bowed.

"Is it well with you, my child, before the Lord and before the gods of the land?" asked Jacob. "You see, my illness is so much weaker than I that I can permit myself to ask after another's health. At least that of those whom I love. Are you getting in your tax properly from the children of the land? It is not right, Yehosiph, for to the Lord alone should the fifth belong and not to any king. But I know, I well know, my exalted one. Do you probably burn incense to the sun and the stars as is due to your station in life?"

385

"Dear Father—"

"I know, my snatched-away lamb, I know so well! And how lovely it is of you to come of your own free will between the first time and the third to see the old man, despite the demand upon you with all your affairs and your incense-burning! I will avail myself of your visit to come back to a matter we have not spoken of since you appeared to me again at the plain, sore missed and found again. Then I said in your ear, my darling, that I will divide you up in Jacob and disperse you in Israel and split you up into the tribes of the grandsons that the sons of the sons of the true wife may become like Leah's sons, but you shall be one of us and rise into the rank of the fathers in order that the words may be fulfilled: He is the exalted one."

Joseph bent his head.

"Lo, there is a place in Canaan," Jacob began to give voice, his eyes lifted up. He was excited by the fever and most grateful to it for the stronger pulse of his blood. "A place once called Luz, where they make a wonderful blue for dyeing wool. It is no longer called Luz but Beth-el and E-sagila, the house of the lifting up of the head. For there Almighty God appeared to me in a dream when I slept in Gilgal with my head propped on a stone—for there above on the ramp, the navel cord between heaven and earth, where the starry angels streamed up and down amid harmonies. He appeared to me in kingly guise, blessed me with the sign of life, and cried out abundance of consolation to the sound of the harps, for He promised me His mighty favour and that He would make me to wax and increase to a great multitude and to countless children of His election. Therefore now, Yehosiph, shall your two sons who were born to you in Egypt before I came to you, Ephraim and Manasseh, they shall be mine, just like Reuben and Simeon, and shall be called after my name; but those whom you will have begot later on, they shall be yours and called after their brothers' name that they shall be like their sons. For you have been exiled from your seat in the circle of the twelve, but with so much love that the fourth seat is there prepared for you next the three most important ones."

Here Joseph got ready to present the heirs to him. But now the old man began to speak of Rachel. Once more he told how she had died and left him when he came out of Mesopotamia, in the land of Canaan—it was on the way, only a little way towards Ephrath; and how he had buried her just there on the way to Ephrath, which was now called

Bethlehem. All this was in passing as it were, it had not much to do with the matter in hand. Perhaps he wanted to invoke the presence of his dear one at this hour. Perhaps his idea was to point out to the descendants of Rachel their own special shrine; since Machpelach, the double cave, was the place of pilgrimage for the rest of the brothers. It is possible that he was thinking of the little sleight-of-hand trick he had long had in mind and was trying to justify it. Our teachers disagree about his intentions in the matter; but most likely he simply had none at all, and talked about the lovely one because he was in his solemn mood and thinking of his tales. Anyhow, he simply loved to speak of her, even where there was no point at all—just as he loved to speak of God. Perhaps he talked about Rachel because he feared he might never have a chance to do it again.

And now, after he had buried her for the very last time in her wayside grave, he looked about him, laid his hand over his eyes, and asked:

"And who are these?"

"These are my sons, dear and reverend Father," answered Joseph, "the ones God gave me, as you know, here in this country."

"If they are, then bring them here to me, that I may bless them."

What was there to bring? The heirs came forward of themselves, bowing from the hips with exaggerated good form.

The old man wagged his head and made clucking noises with his tongue.

"Lovely youth, so far as I can see," said he. "Fine and charming before God, both of them. Bend down to me, treasures, that I may caress the young blood in your cheeks with my hundred-years-old mouth. Is this Ephraim I am kissing, or Manasseh? No matter. If it was Manasseh before, it is Ephraim now whom I kiss on the cheeks and on the eyes. Lo, I have seen your face again," he turned to Joseph, still holding Ephraim embraced, "that I thought not to see, and not only that, but God has now showed me your seed. Is it too much to call Him the source of infinite goodness?"

"By no means," Joseph answered, rather absently; for he was concerned that his sons should stand in the right order before Jacob, who plainly did not distinguish between them.

"Manasseh," he said in an undertone to the elder, "take care! Come here, and stand in your right order. Ephraim, stand there!"

And he took Ephraim by his right hand and pushed him towards

387

Israel's left; and with his left he took Manasseh and put him at Israel's right, so that everything should be in order. But what, with surprise and annoyance, if with suppressed laughter at the same time, did he see? He saw this: the father, his blind face uplifted, laid his left hand upon Manasseh's bowed head, and crossing his arms, put his right hand over upon Ephraim's. With his blind eyes staring into space, he began, before Joseph could interrupt him, to speak and to bless. He invoked the three-fold God, the Father, the Good Shepherd, and the Angel, who should bless the lads, and see that his name and the names of his fathers should be named upon them; and that they should grow into a multitude, like to a multitude of fishes in number. "Yea, so be it. Stream, blessing, sacred gift, out of my heart, through my hands, upon your heads, into your flesh and your blood. Amen."

It was quite impossible for Joseph to interrupt the blessing, and his sons did not notice what was happening. They were rather distrait, and a little out of sorts, particularly Manasseh, because this ceremony had made them miss the gazelle-hunt in the desert. Each of them felt the blessing hand on his head, but even if they could have seen that the hands were crossed and the right hand lay on the younger brother's head, the left on the elder's, they would have made nothing of it and simply thought it had to be that way on account of the outlandish customs of their foreign grandfather. They would not have been so far wrong. For Jacob, brother of the hairy one, was of course repeating a pattern. He was copying his own father, the blind man in the tent, who had given him the blessing before the red one. And to his way of thinking, the blessing did not work unless there was a trick in it. There must be an exchange; therefore he changed at least his hands, so that the right one rested on the younger's head and he became the right one. Ephraim had Rachel's eyes and was obviously the more agreeable of the two: that very likely influenced him. But more important still was the fact that Ephraim was the younger, as he himself, Jacob, had been, and had been exchanged through the skin and through the fell of the beast. As he shifted his hands, there were humming in his ears the incantations which his stern-willed mother had muttered as she got him ready, but which themselves echoed hither from much further off, and were, in their beginnings, much older than his own experience: "I cover the child, I cover the stone, let the master eat, let the father eat, at thy feet must fall the brethren of the deeps!"

Joseph, as I said, was both amused and annoyed. His sense of humour was strong; but the statesman in him felt bound to come to the rescue of such order and justice as could still be saved. So soon as the old man had exhausted himself and his blessing, Joseph said:

"Father, forgive me; but I had placed the lads in their right order before you. If I had known you meant to cross your hands I would have placed them differently. May I call your attention to the fact that you put your left hand on Manasseh, my elder son, the right on Ephraim, the later-born? The bad light here is to blame for your having mis-blessed, so to speak. Will you not quickly correct it, change your hands back again, and perhaps just say Amen? For the right hand is not the right hand for Ephraim, it belongs to Manasseh."

And as he spoke he even took the old man's hands, which still lay upon the young heads, and would have respectfully changed them. But Jacob held them as they were.

"I know it, my son, I know it," said he. "And let it be so! You rule in Egypt and take your fifth; but in these things I govern and I know what I do. Do not grieve. This one—" he raised his left hand slightly— "will also become a people, and he also shall be great. But truly his younger brother shall be greater than he, and his seed shall become a multitude of nations. As I have done it I have done it; and indeed it is my will that it become a saying in Israel, so that when a man will bless anyone he shall say: 'God make thee as Ephraim and Manasseh.' Mark it, Israel!"

"As you command," said Joseph.

The young men drew their heads away from under the hands of blessing, adjusted their waists, smoothed their hair and were glad to stand up straight again. They were not much moved by the incident; and they were right, in so far as the time-honoured fiction which made them the sons of Jacob and at the same time descendants of Leah had no effect upon their individual destinies. They passed their lives as Egyptian nobility; it was only their children or, more correctly, some of their grandchildren who gradually, by marriage, intercourse, and religious adherence, went over to the Hebraic side. Finally some of them moved from Keme to Canaan; and in the end there was a posterity descended from Ephraim and Manasseh. But there was also another point on which the indifference of the young men was justified. For our researches indicate that at the height of their increase the tribe of

Manasseh counted a good twenty thousand more souls than Ephraim's tribe. However, Jacob had had his little game with the blessing.

He was really exhausted after the ceremony, and not quite clear in his head. Joseph begged him to lie down; but he still sat up straight in his bed and talked to his favourite about a parcel of land he was making over to him, as a portion apart from his brothers, which he had "taken out of the hands of the Amorites with his sword and with his bow." That could only be the piece of cornland before Shechem, by the gate of the city, which Jacob had once acquired of the gouty Hamor or Hemor for a hundred pieces of silver, certainly not by his sword and his bow. And anyhow, how did Jacob, the man of tents and of peace, come by a sword or a bow? He had never cared for nor used such tools, and never ceased to take it ill of his sons that they had laid about them so savagely at Shechem—indeed, by reason of their conduct it was doubtful whether the purchase was still valid and Jacob could still dispose of the triangle of land.

At all events, he did so, feebly, and Joseph thanked him, with his forehead on his father's hands, for this special gift. He was touched by this token of Jacob's love, and at the same time by the strange phenomenon that it was precisely the old man's feebleness which made him see himself in the heroic rôle of a warrior. Joseph judged that it betokened the nearness of the end, and decided not to go back to Menfe, but to await at Pa-Kos the summons to the final gathering.

THE LAST ASSEMBLY

"Gather yourselves together, ye children of Jacob! Come in your hosts and assemble together round Israel your father, that he may tell you who you are and what shall befall you in future times!"

That was the call which Jacob made to go forth out of the tent to his sons when he judged the hour to have come when he should hold his dying speech. For he held his life in his own hands and precisely knew what strength he had left, that he might expend it in his last words and so die. Through Eliezer, the old young man his head servant, he sent out the call; he told it to him, and then had him repeat it several times, so that Damasek might have it not only more or less right, but letter-perfect. "Not 'Come hither,' but 'Come in your hosts'; and not 'present yourselves before Israel,' but 'assemble together.' Now say it all again and forget not the two things: 'who you are,' and 'what shall befall you.' There, at last, that is right. I fear I have spent too much strength instructing you. Now be off!"

And Damasek kilted his garment and ran in all directions, so fast that the earth seemed to spring towards him. He put his hands round his mouth and cried: "Assemble ye together, ye sons of Israel, and gather together as you are, that good may come to you from day to day!" He ran to all the settlements, to the fields, to the herds and flocks, the royal ones over which the five were set, and to the others; ran to and fro through moor and fen, with muddy water splashing his lean legs, for it was ebb-time, the fifth day of the first month of the winter season, what we should call the beginning of October; and in the delta, after a long spell of late heat, it had rained a good deal. He kept shouting aloud with his hands round his mouth, into the open country and into the dwelling-houses: "Whoever you are, assemble, sons of Jacob, and meet in your hosts about him for future times!"

He ran into Pa-Kos close by; Joseph was stopping there with the magistrate and there were guards before the door. Damasek, with disgraceful inaccuracy, shouted out the words which Jacob had so carefully composed and designed for posterity. But it did not matter, their effect was the same, and they were straightway obeyed in haste by all who heard them. Pharaoh's friend hurried to his father's house, with him Mai-Sachme, his major-domo; and many curious outsiders heard the call and came to hang about.

The eleven awaited their brother at the entrance to the curtained tent. He greeted them in a suitably grave and weighty manner, kissed Benjamin, the little man of forty-seven, and talked with them all a short time in low tones about their father's condition and the probability that he thought to hold his last speech and depart. They answered him with their eyes cast down, and rather tight-lipped; for as usual they were afraid of the old man's tongue and knew that the stern old father-tyrant would probably spare them nothing in this final hour. Each one was privately telling himself, as human beings do: "Good lord, probably it will turn out all right!" Reuben, the seventy-eight-year-old shepherd tower, was clenching his jaw until his facial muscles were taut. He had behaved badly with Bilhah, he would certainly get to hear most explicitly about that on this solemn occasion, and he armed himself accordingly. Simeon and Levi, who in their young days had laid about them like savages at Shechem on their sister's account—that was long, long ago, but they could count on getting it dished up again, with due solemnity; they too braced themselves for the ordeal. There was Jehudah, who had had an affair with his daughter-in-law, by mistake. He had no manner of doubt that the old man would be harsh and cruel enough to hold it against him, even on his death-bed—the more so because he had been a little in love with Tamar himself. There they all were; and all of them but Benjamin, the stay-at-home, had once sold Dumuzi down into Egypt. Jacob on this occasion would be quite capable of making a song about it—they all expected it, and set their teeth accordingly. Particularly the sons of Leah did, for none of them had forgiven their father for choosing, after Rachel's death, not Leah their mother but Bilhah, Rachel's maid, for his first and favourite wife. Jacob had had his failings, and all his life he had been arbitrary in his exercise of feeling. They thought defiantly that he had been just as guilty as they were in the Joseph affair; he ought to remember that, before he used the occasion of his grand dying harangue to take them to task. In short, dread of the coming scene made them all awkward; they were putting on hurt faces beforehand. Joseph saw it, and spoke in the most friendly way. He went from one to another putting out his hand and saying:

"Let us go in to him, brothers, and let us in all humility bear the judgment which our dear one inflicts on us, each one his own. Let us hear him, if necessary, with forbearance. For forbearance, indeed, ought to descend from God to man and from father to child; but if it does not, then the child must practise reverent forbearance and be great in pardon towards the greater for that he is weak in pardon. Let us go in; he will judge us with a feeling for truth, and we shall all get what is coming to us, myself too, believe me!"

They went quietly into the tent, the Egyptian Joseph with them. He did not go first, although they would have had him lead them; he went with Benjamin behind the sons of Leah and only in front of the children of the maids. Mai-Sachme, his steward, went in too; partly with the justification that he had long been in the story and played his part in its embellishment; but partly too because the gathering was to a large extent public, and it turned out that everybody might go in who chose. It was very full in the room of death when the twelve were inside, for besides Damasek the crier there stood round the master's couch a number of under-servants of his household staff, and many of his descendants either stood or lay on their faces farther off. There were even women with children, some giving them the breast. Boys sat on the chests along the walls, and their conduct was not always seemly; but all incorrectness was quickly suppressed. The hangings before the tent had been flung wide open; the courtyard folk and the little people from the hamlet of Pa-Kos, a great host in all, had a clear view and were in a way included in the gathering. The sun declined, and the crowd outside was outlined against an orange-tinted evening sky, a shadowy mass with indistinguishable forms and faces. But the two oil-lamps, flaring on high stands at the head and foot of the bed, sent their rays from within to pick out a striking figure: a gaunt matron in black, between two very broad-shouldered men. Her grey hair was covered with a veil. She was Tamar, the resolute woman, with her doughty sons. She had not entered, she kept outside; for it might be that Jacob in his dying speech would come to speak of Judah's sin with her. But she was here, present and on the spot—and *how* was she present, now that the time had come for Jacob to hand down the blessing to him with whom she had sported by the way and brought herself into the succession! Even without the lamplight that proud profile would have been unmistakable against the sallow rainy sky.

He who had once instructed her in the world, and in the great history into which she had wormed her way, he who had summoned this death-bed gathering: Jaakob ben Yitzchak, blest before Esau, lay propped on his cushions, under a sheepskin, on his death-bed at the back of the tent, in just so much command of his powers as he needed to be. The waxen pallor of his skin was faintly tinged by the tinted twilight and the glow from the charcoal in the basin near by. The look on his face was exalted and mild. A white band which he usually wore when he sacrificed was round his forehead; the white locks came out under it on the temples and ran down in even width into the patriarchal beard that covered all his chest, thick and white beneath the chin, farther down sparse and grey; through it showed the fine, witty, rather bitter mouth. He had not moved his head; but the soft eyes with the swollen ducts beneath were rolled sidewise so that they showed much yellowish-white eyeball. His gaze sought his sons as they entered and a lane quickly opened for them to the bedside. Damasek and the servants drew back; and those begot across the Euphrates, together with the little one whose

393

mother had died of him in Abram's land, bowed down on their foreheads and then stood drawn up round their father and head. Complete silence had fallen, all eyes were fixed upon Jacob's ashen lips.

They parted in an effort to speak, several times before they shaped any words. Painfully, in a low voice, his speech began. Later he got more freedom and his voice a fuller ring; only at the very last, when he blessed Benjamin, did it die away in weakness.

"Welcome, Israel," he said, "girdle of the earth, zone of your courses, stronghold and dike of the skies, ordered in sacred pictures! Lo, obediently you came in your host and stoutly gathered yourselves full-numbered round the bed of my death, that I may judge you according to the truth and foretell to you out of the wisdom of my last hour. Praise be yours, my ring of sons, for your readiness, and commendation for your courage. Blessed be ye all together by the hand of the dying and glorified altogether. Be blessed by my well-saved strength and blest to eternity! Mark now: what I have to say to you, each by himself in your order, is said within the bond of the general blessing."

Here he paused in his speech and only moved his lips awhile to himself, without any sound. Then his features became concentrated, the skin of his forehead wrinkled with strain as he drew his brows together to fight his weakness.

"Reuben!" came the summons from his lips.

The shepherd tower strode out on his girded legs like strong columns. He was quite grey-headed, and his red, smooth-shaven face worked like that of a chidden child about to cry. The eyes with their inflamed lids kept up a blinking beneath the white brows; the corners of his mouth were drawn down in such bitterness, so violently, that they made thick ridges of muscle at the sides. He knelt at the bed's edge and bowed himself over it.

"Reuben, my eldest son," Jacob began, "you are the beginning of my strength, the firstling of my manhood, yours was the right of the first-born, and a mighty pre-eminence. In the circle you were the highest, the nearest to the sacrificing and the nearest to the kingship. But it was all wrong. A heathen god showed it to me on the field in a dream, a biting beast, a dog-boy of the desert with beautiful legs, sitting on a stone. Begot by a mistake, begot with the wrong one in the blind night to which everything is the same and knows naught of distinctions in love. So I begot you, my eldest, in the windy night with the wrong one,

394

the strong one, begot you in my delusion. I gave her the flower, but there had been an exchange, the veil was exchanged, and daylight taught me that I had only begot where I falsely thought to love—and my heart and my bowels turned over and I despaired of my soul."

Now there was a time when they did not understand what he said; he moved his lips and soundlessly talked to himself. Then his voice came back, stronger than before, and part of the time he spoke of Reuben in the third person, no longer to him.

"He shot away like water," said he. "Like water bubbling over out of a pot. Not he shall be the head, not he the king-post of the house, he shall have no pre-eminence. For he went up to his father's bed, and has defiled his father's bed with his going up. He has bared and mocked his father's shame and come near him with the sickle and committed naughtiness with his mother. Ham is he, black of face, and goes bare with naked shame, for as the dragon of the slime has he borne him and after the ways of the hippopotamus. Hear you, my early strength, what I say of you? May you be accursed, my son—that is, accurst within the scope of the blessing. For the first-born right is taken away from you, the priesthood revoked and the kingly headship recalled. For you are not worthy of the leadership and your first-born right is done away. Beyond the Salt Sea shall you live and border on Moab. Your deeds are weakly and your fruits are poor. Thank you, my eldest son, that you so stout-heartedly came to the gathering and boldly put yourself in the way of judgment. You are like a shepherd tower, and move on your legs like moving columns of a temple, because I scattered my first strength and manhood so mightily in the madness of the night. Receive a father's curse and so farewell!"

He ceased, and the aging Reuben stepped back among the ranks, all the muscles of his face grim with dignity and his eyes cast down just as his mother used to cast hers down to hide her squinting.

"The brothers!" Jacob next commanded. "The twin sons, inseparable in the skies!"

And Simeon and Levi bent and bowed down before him. They were seventy-five and seventy-six years old (for of course they were not twins, only inseparables); but they had astonishingly preserved their rough and blustering outward appearance.

"Oh, oh, how scored and scarred with ingrained savagery!" exclaimed their father. He even started back as though in fear. "They kiss the instruments of cruelty, I will know naught of them. For I love it not, ye savage ones, may my soul come not in their counsels nor my honour have any part with theirs. Their anger slew a man and their self-will mutilated the cattle. Therefore the curse of the injured struck them down and they were appointed for destruction. What have I said to them? Cursed be their anger that it was so fierce and their wrath for that it was stubborn. That have I said to you. Be accursed, my dear ones, accurst within the blessing. Ye shall be divided and scattered that ye commit not misdoing together for ever. Be dispersed in Jacob, my Levi! Yours be a lot and land none the less, stout Simeon, but I see it stands not alone but is consumed in Israel. Take your place in the background, double star, having heard the death-bed second-sight of the blessing one. Step back!"

They did so, not vastly upset by the judgment. They had long known it and expected nothing better. Having it once more expressly served up in open meeting did not cut them up, for everybody knew it before—and they still remained "Israel." Their rejection was only within the scope of the general blessing. Besides, they and the whole audience espoused the view that rejection is a destiny like any other, with a dignity of its own. Every condition is a condition of honour: such was their view, and the view of all the others. After all, it was pretty plain that part of what their father had said did not refer to them, but to the constellation of the Twin Brethren. Partly out of his native weakness for the allusive, partly in the mental confusion of his state, to which, on the same ground, he solemnly gave way, he had mixed them up with Gemini and brought in Babylonian allusions well known to them all, even to the lads sitting on the chests along the walls. Deliberately and blatantly he had at times confused them with Gilgamesh and Eabani in the song, so enraged about their sister that they had cut in pieces the heavenly steer and for this blasphemy been cursed by Ishtar. But they had not paid particular attention to any steer at Shechem, the city of Sichem, the scene of the butchery; nor did they recall having mutilated any. Jacob, however, had had this fixed idea about a steer from the beginning, and always brought it up when they came back to the subject. But can anyone be more honourably cursed than to be confused with the Dioscuri and the sun and moon? That is a rejection one can take, even in public: it is only half personal; the other half is spun out of the dream fancies of a dying man.

396

It is necessary to emphasize here that many astral allusions were thus mixed into these pronouncements of Jacob to his sons. They gave elevation to his discourse and also imparted a certain touch of human fallibility. That was both weakness and wilfulness—with a good deal of wilfulness in the weakness. There was a hint of Aquarius in what he had said to Reuben. Now it was Judah's turn. And Jacob so nearly expended himself in the decisive and tremendous blessing he now bestowed that after it he had repeatedly to call on God for help, fearing he might not last out, and particularly that he might not get round to Joseph. Judah had always been called the lion. But Jacob's dying words to him played so untiringly on the epithet and showed him so explicitly lionlike, that Judah writhed in torment and nobody present could possibly fail to recognize the heavenly phenomenon. A great deal of Cancer came out in Issachar—the constellation of the little asses, which stands in this sign of the zodiac, was brought into cosmic connection with his everyday nickname of the bony ass. In Dan everybody made out the scales, the metaphor of law and justice, though the adder in the path came out as well. And Naphtali's stag-and-hind passed over, intelligibly to most of the audience, into the Ram. Joseph himself was no exception. On the contrary, in his judgment the astral implication was double: the Virgin and the Bull alternated therein. Benjamin's judgment seemed to be conditioned by Scorpio, for the good little man was pronounced a ravening wolf, only because Lupus stands near by, south of the sign with a sting in its tail.

Here the mythological coloration and the divorce from the personal became clearest of all—it was that which made it so much easier for the big twins to take their condemnation with equanimity. They lived in an earlier time, but also in a time that was already a later one; in some directions they possessed a good deal of insight—for instance, into the not absolutely reliable character of death-bed prophecies. The gaze which the departing one sends into the future is impressive and hallowed; much faith may be put in. Yet not too much, for it has not always been entirely justified; and it seems that the already unearthly state of the dying which produces it can also be a source of error. Jacob solemnly made some solemn misfires—along with some prophecies that amazingly hit the mark. Reuben's descendants never did amount to much, and Simeon's stock was never independent and was absorbed into Judah's. But that the blood of Levi would in time attain to the highest honour and achieve permanent election to the priesthood—as we who are in the story but also outside it already know—that was obviously hidden from Jacob's parting gaze. In this respect and in some others his dying prophecies were a dignified failure. Of Zebulon he said that he would dwell at the haven of the sea and before an haven of ships; his border should be unto Sidon. That was a natural guess, on account of Zebulon's well-known fondness for the sea and the smell of pitch. But the location of his tribe was not to be by green water at all nor did it ever border on Sidon. It lay between Sidon and the sea of Galilee, separated from the latter by Naphtali's portion and from the sea by Asher's.

For us such errors are valuable. For are there not clever people who assert that Jacob's blessing-speech was composed after the time of Joshua and should be regarded as prophecy after the event? We may shrug our shoulders at this: not only because we are present at the death-bed and hear the dying man's words with our own ears, but also because prophecies which are given out with history to go upon, back-dated prophecies, so to speak, have no trouble in being correct. The best evidence for the genuineness of a prophecy is its incorrectness.

And now Jacob summoned up Judah. It was a great moment. Deep stillness reigned in and without the tent. It is seldom that such a large assemblage preserves such a profound, motionless, and breathless stillness. The ancient raised his pallid hand towards his fourth son and Judah stood there ashamed to his very depth and bending low his seventy-five-year-old head. Jacob lifted his finger and pointed to him and spoke:

"Judah, you are the one!"

Yes, it was he, the tortured one, the man utterly unworthy in his own mind; the slave of the mistress, who had no lust to lust, but she to him: sinner and religious man in one. It might be supposed that at seventy-five years this slavery to desire cannot be so abject. But to suppose so would be wrong. That lasts to the last breath. A little blunter the spear may become, but that ever the mistress frees her slave is unheard of, it does not happen. Deeply abased, Judah bowed himself for the blessing. And now a strange thing came to pass: in proportion as the flood gushed out over him and the oil of the promise poured out upon his head, so his tumultuous feelings were calmed, he listened and in waxing pride he told himself: "Well, well, in spite of everything! Then it was

398

not so bad after all, and apparently it does not affect the blessing! Perhaps it is not taken so seriously—maybe the purity I so craved was not so indispensable to salvation; maybe it is all taken in together, even hell itself is taken in—who would have thought it? For the oil is trickling down on my head, God have mercy on me, for I am the one!"

It did not trickle, it poured and roared. Jacob expended himself almost recklessly in blessing Judah; several of the brothers were cut off with a hasty mention and Jacob's voice quavered with weakness as he gave it.

"Judah, you are the one! Your hand will be in the neck of your enemies, your brethren shall praise you. Your father's children and the children of all the mothers shall praise in you the anointed one!"—Then came the lion. For some time there were only lions, and powerful lion metaphors. Judah was a lion's whelp, from the litter of a lioness, a veritable king of beasts, from the prey he went up ravening, he purred, he mewed, he roared. Upon his desert mountain he withdrew, there he couched and stretched like a maned king and like the son of a fierce lioness. Who shall dare to rouse him up? No one shall dare. It was surprising to have the father praise as ravening beasts those sons whom he blessed while those whom he did not bless he blamed unmercifully precisely because the instruments of cruelty were their familiars. As he himself in his dying weakness had seen himself in the rôle of a hero with sword and bow, so now he lauded his sons, first the tormented Judah and then little Benjamin, as savage warriors and beasts of prey rejoicing in blood. Remarkably enough, the foible of the mild and intellectual type is a weakness for the heroic.

But Jacob did not end his Judah-scene on the beast-of-prey note. The hero he had in view, whom he had sought out long since, was not the kind to make weakness forget itself in hero-worship. Shiloh was his name. From lions to him was a long way; therefore the old man made a transition in his blessing; he introduced a great king. The king sat on his throne and the sceptre leaned between his feet and should not move from there nor be taken from him until "the hero" appeared, until Shiloh came. To Judah, the king with the sceptre between his legs, this promise-name was quite new—indeed, it was a surprise to the whole gathering. They listened amazed. One only among them all knew it and had waited eagerly to hear it. Our gaze turns involuntarily out to the shadowy profile: she stood there erect, in darkling pride, to hear Jacob

399

pronounce the seed of the woman. From Judah favour should not pass, he should not die, his eyes not close until his greatness should wax immense, for that out of him should come one upon whom all the people should depend, the bringer of peace, the man of the star.

Thus it went on beyond all expectation above Judah's abashed head. His own figure, or rather his tribe, mingled—whether intentionally or out of mental confusion or perhaps out of both, that is to say, the confusion being used to heighten the high-flown poetic effect—it mingled and melted in with Shiloh's figure so that in this vision of the fullness of the blessing and the grace no one knew whether Jacob was talking about Judah or about the promised one. Everything swam in wine— everything shone red with the red sparkle of the wine before the eyes of the host as they listened. It was a land, the kingdom of this king, where one bound his foal to the vine and his ass's colt to the choice vine. Were they the vineyards of Hebron, the wine-clad hills of Engedi? Into his city "he" rode on an ass and on a colt the foal of an ass—there was nothing but drunken desire as of red wine at the sight of him, and he himself was like a drunken wine-god treading the press, high-kilted, exalted; the blood of the wine sprinkled his apron and the red juice of the grape his garment. Lovely was he as he trod, wading and dancing the dance of the winepress—lovely above all mankind: as white as snow, as red as blood and as black as ebony.

Jacob's voice died away. His head bobbed down, his eyes rolled up from below. He had expended himself very much, almost too much, in this blessing. He seemed to be praying for a renewal of strength. Judah, finding his blessing blessed out, stepped back, amazed and abashed because it had turned out that impurity was no hindrance. The uproar in the assemblage at the appearance of Shiloh and the entirely new revelation and declarations brought out in this blessing were almost uncontrolled. A loud whispering went round both within and without the tent. Outside it was even vocal, voices were heard excitedly repeating the name of Shiloh. But all movement ceased again as Jacob once more raised his head and his hand. The name of Zebulon came from his lips.

The man of sixty-eight years put his head under the old hand. Since his name actually meant dwelling and habitation, it surprised no one that Jacob should point out his dwelling and his habitation: he should dwell at the haven of the sea and live near the treasures of ships and should border on Sidon. Very good: he had always wanted it, so now he got it—in a tired, perfunctory voice. Issachar. . . .

Issachar would be like a strong ass crouching down between the folds. The little asses in Cancer were his sponsors, but despite this connection Jacob seemed not to expect much of him. He spoke only briefly of him and in the past tense, which meant the future. Issachar saw that rest was good and the land that it was pleasant. He was strong and phlegmatic. He thought nothing of lending his bones as a beast of burden. To serve came easy to him and he bowed his shoulders to be laden. So much of Issachar. He touched the Jordan, so Jacob claimed to be able to see. Enough of him. Now for Dan.

Dan guided the scale and judged with wisdom. So subtle was he of mind and tongue that he was like a biting adder. Jacob took occasion here, lifting his finger to give his audience a little lesson in zoology: in the beginning, when God was creating the animals, He had crossed the hedgehog with the lizard and so produced the adder. Dan was an adder-serpent. A snake he was by the way and an horned adder in the path, not easy to see in the sand and very tricky. In him the heroic took the form of knavery. The enemy's horse he bit in the heels so that the rider fell backwards. Thus Dan, Bilhah's son. "I have waited for thy salvation, O Lord!"

In his exhaustion Jacob gave his sigh and ejaculated his prayer, distressed lest he should not get to the end before his end. He had begotten so many sons that in his last hour the number of them was almost beyond his strength. But with God's help he would win through.

He summoned the stocky Gad, whose clothes were besewn with bronze.

"Gaddiel, a troop shall overcome you, but you will overcome at the last. Stoutly, my stout one! Now Asher."

Asher, the sweet-tooth, had fat land from the mountain to near Tyre. The lowlands were full of waving corn and dripped with oil, that his bread should be fat and he should make fine ointment such as kings send each other for their pleasure. From him came pleasure and the love of bodily pleasure, which amounts to something too. "Asher, you will also be somebody. And since song came from you and joyous tidings, be praised for it before your brother Naphtali, whom I now summon beneath my hand."

Naphtali was a hind who leaps over ditches and a springing doe. His was the nimble gait, he was a running he-goat when he draws in his horns and leaps. His tongue too was nimble, it gave glib information and the fruits of the plain Gennesareth ripened apace. "Of quickly ripened fruits, Naphtali, may your trees be full, and quick success, if not too great, be your judgment and lot."

Then this son too, having been blessed, stepped back into the ranks. The old man rested, with closed eyes, in a deep silence, his chin on his breast. And after a little he smiled. They all saw and were touched, for they knew what summons it meant. It was a happy, yes, an artful smile and somewhat sad withal, though it was artful too, for the love and tenderness within overcame the sadness and renunciation. "Joseph!" said the old man. And a fifty-six-year-old man, who had been thirty and seventeen and nine, and lain in the cradle as a lamb of the mother sheep, a child of the time, beautiful of face, in Egyptian white, Pharaoh's sky-blue ring on his finger, fortune's minion, bowed beneath the ashen blessing-hand.

"Joseph, my scion and seed, son of the virgin, son of the dearest, son of the fruit tree by the spring, fruitful bough whose branches overhang the wall, I greet you! Who is the heart of the spring, first-born bull in his adornment, greeting!"

Jacob had spoken loud and clear, a solemn address, to be heard by all. But then he dropped his voice almost to a whisper, obviously minded, if not to shut out the public, at least to limit its numbers during this blessing. Only the nearest heard his words of farewell to the set-apart one; those farther off only got a word here and there and those outside for the moment nothing at all. But afterwards it was all repeated over and over, reported and discussed.

"Most dearly beloved," came from the painfully smiling lips. "Chosen and preferred by the daring heart for the sake of the only beloved, who lived in you and with whose eyes she looks, just as once she first looked at me at the well, when she appeared among Laban's sheep and I rolled away the lid for her—I was allowed to kiss her and the shepherds shouted in delight: 'Lu, lu, lu!' In you I kept her, my darling, when the almighty tore her from me, in your loveliness she lived, and what is sweeter than the double and the doubtful? Well I know that the double is not of the spirit, for which we stand, but is the folly of the peoples. And still I yielded to that ancient mighty spell. Can one be ever and entirely of the spirit and avoid folly? Lo, I am double now myself, I am Jacob and Rachel. She am I, who went so hardly away from you into the summoning land, for me too it summons today away from you—it summons us all. You too, my joy and my care, have already made half the journey towards that land and yet you were once little and then young and were all that my heart understood of loveliness and charm. Serious was my heart but soft, therefore was it soft before beauty. Called to the heights and to the sight of diamond-sharp steeps, secretly I loved the gentle hills."

His voice failed for some minutes and he lay smiling with closed eyes as though his spirit wandered in the charming rolling landscape which had risen to his eyes as he gave Joseph his blessing.

When he began to speak again he seemed to have forgotten that Joseph's head was under his hand, for he spoke of him awhile as of a third person.

"Seventeen years he lived with me and another seventeen by God's mercy he lived: between them lay my stiffness and the destiny of the set-apart one. They lay in wait for his loveliness and that was folly; for with loveliness wisdom was ever one. On that their strong desire was wrecked. More alluring than has ever been seen are the women who climb up to look after him from house-tops and towers and windows, but they had not their desire. So it was made bitter to him and they attacked him with arrows of ill report. But his bow abode in strength, the arms of his hands were made strong and the hands of the Everlasting held him up. Not without rapture will his name be remembered, for he succeeded as few succeeded in finding favour before God and man. That is a rare blessing, for mostly one has the choice of pleasing either God or the world; but the spirit of charm and mediation gave it to him that he pleased them both. Be not proud, my child—have I need to warn you? No, I know your shrewdness saves you from presumption. For it is a charming blessing but not the highest and sternest. Lo, thy dear life lies open in its truth before the dying gaze. Play and playing it was, familiar, friendly appealingness, approaching salvation yet not quite seriously a calling or a gift. Love pierces my heart at sight of that mingled gladness and sadness; not so can anyone else love you, my child, who see, not as the father-heart can the sadness, but only the brilliance of your life. And so I bless you, blessed one, with all the strength of my heart in the name of the Eternal who gave you and took you and gave you again and now takes me from you. Higher shall my blessing mount than the blessings of my fathers upon my own head. Be blessed, as you are blessed, with the blessing of heaven above, blessings of the deep that lieth under, with blessings gushing from the breast of heaven and the womb of earth! Blessings, blessings on Joseph's head, and in your name shall they sun themselves who come from you. Songs shall stream far and wide singing the story of your life, ever anew, for after all it was a sacred play and you suffered and could forgive. So I too forgive you that you made me suffer. And God forgive us all!"

He finished and drew his hand back, slowly, from this head. So one life parts from another and must go hence; but in a little the other goes too.

Joseph stepped back among the brothers. He had not said too much in saying that he would receive his share and be judged with the truthfulness of the dying. He took Benjamin by both hands, since the old man failed to summon him, and brought him forward. Clearly Jacob was at the end of his strength and Joseph had to guide the blessing hand upon the little brother's head, for it would no longer have found the way. That it was the youngest who awaited his judgment he probably knew, but what his failing lips murmured had little to do with the little man. Possibly it would fit his descendants better. Benjamin, so they heard, was a ravening wolf, in the morning he would devour his prey and at night divide the spoil. He was vexed at what he heard.

Jacob's last thought went back to the cave, the double cave on the field of Ephrath, son of Zohar, and his wish that he be buried there among his fathers. "I enjoin upon you," he breathed, "it is paid for, paid by Abraham to the children of Heth with four hundred shekels in silver by weight, as it . . ." Here death interrupted him, he stretched out his feet, sank deeper into his bed, and his life stood still.

They all held their breath and their lives stopped a little too, when it came. Then Mai-Sachme, Joseph's steward, who was also a physician, stepped up quietly to the couch. He laid his ear to the quiet heart, watched with serious pursed mouth a feather he had laid on the muted lips—it did not stir—and struck a little blaze before the pupil, which gave no sign. So then he turned to Joseph, his master, and announced to him:

"He is gathered to his fathers."

But Joseph motioned him with his head to Judah, to whom, not to himself he should make the announcement. And as the good man went

404

up to Judah and repeated: "He is gathered up," Joseph stepped to the death-bed and closed the eyes of the dead; for to that end he had motioned Mai-Sachme towards Judah. Then he laid his forehead on his father's brow and wept for Jacob.

Judah, the heir, made the necessary arrangements: the mourners, male and female, were ordered and male and female singers and flute-players; and the body was washed, anointed, and wrapped up. Damasek-Eliezer kindled an offering of incense in the chamber: stacte, neat's-foot oil from the Red Sea, galbanum and olibanum, mixed with salt. And as the spicy clouds floated round the dead, the guests streamed out, mingled with those outside, and moved away, eagerly discussing the judgment and the pronouncement that Jacob had made to the twelve.

JACOB IS SWADDLED

And so now the story, grain of sand by grain of sand, has run steadily and silently through the neck in the glass; it lies below in a little heap, only a few grains are left to run. Nothing remains of all the happenings except what happens to a dead man. But that is not a little: you will be well advised to look reverently on as the last grains run through and fall gently on the heap beneath. For what happened to Jacob's husk was extraordinary, an honorific expenditure of an almost unique kind. No king has ever been borne to the grave as was Jacob, the man of years and dignity, by his son Joseph's command and disposition.

Joseph, of course, after his father's death left to Judah, the heir of the blessing, the first and immediate arrangements; after that he took mat-ters in hand himself, since only he could attend to them, and embarked on certain measures, empowered by a quickly assenting council of the brothers. The measures followed upon the circumstances: upon Jacob's command and last wishes; and that they did so was dear to Joseph's heart. For the set-apart one thought as an Egyptian, and his ardent de-sire to do honour to his father in the best and most expensive way fol-lowed quite naturally an Egyptian train of thought.

Jacob had not wanted to be buried in the country of the dead gods. He had exacted a pledge that he be gathered to his fathers at home in the cave. That meant a far journey, for which Joseph had extravagant plans, very large in their scope and requiring time to carry out: time, that is, for the transportation itself, a period of at least seventeen days. To that end the body must be preserved, preserved by the art of Egypt, pickled and embalmed; and if he who had gone hence would have rejected the idea, then he should have forborne insisting upon being carried home. For it followed from his own stipulation that he should not be buried in Egypt that he had to be buried in the Egyptian way, magnificently dried and stuffed into an Osiris-mummy. The idea may be unpleasant to some of us. But we have not, as his son Joseph had, lived forty years in Egypt and been soaked in the sap and the spirit of that strange land till they were his pith and marrow. To him it was a joy, a consolation in the midst of grief, that his father's command allowed him to deal with the beloved shell after the most honourable and exquisite customs of the country and give it a permanence only imparted by the most costly methods.

Accordingly, as soon as he got back to his house in Menfe, where he spent the period of mourning, he sent to Goshen men whom the brothers called his "physicians." Actually they were not physicians but professional embalmers, masters of the technique of making the dead undying; the most sought-out and skilled in their line, who lived—not at all by chance—in the city of Menfe. With them came masons and carpenters, goldsmiths and engravers, and these set up their workshop next the house of hair and death, while within it the "physicians" did upon the body what the brothers called anointing. But that was not the right word. They drew his brains out through his nostrils with a bent iron and filled the empty skull with spices. They had an Ethiopian knife, made of obsidian and extremely sharp; they wielded it with great elegance, their fingers spread out, to open the left side of the abdomen in order to remove the entrails. These were preserved in special alabaster jars with the likeness of the deceased's head on the lid. The cavity they thoroughly washed out with date wine and in place of the mesenteron put the very best materials inside: myrrh and spice-bark from the shoots of a laurel. They took professional pride in their work, for death was their province and they enjoyed making a man's body so much cleaner and more attractive than when he was alive.

Then they carefully sewed up the cut and put the corpse into a bath of saltpetre for a full seventy days. During that period they made holiday, ate and drank, and were paid high wages by the hour. When the time was up and the body salted, the bandaging could begin; and that was a considerable labour. Byssus bandages four hundred ells long daubed with gum, endless strips of linen, the finest of which came next the body: these they wound round Jacob, round and round, now alongside, now on top of one another, and among them on the shrunken neck they laid a gold collar and on the breast another ornament, a vulture with outspread wings, made of flat hammered gold. For during the seventy days the other artists had got on with their task and now contributed these ornaments; likewise ribbons wrought out of sheet gold, inscribed with the name of the dead and with laudatory phrases. These were drawn round the bandages, round the shoulders, the middle, and the knees and fastened to other gold bands running vertically front and back. Not content with this, that which had once been Jacob and was now in death an adorned and durable doll, purified from all corruption, was wrapped from head to foot in thin flexible plates of purest gold and then lifted into an *aron,* the chest which the cabinet-makers, jewellers, and sculptors had meantime made to measure: in human form, richly decorated with precious stones and vitreous paste. The figure fitted into the figure; the outside head was carved out of wood and covered with a mask of thick sheet gold; it had the Usir beard on its chin. Thus it went with Jacob, in all honour and splendour if not just according to his wishes but rather those of his transplanted son. However, it is probably right to have things done according to the feelings of him who still has his living entrails in his body; to the other it cannot matter.

To honour his father in death, to make his last wish the occasion of exceeding pomp: such was Joseph's dearest wish, the mainspring of all his actions. While the corpse was being got ready for the journey, the exalted one had taken steps to make the expedition an occasion to remember and marvel at, a tremendous triumph. To that end he needed Pharaoh's consent; but the mourning ritual and prescribed neglect of his person prevented him from speaking before the King. Instead he sent up an embassy to him to the city of the horizon in the hare district, and begged the lovely child of Aton for permission to accompany his father's body over the border into the land of his last resting-place. It was Mai-Sachme, his steward, whom Joseph entrusted with this mission, to give the good man the chance of being in the story up to its end. Indeed, he might confide in Mai's loyalty and poise for the accomplishment of the diplomatic mission which in fact it was; for it meant getting commands from Pharaoh which could only be suggested to, not asked of him. It meant procuring his consent for a highly solemn state funeral for the begetter of his first servant, or, in other words, to bring him to the point of ordering a so-called "great progress."

Again we see how much the thoughts of Rachel's lamb had got used to going Egyptian ways. The great progress was a peculiarly Egyptian concept, a favourite festival and ceremonial of Keme's people. Joseph had derived from Jacob's command not only the embalming in the highest price-range, but also the design of having a great procession which should be talked about beyond the Euphrates and the islands of the sea. It should vie with the most famous embassy ever sent out to Babel, Mitanniland or to the great King Hattushilish of the Hittite lands and be worthy to be entered in the annals of the realm for posterity to read. It was necessary that Pharaoh should grant him official leave for seventy days in order that he with his eleven brothers, his sons, and his brothers' sons should take their father across the border to his grave on the route of honour which he had chosen for him. But that was only a part, it was even the least part of the programme. For so far it constituted no great procession, no royal progress; and Jacob's worldly son designed to bear his father to his grave not otherwise than as a king is borne. Pharaoh must be brought to consent and to direct; state, court, and military must he command as retinue; and that meant a considerable force of troops to cover the long desert route. And Pharaoh so thought and so ordered, after the steward had spoken before him. He so arranged partly out of feeling and the wish to show love and favour to his most deserving servant, who had done so much for him. But it was also out of the fear lest Joseph, if left uncovered by the power of Egypt to go into the country of his origin, might end by not coming back. That Meni seriously feared this, and also that Joseph reckoned with this fear, shows in the words which the basic tradition puts into his mouth in his dealings with the court: "Let me go up, I pray thee, and bury my father and I will come again." It may be that he made the promise voluntarily in advance; it may also be that Pharaoh asked it of him. But it is clear that the suspicion was present and it must have been a satisfaction to Pharaoh that he could combine favour with foresight and by means of a very heavy Egyptian escort secure himself against the loss of the irreplaceable.

The lord of the two crowns was no longer of the youngest; the years of his life were more than forty and that life was precarious and sad.

408

He was already familiar with death: one of his daughters, the second of six, Meketaton, the most anaemic of them all, had died at nine years old; and Ikhnaton, the father of daughters, was far more dissolved in tears at the loss than was Nefernefruaton, his Queen. He wept much; tears came easy to him on all occasions, for he was lonely and unhappy and the preciousness of his life, the soft refinements among which he lived, made him more and more sensitive to loneliness and misunderstanding. He liked to say that a man who suffered much should live well. And in his case the good living went hand in hand with the tears; he lived too well to bear to suffer much; and he wept a great deal over himself. His dawn-cloud, golden-seamed, the Queen, and his transparent daughters had constantly to dry with fine batiste handkerchiefs the tears on his already elderly childish face.

It was his great pleasure to make offerings of flowers and choral services in the splendid court of the magnificent temple he had erected at Akhetaton, his only capital, to his Father in heaven, that mild friend of nature, whom he conceived as weeping a good deal too. But his pleasure was embittered by mistrust of his courtiers, whose sincerity he doubted. They lived on him, and they had accepted the "teaching." But all the evidence showed that they neither understood nor were capable of understanding it. Nobody was in the very least capable of understanding the teaching of his Father in heaven, who was infinitely distant yet tenderly concerned for every little mouse and worm; that Father of whom the sun's disk in heaven was only a symbol and a parable and who whispered the truth about his nature and essence into the ears of Ikhnaton, his beloved child. Nobody—he did not conceal the fact from himself—nobody had the least or faintest idea about it. He was remote from the people and afraid of contact with them. With the state religion of his country—the temples, the priesthood, not only with Amun but also with the rest of the ancient and traditionally honoured deities, the house of the sun at On being the only exception—between them all and him was hopeless strife. In his anguished zeal for his own revelation he had even gone so far as to take measures for their suppression and dissolution—again not only against Amun-Re but also against Usir, Lord of the West, and Eset, the mother, against Anup and Khnum, Thoth, Setekh, and even Ptah, the master of the arts. Thus the gulf widened between him and his people, a people profoundly practised in ideas and profoundly bent on loyalty to the old and its preservation everywhere. It made of him, shut off in his royal luxury, a stranger in their midst.

What wonder that his narrow grey eyes, the eyes of a dreamer, were almost always red with weeping! When Mai came before him to ask in Joseph's name for leave and to bring him the news of Jacob's death, he wept at once—he was always just about to weep and his tears found the occasion not one to miss.

"How frightfully sad!" he said. "So he is dead, that old, old man. That is a shock to My Majesty. He paid me a visit, I remember, when he was alive and made no little impression on me. He was a great wretch in his youth, I know some pranks he played, with his skins and his wands—My Majesty could still laugh till I cried at them. So now a term has been set to his years and my little uncle, who administers all the gifts of heaven, is bereaved? How infinitely sad! Is he sitting and weeping, my universal friend? I know he is no stranger to tears, that he is easy to weep, and my heart goes out to him, for it is always a good sign in a man. I know that when he revealed himself to his brothers and said to them: 'I am he!' he wept too. And he is asking for leave? Leave for seventy days? That is a long time to bury a father, however great a wretch he was! Does it have to be seventy days? It is so hard to spare him! Easier now, of course, than in the times of the fat and the lean kine, but even in these more equable years it will be very hard for me to lack him, who is over the kingdom of the blackness, for My Majesty has little understanding for such things. My field has always been the upper one and the light. Ah, it is a thankless task; human beings understand better a man who brings dark tidings than they do one who is the herald of the light. Do not think I am envious of your dear master. He shall be as Pharaoh to the very end of his life, for he has helped my poor Majesty beyond my power to thank him—in so far, that is, as I could be helped."

He wept again a little, and then he said:

"Of course he must bury his reverend father, the prankish old man, with explicit honours and carry him abroad with his sons and brothers and the sons of his brothers and all the male seed of the house—it will be a whole procession; it will be like a progress, and to the people it will look as though he went out of Egypt with all his family thither whence he came. Such a misleading impression should be avoided. It might cause unrest in the land and lead to scenes and disorder if the people thought the provider was departing—I think they would feel it much less if My

410

Majesty departed and forsook the land out of grief over its ingratitude. Hearken, friend! What sort of retinue would that be, of only the children and the children's children? In my opinion there is nothing else to do, and this conveyance is a perfectly good occasion for it, but to make a great progress. It must be one of the biggest that ever went abroad from Egypt and in equal pomp returned again. What should I be if I granted a favour to my universal friend and did not make the granting of it far outbid the favour asked? Say to him: Pharaoh grants you five and seventy days and covers you with kisses, that you may convey your father to Asia, and not only your family and their entourage shall attend you and the corpse but Pharaoh will command a whole great progress, a journey of state, and the cream of Egypt shall bring your father to his grave; I will order my whole court, Ikhnaton sends word to you, the highest of my servants and the most aristocratic in all the land, the heads of state with their retinues, wagons and armed men in very great strength. They shall all go with you, O apple of my eye! and follow the bier in front and behind and on both sides, and then just so escort you back to me, when you have deposited your dear burden in the place where he would lie."

THE GREAT PROGRESS

Such was the answer which Mai-Sachme brought back from Akhetaton to Joseph, and all was arranged and put in train accordingly. Invitations which were of course commands were issued by a high palace official called privy councillor of the levee and of the privy council and sent out by running footmen; and the day was fixed when the participants were to come from all parts of the country and assemble in the desert outside Menfe. It was a burdensome honour that was thus bestowed on Pharaoh's servants and the great ones of his house and of the land of Egypt. But there were none who would not have taken care not to refuse; yes, some notabilities who were not bidden had to listen to the taunts of the favoured ones and were like to fall ill with chagrin. It was no small undertaking to organize the huge procession which assembled together in the desert by members and groups; it fell to a captain of troops whose regular title was "Charioteer of the King, high in the Army." For this occasion, however, and for the duration of the progress he received another title: "Organizer of the great funeral train of the Osiris Jaacob ben Yitzchak, father of the great vice-spender of the King." It was this field officer who drew up the order of the procession with the list of particulars in his hand, and reduced to order the confusion of wagons and litters, riding animals and beasts of burden, into a properly graded procession of regularity and beauty. He also had charge of the military taken along for protection.

The order was this: A host of soldiers, trumpeters, and drummers came first, then Nubian bowmen, Libyans armed with sickle-shaped swords, and Egyptian lance-bearers. Then followed the pride of Pharaoh's court, as many as could be spared from his entourage without derogation to the person of the god: friends and unique friends of the King, fan-bearers on the right hand, palace officials of the rank of the head of the privy council and privy councillors of the royal commands; highly placed personages such as His Majesty's chief baker and chief butler, the lord high steward, the keeper of the King's wardrobe, the head of the Fullers of the Great House, Pharaoh's sandal-bearer, his head wigmaker, who was also a privy councillor of the two kingdoms, and so on and so forth.

These elegant toadies formed the advance guard before the catafalque, which was taken into the procession when they reached Goshen and thereafter towered above it in glittering splendour. Jacob's coffin, shaped like a man, sparkled with gems and with the gold mask and beard it wore. It lay on a bier which in its turn rested on a gilded sledge and this again on a car with draped wheels drawn by twelve white oxen. The lofty vehicle swayed along, frequently accompanied by the wailing of flutes and the song of the professional mourners. It passed the houses of the dead and his connection, who now joined the train. There was Joseph with his sons and his household staff, of which Mai-Sachme was the eldest servant and head; there were Joseph's eleven brothers with their sons and the sons of their sons—all that bore male names in Israel followed Israel's bier, with the closest attendants of the dead, foremost among them Eliezer, his oldest servant, and a very long and numerous train. But what a host now followed after it!

For now came the administrative bureaucracy of the two lands: the Viziers of Upper and Lower Egypt, Joseph's immediate subordinates, the head bookkeeper of the office of supply; such people as the inspector of the King's bulls and of all the cattle in the land (he had also the title of steward of all horned and clawed and feathered creatures), the head of the fleet, the actual steward of the privy chamber, the warden of the scales of the treasure-house, the general overseer of horses, and numerous actual judges and head scribes. Who could set down all the titles and offices whose wearers were honoured by the command to accompany to foreign parts the mummy of the father of the provider? Military, with standards and cornets, followed the officers of the state. And after that came the baggage train with luggage and tents and the forage wagons with mules and drivers—for what immense quantities of food and drink in the desert did not such a train require!

A very great company, as the tradition rightly says; one can only try to picture this long-drawn-out caravan of splendid riding-horses and luggage-carts, of bright feathers and glittering weapons; all the snorting and rolling and marching, the whinnying of steeds, the braying of donkeys and bellowing of bulls; the crashing of trumpets, the throbbing of drums, the wailing of the professional mourners—and out of the midst of it all the amazing, towering structure of the hearse with the mummied corpse inside. Joseph might be well pleased: into Egypt the father-heart had once lost him; now all Egypt must pay tribute to that agony and bear the dead Jacob on its shoulders to his grave.

The amazing host wound its way eastward to the border, stared at everywhere on its way. Now it entered the desolate stretches which had to be covered in going from the bottom-land of Hapi in Pharaoh's eastern provinces to the land of Haru and Emor. It went along the upper edge of the desert tableland of Sinai; but then it took a direction which would have surprised anyone who knew its goal; for it did not go by the usual and shortest way, to Gaza on the sea, through the land of the Philistines and via Beersheba to Hebron; it followed the fall of the land which runs south of the port of Khadati eastwards, to Amalek and towards Edom to the southern end of the Salt Sea. It skirted this and went along its eastern shore to the mouth of the Jordan and a little way up the river valley, and thence—that is, from Gilead and from the east—across the river and into the land of Canaan.

A long detour for Jacob's great funeral procession! It made a journey of twice seventeen days and was the reason why Joseph had asked for seventy days' leave. Even so he had not asked enough and overstepped the seventy-five that Pharaoh in his love for his favourite had granted. But he had early decided on this long way round and disclosed his intention to the officer who organized the procession and he had at once approved. For he had been doubtful of the effect of an Egyptian irruption in such strength, with so many soldiers, from Gaza up on the military highway, lest it make difficulties and arouse excitement and mistrust. He had himself preferred to go around through more tranquil country. But in Joseph's mind the long detour meant greater honour for the progress. The solemn convoy could not be too extravagant in time and trouble to please him; no distances were too far through which the pride of Egypt should carry his father on its shoulders. That was the thought which had determined him to make this detour.

When they had circled the Sea of the Plain and gone a piece upstream along the Jordan, they came to a place near its bank called Goren Atad. In olden times there had been nothing but a threshing-floor there, grown round with thorns; but now it was a populous market. Near by, on the river, was a great grassy place; there they spread out and made camp, watched curiously by the people of the neighbourhood. They stopped seven days and held a wailing, renewed every day, a seven days' service of mourning and lamentations, very shrill and bitter, so that the children of the land were much impressed—as was indeed the intention, since even the animals were in mourning. "A very important encampment," said the inhabitants, with their eyebrows raised, "and a grievous mourning to the Egyptians is this!" So they called the meadow thenceforward nothing but Abel-Mizraim or the Wailing Meadow of Egypt.

After this ceremonial pause the procession formed again and crossed the Jordan by a ford, which the children of the land had made easier for their own use by laying stones and sinking tree-trunks. The sledge with Jacob's mummy was taken from the wagon for the crossing and the twelve sons together bore it over the river on poles.

Now they were in their own country and went up from the steaming river valley to the fresher heights. On the ridge they followed the well-kept roads and came on the third day before Hebron. Kirjath Arba lay surrounded on the slope and a multitude of folk hurried down it to see the splendour which was moving in with its sacred burden and taking its place in the valley where the walled hollow was, the double cave, the ancestral burial place. Adapted by nature but enlarged and built up by the hand of man, it was not double on the outside and had only one door. But if you opened up the masonry, as they now did, a round shaft was revealed, leading downwards, and from it right and left two passages, closed by stone slabs, branched off and led into the two barrel-vaulted tomb cells which gave the place its name of the double hollow. But if one thinks of how many and who had found their eternal home in this hillside chamber, one pales with fear, as the brothers paled when they opened it. The Egyptians were not affected; some of them might even have stuck up their noses at such a home-made affair. But all that was Israel went pale.

Shaft and passages were very low and narrow. Only two people of Jacob's house, his eldest servant and his second eldest, one in front and one behind, could enter, and even they could hardly squeeze in to carry the mummy down and lay it in the chamber—whether the right or the left one is no longer known. If dust and bones could be surprised certainly there must have been great astonishment in the hollow when the newcomer arrived decked out in his foreign folly. But absolute indifference reigned and the two bearers hastened out of that ban of corruption and stooped through the shaft into the sweet air of the living world. There slave artisans stood ready with mortar and trowel and in a trice the lodging was closed again, for it should receive no one else after Jacob.

The father bestowed, his house closed after him, the ten stared as the workmen filled the last hole. What were they thinking? They looked so sallow; and they bit their lips. They stole glances at the eleventh and cast down their eyes. To be quite frank, they were afraid. They felt lost, forsaken and forlorn. The father is gone, the hundred-year-old father of these seventy-year-old sons. Till this moment he had been present, if only as a mummy—but now he was walled away and their hearts sank. Suddenly they felt that he had been their shield, he alone; he had stood where now nothing and nobody stood, between them and the payment.

They stuck close together and whispered in the fading light of day. The moon rose, the everlasting pictures hung themselves in the sky, the dampness of the mountain regions rose in a mist among the huts of Jacob's train. Then they called the twelfth, Benjamin, Rachel's son.

"Benjamin," said they, stiff-lipped, "listen to this. We have a message from the departed to Joseph your brother, and you are the best one to give it to him. For shortly before his death, in his last days, when Joseph was not there, the father summoned us and said: 'When I am dead, you are to say to your brother Joseph from me: Forgive your brothers their misdeed and their sin that they did so evilly by you. For between you and him will I be, in death as in life and I lay it upon you as my last wish and command that you do them no ill and forbear to take revenge for things gone by, even when I seem not to be there. Leave them to shear their sheep, unshorn.' "

"Is that so?" queried Benjamin. "I was not by when he said it."

"You were never by at anything," they answered, "you cannot talk. A little chap like you does not have to be by at everything. But you will not refuse to give his grace your brother Joseph the father's last wish and command. Go to him at once; we will follow you and wait to hear what he says."

So Benjamin went into the tent, to the exalted one, and said hesitatingly:

"Joseph-el, forgive me if I disturb you; but the brothers desire to say to you through me that on his death-bed our father solemnly adjured you not to do them harm after he was dead and gone, for what happened years ago, for even after death he would stand between you to protect them and forbid you your revenge."

"Is that so?" asked Joseph, and his eyes got wet.

"So particularly true it most likely is not," answered Benjamin.

"No, because he knew there was no need of it," added Joseph, and two tears rolled down from under his lashes.

"They are probably outside now and have followed you?" he asked.

"They are out there," the little man answered.

"Then let us go out to them," said Joseph. And he went out into the starlight and beneath the weaving beams of the moon. There they were. They fell down before him and said:

"Here we are, servants of your father's God, and we are your servants. So forgive us our trespasses, as your brother here has said to you, and repay us not according to your power. As you have forgiven us while Jacob lived, so forgive us likewise after his death."

"But brothers, my dear old brothers!" he answered, and bent down to them with his arms stretched out. "What are you saying, as though you were afraid—you talk as though you were and want me to forgive you! Am I then as God? Down in Egypt they say I am as Pharaoh and he is called god; but really he is just a sweet pathetic thing. When you talk to me about forgiveness it seems to me you have missed the meaning of the whole story we are in. I do not blame you for that. One can easily be in a story and not understand it. Perhaps that is the way it ought to be and I am to blame myself for always knowing far too well what was being played. Did you not hear from the father's own lips, when he gave me my blessing, that my life has always been only a play and a pattern? Did he remember, when he pronounced judgment on you, the bad things which happened between you and me? No, he kept quiet about them, because he too was in the play, God's play. I was protected by him when I had to rub you all the wrong way and provoke you to evil in my crude childishness that cried to heaven. God turned it all to good, for I came to feed many people and so I was forced to mature somewhat. But if it is a question of pardon between us human beings, then it is I myself must beg for it, for you had perforce to be cast in the villain's part so that things might turn out as they did. So now am I to use the might of Pharaoh simply because I command it, to avenge myself for three days' discipline in the well and so make ill again what God has made good? I could laugh at the thought! For a man who uses power only because he has it, against right and reason, he is absurd. If he is not today, he will be. And it is the future we are interested in. Sleep in peace! Tomorrow in God's good providence we shall take our way back into that quaint and comic land of Egypt."

Thus he spoke to them and they laughed and wept together and stretched out their hands as he stood among them and touched him, and he too caressed them with his hands. And so endeth the beautiful story and God-invention of

JOSEPH AND HIS BROTHERS

The Principal Works of Thomas Mann

৶

FIRST EDITIONS IN GERMAN

DER KLEINE HERR FRIEDEMANN
[Little Herr Friedemann]. Tales   Berlin, S. Fischer Verlag. 1898

BUDDENBROOKS
Two volumes. Novel   Berlin, S. Fischer Verlag. 1901

TRISTAN
Contains Tonio Kröger. *Tales*   Berlin, S. Fischer Verlag. 1903

FIORENZA
Drama   Berlin, S. Fischer Verlag. 1905

KÖNIGLICHE HOHEIT
[Royal Highness]. Novel   Berlin, S. Fischer Verlag. 1909

DER TOD IN VENEDIG
[Death in Venice]. Short novel   Berlin, S. Fischer Verlag. 1913

DAS WUNDERKIND
[The Infant Prodigy]. Tales   Berlin, S. Fischer Verlag. 1914

BETRACHTUNGEN EINES UNPOLITISCHEN
Autobiographical reflections   Berlin, S. Fischer Verlag. 1918

HERR UND HUND
[A Man and His Dog]. Idyll
Contains also Gesang vom Kindchen, *an idyll in verse*
     Berlin, S. Fischer Verlag. 1919

WÄLSUNGENBLUT   München, Phantasus Verlag. 1921

BEKENNTNISSE DES HOCHSTAPLERS FELIX KRULL
     Stuttgart, Deutsche Verlag-Anst.

BEMÜHUNGEN
Essays   Berlin, S. Fischer Verlag. 1922

REDE UND ANTWORT
Essays   Berlin, S. Fischer Verlag. 1922

DER ZAUBERBERG
[The Magic Mountain]. Two volumes. Novel
     Berlin, S. Fischer Verlag. 1924

UNORDNUNG UND FRÜHES LEID
[*Disorder and Early Sorrow*]. *Short novel*   Berlin, S. Fischer Verlag. 1926

KINO
[*Romanfragment*]   Berlin, S. Fischer Verlag. 1926

PARISER RECHENSCHAFT   Berlin, S. Fischer Verlag. 1926

DEUTSCHE ANSPRACHE
Ein Appell an d. Vernunft   Berlin, S. Fischer Verlag. 1930

DIE FORDERUNG DES TAGES   Berlin, S. Fischer Verlag. 1930

MARIO UND DER ZAUBERER
[*Mario and the Magician*]. *Short novel*   Berlin, S. Fischer Verlag. 1930

GOETHE ALS REPRÄSENTANT DES
BÜRGERLICHEN ZEITALTERS   Berlin, S. Fischer Verlag. 1932

JOSEPH UND SEINE BRÜDER
[*Joseph and His Brothers*]. *I. Die Geschichten Jaakobs. 1933. II. Der junge
Joseph. 1934. III. Joseph in Ägypten. 1936. IV. Joseph, der Ernährer. 1943. Novel*
I, II, Berlin, S. Fischer Verlag.
III, Vienna, Bermann-Fischer Verlag.
IV, Stockholm, Bermann-Fischer Verlag.

LEIDEN UND GRÖSSE DER MEISTER
Essays   Berlin, S. Fischer Verlag. 1935

FREUD UND DIE ZUKUNFT
Lecture   Vienna, Bermann-Fischer Verlag. 1936

EIN BRIEFWECHSEL
[*An Exchange of Letters*]   Zürich, Dr. Oprecht & Helbling AG. 1937

DAS PROBLEM DER FREIHEIT   Stockholm, Bermann-Fischer Verlag

SCHOPENHAUER   Stockholm, Bermann-Fischer Verlag

ACHTUNG, EUROPA!   Stockholm, Bermann-Fischer Verlag

DIE SCHÖNSTEN ERZÄHLUNGEN
Stockholm, Bermann-Fischer Verlag

LOTTE IN WEIMAR
[*The Beloved Returns*].   Stockholm, Bermann-Fischer Verlag. 1939

DIE VERTAUSCHTEN KÖPFE
Eine indische Legende [*The Transposed Heads*]
Stockholm, Bermann-Fischer Verlag. 1940

DEUTSCHE HÖRER
[*Listen, Germany!*]   Stockholm, Bermann-Fischer Verlag. 1942

AMERICAN EDITIONS IN TRANSLATION
ALFRED A. KNOPF, NEW YORK

ROYAL HIGHNESS: A NOVEL OF GERMAN
COURT LIFE
Translated by A. Cecil Curtis. 1916

BUDDENBROOKS
Translated by H. T. Lowe-Porter. 1924

DEATH IN VENICE AND OTHER STORIES
Translated by Kenneth Burke. 1925. Contains translations of Der Tod in Venedig, Tristan, *and* Tonio Kröger *(out of print)* *

THE MAGIC MOUNTAIN
Translated by H. T. Lowe-Porter. 1927. Two volumes

CHILDREN AND FOOLS
Translated by Herman George Scheffauer. 1928. Nine stories, including translations of Der kleine Herr Friedemann *and* Unordnung und frühes Leid *(out of print)* *

THREE ESSAYS
Translated by H. T. Lowe-Porter. 1929. Contains translations of Friedrich und die grosse Koalition *from* Rede und Antwort, *and of* Goethe und Tolstoi *and* Okkulte Erlebnisse *from* Bemühungen

EARLY SORROW
Translated by Herman George Scheffauer. (1930) (out of print) *

A MAN AND HIS DOG
Translated by Herman George Scheffauer. (1930) (out of print) *

DEATH IN VENICE
A new translation by H. T. Lowe-Porter, with an Introduction by Ludwig Lewisohn. 1930

MARIO AND THE MAGICIAN
Translated by H. T. Lowe-Porter. 1931 (out of print) *

PAST MASTERS AND OTHER PAPERS
Translated by H. T. Lowe-Porter. 1933. Thirteen essays (out of print)

JOSEPH AND HIS BROTHERS
I. Joseph and His Brothers. 1934. II. Young Joseph. 1935. III. [two volumes]. Joseph in Egypt. 1938. IV. Joseph the Provider. 1944. *Translated by H. T. Lowe-Porter*

* *Now included, in a translation by H. T. Lowe-Porter, in* Stories of Three Decades.

421

STORIES OF THREE DECADES
Translated by H. T. Lowe-Porter. 1936. Contains all of Thomas Mann's fiction except the long novels

AN EXCHANGE OF LETTERS
Translated by H. T. Lowe-Porter. 1937 *

FREUD, GOETHE, WAGNER
Translated by H. T. Lowe-Porter and Rita Matthias-Reil. 1937. Three essays

THE COMING VICTORY OF DEMOCRACY
Translated by Agnes E. Meyer. 1938 *

THIS PEACE
Translated by H. T. Lowe-Porter. 1938 *

THIS WAR
Translated by Eric Sutton. 1940 *

THE BELOVED RETURNS
LOTTE IN WEIMAR
Translated by H. T. Lowe-Porter. 1940

THE TRANSPOSED HEADS
Translated by H. T. Lowe-Porter. 1941

ORDER OF THE DAY
Political Essays and Speeches of Two Decades
Translated by H. T. Lowe-Porter, Agnes E. Meyer, and Eric Sutton. 1942

LISTEN, GERMANY!
Twenty-five Radio Messages to the German People over BBC. *1943*

* *Also included in* Order of the Day.

PRINTER'S NOTE

This book is composed on the linotype in *Old Style No. 7*. This face is largely based on a series originally cut by the Bruce foundry in the early seventies and that in its turn appears to have followed in all essentials the details of a face designed and cut some years before by the celebrated Edinburgh typefoundry Miller & Richard. *Old Style No. 7* composed in a page gives a subdued color and even picture which makes for easy and comfortable reading.

THIS BOOK WAS DESIGNED BY STEFAN SALTER